I0614457

Luke's Redemption

by

Anni Fife

King Security Book One

This is a work of fiction. Names, characters, places, and incidents are either the product of the author's imagination or are used fictitiously, and any resemblance to actual persons living or dead, business establishments, events, or locales, is entirely coincidental.

Luke's Redemption

COPYRIGHT © 2016 by Anni Fife

Contact Information: info@thewildrosepress.com

Cover Art by *Kristian Norris*

The Wild Rose Press, Inc.
PO Box 708
Adams Basin, NY 14410-0708

Visit us at www.thewilderroses.com

Publishing History
First Scarlet Rose Edition, 2016
Print ISBN 978-1-5092-1168-5
Digital ISBN 978-1-5092-1169-2

Published in the United States of America

Red-hot sex. Searing betrayal.
A passionate and elusive love…

We pulled into the underground parking at King Security and Luke parked the SUV in line with several other huge black Ford Expeditions. It appeared King Security had its own fleet.

Unable to stop myself, I blurted, "You were with Anna when you were undercover with my father, weren't you?"

Luke pulled the keys from the ignition. In the deafening silence I didn't think he was going to answer. Then he turned to me and bit out, "Yes!"

Wow! I didn't expect him to be so honest. I sat back and folded my arms, tight. *Damn, his answer hurt me.* "So you make a habit of lying to your women? Being with them while you're pretending to be someone you're not? Is that your thing?"

"She wasn't *my* woman," Luke growled. "She was just *a* woman. She was there, I was there. It was never deep, and it sure as hell wasn't forever. Then it was over, and I made certain she was clear of the investigation. That was it." He leaned towards me and said impatiently, "That tell you what you want to know?"

"Not even close. You made love to her didn't you?"

"Hell no!" Luke snarled. "I fucked her. Like I have all the other women in my life. There's only one woman I ever made love to Katya. And that was you."

I went rigid, stunned into silence. Luke turned to open his car door. "You didn't make love to me. Michael did."

Dedication

To my Mum and Dad, my very own living pansy shells.
Your unflinching support makes everything possible.

Author Acknowledgments

First, I'd like to thank you, my readers. You're new to me and I'm new to you. I can't thank you enough for taking a chance on me. I hope you enjoy Luke and Katya's story, and I look forward to hearing from you—email me, chat to me on Facebook, or leave a review on any site that works for you.

Thank you to my dear friend, Sarah McGregor from Clockwork Books. You did an amazing job editing my First Draft. It would never have been the same without you.

To my multi-talented mother, Arlene—my most valued beta reader who never misses a beat. You pick me up when I get down, you feed me when I'm too tired to cook, and you never lose faith in me. Words can never express how special you are to me.

And thank you to Ally, my wonderful editor, and the hardworking team at The Wild Rose Press, Inc. May this be only the beginning…

Love,

Anni xx

Prologue
Floating Pumpkins and Winking Scarecrows

Harrison, Westchester County, New York

It's the most anticipated day of the year in the small town of Harrison. Crowds of people line Halstead Avenue, undaunted by the unseasonably hot weather as they eagerly wait for the arrival of the colorful Columbus Day Parade. The air is filled with excited chatter and the delicious aromas of local food vendors.

Katya, clutching the string of a yellow balloon, barrels her way to the front. She beams up at her parents and her papa smiles indulgently back at her. "Look, Katya, here comes the school band."

She spins around, black hair flowing past her shoulders, her pretty, heart-shaped face alight with excitement. For a brief moment she scrunches up her nose, disappointed that she is too young to join the parade. "Next year," she says fiercely to herself, "then I'll be six and big enough!"

The parade approaches and she claps wildly. Cheerleaders throw their batons high and shake their pompoms as they pass. The air fills with a cacophony of blaring trumpets, drums and cheers. Rows of police motorcycles roar past in a deafening wave of sirens, followed by an old fire engine draped in a banner proclaiming, 'It's Great to Live in Harrison.'

Another line of cheerleaders follow, twirling huge

1

flags displaying their school colors. Behind them she sees a giant pumpkin that seems to float through the air. It gets closer and her eyes widen when she spots a scarecrow crouched behind the pumpkin. Entranced, she stares as the float moves closely by her.

Then the scarecrow catches her eyes and winks!

Surprised laughter bubbles inside her. "It's Uncle Sam!" She waves enthusiastically and squeals when he waves back. "Uncle Sam, wait!" She runs after him and he smiles down at her again. She runs harder to keep up. But steadily, the pumpkin floats farther and farther away. She stumbles on the roadside curb and loses her balloon when she nearly falls. As it drifts away, she bends over to catch her breath and giggles to herself. "How does such a big pumpkin fit into the oven?"

Straightening, she turns to look up at her mama. A sea of people tower over her, waving flags, shouting and laughing. "Mama! Papa!" Her alarmed call is drowned out by passing bagpipes. Bumping into legs, she shoves her way through. "Mama! Papa!"

"What's wrong, honey? You lost?" The man bends and his large belly almost knocks her over.

He's a stranger!

She backs away, shaking her head. Her legs are wobbly and she starts to cry. Desperate, she looks around.

Nothing!

Laughing strangers close in on her. Her heart pounds and she gasps for breath. Lost! She was lost!

"Papa, where are you?" she whispers tearfully.

A hand slides over her shoulder.

Warm. Familiar.

She looks up and her tear-filled eyes meet her

father's. The same violet color as her own, they are filled with concern. "Micuta mea, *why are you crying?"*

"Papa!" Overwhelming relief sweeps through her and she scrambles up into his embrace. Her tiny arms and legs wrap tightly around him. "Papa, where did you go?"

"I was right here, micuta mea.*"*

She burrows into his neck and breathes in his comforting smell. "I was lost," she hiccups.

He hugs her harder. "No, prinţesa mea, *never lost. I was watching over you. I will always watch over you. Papa will never let anything bad happen to you."*

His warmth settles over her like a protective blanket and her heart finally slows. Her small arm stays wrapped around her papa's neck as she turns back to the passing parade. The booming noise envelops her again and she smiles, rubbing away her tears. But her earlier joy is muted and as the morning passes, no matter several attempts made by her father to put her down, she refuses to leave his safe embrace.

Chapter One
Sugar Beignets and Deep-fried Po'Boys

The French Quarter, New Orleans
March, Nineteen Years Later
Luke

The first time Luke Hunter saw Katya Dalca in the flesh she was running towards him. Okay, so it wasn't really in the flesh, it was through the vertical crosshair of his scope. And she wasn't running towards him, she was jogging back to her hotel. She was a quarter mile away, but with the jolt he felt deep in his gut, he might as well have been touching her.

As usual his patience had paid off. He'd been in position since her arrival the night before, hunkered down against the balustrade of the balcony. He was in line with her hotel room on the opposite side of the road, a budding azalea acting as good camouflage to create the perfect hide-site for him to track her comings and goings.

Up to an hour ago, she had not shown herself.

Then, deep shadows still blanketing the street, he watched as she slipped out of the hotel entrance. He only caught her dark, flitting shape because he was looking for it. And the flash he glimpsed of her sleek Nike outfit told him she was going for a run.

Good. The perfect opportunity for Gray to search her room.

Now, nearly an hour later, dawn had fully arrived, the sun rapidly chasing away leftover shadows on the quiet street. New Orleans was suffering from its annual Mardi Gras hangover and Luke could sense the lethargy that blanketed the city. He watched Katya run smoothly along the sidewalk, and sent Gray a text warning him of her imminent return. The last thing they needed was to have Katya catch Gray searching her room.

She ran closer and closer, forcing him to constantly adjust his lens to keep her in focus. Her intense frown of concentration seemed to contradict her exotic beauty. She turned to glance over her shoulder and he saw her dark hair was pulled tightly back into a long braid that snaked down her back. Just then, a door opened and a small boy ran out into her path. She swerved into the road to avoid tripping over him. The boy froze and from his expression, Luke thought he was going to cry. Katya walked over and crouched down to the boy's level. He watched her talking to him. And then she smiled.

Christ!

He didn't know about the boy but that smile triggered tingles throughout his body and he actually felt his temperature warm several degrees. *What the hell?* The boy's mother stepped out and called to him. Katya moved away and shifted back into her easy jogger's pace. Her smile faded, leaving behind a wistfulness that stirred up a matching melancholy in himself. She arrived back at her small hotel and slipped quickly inside.

A sense of unease settled over Luke and he remained where he was, perfectly still. Minutes later he heard the sliding door open. Gray was back.

Studying Katya's windows, he made sure there was no movement before he silently withdrew from the balcony. He shook the stiffness from his limbs, determined to set his odd reaction aside and refocus his mind on the task at hand. Gray was helping himself to a coffee from the small tray. Luke moved across to claim a cup for himself. "You find anything in her room?"

"Nope."

"Shit." He didn't ask Gray if his search had been thorough. They had been partners for over eight years and Luke trusted Gray like the brother he had become. "She must have it on her person," he said.

"Yeah. The only way you're gonna get that memory stick is to get close to her. Real close."

He looked sharply at Gray and his jaw tightened in irritation at the sardonic amusement reflected on his friend's face. He turned away, moving back to the balcony window. Why was he wavering about approaching her with an undercover persona? It wasn't like it was the first time he had got close to somebody using a fake identity. And it certainly wouldn't be the last. He took a deep breath, consciously loosening his muscles before he turned back to Gray. "Let's go over Michael Clark's legend. The quicker I can get close to her, the quicker we can be out of here. We need to find that memory stick, before the rest of the dogs pick up her trail."

Gray nodded and moved across to the table where their files were spread out. A black and white photograph of Katya caught his attention. He picked it up and flipped it around to show Luke. "She doesn't look like she belongs in the criminal world does she?"

Luke stared at the photograph. She was

extraordinarily beautiful. The still image exuded a coldness, though. A coldness that wasn't apparent when he had studied her through his scope earlier. Then, she had appeared disturbingly warm and touchable. "She's Nicolae Dalca's daughter. There's no way she grew up in his house without being aware of how he earned his millions."

"There's no record on file of her being involved in her father's business as far as I can see," Gray said.

"Maybe she's not directly involved, but she's had no problem living off dirty money. And picking up a first class degree from Berkeley off daddy's ill-gotten gains screams guilty to me."

Gray studied the photograph again. "Well, I still don't think she looks like a criminal kingpin's daughter."

"Not sure what that's supposed to look like, but looking like an angel doesn't mean she is one."

"You think she looks like an angel?" Gray mused. "I've never seen an angel with a rack like that! She looks more like—"

"Shit, brother, give me a break, yeah? I've gotta make good with this girl."

Gray finished his coffee and seemed about to say something but the look on Luke's face appeared to change his mind. "Right. Any idea why she took that memory stick and turned herself into a bull's-eye?"

"Who the fuck knows? My guess, spoiled princess wanting daddy's attention."

"Well, she sure got it. And the DEA's too." Gray tossed her photo on the table and picked up the file marked *Michael Clark*. "OK, let's see what Michael Clark is all about," he muttered. "Photojournalist. Just completed an assignment for *American Traveler* at this year's Mardi Gras…"

Luke shrugged off the last of his disquiet and concentrated on Gray's brief. Achieving their mission objective was dependent on Michael Clark's successful seduction of Katya Dalca. Failure was not an option.

****

Katya

I hurried along Chartres Street towards Jackson Square. There was no need to rush but I was full of nervous energy, even after my morning run.

The last three days had been hell.

Traveling by bus, I had crisscrossed my way from New York to New Orleans. After each bus changeover, I curled up in my seat and tried to sleep. But my success was sporadic. I was too nervous to settle, constantly checking I wasn't being followed. My situation was made worse by the knowledge that I was on the run from one of the most dangerous criminal bosses in New York. And of course, not to mention the lousy fact that that criminal happened to be my father.

That's right. My shitty shitty father who thought it would be good business practice to marry me off to his partner's son. His Russian drug-lord partner's son!

For as long as I cared to remember my father's idea of good parenting was locking me in a cage made up of security alarms, bodyguards and curfews. His work was dangerous and always had the potential to spill over and stain me with its filth.

It had once before, with devastating consequences.

And he was determined that it would never happen again. So determined that when Arkady Boykov insisted that a marriage between myself and his son was imperative to cement the trust between our two families, he succumbed. Instead of throwing that Russian scumbag out on his ass he traded me to his degenerate son.

I looked up and saw that I was a block from St. Louis Cathedral.

I had never been to New Orleans, but even on my worst day I could not have imagined being here under such frightening circumstances. I also couldn't shake the feeling that I was being watched. My whole body had tingled with it this morning when I returned to the hotel. I looked behind me, trying to catch a glimpse of somebody who didn't belong, but the street was quiet. It was nearly eight thirty and the only activity was a middle-aged woman washing down the pavement outside a small cafe. Probably spraying away leftover sins from the night before.

Whoa girl, melodramatic much?

I shook my head in exasperation and made an effort to appreciate the picturesque buildings that lined both sides of the street. Their pretty balustrades were familiar from countless movies I had seen. I was finally in the French Quarter, the heart and soul of Louisiana!

As I hit Jackson Square, I checked my cell phone. Still nothing. Not even any messages. *Dammit. Where is Hector?* I was undecided—wait for Hector to make contact or go and get some breakfast? I was hungry but the thought of food was vaguely nauseating. Until I got a news update from Hector, I knew I wasn't going to be able to swallow a morsel.

Slowing down, I looked up at the architectural beauty of St. Louis Cathedral. Its three towering spires had a Disney quality about them, reminding me of the castle in Magic Kingdom. From the brochure in my room I knew it was one of the oldest cathedrals in America. I found the building's imposing elegance had a calming effect on my jagged nerves. Noticing a row of benches that ran along the center of the pedestrian's walkway, I walked across and sat down. In front of me, wrought iron gates opened into Jackson Square Park. The artists that traditionally lined the black fence were beginning to arrive and I idly watched them unpack colorful wares, their Cajun chatter washing gently over me. I shivered, the sun barely high enough to penetrate the morning chill. Lifting my face to catch a few rays, I chanted my new mantra: *It's going to be okay. I'm going to be safe.* I wasn't yet convinced, but saying it over and over helped to settle the butterflies building in my stomach.

"Mm-hmm, *cher*, ain't you a sight for sore eyes." The distinct bayou drawl drew my attention. I looked over my shoulder and caught my breath. Crouched down on one knee was the most beautiful man I had ever seen. He was smiling at the wizened Cajun flower seller who was happily sipping her coffee and ogling him. Part of his face was obscured by a professional-looking camera that he held aloft, but this didn't mask his chiseled good looks. Nor did it hide his powerfully built body. *Oh yes!* I could see his defined chest clearly beneath the white T-Shirt he was wearing, biceps straining at the sleeves. His hair was dark blond, thick and probably hung to his shoulders. Right now it was tied back untidily with a leather cord of sorts.

Distracted, I felt my cell phone vibrate and realized it was ringing. Dragging my attention away from the gorgeous man, I fumbled with the answer button.

"Hello. Hector?"

"*Hola,* Katya."

"Oh, thank goodness! It's late, I was getting worried."

"Calm, *mi querida*. I know you are frightened but it's important you keep your head. *Sí?*"

Hector's steady voice with its familiar Spanish intonations settled me like nothing else could. "Yes, I'm okay now."

"Good girl."

"Where are you?"

"Still in Mexico. I'm about to board a flight now. I'll be there by midday."

"Tell me you have my passport?" I pleaded.

"I have everything you need, *cariña*. Now promise me that you'll meet me in Jackson Square at one o'clock. Can you do that?"

"Yes."

"I'll be waiting by the statue of the man on a horse. You know the one?" Hector asked.

"Yes. I ran by it this morning."

"*Bueno*. I have to go now, they're calling my flight."

"Okay. Bye then."

"*Adiós por ahora,* Katya." I heard dead space. Hector had hung up. I immediately missed his comforting voice and reached for the memory stick hanging on a chain around my neck. Even though it was lying beneath my shirt, I rubbed it like a talisman. *It's going to be okay. I'm going to be safe.*

I slipped my phone into the small, brown leather bag strapped across my body. The street traffic was picking up, the day moving comfortably forward, indifferent to my plight.

It was time for breakfast.

I stood to go and remembered the striking photographer. Looking over to the cathedral, my shoulders drooped. *Damn.* The man hadn't even glanced my way but I couldn't stop the pang of disappointment that he was gone.

Oh well. I would go to the cafe that I had jogged by this morning. The mouth-watering aroma of freshly baked beignets had wafted into the street and it had taken all my self-control at the time not to stop. I picked up my pace. Sugar was the perfect antidote to my vague sense of loss.

****

Katya

I entered *Café du Monde* through a fine mist of powdered sugar, and was immediately assaulted by an aroma of fresh baked patisserie and richly brewed coffee. It was just past nine, but the traditional French café was already busy with tourists queuing for tables so I opted for the takeout counter. Waiting my turn to place an order, I took in the European-style decor. Green and white striped awnings, plenty of small round tables full of people happily devouring beignets, the famous French-style donut, lavishly covered with powdered sugar. There was a happy buzz, overlaid with nondescript jazz piped through the restaurant speakers. It was impossible to remain tense in such a non-threatening setting.

"Next."

I turned back to the small take-out counter as the couple in front of me moved away. "Single order beignets and a *café au lait* please."

My order was served up less than a minute later. Grabbing my coffee and packet of three beignets generously covered in sugar, I turned to leave. And bumped into a solid wall of muscle. *"Oomph!"*

A hand shot out and steadied me, making sure I didn't spill my coffee. "Careful there, honey," a deep voice rumbled.

I felt his hand wrap around my elbow like a hot brand. I was too close to him, my eyes level with his powerful chest covered in a thin white T-shirt. I knew it was him. I just knew it!

"Hey, you okay?" he asked.

I looked up slowly. *Oh Lord, he was built!*

"Um, y-yes." I felt the heat move up from my chest. "Fine. Sorry." I didn't have the courage to raise my eyes further than his full lips which were tipped into a very sexy smile. I knew my face was glowing red and I ducked my head to allow my hair to sweep down and cover my embarrassment. "Excuse me." I pulled away from his gentle hold and brushed past him, hurrying outside.

The gorgeous photographer!

Why was I such an idiot? Scampering away like a scared mouse instead of snatching the opportunity to chat him up. Where was my normal cool persona? It had melted to goo in the face of all that testosterone. A few steps from the cafe entrance, I sagged against a lamppost and lifted my heated face to the soft breeze. My blood pressure slowly returned to normal and I wondered if I should wait for him to come out. *Argh*! Why did I feel such a powerful urge to connect with this man? *What was up with that?*

The smell of beignets wafted up and distracted, I

lifted the bag and took a deep breath. *Whoosh!* Fine sugar blew up out of the bag and coated me.

"Shit, honey, you look sweet all over."

Oh, just great.

Blinking sugar out of my eyes I looked up. And up. He was tall, well over six foot. Midnight-blue eyes rimmed by a deeper blue-black smoldered lazily down at me. "You're holding the best beignets in the world. You gonna stand there or you going to take a bite?"

"Umm." *Jeez, Katya. Say something.*

"Here, let me hold that for you." He took the coffee from my hand. "Go on, babe. Take a bite. It'll be the best thing you'll ever taste."

Still struck dumb, I did what he asked and lifted a beignet out of the bag and took a big bite. *Oh!* It was like sinking my teeth into a sweet pillow of ambrosia.

"Good huh?"

I nodded and stared back at him. Then, without uttering a word, I stuffed the rest of the beignet into my mouth. He grinned at me, shaking his head. "Want to wash it down with this?" He held out my coffee.

My fingers brushed against his. *Yikes!* I couldn't stop the slight tremor caused by his touch. I took a gulp of coffee—half rich chicory, half hot milk—and finally found my voice. "Would you like one?" I offered the bag of beignets to him.

"Would be like taking candy from a baby," he grinned. "But don't worry, I've got my own." He dangled a packet like mine in front of me.

Then we both stood there and smiled at each other while we gorged on sugary donuts. He would reach for my coffee to free my hand. Then after I ate some fluffy yumminess, he'd hand it back to me so I could take a sip. We swallowed the last of our beignets and licked our fingers.

I didn't even know his name, yet I was more turned on than I had ever been in my life.

"You want to go back for a reload?" He raised an eyebrow. "We can grab a table if you like? You can take your time on the second batch, savor them." His magnetic gaze caressed my face and his lips quirked. "You're still dusted in sugar, it suits you."

I tried to brush the sugar off. It was everywhere, even catching on the ends of my hair.

"Come on, beautiful. The place is packed and there's sugar floating in the air. Nothing bad can happen here. Join me." He reached his hand out and waited patiently for me to take it.

I don't know why I did it, but I reached out and slipped my hand into his. Warmth. It traveled up my arm and spread through my body. Looking up to meet his intense blue regard I felt the world as I knew it shift. Something was happening here. I didn't know what it was, but I was ensnared.

I could no more flit away than a fluttering butterfly could escape a silken web.

****

Katya

It was nearly one o'clock and I was in the middle of Jackson Square Park by the statue of General Andrew Jackson, triumphantly astride his horse. I was impatient to see Hector. Not because I was anxious for my passport and escape plans. No, I was impatient because I wanted to go and buy a new outfit. I had a date with Michael Clark.

How crazy was that? I had a date with Mystery

Man himself. I wanted to be with him so bad that I refused to pay attention to the niggling doubts lurking on the edge of my subconscious. I pushed these aside, together with my exhaustion and panic that my father's henchmen would soon catch up to me.

The morning had been a blur.

I'd followed him back inside that sugar palace and ordered another serving of beignets. Just as he suggested, I took my time, only it wasn't to savor the crispy donuts. It was to savor Michael Clark. That was his name. It seemed rather a mundane name for such a striking man, but I brushed this inane thought aside as I allowed myself to be swept up in his charming banter.

He told me he was a photojournalist, a freelancer specializing in lifestyle and travel for a range of magazines. He distracted me with amusing anecdotes about his week at Mardi Gras, but something about him was off. His eyes missed nothing, belying the casual, laid-back appearance he tried to portray. He was alert, in a state of constant readiness that reminded me of Hector. Ready for what, I didn't know.

Then he asked me my name and I just answered him straight out, "Katya," I said. "Katya who?" he asked. "Just Katya." His questioning eyes held mine. After a moment he gave me his panty-melting smile. "Okay, just Katya. I'm going to take a walk along the river to the French Market. You coming?" Of course, I said 'yes'.

We walked down to the flea market and the morning passed in a jumbled collection of craft stalls, specialty shops, engaging artisans and food. So much fresh and delicious food, which Michael took great delight in eating. He fed me samples of local produce, refusing to accept my entreaties that I was too full. And how could I not be seduced when he hand-fed me warm *muffuletta* stuffed with salami, mortadella, provolone and dripping with garlicky olive spread? And how could I not be mesmerized when he thumbed off the olive oil that had escaped down my chin. And then proceeded to lick his thumb clean, never taking those inky-blue eyes off me.

Clichéd moves? Um, YES! Did they work? Oh yes. I was totally captivated by him.

It was my father's fury I had fled, but in a strange way my decision to cut ties with him had liberated me. At twenty-three I was finally free of his claustrophobic protection. Free to engage with a man that completely enchanted me. I didn't care that Michael might be dangerous, I just believed that he wasn't dangerous to me. And I desperately wanted to lose myself in him, even if it was for only one day. Very soon I was going to disappear. I was going to lose my name and my identity, fading into the new life that Hector had arranged for me. Why couldn't I have just one taste of Michael before my life ended?

"*Hola,* Katya."

"Hector!"

"I surprised you?"

I reached up to hug him. "I was day-dreaming."

"How are you doing, *mi querida*?" Hector hugged me back warmly.

Stepping back, I smiled up at him. "All things considered, I'm doing okay. Better now that you're here."

Hector was my best friend Dani's brother. He was naturally macho and overprotective, reinforced by his career in law enforcement. He was very secretive about which agency he worked for and Dani and I had never been successful in squeezing him for further information. When we were at Berkeley, Hector made it his business to stop by regularly to check on his sister. As I was often with her, it became his habit to check up on me too. He became adept at reading us, and right now his handsome face was full of questions.

"Come on, let's go sit down over there." I indicated a bench nearby. "We have a lot to talk about." I needed Hector to stay focused on my escape. He couldn't find out about Michael. Not because I didn't trust him. I didn't want to take the chance that he would warn me off. Even if it delayed my departure from New Orleans, I wanted to be selfish. Michael was my guilty pleasure and I wasn't going to give him up.

"Buena, mi hermana. Now talk to me." Hector sat down, one arm stretched along the top of the bench and one ankle lifted to rest on a knee. He leaned forward and his dark-brown eyes scrutinized me. "Tell me what happened."

"Where do I start?"

"Tell me what frightened you enough to run. You have always had a difficult time with your father but I never understood you to feel unsafe. You told Dani he had crossed a line, that he was going to force you to marry some Russian criminal. I need to understand, Katya."

"Okay. Well, things between us have been getting worse over the past year. I got a promotion at the advertising agency in Chelsea and my work hours were getting longer. I told Father I wanted to move out and get an apartment in lower Manhattan, you know, somewhere closer to work."

Hector nodded encouragingly.

"He got so angry. Said I was being selfish, that I knew he couldn't focus on his work if I was exposed to his enemies. I told him it was his work that made me unsafe. If he loved me and wanted me to be safe then why didn't he sell Lightning Transport to his competitors and then he wouldn't have any enemies."

I shivered, cold rippling through me at the memory of his response. "He said I was behaving like a child, that I was a disgrace to the Dalca name. Then he walked out and we didn't speak for over a week."

"A spat. It is not so unusual for a father and daughter to butt heads. No?"

"Maybe not for normal families. But you have to understand, Hector, my father and I are not a normal family. We do not have spats, we have formal discussions, usually resulting in my compliance with his wishes." I leaned closer to him. "I have never had the courage to go against my father. I learned at a young age that rebellion was unhealthy for all concerned."

"What do you mean? Nicolae hurt you?"

"No, not how you think. There are more ways to hurt a young girl than physically." Sighing, I leaned back again. I sounded cryptic, but I didn't want to rehash my past. "That's over now. I'm more concerned with his latest plan for me."

Hector took his time, studying the constant stream of tourists passing by. I was suddenly nervous. What if he changed his mind? What if he sent me home?

"All right, Katya. What made you run?"

I rubbed sweaty palms on my jeans. "It was

Father's fiftieth birthday. He had a cocktail party at the house. We had reached a truce of sorts and he asked me to help host his party. Most of his work friends were there, including the Boykovs. God, they give me the creeps, especially Lev."

"Lev?"

"Arkady Boykov's son. I think Arkady controls the Russian Mafia in New York, or at least, he's one of the big bosses. He's actually not so bad, always polite and charming. But his son is a pig. I've only met him once before, but he was at the party. Made a point of brushing against me." I got goosebumps remembering how I had physically recoiled from that disgusting man.

"What does your father have to do with the Boykovs?"

"Why are you asking me that?"

"Calm." Hector covered my fluttering fingers with his hand. "I'm not accusing you of anything."

I stared back at him. I had to trust him. There was nobody else I could go to. I rushed to finish my story. "Lev kept following me around and I couldn't see my father anywhere. I slipped into the library to get away. I was sitting on a reading chair that was hidden behind a large shelf. It's my favorite place to go when I want to be alone. The door opened and I heard my father inviting somebody in to join him. It was Arkady Boykov. Before I could tell them I was there, Arkady started telling my father that he had a very important offer to discuss with him. He said it was vital for it to succeed if they were to continue in business together."

"They could not see you?"

"No. The room had low light and they moved to the fireplace. I was hidden by the large bookshelf."

"Go on, *mi querida.*"

"He said Lightening Transport was too powerful. That my father, as sole owner, wielded too much influence over their business. It made them vulnerable if he should become difficult. My father asked him why he was suddenly so concerned. I couldn't hear Arkady's response but then I heard him say that the solution was for our families to become bonded and the way to achieve this was by a marriage between his son and me. I barely stopped myself from making a noise. I couldn't believe what I was hearing." Shaking my head, I forced myself to tell Hector the worst of it. "My father told Arkady that if he believed a marriage between our two families would strengthen loyalties to his satisfaction, then he would not stand in its way. Arkady asked him to shake on it and even though I couldn't see it, I know the betraying bastard did just that. I heard Arkady say, 'Good, we are in accord. Now it's a real party, let us go and drink vodka to celebrate.'"

"I cannot believe that Nicolae would do this. I know he has been a distant father but I never doubted he put your happiness and safety above all else."

"Safety? Yes. Happiness? Never!" I said vehemently.

"Did you speak to him after the party?" Hector brushed his fingers through his short dark hair, his brow creased in agitation.

"No. I went straight to my room. I wanted out of there." I looked away to blink back tears. I was not going to cry again. My father was a bastard and that's just how it was. He didn't deserve my tears. "I packed a bag. I knew I had to get away." Angrily pushing my hair back I turned back to Hector. "Before I left I took some insurance."

"What?"

"A memory stick."

"What memory stick?"

"A small flash drive. My father normally keeps it on a chain around his neck but sometimes he leaves it by his computer in his study. On my way out I looked to see if it was there and it was. So I grabbed it and just left."

"Security didn't follow you?"

"I'm normally very cooperative with my comings and goings. I caught them by surprise. By the time they got it together, I was gone. I checked into a motel near LaGuardia and called Dani. You know the rest."

Hector nodded. "Tell me more about this drive that you took."

"I'm not sure what's on it but I think it's significant. My father's not IT savvy. He doesn't understand about off-site data storage or secure cloud back-ups. He always has this drive with him or nearby so I guess he must back up important information to it." I couldn't stop my fingers going instinctively to my chest to feel the shape of the memory stick hanging there. "I needed some insurance if he came after me," I said defiantly.

"That's it?" Hector pointed at the chain around my neck.

I nodded.

"Have you looked at what's on it?"

"Not yet."

"Do you want me to take it? Keep it safe for you?"

Did I? What if there was really incriminating information on it—information that could send my father to jail? I knew that I trusted Hector with my life, but did I trust him with my father's? Did I care?

After a moment I said, "No thanks. I think I'm going to hang on to it for now."

Hector just nodded.

We sat quietly. It was getting hot and Jackson Square was teeming with people. Hector stood up and reached for my hand. "Come. Let's walk back to your hotel. I need to give you your passport and familiarize you with your new legend."

"Legend?"

"*Si*. The background story for your new identity. You will only use it to travel to Mexico, but it's important you have it all clear in your head."

Taking his hand I let him help me to my feet. "It all sounds a little scary."

"It is scary, Katya, but you're going to be safe. I'll make sure of that. Now let's go. We have a lot to cover and I have to be back at the airport by four o'clock."

****

Luke

Gray was waiting for Luke outside *Domilise's Po-Boy & Bar* in Tchoupitoulas Street, just outside the French Quarter.

"Find it okay?"

"Sure, after getting directions from two locals," he said.

Ignoring his gripe, Gray led him into the small cafeteria. Luke took in the ramshackle interior and noted it was filled with what appeared to be regulars. There was a hodgepodge of tables placed closely together and crammed full with customers. A no-nonsense bar counter stretched the length of one wall with bar-stools along one side and two cooks manning the fryer and dressing up po'boys on the other side. Most of the space was filled with locals eating and chatting, washing everything down with plenty of beer. Luke followed Gray to two empty stools at the far end of the bar. "They keeping these for you?"

"Yeah. I'm a regular here and a definite favorite of Miss Dot's."

Like he conjured her up, a slight woman of indeterminate age walked through the swing door from the back kitchen. "Grayson Walker! As I live and breathe, aren't you a sight for these tired eyes."

"Miss Dot." Gray leaned over the counter to kiss both her cheeks in greeting.

"It's been too long, *cher*."

"I know." Sitting down he indicated Luke, "A good friend, Luke Hunter."

Giving him the once over, Miss Dot slowly smiled. "We-ell, aren't you a good-lookin' one?" He couldn't help smiling back at her blatant flirtatious manner. "Let me get you both fed and we can talk up a storm after. Shrimp and oyster po' boys for you both?"

"That would be great, Dot. And a couple of cold ones as well," Gray said.

Luke took a seat and looked around. They were tucked away in the corner of the bar which offered them a bit of privacy. "Any more information on the Russians?"

"What's she like?"

"She's fine. The Russians?"

"You got a date with her later?"

"It's not a fucking date. Shit, I don't know what it is. I'm taking her to dinner."

"Where?"

"*Cochon.*"

"Oh yeah, it's a date."

"For Chrissakes! You going to tell me about the Russians or not?"

"Sure, Hunt, whatever you need." One of the cooks slid two ice-cold beers across the counter and Gray contentedly picked his up and took a long swallow.

Luke pressed his lips together to contain his irritation. He knew Gray enjoyed fucking with him. He'd relay the relevant information in his own time. He looked up and read a slogan hanging over the bar—*It's Good!* The way people were happily tucking into their food, he had no doubt it was very good.

"The latest sit-rep is unchanged," Gray said, his tone taking on a serious note. "The Russians still seem ignorant that Katya has even rabbited. Nicolae Dalca has gone silent. HQ doesn't want to overplay their hand and risk Dalca finding their wire, so they're keeping it inactive for now."

"Where is Grigori Petrov?"

"Off the grid for the last two days. We think Nicu sent him after Katya. He's the only one Nicu would trust to retrieve his daughter and the memory stick without killing her."

"Nicu?" Luke raised an eyebrow.

"Short for Nicolae. Seems Dalca's friends and enemies alike call him Nicu."

"Cosy." He reached for his beer. "Petrov's smart and dangerous. He can't be far behind."

"Agreed. You need to make your move tonight. Get that memory stick so we can pull out and get back to—"

"Here you go my lovelies." Miss Dot pushed plates in front of them, steaming with freshly fried po' boys. "Two shrimp and oyster. Eat up while it's hot."

Luke pulled his plate closer. Even though he had generously sampled the local foods on offer when he was with Katya, he had no problem digging into the delicious Cajun-style sandwich. He bit through the flaky exterior and savored freshly-fried shrimp and oysters soaked in an unidentifiable sauce. *Yeah*, as he had expected, the bar slogan said it all—'*It's Good!*'

"Damn. The first mouthful's always the best," said Gray, and washed down the fried goodness with his beer.

They ate, the easy silence between them earned from hundreds of hours together in hide sites scoping designated targets. Gray was the finest spotter Luke had ever worked with. As a marine force recon sniper team, they were up there with the best. And even now, since they had opted out on an honorable discharge, they remained partners.

Pushing his empty plate aside, Gray finished his beer. "So, do you know where she keeps the memory stick?"

"On a chain, around her neck." Luke swallowed the last of his food and washed it down with the dregs of his beer. "She's not how I thought she'd be," he said.

"Not as beautiful, you mean?"

"Shit no, she's the most beautiful woman I've ever seen." He remembered her face covered in sugar dust. *So fucking beautiful and so fucking sexy.* Dark-violet, almond-shaped eyes, surrounded by the longest fucking eyelashes, so long he had thought they were fake until he looked closer. She had a perfectly symmetrical heart-shaped face, high cheekbones and her lips, *Christ!* Full and pouty and covered in sugar. It had taken everything he had not to lean down and take a taste. "What I mean is, she's not as cold as I thought she'd be. Not as shallow. She's funny, quirky. But she's also a little fragile, sad—"

"Careful, Hunter. Michael Clark can be as sensitive as the job demands, but *you* need to keep focus. Don't let this woman take you off your game."

"I won't lose focus!" Luke shoved his stool back and stood up.

"All right then. It just sounds like you're real taken with her."

"She's the target, that's all she is. Have you ever known me to lose focus of the target? Ever?"

Gray stared at Luke and then sighed softly, "No."

Chapter Two
I Just Want to Make Love To You

Katya

By the time Hector left it was late afternoon. I had three hours to shop for an outfit and get ready before I was to meet Michael at six-thirty. When he had asked me for my hotel details, I panicked and insisted on meeting him outside *Harrah's Casino*. He'd raised a brow but thankfully hadn't argued.

My hotel concierge understood exactly what I was looking for. She arranged a taxi to take me to the Garden District and gave the driver clear directions of where to find the boutique she recommended—*A Girl is a Gun*—*Wow, how perfect is that name?*

The shop was easy to find. A red sign hung from chains above the door, just like an old style saloon would have. The interior was stylish and retro-modern, the clothing an excellent mix of vintage chic and funky labels like Bettie Page, Bernie Dexter and Stop Staring. Hair accessories with feather and jewel appliqués, Lux D'Ville purses and a range of in-house designed T-shirts and sweatshirts filled the shelves lining the walls. Dani would have loved it.

When I arrived at Berkeley University, my wardrobe had been conservative and unexciting. Dani was studying Fashion Merchandising and wasted no time taking me under her fashionista wing. It helped that her and her posse sub-majored in where to unearth top brands for a fraction of their retail price. With her blunt but well-meant advice, we slowly replaced my prim and boring wardrobe with high-street elegance mixed with retro pieces that tended towards vintage.

I spent several minutes browsing the labels, but was irresistibly drawn to the vintage rail. A savvy looking saleslady approached and introduced herself as Hazel. I explained I was looking for something special for my date. While I rambled on about the style I preferred, she pulled items off the rail and then expertly maneuvered me into the change room.

The minute I slipped on the violet-purple top I knew it was perfect. The satin oozed Old Hollywood glamour and totally matched the color of my eyes. The lapels hugged my breasts then dipped into a plunging neckline with a faux wrap front tying on my hip. The back and long romantic sleeves were transparent chiffon, the cuffs lined in satin frills.

"Oh, honey, that looks like it was made for you," Hazel drawled.

"You don't think it's too revealing?" I tugged at my exposed cleavage.

"You're young and you're beautiful. You can never have too much cleavage!" I gulped at her no-nonsense tone. "You got a pair of decent black pants to go with that?"

"Yes." And I did. A pair of Armani cigarette trousers in a stretchy faux leather. I also had the perfect black Gucci ankle boots that Dani had snatched up for me when she interned at Marie Claire. They were super high with steel zip inlays that added a sexy edge. Both pants and boots were firm favorites of mine, so had made the cut in my hastily packed bag.

I paid for the top before I could change my mind. The purchase made a serious dent in my cash reserves, which wasn't ideal as I couldn't use any of my credit or charge cards. But I shoved this problem aside, preferring to picture Michael's reaction when he saw me. I didn't want him to just find me hot. I wanted him to be totally smitten with me like I was with him.

I arrived back at my hotel with less than an hour to get showered and dressed. I never once considered taking Hector's advice that it was best to leave for Mexico immediately. Kissing my lips with a final touch of cherry-red lip gloss, the only thing on my mind was the potent and irresistible package that was Michael Clark.

****

Katya

I dashed down to the riverfront where there was an electric trolley service. The concierge called them streetcars when she gave me directions. I got lucky and one pulled up just as I arrived at the station. I jumped off at *Harrah's Casino* and arrived only three minutes late. Michael was already there, lounging casually against a pillar. He stepped forward to meet me and his tall frame filled my vision. He took his time, blatant in his regard. When his eyes lifted to meet mine they were midnight ink, burning with his appreciation. He lifted a hand and boldly stroked one finger down the edge of my satin lapel, stopping just short of my cleavage. I held my breath, every hair on my body raised at his whisper-light caress.

"Breathe, Katya."

I exhaled noisily and heat flushed through me. His

sensual lips tipped into that lazy smile that I was already addicted to. *Yes!* The splash-out on my outfit was worth every reckless cent.

"I love it when you blush like that."

"Like what?" I knew exactly what he meant. My fair skin cursed me with a blush that was easily triggered and deepened to a crimson-red the more mortified I became.

He lifted his hand and I watched, mesmerized, as his finger returned to my cleavage. "It starts at these gorgeous breasts, then moves up this long, bitable neck." His finger brushed lightly along my skin, stopping briefly at my frenetic pulse and then he lifted both hands to gently cup my flushed face. "And finally, it brings an incredibly sexy but innocent glow to this beautiful face."

My lips parted. *Kiss me, please kiss me.*

His thumb caressed my lower lip and then he stepped back. "Come on, babe. The restaurant's not far and we don't want to lose our reservation."

My pulse fluttered. I loved it when he called me 'babe'.

"You okay to walk in those heels?"

"Um, yes, it's fine."

"Great, 'cos they're sexy as all hell." He took my hand and urged me along.

We joined the throng along the busy sidewalk, my hand engulfed by his much larger one, and I experienced a sense of belonging and safety that had been missing in my life since I was a child. That awful feeling I had sensed earlier of being watched was also gone. It was like his sheer presence kept all the evil in my life at bay. I was probably being melodramatic.

Dani said I should have studied drama instead of graphic art, but what she didn't realize was that I only ever displayed this behavior with her. Her unconditional acceptance of me made it safe to be myself. At home, I learned to hide this side of my nature and suppress my propensity for over-exuberance.

"I hope you eat pork."

"Sorry?"

Michael gestured towards a restaurant where a long queue of people waited at its corner-street entrance. "Here we are." He nudged me in front of him and guided me through the door.

The inside was buzzing with people too. I looked up at him "What did you say about pork?"

"This place specializes in pork, hence its name, *Cochon*." He lifted his brow expectantly and grinned when I didn't answer. "*Cochon*, French for pig," he clarified.

I ignored his cockiness. "Is it okay for us to jump the queue like this?"

"Yeah. I've got a mate who runs the bar. He made a special booking for us."

Inside, the restaurant looked like a renovated warehouse with a rustic yet elegant decor. The kitchen area was mostly open with a wood fire oven. Clever mood lighting gave the place a chic but casual vibe, though it was clear to see that jeans or shorts were just as welcome. My get-up was fairly dressy so I was glad that Michael had made an effort as well. His dark Levi jeans were matched with a navy shirt molded to his beautifully toned body. It wasn't tucked in and fell just to his hips, which allowed enticing glimpses of his black leather belt that had a hammered silver buckle.

Over this, he wore a tailored three-quarter length black leather jacket. *Stylish and crazy sexy.*

Michael caught the hostess's attention and we were shown to a corner booth with one curved leather seat, obviously meant for only two people. We sat and the hostess wasted no time handing over menus. "Jules will be along in a mo', he said he'll take care of your drinks. And I'll send your waitress along in five, give you some time to look over the menu."

Michael nodded at her then turned to me. "Jules is a mate of mine, met him when I was doing my service."

"Service?"

"Yeah, I was in the Marines."

"Oh. How long for? When did you get out?" He stiffened and I was surprised to see his face shutter.

"I joined soon after 9/11. Got my discharge about a year ago."

His tone didn't encourage further questions but I was curious. "For somebody who's been out of the military for some time, you still seem super alert."

"How so?"

"You have this watchful quality, like you're expecting danger. You remind me of a cop friend of mine."

He didn't answer, just flattened his lips and stared out at the restaurant. His abrupt withdrawal stung and I was suddenly sorry I had said anything. "I didn't mean to upset you or anything—"

"It's fine," he said, turning back to me. But it didn't feel fine. Something was off, I just couldn't put my finger on it.

"Hey, Mikey, good to see you brother." Michael stood up to shake his friend's hand and they did that backslapping thing that guys always do. "And who is this gorgeous creature?"

Very pretty gray-blue eyes twinkled down at me and I spontaneously smiled back.

"This is Katya. Katya, meet Jules."

"*Enchanté*." Jules drew out the French greeting and placed a bottle he was carrying on the table. Then he dramatically bowed to take my hand in his and place a light kiss on my knuckles.

I giggled. His dark good looks and flirtatious manner was a relief after the intensity that always seemed to brew between Michael and myself.

"Sit," Jules said to Michael. "I've got a homemade specialty of the house for you both to try."

I bit the inside of my lip, uncertain of the unlabeled bottle he had brought to the table. It was a pale orange color and was stuffed full of jalapeños! Popping the cork with a flourish he filled three shot glasses to the brim. "This is homemade jalapeño tequila, best you'll ever taste." And with that he clinked our glasses and threw back his shot.

I expected some wincing reaction on his face but there was none. Licking his lips he drawled, "Nectar of the gods."

I turned to Michael and caught my breath. He was watching me, his glass aloft. "Chicken?" he challenged, his eyebrow raised wickedly.

Yikes. There was no way I was wimping out. Mentally crossing my fingers, I tossed back the concoction in one hit—*Yowza!* I was on fire. Breathing out fumes, I eyed both of them through a haze of tears. They were laughing at me. I pointed at Michael and gestured at his still full glass but I couldn't actually speak. He shook his head at me, then casually lifted his glass and tossed back the contents. I waited to see his reaction but I was disappointed as, just like Jules, he looked blandly back at me.

"What?" I gasped, still trying to catch my breath. "Do you guys have mouths of steel?"

"You prefer something a little sweeter, darlin'?" Jules asked facetiously.

"Yes, please," I answered instantly, deciding it was best to take him at face value.

Laughing, he turned back to Michael. "I think she's a keeper, Mikey. Careful she doesn't slip through your fingers."

Michael leaned back, he seemed oddly irritated by Jules' comment.

"All right then. One Ramos Gin Fizz coming up for the pretty lady and I'll send you a beer, yeah?"

Michael nodded.

Our waitress came to take our order and thankfully, by the time our drinks arrived, Michael had returned to his previous good humor. My Ramos Gin Fizz was sublime—a combination of gin, lemon and lime juice, egg white, sugar, cream and surprisingly, orange flower water. All topped up with soda water to add a sparkle. Without much delay, our shared starter arrived—fried alligator bites served with chipotle mayo and a chili garlic aioli that had a slow, creeping heat. Biting into the tender alligator and sipping on my delicious Gin Fizz, I was hyper aware of Michael who was seated close to me, his knee frequently rubbing against mine.

"Where are you from, Katya?"

"What do you mean?" His question caught me off guard.

"Where are your family from? Katya is an unusual name, not American."

"I was born in America. My mother was American but my father is Romanian."

"Your mother *was* American?" he said gently.

"Uh, yes. She died when I was ten." I looked away, taking a sip of my drink, which was suddenly tasteless. I hated talking about my mother.

"I'm sorry, baby. That must have been real tough on you."

Baby? I liked that even more than 'babe'. And the gentleness in his voice when he said it helped dilute the painful memories.

"So, you were named for your father?"

"No, after his mother, Ekaterina."

"Is she as beautiful as you?"

"I never knew her, but then neither did my father. She died giving birth to him. I've seen photos and she was lovely. But I look more like my mom."

"Yeah?"

"Mmm, just like her in fact. But I have my father's eyes and hair." Suddenly uncomfortable, I reached for the memory stick that normally hung around my neck. My heart stuttered when I felt nothing, and then I remembered I tucked it in my purse because it had ruined the effect of my new top.

"You okay?" Michael leaned closer and his hand settled on my jaw, turning me to face him.

I didn't feel okay. Shit! Tears welled up and I tried to move my head away as they began to overflow.

"Christ, Katya, what's wrong?"

I shook my head. My father's betrayal and talking about my mother had loosened something inside me and I was suddenly overwhelmed with a deep, clawing sadness.

"C'mere, baby." He reached to wrap me in his arms. As he nestled me into his chest, his hand stroked my head and combed through my hair. "Shh, it's okay," he crooned.

"I don't understand—"

"It doesn't matter. You're hurting for whatever reason but I've got you, sweetheart. Just let go, I've got you."

And he did have me. Right in the palm of his hand.

****

Katya

Michael slipped the keycard from my trembling fingers and inserted it into the slot. The green light lit and he pushed my hotel door open but didn't enter.

"Are you sure this is what you want?"

"Yes." My voice was husky as I returned his heated stare.

"Then why are you trembling?"

"Because I'm nervous. And excited." *Jeez girl, could you sound any more dorky?* I didn't know how to tell him I ached because I wanted him so bad.

His gorgeous eyes glinted and he gave me that lazy smile. "Excited's good. I'll definitely take excited."

"Okay, good then. Um, you, uh… Damn." I grabbed his hand and pulled him into the room.

I invited Michael into my bedroom with no misgivings, even though I knew it would most likely result in losing my virginity to him.

Yes. I was still a virgin at twenty-three. Of course, he didn't know this, and I hadn't yet worked out how to impart this tiny bit of news to him.

Back at *Cochon* I was mortified over my crying jag, but Michael had gently brushed it aside. He made a point of not asking me any more personal questions, distracting me instead with innocuous chitchat as we polished off our mouth-watering main course—roast pork with crackling and a special of sweet smoked ham with fresh corn and figs. *Yum!* He tried to tempt me with the German chocolate ganache but admitted defeat when I threatened to sic Jules on him with the Jalapeño Tequila.

I was tired and Michael urged me to get some sleep, but I wasn't ready to call it a night. He must have seen something in my expression because he suggested we take in a club in Frenchmen Street that had a reputation for excellent music, and I gratefully agreed. I went to the restroom to freshen up, and when I came out he was by the reception door in an intense discussion with Jules. It looked like they were arguing but when they saw me, Jules walked away and Michael approached me, reaching for my hand. Worried I would be cold, he'd arranged for a taxi rather than use the streetcars. I didn't question him about his argument with Jules. I didn't want to risk him shutting me out again and spoiling the evening.

The club, *The Apple Barrel Bar*, was really small and crammed full of people. It was the perfect place to shake off any lingering doubts. Michael ordered us bourbon and then pushed his way through the foot-tapping crush, with me in tow, to a pillar next to the small stage. He leaned against it and smoothly turned me to face the band. My breath hitched as he pulled me up against his body, one arm wrapped protectively around me. His move seemed natural as the space was so tight but it didn't feel natural. It felt electric. The heat from his chest easily penetrated my thin top and with his muscled arm enfolding me, I was immersed in all that was Michael.

The smoky bourbon went perfectly with the band, their music a combination of New Orleans Dixieland mixed with the sound of Muddy Waters. Encased in our own simmering heat, we listened as they played a mix of unfamiliar songs, interspersed with some popular favorites, including Bessie Smith's famous *Baby Please Come Home*. I couldn't stop myself swaying to the music and this meant my body was constantly moving against his. *Oh Lord, it was hot.*

And just when I thought it couldn't get any hotter, the opening cords of Muddy Water's "I Just Want To Make Love To You" slid over us with all of its sensual power. Michael turned me to face him and took the empty bourbon glass from my hand. I didn't notice where he put it because both his arms wrapped around me and pulled me tight up against him. I went up on tiptoes to meet his descending mouth. And then, with the classic blues song thick in the air, he claimed me.

And it was a claiming!

His mouth fused with mine and a place deep inside me unfurled in response. Waves of heat cascaded through me as his tongue swept into my mouth. It filled my senses and created a voracious need that I knew, with absolute certainty, only he could ever fill.

I clung to his shirt when he pulled back slightly, feeling the warmth of his hand on my jaw. When his thumb feathered my cheek I forced my eyes open. I could feel his breath kiss my lips.

"Jesus, babe!" he whispered hoarsely.

I couldn't speak.

His hand threaded into my hair, pulling my face impossibly closer and his lips settled back on mine. This time he went slower, our tongues endlessly entwining with each other. The people around us faded away as his kiss consumed me. I couldn't get enough. His taste was intoxicating.

Then he caught my lower lip between his teeth and bit me, gently. My knees sagged and he was forced to catch my weight, pressing me tightly to his body. His erection beneath his jeans pressed into me and wetness surged between my legs.

Oh God! Unable to stop myself I whimpered into his mouth.

His hand fisted my hair and he pulled my head back, not so gently. His eyes were liquid ink and he was breathing so deeply his nostrils were flaring. Completely ensnared, I was a willing partner to whatever he wanted to do with me.

"It's time to go, baby." His voice was deep and husky. "Come on." He pulled me through the crowd and out on to the street. In the cool air, he removed his jacket and slipped it over my shoulders. It enveloped my much smaller frame and I pulled the leather around me, inhaling his spicy, masculine scent. It settled around me like a cocoon. And I felt safe. Protected.

In the taxi he asked for the name and location of my hotel. I gave it to him without hesitation.

As we drove past the lively sidewalks, I turned to him. "You'll stay with me tonight?" My voice was tremulous, but even I heard the bold challenge in my question.

"Is that what you want?"

"Yes."

He searched my face then leaned over and dragged me across the seat, tucking me into his side. I rested my face against his chest and soaked up his addictive heat, surrounding myself in the heady scent of Michael Clark.

****

Katya

And now, here we were, alone in my hotel room.

Thankfully, housekeeping had been in and tidied up the mini-cyclone I left behind when I dashed out earlier to meet Michael. *It felt like a lifetime ago.*

I let go of his hand and moved over to a corner chair to drop my purse on the seat and lay his leather jacket over the back. Flipping my hair nervously, I turned to face him.

He was standing in the middle of the room, hands resting arrogantly on his belt buckle. "Come here, Katya," he drawled.

I wavered. I wanted him so badly, but his arrogance irked me.

"If I come to you, baby, I'm going to rip that sexy top in half and I don't think that's what you want."

Yikes! I guess he was a lot tenser than he appeared. *Maybe he wants me as much as I want him?*

I slowly approached him, stopping less than a foot away. Just below his jawline, a muscle jumped and my pulse picked up speed in response.

"You going to take that top off, baby?"

I didn't answer. Just reached to undo the tie at my hip then raised my arms, widening my eyes back at him.

And then I smiled.

His ragged breath sent a bolt of electricity through me and I bit my lip. *Oh yes! He wants me.*

Eyes narrowed, he frowned down at me. "You like to challenge me, baby?"

He didn't wait for my answer, just moved to unceremoniously slip my top up and over my arms. He tossed it on the chair and brought his hands quickly back to my body, smoothing them down my waist and over my ass. Then he tightened his grip and lifted me up against him until my breasts were within easy reach of his mouth. My legs automatically moved to wrap around his hips, my hands braced on his shoulders.

"Gorgeous!" He sighed and dipped his head to run his lips along the edge of my black lacy bra. My breath quickened when he used his strength to support me with one hand and used the other to pull my bra aside and reveal my hardened nipple. Before I could say anything, he sucked the peak into his mouth. He didn't take it slow. His mouth was wet and demanding. Each pull on my nipple an electric conductor attached directly to my throbbing clit.

Swamped with pleasure, I clung to him.

He lifted his head and rasped. "Prepare the other one for me, Katya."

"What?" I gasped.

"I want to taste your other tit, baby. Lift it up for me."

Oh God! My pussy wept as I pulled the lace away from my swelling breast and lifted it to meet his mouth. His face was tight with lust as he closed his mouth hungrily over my offering. A long moan escaped my throat and my legs started to shake around his hips. Only his hand under my butt stopped me from sliding into a puddle at his feet.

I groaned in protest when he lifted his head, both arms wrapping tightly around me. "Hold on to me, baby, don't let go and I'll give you what you need."

There was nothing in this world that could make me want to let go.

I ran my lips along his stubborn jawline and dipped my tongue into the cleft at his chin. Feeling for the leather cord holding back his hair, I pulled it out. I didn't care if I was a little rough. My fingers luxuriated in the untamed length, then curled into fists and pulled his mouth down to mine. I was starved for more of his taste.

I caught his lower lip between mine and sucked on it.

He jerked his head back and climbed on to the bed with me still clinging to him.

"Christ! You're going to be the death of me," he growled. He lowered me to the mattress and his lips covered mine. I arched helplessly into him, desperately rubbing myself against his rock-hard erection. I couldn't get enough, I wanted to be consumed by him. If I could crawl inside of him I would have.

Easing back, he licked at my lips. "Fuck, if the rest of you tastes half as good as your mouth—"

My breath caught as he reached up to yank his shirt over his head and toss it to the floor.

God, he was superb.

I pushed up, greedy to stroke his sculptured chest. It was smooth, warm to my touch, with only a light scattering of dark blond hair. Caressing his hot, taut skin, I thrilled as his muscles contracted in response. He combed his fingers through my hair as I traced chiseled abs, absorbed by the darkening trail of hair that tapered down his flat stomach and disappeared erotically beneath his jeans.

I pressed closer to inhale his musky scent. Craving more, my tongue darted out and flicked hungrily over a flat, hard nipple. He hissed, tightening his hands in my hair. I was eager for more, but Michael undid my bra and nudged me back, slipping the straps down my arms.

"You've got the most exquisite tits I've ever seen," he said huskily. He cupped them in both hands, then ran his thumbs over my nipples.

Fire streaked down to my pussy. I gasped, reaching up to grip his wrists. "Michael, stop, I need—"

"I know what you need, Katya. And you'll get it, I promise." He pinched my nipples between his finger and thumb and gently squeezed. "Now let go of my wrists."

I instinctively resisted.

He increased the pressure and the pleasure was indescribable. "Be a good girl for me and lie back down."

Confused by the pleasure-pain and terrified he might stop, I slowly released his wrists and lowered myself back to the pillows.

"Such a good girl," he drawled, and lowered his body to cover mine. He deliberately rubbed his chest against my aching breasts then lowered his mouth to tease my lips.

Whisper-soft, his lips moved across to my ear. "Grip the headboard, Katya, and don't let go."

Helpless to defy his sensual demand, I did as he asked. I was completely out of my depth and I didn't care. I chose to abandon myself to the spiraling pleasure.

Resting back on his knees, he undid my faux leather pants and slid them down my hips. My hands curled around the wooden headboard as he edged down the bed. When he reached my boots he cradled the crazy sexy heels in his hands. "Next time we fuck, you're going to be wearing these and nothing else."

Then he unzipped them and slipped them off, taking my pants with them.

I was naked except for a pair of tiny black lace panties. Soaking wet panties!

My heart was beating madly and I knew I was flushed, probably a combination of excitement and embarrassment. I had never been naked in front of a man before. *Oh jeez, how am I going to tell him this is my first time?*

Taking an ankle in each hand he moved my legs apart and then settled between them.

Tell him, Katya, tell him now.

His lips were like hot velvet moving up my thigh.

Oh God. I knew where they were heading.

Before I could say a word, his mouth settled right over my pussy and he kissed me deeply through my lacy underwear. I arched up, pushing desperately against his hot mouth. "Michael, oh Lordy, ple-ease!"

A moment of cooler air as fabric was pushed aside and then his tongue was on me, branding me. "Oh! *Oooh.* Don't stop."

His hands cradled my hips and his thumbs spread me open. Then his hungry tongue began to devour me.

Wild streaks of pleasure pounded through me as he stabbed his tongue into my pussy. His strong grip held me down, preventing me from arching into him. I let go of the headboard and buried my hands into his hair, trying to pull him ever closer. I didn't understand but I knew I needed more.

Lifting his head he casually licked my wet from his lips. "Hands, Katya." His voice was rough, his eyes glinting.

Then, as if he realized I was about to buck out of control, he moved his thumb to gently circle the hard bud of my clit. "Come on, baby, trust me," he coaxed.

I knew he wouldn't continue unless I did as he asked. *Oh God, I needed him to continue.* So I eased my hands from his hair and slowly curled them back around the headboard.

Watching me intently, he moved his hand and I felt a finger enter me.

"Jesus, you're tight,"

"Don't stop," I begged.

"I promise, babe, I'm not going to stop but if I don't ease you I'm gonna hurt you."

I had to tell him, I knew I had to tell him.

"Michael?"

His finger slid in and out of me. As it picked up speed, he lowered his mouth and circled my clit with his tongue.

Explosions of light erupted behind my eyelids and pleasure like I had never known cascaded through me. The sensations were both terrifying and exhilarating. I was close to orgasm but I didn't know how to let go.

It was like he read my mind. He lifted his head. "Let go, baby. Come for me."

Oh God, I wanted to.

Then he added a second finger and started to rub at a point deep inside me. His mouth covered my clit but instead of tonguing it he started sucking it. Explosions rippled through me, building quicker that I could control. My body spasmed. Only his restraining arm stopped me from lifting off the bed.

"Michael!" My cry was one of desperation and clawing need.

Then my orgasm burst. It moved through me like hot lava, burning me up, consuming everything in its wake. As my body shuddered in ecstasy, I couldn't stop my hands moving back to clutch his hair. I needed something to hold on to, something to anchor me.

Michael continued to lave my pussy, sliding his tongue gently through my wet heat. His touch no longer demanding but rather comforting as he helped calm my quivering limbs.

****

Luke

Luke slowly inhaled Katya's erotic heat as she untangled her fingers from his hair and sank back onto the bed, shudders still shaking her glistening body.

Christ, she was lovely. When she finally let go and exploded around his tongue, he barely managed to stop himself from going over the edge with her.

He stood and stripped off his socks and jeans. Silently swearing, he reached back down for his wallet and slipped a condom out from the side pocket.

His skin burned under her heated stare as he tore the packet open and sheathed his cock. He was so fucking hard. If he didn't sink himself inside her, the pressure building inside his balls was going to tear him apart.

He climbed back on the bed and slid between her sprawled legs. She was flushed, tendrils of hair sticking to her face and shoulders, and her eyes—*damn! Huge pools of violet, impossibly beautiful.*

Supporting most of his weight with his arms, he let his hips nestle into her. His dick was desperate to feel her silky heat. "You still with me, baby?"

She nodded, still languorous from coming so fucking hard.

Unable to resist, he lowered his mouth to her plump lips. Nibbling on them, he used his tongue to soothe the sting. Starved for more of her taste, he slanted his head and kissed her deeply. He took his time, enjoying her hungry response.

"You taste of innocence and hot sex," he rasped. "Christ, Katya, you're dangerously addictive."

Sliding his cock between her wet, soft folds, he coated it in her juices then reached down to position himself to take her. "Wrap your legs around me, baby."

"Wait," she begged, lifting her hands to cup his face.

What the fuck?

"Please, Michael." Her eyes filled with tears. "I'm sorry."

"Christ, babe, what's wrong? Are you hurting?"

"No! It's just, I meant to tell you earlier but then you made me feel so good I didn't want you to stop and—"

"Slow down." He moved his hand away from his aching dick and threaded it through her hair, cradling the side of her face. "Tell me."

"It's my first time," she blurted.

He froze. What did she say?

Rolling her eyes impatiently, she said, "I'm a virgin!"

Shit! Fuck!

"And you're only telling me this now?" He knew he sounded pissed but *fuck it*, he was pissed.

"I'm sorry, I really am. I know I should have said something but—" She started struggling, pushing against his shoulders to move him back.

"Calm down," he said quietly and lowered his body to stop her flailing.

She quieted, but the deepening flush on her flawless skin screamed her embarrassment. Her eyes flickered away unable to meet his and his gut churned at her obvious withdrawal.

"Look at me, Katya, please."

Slowly she lifted those incredibly long lashes and looked up at him. Her eyes were glistening again. *Christ, she really was like his own brand of kryptonite.* Gray warned him he was in trouble with her. As usual, he wasn't wrong.

"You been saving this all up for me?" he asked.

And he couldn't help smiling when she snapped back at him.

"No!"

"No?" he queried mildly.

Taking a deep breath, she blew out her cheeks. *She was so damn cute.*

"Well, I wasn't really saving it, it just worked out that way."

"Yeah?"

"Yeah!"

His dick jerked at her exasperation and he knew she felt it when her eyes widened. He deliberately pressed his hard-on into her and her breath hitched as she instinctively moved to meet his thrust. The heat between them was spiraling quickly. He knew it wouldn't be long before it ignited into an inferno again.

"I don't want you to stop," she whispered.

"You barely know me, Katya."

"It doesn't matter. The way you make me feel, that's all that matters."

"Christ, baby, you're breaking my heart."

"Don't stop, Michael, please don't stop."

She moved urgently against the thick wedge of his erection, her eyes begging him to give her what she ached for.

"All right, baby." He'd just sealed his place in hell, but there was no way in this lifetime he had the strength to refuse her heartfelt pleas. Sliding his body to the side, he rested his weight on one arm. "Spread your legs for me and relax."

"What? But—"

"Do it, Katya, now."

He held back his smile at her slow compliance, both amused and turned on by her uncertainty at his bossy commands.

"Now lie still." He slid his hand between her legs.

She gasped as he eased a finger into her hot cunt. Unable to resist, he leaned down and sucked her nipple into his mouth.

"Yes-ss," she sighed, pushing her breast up to him as he increased the pressure.

Luke loved that her breasts were so sensitive, and hungrily moved from one creamy mound to the other. He didn't hesitate to nip down on her pebble-hard nipples. He knew she enjoyed the bite of pain, because her cunt clenched around his finger every time he did it.

She was whimpering now. Her head tilted back,

exposing the vulnerable curve of her neck. Moving his lips to cover her pulse, he gently bit down. He thrust into her with a second finger and rolled her swollen clit with his thumb. Her whimpers turned to deep-throated groans.

"That's it, Katya, burn for me."

"Oh God, Michael, I need more."

And so did he.

He rose over her, still keeping most of his weight on his bent elbows. Reaching down, he lifted one of her legs to wrap around his hips.

Her hands fluttered over his shoulders.

Gripping his cock, he guided it to her entrance.

"This is going to hurt, baby."

"It's okay. Don't stop, Michael. Please. I want you so bad."

Entering her slowly, Luke fought for breath, for control. It killed him to hurt her but he knew it was unavoidable. She rose up to meet him and he slid further into her. *Christ!* She was so tight and hot around his cock.

Then he nudged against her barrier. "Hold tight, baby." Before she could react he eased back then surged forward.

Her body went rigid and she clung to him.

"That's it, beautiful, hold tight." He gritted his teeth and stayed perfectly still, waiting for her to ease around him.

Before long she restlessly nudged against him. "Move," she begged, "I can't stand it. You have to move."

Sliding his aching cock slowly back, he settled his body closer then stroked back deep inside her. "Is that what you want?"

"Y-yes! Oh God, yes." Her hands curled around his shoulders, her nails biting into his skin.

Shit yeah. He also liked a touch of pain. It hardened his cock even further. Feeling how wet her cunt was, he picked up his pace, fucking her harder. She was arching beneath him now, her sweat-soaked body writhing out of control.

Fuck! The friction was unbelievably pleasurable.

Lifting her tits to his hungry mouth, he began to suck. Her cunt tightened around him with each pull he took. She was close and he wanted her to come with him this time. Moving his free hand he slid it between their slick bodies and then he pinched her engorged clit between his thumb and finger.

"Michael!" She screamed.

Fuck, he hated that name on her lips!

As she exploded around him he couldn't hold back any more. He let her drop back to the bed and surrendered to the savage need. Thrusting one last time, he emptied himself deep inside her.

Jesus fuck! This woman had him by the balls and she didn't even know his name!

Chapter Three
Pavlov's Bitch

Katya's Hotel Room, New Orleans
The Next Morning
Katya

I snuggled deeper into the bedding, lazy and heavy-limbed. Shifting slightly, warmth spread through me as the slight stickiness between my legs brought with it delicious memories of the night before. I never dreamed that I could be so wanton, so wildly desperate for one man's touch.

And boy, did he touch! His potency evident in every aching muscle in my body.

Mmm. Heat flickered as his musky scent infused my senses.

"Katya."

I loved his voice. Especially when he said my name, so deep, rich like dark molasses.

"Katya!"

I forced my lids open. And drowned in sensual, male beauty. "Hi," I purred. And it was a purr. I sounded like a sated cat. Inching a hand out from under the covers, I reached up, hungry to stroke his rough morning stubble.

He reared back as if stung.

What?

My hand hovered mid-air as he lowered himself to

a chair that was pulled up close to the bedside.

How did that chair get there? Was he watching me sleep?

Sluggish, I looked at the window. The curtains were drawn together but didn't quite meet. Faint light trickled in. It was barely morning. I looked back at Michael and cold started to seep in. *Shit.* He was fully clothed, he was even wearing his jacket. Only his hair looked out of place. He obviously couldn't find the cord that I'd enthusiastically pulled from it like a wild woman, and now it hung loose to his shoulders. Bed-hair. *Do men get bed-hair?*

He was still. Hands clasped together, elbows resting on his knees. Here, but not here. Only his eyes flickered as they roamed intensely over my face. Such wickedly, beautiful eyes. After he came inside me they had turned an inky-blue, almost black.

Now, they were deep shards of navy. And they sent ice cascading through me.

I was still naked and he was fully clothed. I jerked upright and pulled the covers to my chin. My stomach quivered, only it wasn't in a sexy way.

"What is it?" He was so remote it put me on edge. "It's still early, isn't it?" The warm glow I awoke with was gone. "Michael?"

His silent regard was awful, so oppressive I looked away. My gaze dropped to his hands. They were clasped tightly together, his knuckles white. Forcing a breath through my nose, I swallowed hard.

"I'm sorry, Katya. I fucked up."

"What? How?"

"Last night was a mistake."

A mistake? The pain cut so deep it forced the

breath from me.

"I didn't mean for it to go so far."

He stood up quickly, moving restlessly to the end of the bed. "Christ! You're just so fucking addictive!"

How was I supposed to answer that? I was still reeling. My chest constricted. He believed what we did was a mistake? My lungs tightened further. *The most beautiful night of my life was just a damn mistake?*

"Goddammit! Don't look at me like that," he growled. "This wasn't supposed to mean anything. Shit!" He pointed a finger at me accusingly. "You haven't even told me your full name."

Pulling the bedding tighter around me, I remained mute.

"Just Katya?" he accused. "I'm not the only one with secrets."

What is he talking about? What secrets does he have?

I didn't ask him that. Instead I asked, "Why was it a mistake?"

He combed his fingers roughly through his hair. "I have secrets too, Katya. And they aren't the type of secrets I can share with you, at least not now. Making love, taking your virginity, that was fucked up. The timing is all wrong."

My jaw clenched. "I gave it to you."

"What?"

"You didn't take my virginity," I insisted. "I gave it to you." I kept my trembling hands under the covers, relieved to find my voice steady.

"Jesus." He collapsed back into the chair.

I cleared my throat as he dropped his head into his hands and roughly rubbed his face. "Why are you so angry with me?"

"I'm not angry with you," he sighed. "I'm angry with myself. I'm pissed that this thing between us has taken me off my game."

"Game?"

"I told you, there are things I can't share with you. But that doesn't mean I can deny the strength of what's between us."

"You said fucking me was a mistake!" I cried. "Jeez, Michael! I don't understand anything of what you're saying. Secrets? Games?"

What he was saying.

How he was behaving.

It was terrifying and my control started to slip.

"Listen to me, babe, please."

That was the first time he called me babe since I woke up. It cut through the fear like nothing else could.

Yeesh, I was like Pavlov's dog. Or maybe Pavlov's bitch! Trained to respond without thought.

"I have to go. I can't explain any of this to you." Agitated, he leaned forward. "But you need to know, when I said last night was a mistake, it's not like you think. Christ, it was the single most important thing anybody ever gifted me. You have to know that," he insisted.

The relief was so huge I couldn't stop the sudden welling up of tears.

He stood and leaned over the bed. "I need you to promise me something." I huddled back as his arms settled on either side of me. His powerful torso had me caged against the headboard. "One year from now, thirty-first of March, I want you to meet me in New York. Will you do that for me?" His voice was a gentle plea.

"What? I don't—"

"I know you don't understand, but I need you to take a leap of faith for me. Can you do that, Katya? Can you believe in the beauty of what we had last night and make a promise to me?"

His face was so close to mine, I felt his breath soft on my lips.

"Union Square, by the George Washington Statue. Four o'clock, thirty-first March." He reached up to thread his fingers through my hair. Then his palm stilled and his thumb gently stroked my cheek. "Promise me, baby."

I was mesmerized. His eyes scorched right through to my soul.

And just as I had less than twenty-four hours ago, when I placed my hand so trustingly in his and followed him into that sugar palace, once more I reached out. "Okay, Michael, I promise."

He closed his eyes. His relief was so palpable my eyes started to burn again. Then his thumb briefly whispered along my lips before he straightened to his full height.

"One last thing, babe, then I gotta go."

What more could he want from me?

"Last night, the condom broke."

I flinched. I couldn't help it. "I'm not on the pill or anything—" I whispered, tingling all over as adrenaline surged through me.

"It'll be fine," he reassured me. "It's going to be fine, I promise. But just in case, I've left a number you can call."

"A number?"

"Yeah, you call it, whoever answers will know how to contact me. It's there, on your purse."

I looked to where he pointed and saw my purse on the dressing table. I could see a small piece of paper resting on top of it.

Then he moved rapidly to the door.

Alarm bells were going off in my head as I looked between his departing body and my purse.

"Michael!" I called. Fragmented pieces of everything he said were imploding in my brain.

"Sorry, baby, I've gotta go."

He opened the door, and just like that, he was gone.

I stayed motionless in the bed. The sound of the door clicking closed was an ominous echo of the chaos resounding in my head.

Secrets! Games! He fucked up making love to me?

I stared with dawning horror at my purse. *Please no. Oh God, please no.*

The bedding slipped as I hugged my knees to my chest. I forced air into my lungs and slowly started to rock.

It's going to be okay. I'm going to be safe.

But my stupid purse just sat there, like it was mocking me.

And I knew it wasn't going to be okay, it was never going to be okay.

Dammit, Katya, do something.

I leaped from the bed and stumbled as the bedcovers got caught up in my legs. Flinging my arms out I managed to keep my balance without slamming into the dressing table. I grabbed my purse and flicked it open.

It wasn't there.

No, no, no, no—I kept mumbling, as I rummaged desperately through the small purse, but it wasn't there.

Turning my purse upside down I shook it violently—and watched as my lip gloss, phone and a few dollars tumbled to the floor.

No memory stick!

My stomach contracted as a sour taste in my throat welled up. Pressing a fist against my mouth, I dropped my purse and ran for the bathroom. I barely made it to the toilet as toxic bile spewed out of my mouth. Sinking to my knees, I clung to the toilet seat and continued to vomit my guts out.

My hair draped over the edges of the toilet and stuck to my clammy face but I didn't have the strength to hold it back as my stomach continued to heave uncontrollably.

Stupid! So damn stupid. How could I be such an idiot?

The retching eased and I moved back from the toilet bowl. My throat burned from the stomach acid and my mouth tasted foul. The stench of vomit filled my nostrils, making my eyes water and my stomach clench again. Taking a deep breath through my mouth, I shifted to my ass and leaned against the bath. Slowly, the nausea eased, leaving in its wake a terrible loneliness. I rested my head against the bath rim, exhausted.

I'd fallen for him and he reeled me in like a stupid fish, and then dangled me on his line. And now here I was, naked, sprawled on the bathroom floor, gawping for air. I glanced down and saw a faint bruise on my breast.

He had marked me. I still felt him between my legs

and his smell lingered on my skin. My body was covered in him. I started to rub frantically at my skin, my hands slipping between my legs to cup myself.

Oh God, I felt so dirty. I gave my body to him willingly. But I knew, in every fiber of my being that his betrayal had stripped my soul.

I forced myself up and moved woodenly to the shower, turning it to hot. I needed him gone from me. His smell, his touch. Stepping into the steaming spray, I started to scrub. I was sobbing so hard I didn't notice I was abrading my skin.

I don't know how long I stayed under the water but by the time I stepped out I felt deadened. I heard the hotel phone ring by the bed. *Maybe it's Hector?* I grabbed a towel and dashed into the room to answer.

"Katya!" The sound of Michael's voice reignited the pain inside me.

"You bastard! Do you know what you've done to me?"

"Dammit, woman, listen to me."

"No! I'm done listening to you, you lying low life—"

"Grigori Petrov is here"

I froze. "What? Where?" I whispered hoarsely.

"He just landed at the airport. You have to get out of there, now. Out of New Orleans."

"Who the hell are you, Michael? Why do you even care if my father's thug finds me? You lied to me! Oh God, you stole from me." I sank to the bed, crying uncontrollably.

"Just leave, Katya. Leave now! There's no time, baby." His fierce demand echoed through the phone. "No matter what happens, you better be in New York in one year. One year, Katya!" And then he was gone, silence ringing through the handset.

I sat there, gripping the phone and cursing him. But I knew I had to pack. I had little time and I had to get out of there before Grigori tracked me down.

I dressed quickly and threw my few belongings into my bag. The purple top brought me up short. I bought it with such high expectations. And he had loved it, his eyes darkening when he saw me wearing it.

Fuck you, Michael! I hope you rot in hell!

I dumped the purple top in the dustbin, grabbed my bags and walked out of the room.

And the piece of paper with his contact number? I left *that* on the floor exactly where it fell when I grabbed my purse.

Pushing the button for the lift I nervously fiddled with the leather cord around my wrist. I had found it on the floor next to the bed, the memory of how I tore it from his hair slipping insidiously through my defenses. Spontaneously, I had wrapped it around my wrist, something deep inside me unable to casually discard it.

****

Red Hook, Brooklyn, New York City.
Two Days Later
Luke

Luke stood at the window, his hands buried deep in the pockets of his sheepskin-lined leather jacket. He looked past the giant cranes in the Red Hook Container Terminal and across the bay where he could just make out the skyline of lower Manhattan.

He'd been in the same position for the last thirty minutes, watching the freezing rain slowly turn to sleet. Nobody interrupted his vigil. He was alone in the boardroom of Lightning Transport, the heart of Nicolae Dalca's self-built empire.

He idly wondered how much longer Nicolae was going to keep him waiting. He touched the memory stick in his pocket and knew he would wait for as long as it took.

The weather closed in, sleet driving against the windows. His view of the port faded into gray fog and unbidden, images of Katya invaded. Her bewitching eyes dilating as he licked her to climax.

Fuck! Blinking to clear her image, he flinched as her ringing accusation reverberated through his head. 'You stole from me!' It was a litany that continued to repeat itself, searing her pain into every nerve in his body.

Breathing deep, Luke called on his training to force her from his mind, replacing his guilt and her evocative image with the stillness necessary to complete his mission.

The door clicked open and he briefly closed his eyes in relief. He turned and studied Nicolae. He was surprised to see him alone. The man usually had at least one of his henchmen hovering nearby. Nicolae calmly walked over to join him by the wall of windows and Luke was careful to show no sign he was pissed at being made to cool his heels. He remained still and stonily returned Nicu's—as Gray had reminded him he preferred to be called—impassive appraisal.

Nicu was a good-looking man. Just under six feet, he was fit and strong for his age, which Luke knew to be fifty. There was little evidence of grey in his immaculately combed hair or groomed beard. Hair, he noted not quite as dispassionately, the same blue-black as Katya's.

Their eyes met and Luke found himself in a classic alpha stare-down. *Fuck!* Nicu's eyes were the same color as Katya's. Deep violet. Only his were cold, dead. Katya's were full of fire and mystery, life and pain.

Dammit. If he didn't get his head in the game, he was going to get himself dead.

"What are you doing here? The DEA has no business with me." Nicu's arrogant voice was devoid of any accent, Romanian or American.

It was the very lack of an accent that marked him as foreign, Luke realized. "I'm no longer with the DEA," he said.

That disclosure only garnered a raised eyebrow.

Luke pulled the memory stick from his pocket and dangled it in front of Nicu. "I thought you might want this returned."

Nicu unfolded his arms, but instead of reaching for the memory stick, he slipped his hands in his pockets. "How did you retrieve that from my daughter?" he said evenly.

"I asked nicely."

"Did you hurt her?"

Luke couldn't read his tone. Was he asking as a caring father or just out of curiosity?

"Not physically, no." Luke ensured he sounded cold, even cocky. He tossed the memory stick on the table and forced back the bile that coated his throat. He knew he had done much worse than hurt her physically. He had destroyed her trust.

His gaze never wavering from Luke, Nicu reversed gears. "Did you look at it?"

Luke nodded. *Is he even a little bit concerned*

about his daughter's wellbeing?

"Then you know it contains little of consequence that can damage me."

"Maybe." Luke shrugged. "But you can't say the same for Arkady Boykov."

Nicu stilled and, so slightly that Luke thought he might have imagined it, rocked back on his heels. "Tell me, Mr. Hunter, what exactly do you want?"

"A job."

"I don't hire cops. I buy them."

"Good thing I'm not a cop, then. At least not anymore."

"Really?" Nicu sounded skeptical. "Now why should I believe that?"

"I don't expect you to. Check me out. Put your sources to work and they'll verify that I got caught with my hand in the cookie jar, so to speak. The DA didn't have enough to indict me but it was just enough," he said resentfully, "to shove me out the door."

Nicu turned his back, drifting closer to the window. The freezing sleet obscured any possibility of a view. He stared at his reflection in the glass, then his eyes moved to Luke. "So, you're returning that to me with no strings? Why?" He turned back to the room. "As a means of getting close to me?"

"No. As a gesture of goodwill. Or better yet, think of it as my business card. We both know you're not going to let me back through your door until you trust me and that could take a while."

"Perhaps forever," Nicu sneered.

Luke walked over to the table and picked up the memory stick. Tossing it in his hands, he turned to contemplate Nicu. "You do know that if I was DEA, there's no fucking way I would still have this drive? There's enough on here to burn Arkady Boykov, his son and his whole organization." Swinging the drive on its chain, he stepped closer to Nicu. "And if Arkady believed it would save his son's ass, he wouldn't hesitate to spill everything he has on you."

"There's not enough on that stick to indict him." Nicu scoffed. "And even if there was, Arkady's old school. He will never talk, not even to save his son. The DEA has nothing on me."

"You're right, they don't," Luke agreed.

"So what don't I know, Mr. Hunter?"

"Your security is crap. I've scoped you out for weeks now, looking for a weakness, a way to get your attention. Penetrating your outer perimeter was child's play and your men have loose tongues. Don't you want to know how I knew Katya had your drive? Was on the run with it?"

Nicu stood motionless. Luke sensed he had finally made a dent in that fucking ice-cold arrogance. Wanting to maintain the momentum, he forged ahead. "The night of your fiftieth, I breeched your residence and overheard Petrov brief your security detail. He's a loud bastard and indiscreet. Why the fuck was he briefing grunts on confidential family matters?" Again, he didn't wait for a response. "He made it clear Katya had dangerous information and you wanted it back. Urgently." He strolled back to the table and tossed the memory stick back down. "I knew I had found a way in. All I had to do was find your daughter and steal that back for you." He pointed at the drive. "And that's exactly what I did."

He knew he had reached the critical point: Nicu

would either buy what he was selling or shoot his ass. He delivered his punchline with care. "You're the best at what you do. You should hire the best. There's nobody better than me to work security. I have the military training and the street contacts, inside law enforcement and out. If you give me the opportunity, I can turn your company into a fortress."

The son-of-a-bitch just stood there, assessing him with that fucking hypnotic stare. Luke knew he had to stand his ground. He concentrated on staying outwardly relaxed and hoped to hell he'd done enough for Nicu to take the bait.

"Do you know where she is?"

Damn. The guy just didn't let up. He was beginning to believe he really did give a damn.

"No," Luke replied. "I saw Petrov at the airport. I thought I owed her, so I made a call and warned her to take off. She didn't leave a forwarding address."

"If you want a job with me, Mr. Hunter, it would be best for you to forget about her."

"If you say so."

"I do."

Luke didn't miss the deadly warning couched in that assertion.

It did cross his mind whether Nicu realized he had no intention of heeding that warning. None whatsoever.

"If your story checks out, we'll see." He turned to face the window in an obvious dismissal.

"Good," Luke grunted, and then got himself the hell out of there.

****

One Week Later
Luke

"I'm in."

"He called?"

"Yeah, just got off the phone now."

"Where are you?"

"Heading for Red Hook. He wants a meet now."

"Shit, that's quick. He say much?"

"Nope. Just that he had a job for me."

"You're at point blank range, brother, and out in plain sight. You concerned?"

Luke considered Gray's question before replying. "Instinct says it's a go, but it's gonna take some time to build trust. Longer than we had hoped."

"I butted heads with the Commander but he still thinks this is our best shot."

"And the DEA?"

"They and the DA have studied every bit of info on that stick and they're convinced it's a crapshoot. Fifty-fifty that Arkady and his ring will wriggle off the hook. Nicu's a clever bastard. All the info on collections and deliveries are coded. Difficult to pin the drugs on any one person in a court-room."

"Yeah, that's what I thought."

"DEA also got wind of another player. Looks like Nicu is doing business with the Armenians now as well."

"Christ! If he's not careful, he's gonna get his ass fried."

"You're gonna be in the middle of it, Hunt, it's your ass I'm worried about."

"You mothering me, Gray?"

"Shit, Hunter, this is different to Fallujah. This time, I'm not there to have your six."

Luke heard the concern in his friend's voice. Gray

only ever called him Hunter when he was being serious. "Take it easy, man. I'll be vigilant. Listen, I'm coming up on the tunnel, I might lose signal for a while."

"Okay. You been in touch with your family?"

"No."

"They worry when they don't hear from you. You want me to give your aunt a call?"

"No," Luke sighed. "I'll call her later. But I won't be able to keep in touch, not while I'm on Nicu's payroll."

"I get it, it'll mess with your head. I'll keep in touch while you're under, make sure they know you're okay."

"Appreciate it."

As the line of cars approached the Brooklyn-Battery Tunnel, Luke hesitated about asking Gray for the information he was burning for. *Fuck it.* They weren't going to speak for a while and he needed to know. "You got any more info on Katya?" He tried to keep his tone neutral but Gray knew him too well.

"Shit, Hunter. You need to get that girl out of your head. Jesus, you're working on taking down her father. She might hate his guts, but you reckon she's gonna be cool with you about that?"

Luke clenched his jaw. "Dammit, just answer my fucking question!"

He could hear Gray cursing. The cars in front of him flowed into the tunnel and he knew he had no time left. "Gray, please, answer my question," he said quietly.

"No. There's no sign of her. The last we know she crossed into Mexico, but we've lost track of her since. If she pops up, I'll find a way of connecting with you."

"Right. Thanks."

"Yeah. Be safe."

Shutting off his phone, Luke thought about what Gray had said. Then he thought about what he knew about Katya. *Damn.* Not nearly enough.

But it was time to lock all thoughts of her away. He had a job to do and he was about to enter enemy territory. If he didn't stay on-point he was going to fuck it up. And that would likely equate to his bullet-ridden body floating face down in the Hudson.

****

Six Weeks After Katya Departs New Orleans
Katya

I folded away the TV monitor and pressed the button to move my seat upright. My stomach rolled as the plane descended, and I swallowed back the slight queasiness as I leaned over to peer out the window. I had promised Dani I wouldn't miss the view as I flew into San Diego. She always carried on about how much she loved the sight of her city set against the backdrop of the ocean.

She was right, it *was* beautiful and I tried to stir up some enthusiasm worthy of Dani's fervor. But I failed. The numbness I had embraced was firmly rooted, deadening my senses. I wasn't really annoyed by this— I knew it was the only thing keeping me sane.

The past six weeks were like a jagged kaleidoscope.

I had retreated into myself, licking my wounds and trying to shore up the emotional strength needed to start my life afresh. Hector had arranged my escape through Mexico. The bright colors and vibrant culture were a welcome distraction as I journeyed deeper south. With each mile I covered, another layer of my identity was left behind. I was greeted in each town by friendly faces that eased my passage, secreting me away to their terracotta haciendas. I played my role and participated in their warm chatter, cooked meals with curious children and exclaimed over fresh tomato, lime and chili concoctions that were fed to me. But it was just that, role-play. I was exhausted, my nerves fried. For no reason, I would suddenly become short of breath or start crying uncontrollably. I was forever excusing myself from company to disappear into my room, the solitude a balm to the anguish that continued to surface unexpectedly.

By the time I reached Tijuana, six weeks had passed since my madness with Michael. I had become practiced in conquering my crushing despair. I achieved this by burying it so deep that it suffocated, my lack of attention cutting off its oxygen supply. The result was an emotional detachment that might have seemed bleak but it made my daily existence manageable.

Yesterday, when Hector arrived to join me, I was able to smile, breathe evenly and show interest in my new future. I'm not sure I fooled him, but for whatever reason, he chose to let me make this play.

And then this morning, my hard-earned equilibrium was completely shattered. A wave of nausea forced me to pay attention and I realized my period was late. Too late. I dashed out to the corner pharmacy and bought a three-pack of pregnancy test sticks, desperate to hold off the tsunami I sensed coming.

I did the test.

Three times.

Each time with the same result.

I stood at the bathroom vanity and shook my head in denial. The last white stick was gripped in my trembling hand. *No, no, no! How could this be? Michael promised it would be okay.*

I should have known better! The evidence was right there in my hand, the little pink lines a screaming accusation that robbed me of breath. Light-headed, I sank to my knees.

Once again I was sprawled on a bathroom floor, alone and exposed by my own stupidity. Michael's face shimmered behind my closed eyelids but I determinedly blinked it away. I had to get my act together. In less than four hours I would board a plane with Hector to return to the United States.

****

Several hours later, I was still struggling to absorb the shock and anesthetize my aching heart. Katya Dalca is dead I kept reminding myself. And with her, my memories of Michael Clark, and my dream of having a family like the one I was a part of when I was a little girl.

My new name was Katalina "Kat" Molina. I was the distant cousin of Dani and Hector Molina, relocating to San Diego to live on their family flower farm in Encinitas.

Lingering nausea reminded me I was also a single mother-to-be.

And as the wheels of the plane touched down, my hand slid to my stomach and I silently chanted: *We're going to be okay. We're going to be safe.*

Chapter Four
Dani Dialogues

Encinitas, San Diego
Katya, Thirty-four Weeks Pregnant
"Surprise!"

I waddled into Mama Carmen's sitting room and excited screams hit me. I had no time to protect my carefully nurtured reserve in the face of such a barrage of cheers.

"Surprise! Baby Shower!"

"Yay for Kat!"

"Surprise, surprise!"

"We got you didn't we? You never even guessed!" Screeched Gabi, one of Dani's friends that studied with us at Berkeley. The other two, Lisa and Gloria, who completed Dani's San Diego posse, stood nearby, laughing and clapping at, what I'm sure, was my open-mouthed shock.

Then Dani was there, folding me in the tightest embrace. "Surprise, KitKat," she whispered.

I hugged her back and my huge tummy nearly pushed her over. But she was taller than me and circled behind to wrap her arms around my pregnant stomach. I looked around the familiar open-plan living-room with its huge picture window that looked out over the flower fields. Right now, it was festooned with pink balloons. The long dining-room table was covered in mountains of food and the center coffee table—*that* was piled high with gaily wrapped presents all obviously meant for a baby, a baby girl. I stood there dumbfounded, wrapped in Dani's arms as she rocked me side to side. Then I caught Mama Carmen's smiling face approaching, and smiled back at her through my tears.

"Tears, *mi hija*?" She raised an arched brow.

"Happy tears," I insisted.

"Mmm." She perused my tear-stained face. Then she smiled and nodded, "*Sí*, I see this to be true. Come." And I went into her beckoning arms.

Mama Carmen was not how I had pictured her. When Dani had talked about her warm and loving mother, how funny and fiery she was, what a fabulous cook she was, I pictured a portly, middle-aged woman stirring a pot in the family kitchen. She was anything but! Carmen was tall and built like a penthouse model. Olive skin and dark flowing hair. Big hair! With an even bigger smile. She was drop-dead gorgeous. But when her arms embraced you, it was like you were enfolded in maternal heaven.

I reluctantly moved from her comforting embrace to be enveloped in the thick arms of Aunt Rosa, Carmen's younger sister and the office manager at Molina Flower Farm. Unlike Carmen, Rosa was the stereotypical Hispanic mama: short and rotund, as quick to laugh as she was to let loose with her notorious temper.

"So happy for you child. A daughter is a blessing," she declared.

I glanced over her shoulder and saw Daisy giggling with Lisa and Gloria. Daisy worked with me in the office at the Flower Farm. She handled all the admin and helped me out with the graphic artwork and event management I did for the family. She waved happily at me, obviously deciding not to rescue me from Rosa. I smiled back at her, pleased that Dani had included her amongst our friends.

When I arrived in San Diego six months earlier, I was broken and adrift. The Molina family didn't hesitate to reach out and enfold me into their family as if I was born to them. This included Carmen and Antonio, Dani's father, ensconcing me in a beautiful little cottage a stone's throw from the main farmhouse and insisting that I was now an employee of the family business, the Molina Flower Farm.

The farm was just twenty-five miles north of San Diego, near the small town of Encinitas. When Carmen's grandfather started it, he literally parked a caravan and began to clear the undergrowth with his wife and young children. Over the years, the caravan became a small family home, then a larger farmhouse that easily accommodated four children and extended family members. The farm also expanded from a couple of acres with a small selection of day lilies to over twenty acres, eighteen greenhouses and over five-hundred different day-lilies.

I was constantly amazed at the thriving success of my friend's family business that had started from such humble beginnings. The farm was not only a wholesaler that supplied day-lilies throughout California, but it was also famous for special event floral design, Carmen's gift. In fact, Carmen was such a goddess at arranging flowers for weddings that brides from all over the region booked her services. Sometimes, when bookings were swamped, we were forced to deny them their wishes and it wasn't unusual to see brides arrive on our doorstep, demand to see Carmen and beg her to find a way to do the flowers for their special day. Carmen's big ol' heart normally gave in too easily and when Rosa threw a hissy fit, insisting we were too busy, Carmen would just look at her enigmatically and shrug, 'Who am I to refuse a bride flowers? Every bride wants the best, *cariña*, and I am the best, *no?*'

"Here we go everybody, mojitos all around!" Dani's cheerful call interrupted my musing and Rosa pulled me across to the table set up as a bar.

"A virgin one for you." Dani thrust a glass at me, overflowing with crushed ice and fresh smelling mint.

The next hour was spent chatting with the circle of woman that had become my whole world. They were, by now, used to my reticence and never asked nosy questions. They were content to gossip happily about clothes, favorite restaurants, and of course, sex. Dani kept the mood light and fun, regaling us with hilarious tales of her latest escapades in the fashion world. Like Hector, she had chosen not to join the family business, preferring to pursue her obsession with fashion.

Soon, everybody insisted it was gift-time. Over virgin mojitos and red-velvet cupcakes, I undid ribbons, peeled open gift wrap and exclaimed over their generosity. By the time I opened the last present, I had the main ingredients to outfit my daughter-to-be's nursery. Dani's posse had bought me a premium all-terrain stroller that I would be able to wheel through the fields I loved to trudge every day. There was a huge assortment of baby clothes from Dani that ranged in size from zero to one year, plus plenty of blankets, crib mobiles, a small bathing cot and even three months' worth of diapers.

Then Carmen handed me a large envelope with a flourish. "From Tony, Hector and me," she said.

With shaking hands, I opened the envelope and slipped out a photograph of a beautiful hand-carved crib. My eyes blurred in the face of such overwhelming kindness and I clung speechless to the beautiful picture.

"Hector will be home next weekend and he and Antonio will be over to erect it. They will also help to prepare the nursery, painting it and everything else you are going to need. *Si!*" And with that announcement, she stood up and clapped her hands. "Come, everybody, time to take a little walk. The sunset is soon and the view from the ridge is not to be missed today. Come."

None of us would dare ignore a Carmen dictate, so we jumped to attention and followed her out into the gardens. The sun hovered on the horizon and the sky was turning beautiful shades of pink and orange.

Strolling along, Dani looped her arm with mine. "Happy?"

"Yes." I cuddled in towards her as we walked. "Thank you, honey. I didn't realize how much I needed that. But *you* did, didn't you?"

"Hey, what are besties for?"

"It's more than that, Dani. So much more. I've been drifting. No matter how much I understand that I have to pull myself together, that the baby is coming soon, I just can't seem to do it. It's like I've been trapped in a silken cocoon. Each day rolls into the next, one week follows another, and I just can't shake off this lethargy." We lagged a little behind the others, still walking arm-in-arm as I tried to describe my awakening spirit. "But today was different. When I walked into the house and everybody was so happy for me, I didn't have time to throw up my defenses. It was like I was hit by a tidal wave. Instead of being sucked under, drowning, I'm out on top. I'm riding it!"

"Hallelujah! If you don't mind my saying so, it's about damn time."

I smiled at my friend's familiar bluntness. "I've got butterflies in my tummy, Dani. It's like the sunshine finally crept in." We stopped on the edge of the small hill and turned to watch the sun as it majestically set over the glorious lily fields. The scent of flowers wafted gently over the valley and the sky turned a luminous red. "I'm having a baby daughter, girlfriend, how amazing is that!?"

"Totally out-of-this-world amazeballs, KitKat. Now what are we going to name her?"

****

Three months before my baby shower I went to pieces. A total meltdown.

It started soon after I arrived in Encinitas. Dani began to accost me with questions. When my responses proved dissatisfying, she ramped up into a series of conversations I started calling the Dani Dialogues. Named such, because Dani did most of the talking while I did my best to block out her entreaties and nurse my anguish.

Most of our conversations started with her favorite "Talk to me, KitKat, please."

This got her my standard response—a small smile and a shake of my head. She usually followed this up with a reassuring, "Okay then, I'll do the talking."

Her talking started with gentle coaxing. "Do you think you might have over-reacted? Do you really believe your father would ever actually hurt you, or force you to marry a drug criminal?"

This plea for rationality where my father was concerned was the easiest to ignore. Even though Michael had stolen the memory stick from me, I quickly figured out I no longer needed this leverage to keep my father at bay. Just by leaving home in such a messy way, I sent a clear message to him. It was not in my father's nature to drag me home, and once he learned I was no longer in possession of the memory stick, he would not endanger my life further by sending more goons after me. I had no idea what Michael had done with the drive but whatever it might be, I was convinced my father was informed about it. As long as I stayed away and didn't attract attention to myself, I was safe, at least for a while. Eventually, he would run out of patience and track me down. But I had time. My departure meant he was occupied with finding alternative ways to keep the Boykovs happy.

I couldn't tell Dani this. I didn't know how to separate my despair with my father from my devastation over Michael. And *that* story I was not ready to tell. I wasn't certain I ever would be.

Dani then progressed to soft demands. "What happened, Katya? How did you end up pregnant?"

To outright threats, "If you won't talk to me I swear I'm going to call Hector and sic him on your trail. You know what he's like, a damn bloodhound!"

But I knew her threats were empty.

She was my best friend. Loyal. Persistent. It was beyond her to betray me, to turn her back on me. Daniela Molina never walked away from those she loved, and she loved me.

My stubborn silence continued until, at twenty weeks pregnant, I went for my second trimester ultrasound.

As usual, I went alone. Both Dani and Carmen were furious about my insistence on attending all my regular check-ups alone. They didn't understand that I was unable to find even a tiny bit of joy at the reality of being pregnant. To be happy conflicted with my deep need to punish myself for my stupidity. My gullibility. How was I ever going to explain to my child that he, or she, was the result of a one-night stand, a moment of lust driven by one man's greed and betrayal?

My obstetrician, Dr. Sally Wheeler, had inquired at my previous appointment if I would like to know the sex of my baby. I immediately demurred without giving her any explanation. But as I lay on the bed this time around, I got caught up listening to the rapid heartbeat of my baby and when she popped the sex-question again, I answered 'yes' without thought. "It's a girl," she said with a gentle smile.

I didn't react.

At least, not until late that night. I was asleep in my little cottage when I jerked awake close to midnight with Dr. Wheeler's pronouncement ringing in my head, 'It's a girl. It's a girl. It's a girl.—"

Soaking wet and feverish, I was curled into a tight ball. My tummy cramped and I panicked, I couldn't seem to get enough air in my lungs. Despair greater than I had ever known settled over me and I felt myself losing control. I was suffocating. I knew I needed help before the blackness completely swamped me. Thankfully, I had enough sense to reach for my phone on the bedside table and speed-dial Dani.

I don't remember much about what happened next, only the comfort of Dani's arms as they surrounded me and her repeated whispers in my ear, "Shh, KitKat. I've got you, I'm not letting go. Shh—"

I wept for hours, wrapped in Dani's arms, shivering and shaking as the pain leaked out of me in unrelenting waves.

By the time I eventually calmed, dawn was filtering weakly through the curtains. We lay snuggled together and against the background of early-morning birdsong, I told her everything.

When I finished, all Dani asked was if I wanted Hector to find Michael. I said 'no' and made her promise not to tell him anything. I tried to explain to her that whatever Michael was doing, however he was involved with my father, I needed to leave him alone to do it. Nodding, she held me closer.

"I have to believe what happened between Michael and myself meant something," I pleaded quietly. "You didn't see his face when he begged me to meet him in New York at the end of March. I have to believe in that. I have to believe that our baby girl is the result of something more than betrayal."

"You're going to meet him then?" Dani asked.

"I haven't decided yet."

"Do you think he'll be there?"

It took me a long time to answer but when I turned to look at her I said, "Yes. He'll be there."

****

Katya, Thirty-eight Weeks Pregnant

"Good morning, baby-girl." I smiled and rubbed the spot on my very pregnant tummy where my daughter kicked vigorously.

I had tossed and turned all night, struggling to get the mountain of pillows propped exactly right to support my humongous stomach. Eventually I gave up on sleep as light cramps and an aching back drove me from my bed.

In the kitchen I sipped on peppermint tea, then pushed my ridiculously swollen feet into the only footwear that now fit, my Crocs. I decided it would be a good idea to take a walk and watch the sunrise from Carmen's favorite spot on the ridge.

A short while later, I watched in delight as the sky lightened and I was treated to a pink and orange extravaganza, made richer by the perfume of awakening lilies. "Soon, baby-girl," I whispered, "soon you get to meet your mama."

My daughter was definitely listening because no sooner had I spoken, than a strong cramp bent me double, and panting for breath, I felt water trickle down my legs.

Wow! I think my water just broke.

And I was one week early!

Instead of being swamped by panic, I smiled.

My baby-girl was coming and I knew that everything was going to be okay.

****

I named my daughter Lily. After the spectacular lily fields where I nearly gave birth.

The moment I looked into her beautiful eyes, I knew that there was nothing I wouldn't do to keep her safe. As I held her to my breast, I promised she would always know she was loved. And most of all, I vowed to do everything I could to give her the family I missed so deeply.

I would go to New York at the end of March to meet with Michael and give him the opportunity to be a part of our little miracle. Hope flared, as each tug of my daughter's mouth sent shards of warmth to melt the walls I had so carefully erected around my heart.

Please be there, Michael, please!

Chapter Five
Saliva Drooling From Her Mouth

Union Square, New York City
March 31 One Year After Luke Left Katya in New Orleans
Katya

   Union Square, by the George Washington Statue.
Four o'clock, thirty-first March. Promise me, baby.

   The memory of Michael's voice rang in my ears as I walked across Union Square to the George Washington Statue. I was fifteen minutes early and wrapped up warmly against the biting cold. Rain was predicted and although the clouds hovered, I was relieved it was still dry. After months of West Coast sunshine, the New York winter bit colder than I remembered.

   When I was at university and then working in Chelsea, the frenetic madness and mercurial nature of Manhattan appealed strongly to me after the bleak and controlled atmosphere of my childhood home in Sterling Ridge. But now, I found I wasn't ready for the energetic buzz, and after less than a day, I was missing the warmth and tranquility of Encinitas.

   I was also desperately missing Lily. It was hard to leave her with Dani and Carmen. Over the last week, I had expressed endless bottles of milk so my hungry daughter had a plentiful supply of mommy's milk, but my breasts still throbbed, a constant reminder of the distance between us.

I stood against the low black fence that surrounded the statue and checked my watch. Still twelve minutes to go. *Why am I early? So dumb.* I should have made him wait for me. What was I thinking?

I wasn't thinking, that was the problem. I was living on my nerves with a constant need to reassure myself this was the right thing to do. Every time I had doubts, I only had to look into Lily's eyes to be reminded of what was at stake.

But Lily wasn't here now and standing alone, I was again racked with misgivings. It was curious how time had lessened the impact of Michael's betrayal. When I lay in bed late at night, trying to grab a bit of sleep before Lily woke me with her hungry cries, I spent more time reliving his touch, his charm, his irresistible lazy smile, than I did his betrayal. I passed countless hours wondering if I had over-reacted. I even found myself looking for reasons to excuse his actions.

I pulled my scarf up to cover my freezing ears. It was time to accept that my decision to return to New York was not just for Lily, it was also for myself. I ached to see him again. He had pleaded with me to take a leap of faith, and here I was. I needed him to fulfill his promise.

Please, Michael, please be here, I silently begged.

****

Luke

Breathe you bastard, breathe.

Luke rubbed damp palms on his jeans when he caught sight of Katya entering Union Square.

Jesus, she was here!

Elation stole his breath as he glimpsed her for the first time in over a year.

She believed enough to come.

He adjusted his lens and focused closer, catching a guarded anticipation on her face. His elation faded. A familiar heaviness crept in as he accepted that her faith in him would soon be ripped apart. His betrayal, once again, would leave only bitter disappointment and shattered hope in its wake.

Dammit. Why does the timing have to suck so bad? Over a month ago his relationship with Nicu changed drastically. This created an opportunity that meant it was unlikely he would be able to meet Katya as promised.

Hell. He hadn't even been confident that she would keep her promise to meet him. But if she did turn up, he knew he had to be there too. No matter that he wouldn't let her see him.

So, in his normal meticulous manner, he reconnoitered the area and selected this eighth floor apartment on East Fourteenth Street, directly opposite Union Square. It was far enough away that, with a good spotting scope positioned at the window, there wasn't a chance of her sighting him.

Goosebumps broke out and he cursed his fucked up predicament. He was desperate to reach out and touch her, feel her soft warmth. Even if it was only to reassure her. But instead he was again stuck behind a scope, so near but too fucking far.

He kept his eyes locked on her as he waited for Gray to arrive. She was obviously cold, huddling deep into her coat. Probably used to a warmer climate.

Maybe she was still living in Mexico?

There was something different about her, but he couldn't put his finger on it. He zoomed the lens in a little closer. Her face had a softness about it, a fullness that he didn't remember. He stiffened at a fleeting thought but discarded it as he heard the door behind him open.

"What's up, Hunt? This isn't our usual meet spot."

Luke watched as Katya leaned against the low fence. He was reluctant to look away but he knew she wasn't going anywhere and he needed to brief Gray. He forced himself to move away from the lens and meet his partner's questioning regard. "You're not going to like it," he warned.

Gray stilled at Luke's tone. He quietly contemplated his friend and partner.

"It's about Katya," Luke said.

"Katya Dalca?"

Luke nodded. "When I left her in New Orleans it was intense."

"I know."

"Yeah, well, something went down and I made her promise to meet me. Here in New York, a year later."

"You're shitting me?"

"Nope." Luke shook his head. "And today is a year later. Four o'clock today, to be precise."

"Jesus Christ, I don't fucking believe this. How do you know she's even going to pitch?"

"Because she's already here."

"What? That's who you're scoping?" Gray pushed Luke away from the tripod that supported the long-range spotting scope. "Let me see."

Luke got up and stepped aside as his friend took a

long look through the lens.

Gray lifted his head to stare enigmatically at Luke. "So tell me, why are you up here and she's down there?"

Luke's hands curled into fists, and he took a slow breath. "With everything that's gone down in the last month I can't take the risk of meeting with her. We got lucky with that fuck-up that went down with the Armenians. Me saving Nicu's ass has finally got us the break we need. We do this right we get to take all those motherfuckers down."

"You think she'll choose her father over you?"

"It's not that. When we pull the plug on Nicu and Arkady's operation, there's going to be a shit storm. I don't want Katya caught up in the middle of that."

"I get that Luke, but what about afterward? Her father will either be dead or in prison. You think she's going to forgive you?"

"It's not about forgiveness, it's about moral strength. Nicu may only be the transporter, but he might as well be the seller. Without him the drugs can't move. He's just as responsible as the drug lords for ruining lives, destroying families." Luke moved to the window and sat back down in the small chair. He looked through the scope and absorbed the increasing concern on Katya's face. "If she doesn't get that, then we won't even make it out the starting blocks," he murmured. His scalp prickled as he felt Gray's laser sharp gaze and he braced for whatever he was going to say next.

"It's four o'clock. You need to be fucking sure about this, Hunter."

"I'm sure," he said resolutely.

"This is twice you've fucked her over. You think

she's going to get over that?"

When the time comes, he wasn't going to give her a choice.

Luke lifted his head and broke the tense silence. "I need you to do something for me."

"Whatever you need. You know that."

"I need you to follow her, find out where she's living. She's fallen off the grid and our techs haven't been able to locate her. Even now, there's no trace of her having re-entered the US."

"Nicu hasn't mentioned her at all?"

"Not a word."

"It's been a year and you still haven't let this woman go. This isn't like you—"

"Just follow her, Gray. Can you do that for me?"

Gray stiffened. Luke knew his curtness had upset him, but he didn't want the questions. He had no answers. His feelings for Katya were completely beyond his understanding. They were instinctive. Primal.

Nodding abruptly, Gray turned to leave. "I'll be in touch. Text me when she leaves."

Relieved, Luke turned back to the scope. He would sit here for as long as necessary.

An hour passed and he didn't move. Neither did Katya. She remained perfectly still except for the emotion evident on her beautiful face.

His gut clenched as he witnessed her pain finally spill over. Tears rolled down her cheeks, clearly visible on her flawless skin. Gripping the scope tightly, he swallowed down the nausea.

Was he making a mistake? Fuck! How could he do this to her again?

Conflicted, a long-buried image flashed through his mind.

His mother, sprawled on the couch, high from meth or heroin or whatever she had managed to score, saliva drooling from her mouth.

Goddammit! He had a job to do, a mission objective.

In spite of that, he couldn't prevent the haunting doubt that his decision today would have long-lasting repercussions for his future.

****

Katya

It was after five o'clock and I was freezing. I hadn't moved in over an hour, stubbornly refusing to accept he wasn't coming. I was crying now, my tears mixing with the ice-cold drizzle that was slowly soaking through my clothes.

Why did he beg me to be here today? Make me promise him?

Here I was, on the other side of the country from my daughter, chilled to the bone and crying my eyes out. *Dammit.* I was furious with myself for being so weak, falling for his charm. I rubbed my wet cheeks. *Such a stupid idiot.*

I needed to leave, but the vivid memory of Lily's trusting eyes kept me rooted in place.

"Miss? Hello, miss?" I flinched as somebody tapped my arm. Oblivious to my surroundings, I hadn't noticed the man approach me. It took a moment to realize his concern. "Are you all right?"

He must have been in his fifties, short grayish hair, a long trench coat likely covering a business suit. "Uh," I croaked, clearing my throat. "Sorry, what?"

"You're standing in the rain, miss, crying. Are you all right?" He moved his umbrella to protect me from the numbing drops.

I blinked. Great, I must look like a crazy person. "I'm fine. It's just, um, a bad day." Wiping away what was probably black mascara running down my cheeks, I tried to smile at him. He didn't look reassured.

"Can I call someone for you? Or get you a taxi?"

His earnest regard shook me from my stupor. *Get a grip, girl.* "Thanks, no, I'll be fine." I yanked my scarf over my head to protect myself from the rain.

"You sure?"

"Yes, thank you," I said with determination. "I'm going to be fine."

Stepping around him I walked quickly away and headed back into the subway.

****

Grayson

Gray furiously pulled at the cord wrapped tightly around his ankles. *Fuck!* He couldn't believe he was lying here on his ass while her train disappeared into the tunnel.

What the hell had happened?

He'd followed Katya into the subway, careful to keep his distance when she switched trains at Grand Central and boarded the Flushing Express. She was probably heading to LaGuardia. He'd hung back and chosen an end carriage to lessen the chances she would spot him. But as he moved to board, he'd been taken out like a green recruit. Laid flat by an over-sized Romanian mobster, throwing, of all things, some sort of modified *bolas,* which entangled his legs and sent him crashing helplessly to the ground. *Shit.* He'd been solely focused on the woman, completely unaware that Petrov was even in the frame.

Goddammit!

Gritting his teeth, he took several calming breaths. Luke hadn't warned him that Nicu was keeping tabs on his daughter, which meant he didn't know. Unwinding the weighted rope with difficulty, he looked up at the computerized board to see how long before the next train arrived. He had a contact at LaGuardia, hopefully he would be able to track Katya down before she boarded a plane and disappeared on them again.

****

Two hours later Gray admitted defeat. There was no sign of Katya at all. Security didn't have her entering the departure terminal. He had them check their cameras in both the domestic and international halls. Nothing. His contact couldn't find her listed on any departing flights. There was also no sign of Grigori Petrov. The Romanian had made like a ghost too.

Fucking great. He was going to have to call Luke and tell him he'd messed up. He couldn't remember a time when he had failed his brother. Never.

It was going to cut Luke. There was something about this woman that screwed with his head. If Gray wasn't careful, she was going to achieve what three tours in Iraq and Afghanistan hadn't. She was going to rip them apart.

****

Nicu

Grigori's name flashed on his phone, and Nicu quickly answered. "Yes?"

"It's good, boss."

"What happened?"

"She was followed, but I interfered. Kept the pig from boarding the train."

"Who was it?"

"Don't know? Maybe DEA. Nobody I recognized from the street."

"Where is she now?"

"She rented a car at LaGuardia. From the look of it, she's heading to Philly."

"Stay with her. See she boards her flight safely."

"*Da*. I see you tomorrow."

Nicu pocketed his phone and closed his eyes. His daughter's image hovered in his mind's eye, as clear to him today as it always was.

****

Katya

I took the pain of Michael's betrayal and buried it in the deepest part of my heart, right alongside the murder of my mother. Then I started the arduous task of sealing it in that box. I'd learned from experience that the seal would never stay true, it was like the pain was just too huge to ever be completely contained. But I'd also learned that as time passed, the raw pain would lessen. Life was relentless like that.

My body felt heavy and I rubbed at my gummy eyelids. I was drained by the long drive from New York to Philadelphia. Hector had been adamant about my method of travel. If I wanted to remain anonymous and protect my new life, I had to follow certain avoidance tactics. So I had gone through the farce of heading to LaGuardia. On arrival, I hot-footed it to the car rental section and rented a vehicle to drive to Philadelphia Airport. The journey took me nearly four hours. The first two I spent intermittently crying and then raging at how Michael had fooled me. The last hour I drove on autopilot, a welcome numbness settling over me.

The departure hall was bleak. I sat alone, yet surrounded by people. Strangers. A sense of familiar abandonment penetrated my deadened emotions and I shivered. Wrapping my arms tightly around myself, I blinked away tears as a distant memory surfaced. I was ten years old. My mother was dead and my father sent me to stay with my maternal grandparents, Mary and Frank Langworth. He promised me it would be for a short time only, but he lied. He abandoned me there for months and months.

The way I felt now was how I felt then. *So goddamn alone.*

My cousin, Julian, came to visit. He was my mother's sister's son and four years older than me. I didn't know him well. Grandma asked him to play with me and he took me outside into the gardens. He was charming and kind, and to a lonely, heartbroken little girl, he was like an angel because he reminded me of my mother. I started to cry and to make me stop he offered to show me his secret hiding place: an old tree house high up in a giant oak. The rope ladder was broken, so he fetched a ladder from the shed and we climbed up. But once I crawled into the little wooden house, Julian removed the ladder and disappeared. He left me there. All alone. I remember my greatest fear was that nobody would ever find me. My terror was so great it paralyzed my voice. I heard people calling for me but I couldn't move. Couldn't shout back. It seemed like forever to my young self before my grandfather eventually poked his head inside and called to me. I crawled into his arms but I didn't feel safe. Not then.

Maybe not ever.

"Ma'am, are you on the San Diego flight?"

I stared blankly at the earnest American Airlines flight attendant. Again, I was caught unawares, stuck inside my head. "Sorry?"

"The gate is closing. If you're on the flight, ma'am, you need to board now."

"Oh, I'm sorry. Yes, I'm coming." I grabbed my bag and followed her to the gate to hand in my boarding pass.

"Thank you, Miss Molina. Have a good flight."

"Thanks." I stiffened my spine and entered the boarding tunnel.

That's right. I'm Kat Molina.

Damn Michael! And damn my father!

Boarding the plane, I made a new vow—Katya Dalca was dead. Gone.

I would not be a sad, sniveling doormat. I was Kat Molina. Single mother, strong, capable. Loved by people who mattered. I would build a life that mattered. For myself. For Lily.

Damn them all!

Chapter Six
Carnage All Around Me

New York City, Five Years Later, May 5
Katya

I was unsettled but also excited to be back in New York. This time I wasn't alone, Lily and Dani were with me. We arrived late and crashed early as we wanted a good night's sleep. Today was going to be a big day.

Yes. Today was my thirtieth birthday. A milestone for sure, but also the age when I could legally claim a legacy bequeathed to me by my mother. It was called the Preston Inheritance, named for my maternal great-grandfather. Blessed with only one daughter, he was paranoid about protecting his fortune from gold-diggers. He drafted a draconian will that allowed only direct descendants to inherit on their thirtieth birthdays. Half his fortune went to his daughter, Mary Langworth, and the other half to her two daughters, Elizabeth and Silvia, my mother. Silvia's untimely death when I was ten years old meant my inheritance had been held in trust by the law firm, Connor & Stanton, for the last twenty years.

I woke up early, dressed and slipped out the room. I had an early meeting with my attorney, Mr. Connor. I had met him once, years before, when he granted me a special dispensation to draw against the trust for my

Berkeley University fees. At the time he offered to brief me on the trust portfolio but I declined. I hadn't been ready to cope with anything connected with my mother. Today, he was as courteous as ever. And remarkably patient when I asked him to repeat himself several times while I tried to absorb the shock of the size of my inheritance.

Oh my God! I'm rich. I mean really, really rich!

When we finished, Mr. Connor handed me a letter from Mary Langworth, my grandmother. I hadn't spoken to her in nearly twenty years.

On the drive back to the hotel I read through the letter, twice. My mind reeled. I stared out the backseat window, barely cognizant of the passing streets. I couldn't get her request out of my mind.

The car pulled up to the New York Palace Hotel on Madison Avenue, and the door was opened by the hotel doorman. "Morning, ma'am."

Distracted, I returned his smile and stepped out of the car. He rapidly backed away, eyes fixed on something over my shoulder. *What?* Impatient, I turned to look behind me.

And my world exploded into a fragmented nightmare. In slow motion.

A black van was parked haphazardly on the other side of my car. The sliding door gaped open and two masked men jumped out.

Oh shit! Are those guns they're holding? The man in front moved quickly towards me. He was huge. Hulk huge. *And yes. That is definitely a gun. A big gun!*

"*Sooka*!" He spat, wielding that horrible weapon at me. "In the van. *Now!*"

I stepped back in an attempt to keep the sedan

between myself and the gun-wielding hulk. *What did he say? Get in the van?* My stomach clenched. Out of the corner of my eye I saw his sidekick closing in. They were going to trap me between them.

Images flashed through my mind. *Lily. Father. Is this his fault? But he's in prison.*

Oh God, what do I do?

I was trapped in a hideous movie. I could actually hear my heartbeat racing.

"Quick. Grab her." The hulk leapt over the front of the black sedan. I scrambled backwards, violently recoiling when I bumped into a hard body. Before I could do anything my arm was yanked behind me and I cringed as steely fingers wrapped around my upper arm.

Hot breath rasped over my ear. "Move it bitch, or I'll blow your fucking head off!"

There was no way I was getting in that van.

I gathered my wits, tried to remember my meager self-defense training from Hector, and kicked backwards. Hard. My high-heeled boot made a dent in his shin. Before he could react, I threw back my head and smashed it into his nose, well I hoped it was his nose. *Take that, you bastard!*

"Fuck!" he roared, rearing backwards.

Yes! I pulled away as his hold loosened. But he clung on, his hand slipping to grip my wrist. Spinning around, I tried to twist loose. I ignored the gun waving in my face because he was overpowering me. I was steadily being pulled towards the van when the air was suddenly filled with the screech of tires. I turned my head and caught sight of two black SUVs. The doors flew open and dark figures dropped out. *Oh no! They've also got guns.* My wrist was released and I instinctively dropped into a crouch, covering my head with my arms.

Ping. Ping. They were shooting!

Shit! Shit! I couldn't hear what they were shouting, my ragged gasps too loud in my head.

A hand gripped my shoulder and I instinctively dropped to my knees to scramble away.

"Katya! Katya!"

My way was blocked. *Oh God!* The gunman who had tried to pull me into the van was sprawled awkwardly across the sidewalk. *Is he dead?*

"Come on, Katya, you've got to move."

The familiar voice triggered a clanging in the pit of my stomach. I looked upwards at the man who had his hand on my shoulder and stared into midnight-blue eyes. Heartbreakingly, beautiful eyes. They were deep navy-blue, fringed with lush, dark-blond lashes. I had only ever seen eyes like that on two people, one was the man who betrayed me and the other was Lily, my daughter.

What is Michael doing here?

****

Luke

Katya's eyes were huge in her white face.

Shit! This wasn't how he had planned their reunion.

Luke was furious. It had taken over five years for her to finally turn up, only to be caught in a hail of bullets. He had no time to sweet-talk her. Grabbing her hand he pulled her to her feet. "Come on, Katya, we've got to get you off the street."

He tucked her against his body and pushed her towards one of their SUVs.

"Secure the scene, cops are on their way," he heard King order, already taking charge of the chaos. "This one's still alive, get him cuffed, now."

Katya resisted him, her body stiff and she still hadn't uttered a word.

"Luke, we gotta move. Her room's been hit." He turned as Gray urgently jogged across to him. "We've got two dead shooters and a woman bleeding out."

"What woman?"

"No idea but it's a fucking mess."

Katya struggled to get loose. "Take it easy, babe." But she wasn't paying him attention, her focus riveted on Gray.

"What room?" she gasped. "Oh my God, you're Jules."

"Your hotel room, sweetheart. We need—"

"No!" Katya screamed, going crazy as Luke's grip on her tightened.

"Jesus, what the fuck?"

But she wasn't listening. She was kicking and screaming. Luke couldn't hold on to her without hurting her. The next thing he knew she was off, running into the hotel entrance.

"King! Something's up. I need back-up," he called and bolted after her.

"What the fuck is up with her?" Gray said, running at his side.

Luke didn't answer, chasing after Katya as she ran up the ornate steps to the hotel's grand lobby. She didn't pause as she raced over white marble floors, past the elevators and crashed through the doors leading to the fire-escape stairs. She still didn't slow, taking them two at time. He tried to make out what she was saying, it sounded like she was pleading. Or praying.

"Katya! Dammit, slow down. There might be more shooters."

"No! No! No!" She screamed hysterically and picked up her pace even more.

When they hit the fourth floor, Luke was right on her heels. He made a grab for her but she shook him off and slammed through the doors and down the corridor.

"Fuck!" He saw Tane, armed and stationed outside her hotel room and shouted as he drew down on her. "Tane, no! She's with me."

Katya ignored Tane and his drawn weapon and pushed into the room.

"Lily! Oh my God, *Lily*!"

"Stay here," Luke instructed Tane as he followed her into the room. There was a dead body lying face down in the entrance hall.

Katya stepped over him. "Dani!"

A woman was sprawled on the floor between the two beds. Matiu was working furiously to stop the blood from flowing out of the bullet holes that riddled her body. Alongside the far bed was another shooter, this one face up and also dead.

"Dani!" Katya cried, bending over the dying woman. "Dani, please, where's Lily?"

"Tane! ETA on ambulance?" Matiu called. "If they don't haul ass we're gonna lose her."

"Two minutes!"

"Oh God nooooo! Lily!" Katya's scream was spine-chilling.

Luke pulled her away from the pooling blood, and pointed to the woman on the floor. "Is that Lily?"

She shook her head. Her eyes were dilated with

shock. He gently shook her. "Who's Lily? Come on, baby, tell me who Lily is?"

"My daughter," she whispered. "She's not here."

****

Katya

I registered the stunned look on Michael's face. Or rather, the man I knew as Michael. I knew that wasn't his name. I didn't care. Dani was shot, dying on our hotel room carpet, and Lily was gone.

"How old is she?" asked Jules.

"Five."

"Describe her."

"She's got long hair, down to her waist, light brown with blonde streaks. And blue eyes."

"Good," Jules said encouragingly. "What was she wearing?"

"I don't know. She was sleeping when I left." I looked around desperately, the panic smothering me. I could see Dani's bare feet out of the corner of my eye. *Don't die, Dani. Oh God, please don't die.*

"Where's your phone, sweetheart? Do you have a photo of her?"

"What?"

"A photo? Come on Katya, you need to focus."

A photo? Shit, of course. "My purse—"

"It's strapped across your shoulder, here let me get it." Jules reached across and unhooked my purse that was miraculously still intact. He dug inside and passed me my phone. "Here you go."

I quickly tapped the picture store and looked for a good image of Lily. *There.* She was in her favorite pink ballet dress, her hair tied in a long ponytail with a sparkling red bauble.

I squeezed my phone tightly. *Yes.* That was my daughter, full of sunshine and sparkles. Forcing myself to loosen my grip, I handed the phone to Jules. "Here she is."

"Luke, I've got a photo," Jules called out.

Luke. His name is Luke.

"Email it to King," he instructed. "I'm on the phone with him now. He'll make sure it gets out."

"Clear a hole, EMS is here."

"King. Katya's got a daughter, she's been snatched. Gray's emailing you with a pic now. You need to question the shooter that's still breathing. Find out what he knows."

I listened to the man who called himself Luke and clutched my arms tightly to control my shaking. It was impossible to comprehend the nightmare in front of me. Medics rushed in to tend to Dani. I moved out of their way and hovered against the wall.

Carnage all around me.

The primal urge to scream welled up and I clenched my jaw, forcing it back. I would not let it overpower me.

I looked back over at Luke. He was talking rapidly to Jules. Or Gray. Or whatever the hell his name was! I could no longer make out their words, their tense chatter a discordant noise. Then Luke walked out and Gray approached me.

"What's happening?"

"We've sent Lily's photo out to our whole team." He handed me back my phone. "King's alerted the police as well."

"Who's King?"

"Thane Kingsley. He owns King Security, that's

who we all work for."

"Who's Michael?"

He gave me a long measured look. "Michael's real name is Luke Hunter," he said. "And the rest darlin'- you're going to have to take that up with him."

"And you? Jules?"

"It's Gray. Grayson Walker."

"Coming through, clear the way."

I sucked in a breath as the medics wheeled out the stretcher. The man called Matiu held a drip above Dani's head. I reached out but she was gone before I could say anything. It didn't matter. What would I say?

I looked over to where she had been lying. Bile rose in my throat. There was so much blood. How could Dani survive such a huge loss of blood?

Luke came back in with two uniformed policemen and a woman who looked like a detective. His eyes caught mine and he said something to the detective. Whatever it was, they stopped and he approached me. The hotel phone on the table beside me rang. Automatically I picked it up. "Hello."

"Katya?"

"Yes."

"Katya, it is Grigori."

"What? Who?"

"Grigori Petrov. I worked for your father. I still work for him."

"What do you want?" I remembered him. He was hard to forget. "Why are you calling me now?"

"Katya, you must listen to me. It's about Lily."

"You bastard! Where's Lily?" I shouted.

"I have her. She is safe."

"Oh my God! Where are you?" The receiver was

grabbed from me.

"Who is this?" Luke said sharply into the phone. "Jesus fuck! Are you insane? Where are you?"

I grasped at Luke, trying to reach for the phone but he was much taller than me. "Dammit, give me that phone!" His arm reached out and a hand curled around my neck, his thumb covering my lips.

"Which room?" Luke stared back at me, nodding. "Forget it, she's not coming."

I grabbed his hand and pulled it away from my mouth. "Don't you shut me up. That's *my* daughter, and I want to know what the hell is going on," I hissed at Luke.

"Hang on," he said into the phone, and then putting his hand over the mouthpiece, he leaned into me. "You have to calm down."

"I am fucking calm. Don't you try and take over. I want to know where that Romanian guard-dog is and where he's taken Lily."

"He's in another room, one floor below. Gray and I will go and fetch her."

"No!"

"Katya, it's not safe."

"My best friend is dying and my daughter is missing. I know it's not safe, but Grigori will never hurt me. If he has Lily he'll be more likely to hand her over to me than to either of you two. Whoever the hell you both are!"

"Hunt, we're wasting time. She's right. Let's go," Gray urged. "You take point. I'll hang back with Katya, keep her covered. That work for you darlin'?" he drawled at me.

I nodded impatiently. "Yes. Let's go."

"Fuck!" Luke lifted the receiver to his ear. "All right, she's coming now. I'll be with her and one of my men. Don't fuck with me Petrov. You know me and you know I'll put a bullet in your head without a moment's thought."

Luke knows Grigori? Of course he does. But I couldn't think about that right now. I moved quickly out of the room, ignoring the policemen who attempted to waylay Luke and headed back to the fire escape.

****

Luke

Katya was trying to pull the fire-escape door open that led out to the third floor, but Luke held it closed.

"Dammit! Let me out," she demanded.

"Not yet."

"He has my daughter, now let me the hell out."

"Do you want Lily to live?"

She glared up at him, those violet eyes spitting with fury. "What do you mean?"

"Christ, Katya, we don't know what's waiting for us." He knew most of her anger was driven by fear and he needed her to hear him. "The only way you're going through that door is if I'm in charge. Do you understand?"

She looked away and visibly clawed back control, taking several deep breaths. Then without looking back at him she nodded.

"Okay. This is how it's going to happen. He's in room 304. I'll take point and will knock on the door and draw him out. You stay here with Gray—"

"No!"

"Katya—"

"You're not going without me. I agree to hang

back with Gray, but that's all."

Luke glanced over at Gray who was leaning against the wall, arms folded. "Don't look at me," he shrugged. "I'm just along to take your six."

He tilted his head down to Katya who mutinously stared at the door. *Fuck. They were wasting time.* "Hold her back until I've cleared the way," he said to Gray. "Let's go."

As he opened the door he was sure he heard her mutter 'finally' under her breath and he couldn't help the small smile. *His woman was still cute.*

They moved down the passage to room 304, which was near the elevators. He lifted his hand to knock but paused to look back at Gray. *Shit.* He was struggling to keep Katya behind him. He gestured for Gray to back up several steps, but Katya was making it difficult. Shaking his head, he knocked sharply on the door.

It opened so quickly that he barely had time to react as the large frame of Grigori Petrov stepped out and closed the door firmly behind him. By the time the door clicked closed Luke had his Glock 22 in Petrov's face.

"*Zhopa!*" Petrov cursed, leaning away.

"You're the asshole!" Luke said. The man always cursed in Russian. "Where's the kid?"

"You think I hurt that child? *Chyort!* She is Nicu's grandchild! I am loyal, not like you. Traitor!" He spat.

"Shit," Luke heard Gray mutter and in his periphery vision saw Katya pull away from him. She quickly approached and he reached out an arm to hold her back.

"Where's my daughter?" She cried, trying to push his arm away. "Tell me where Lily is now, Grigori, or I swear I'll tell him to shoot you."

"Mommy, Mommy!" A child's cry came from behind the door.

"Lily!"

This was escalating. He needed to take control or it was going to be a shit storm. "Katya!" Luke kept his gun pointed steadily at Petrov. "Lily's frightened. The quicker you step back and let me check out the room, the quicker she's going to be in your arms." Pushing her behind him, he added, "Please, baby."

She eased behind him and Luke stared down his gun-barrel at the glowering Romanian. "Give me the keycard." Petrov reached into his pocket. "Slowly," Luke said.

He handed the card over to Luke. "What now?"

"Against the wall, over there." Luke used his weapon to indicate to Petrov to move away from the door. "Gray. You got him."

"Yeah."

"Mommy!"

"It's okay, Lily. Mommy's here."

He slid the card into the slot and eased the door open. A child slipped out before he could stop her.

"Lily!"

He quickly lowered his gun and watched Katya crouch down and wrap the girl tightly in her arms.

"I'm here, baby-girl. It's all okay, Mommy's here."

"Check the room." Luke dipped his head at Gray while keeping an eye on Petrov.

As Gray slipped into the room, Katya stood up, her daughter held tight against her. "I've got you, baby-girl," she crooned, her child's face buried in her neck.

Seconds later, Gray stepped out, holding the door

open. "All clear."

The little girl lifted her head and looked straight at Luke. The hair on his arms stood up and every muscle in his body went rigid.

What the hell? He was staring into eyes the exact midnight-blue shade as his own.

Katya turned to face him, but whatever she was about to say died on her lips when she saw his face.

Luke knew he looked shell-shocked. He could no more prevent it than he could the adrenaline that raced through his body. An elevator dinged and he dropped his gaze. Violet eyes went round and she bit her bottom lip.

"Luke, we need to move inside," Gray said.

Briefly disorientated, he forced himself to move. "Go inside with Petrov," he said to Katya. "We all need to talk." He could see she was anxious, adrenaline crashing, as the fear for her daughter's safety waned. "Go on," he encouraged. "Gray and I will join you now."

Gray closed the door behind Petrov as he followed her into the room. Luke was reeling, goosebumps still raised on his arms. "Did you see the kid's face? Her eyes?"

"Yeah."

"Then you know she's mine."

"Likely."

"Christ! How did I let this happen?" He ran his hand through his hair, then gripped the back of his neck. "I fucked up. I fucked up so bad I don't know if I'm ever going to be able to fix it."

"You'll find a way."

Luke shook his head.

"You don't have a choice," Gray said solemnly. "Inside that room is your family and your first priority, Hunter, is to keep them safe. Yeah?"

Luke stared at his friend. He was right but he made it sound easy. And he knew it wasn't fucking easy, it was anything but.

****

Katya

"Auntie Dani was bleeding, Mommy."

"I know, baby-girl." I was perched on the edge of one of the two beds, Lily curled in my lap.

"Is she dead?"

"No, sweetheart," I crooned. "She's hurt real bad and they took her to the hospital." The image of Dani lying so still, the plush carpet soaked with her blood, was seared on my brain. *How much did Lily see?* I wanted to ask Grigori but I couldn't do it in front of her.

The door opened and Luke and Gray came in. Both totally badass. They oozed testosterone which was intensified by their black combat gear. I had to admit, they were hot. Gray was movie star good-looking: dark tousled hair and muscular, but leaner than Luke. From what I'd experienced so far, he was full of Southern charm that he wielded like a dangerous weapon. And Luke? He was six years older than the last time I saw him and more potent than ever. It didn't escape my notice that even through the madness of the morning, my reaction to him was extreme. And I hated it.

I was still in denial that he was even here. And with all the craziness going on, I hadn't had time to process it. I really didn't want anything to do with him but there wasn't a chance in hell of avoiding him now.

My stomach churned and I hugged Lily closer. He had taken one look at her and known exactly who she was to him.

I watched him stalk past us to join Grigori at the window. I wanted to listen in, but Lily was clinging to me.

"Katya?" I looked down at Gray who had crouched down to talk to me whilst sliding off his flak jacket. "Why don't you let me take Lily and we'll watch some TV together?"

I shook my head, stroking my daughter's hair.

"C'mon, sweetheart. You need to talk with them." He nodded at Luke and Grigori. "The little one doesn't need to hear. Right?"

"She's frightened."

"I know." He looked steadily at me.

He was right. I needed to talk with Grigori and Luke and it couldn't wait.

"Hey, baby-girl." I rubbed Lily's back and leaned away so I could see her face. "Mommy needs to speak with those men. It's really important." My heart ached to see my daughter so cowed. She was usually a ray of sunshine, her exuberance spilling out to infect everybody around her. Now, she sucked her thumb, eyes huge in her ashen face. "Can you be a big girl and watch TV with Mr. Walker?"

She looked down at Gray without moving her head. I gave her time to think. My daughter was stubborn and could rarely be coaxed into doing something she didn't want to do.

"You brave enough to sit with me, sunshine?" Gray encouraged Lily. "Your mommy will be over there." He pointed at the window. "Right where you can see her."

After a moment Lily dropped her thumb and reached up to whisper in my ear. "Can we watch cartoons?"

I blinked to clear the sudden tears and hugged my daughter tight. "Yes, baby, whatever you want."

Gray built up a nest of pillows in the middle of the bed furthest from the window and raided the bar-fridge for sodas and chocolate. He was incredibly warm and gentle with her and she settled quickly. I found a cartoon channel and set the TV volume high to drown out the talk I was about to have with the men who waited for me at the window. I took a deep breath, kissed Lily and walked across the room.

"Tell me what happened." I folded my arms and looked directly at Grigori.

"Katya, I am sorry," he said earnestly, clasping his palms together in apology.

"Did you shoot Dani?"

"*Nu!* No!"

"Then what happened? And what exactly did my daughter see?"

"Okay, okay. Nicu, he call me early today—"

"My father! He's in prison, why would he call you?"

"Babe," Luke said, bending down to me. "You need to cool it and listen."

His face was too close to mine, those damn midnight eyes narrowed on me. "Why are you calling me babe? And why is my father still fucking up my life?" It was a demand but it came out sounding more like a plea.

His face softened and the warmth he radiated touched something inside me. "Give him a chance to tell us what happened. Then we'll decide together what to do from there. Yeah?"

I nodded, the lump in my throat made it impossible to answer him.

"Get on with it, Petrov," he clipped.

"So Nicu call me. He was angry. He say he just receive information you return to New York. You have no protection. He order me to Palace Hotel, give me room number and tell me to watch over you and your little girl. He say nothing about your lady friend."

"Who told him I was coming to New York. And why would he think I needed protection?"

Grigori looked at Luke and shrugged.

"What happened next?" Luke said.

"I am in the stairwell. It is still early, I think Katya in room with her daughter. But soon after I arrive, I see two men at her door. They pull out guns. They are quick, but I recognize them."

"Who?" Luke bit out.

"They are protection for Boykov."

"Arkady?" I said. "But he's dead."

"*Da*, but his son is not dead. They work for Lev Boykov."

Lev. I shivered. Just the thought of that psycho made my skin crawl.

"They shoot out the lock," Grigori continued. "Then they are in the room. I move fast, follow them into room and shoot one in the entrance. Your lady-friend, she is shouting. She push little girl behind bed and before she can do anything the other one, he shoots her."

I couldn't stop the sob. *Oh God! I'm so sorry, Dani. Thank you for saving Lily.*

"I am sorry, Katya," Grigori implored. "I could not shoot him first, she is in the way. Only when she fall do I have clear shot. Then I kill him."

"Lily," I whispered, wiping away my tears. "What did she see?"

"Not so much. She on the floor behind the bed. I pick her up and carry her but she see your friend bleeding. I cover her eyes and take her out, bring her to this room."

"Thank you, Grigori." I said sincerely. If not for this man who had been my father's shadow for most of my life, my daughter would be dead or in the hands of a psycho. "What does Lev want with me?" I turned to Luke. "And how did he even know I was here?"

"We'll talk about that later," Luke said.

"But—"

"No, Katya. Not here," Luke insisted, and his eyes briefly slid to Grigori.

All right. So he didn't want to talk in front of Grigori. But there was something else I wanted to know. "Tell me, Grigori, why is my father still keeping tabs on me. How did he know I was here?"

"Katya, he is your father. Just because you run away, this does not mean you stop being his daughter. You come with me now, to safe place. Then you must go visit him. He wants to see you."

"No!" Lily looked across at me and I clamped my lips together. I had to keep my voice down. "He is not responsible for my safety," I whispered harshly. "What right does he have to insist on seeing me? He's been in prison for the last four years and he's got at least another four to go. He has no rights, especially not with me."

113

There was a knock at the door and Gray got up to answer it.

The room was suddenly quiet except for the lunatic lyrics of SpongeBob Squarepants reverberating from the TV.

My breath was labored and I was finding it difficult to think clearly.

Gray came back in. Thane Kingsley was with him.

I couldn't help noticing Kingsley's incredible good looks, but there was a deadly quality about him. The air positively crackled with it. He appeared older than the others, maybe in his early forties. During the chaos in the street, his sharp British accent had easily cut through the confusion. He reminded me a little of Clive Owen, but so much more dangerous.

He hesitated as he passed Lily and looked down at her. I couldn't see his expression but she smiled back at him.

That was Lily, enchanting Mr. King of the Jungle himself.

He shook his head and then strode quickly over to join us. His eyes briefly took in Grigori and Luke, and then settled on me. "Miss Dalca."

"Molina," I corrected.

"You changed it legally?" And yes, there was definitely a lot of British in his arrogant question.

"Yes. Some time ago."

He nodded abruptly then looked at Luke. "You up to speed?"

"Yeah. Nicu brought in Petrov. He saw Lev's shooters enter the room. Managed to get the little one out, but not before Katya's friend took a few rounds."

"She's going to need to give a statement to the

police. I can't hold them off for much longer."

"They'll have to sit tight until we get her to a safe place."

"Fine. Where're you taking her? The safe house?"

"No. Home."

King's brow raised and a silent communication ensued between them while I tried to make sense of what I had heard. *Home? Luke's taking me home?*

"Mira's arrived," King said. "She can take point with Gray. The twins will take your six."

"Why are you taking me home?" I interrupted, folding my arms and glaring up at Luke.

"Because it's the safest place for you right now," Luke said.

"I'm not going home with you."

"Yes, you are."

"No, I'm not!"

Luke's hand wrapped around my arm. "S'cuse us," he said curtly to King and pulled me aside. Steely-blue shards glinted down at me. "Do you want to end up like Dani?"

"What?" I gasped.

"If you don't care about yourself, Katya, at least give a damn about Lily."

"Don't you manhandle me," I hissed, pulling my arm from his grasp. "And what are you talking about?"

"Lev Boykov is after you and Lily. He had no problem ordering his thugs to shoot your friend and make a grab for you in broad daylight, right outside this damn hotel."

"Why?" I cried. "I don't understand what the hell is going on."

"That's exactly right! And until we do know, you

and Lily are not safe. And I'm sure as fuck not handing you over to Petrov to play guard-dog."

I tore my eyes from his furious glare and looked over at Lily. She was curled on her side but instead of watching TV, she was sucking her thumb, her eyes glued to me. I remembered the promise I'd made to her when she was born. *Whatever it takes to keep you safe, baby-girl.*

The back of my throat throbbed and I swallowed with difficulty. "All right." I turned back to Luke. "But just for now."

He nodded, still scowling down at me.

"And I need to go straight to the hospital, wherever they took Dani."

"I'm sorry, Katya, but no. Until we get a handle on what happened and find out where Lev is hiding out, you need to stay out of the line of fire."

"But—"

"No, it's not gonna happen. But King will call, keep us updated on her condition. And I promise, I'll work out something by tomorrow. Yeah?"

He seemed sincere and at least his expression had softened. Right now I had no choice but to give in. "Okay."

He nodded again and we moved back to King and Gray who were talking quietly.

"All good?" King looked pointedly at Luke.

I bit my lip in frustration. The man was so arrogant, he acted like what I wanted didn't matter.

"Yeah," Luke clipped. "You said the twins will take our back. What about Matiu?"

"What about him?"

"He was with Dani, her friend, when the medics

took her out."

"Right. He stayed to help secure the scene."

"Good." Luke turned to me. "You carry Lily. Stay close to me and you do everything I tell you. The vehicles are in the basement and we're going to move fast."

"Okay," I breathed, my chest tightening. I was terrified.

"It's going to be fine, babe. I promise."

He promised? His promise didn't comfort me. Why would it?

"What about me?" Grigori demanded.

"Leave him to King, go and sort Lily," Luke said firmly. "And don't worry about your stuff, our team will pack up your room and bring it over later."

He stood there, the epitome of an alpha male in his prime. Confident I would follow his instructions. Never in doubt he could keep our daughter and me safe. I wondered if he had any idea how his presence had caused my world to implode. How the very idea of him back in my life made me feel anything but safe.

Chapter Seven
Will This Day Never End!

Katya

King's team moved us down to the basement like a well-oiled machine. Gray and King in front of us. The deadly duo of Tane and Matiu—referred to by the others as The Twins—behind us. I had not paid them any attention during the earlier nightmare, but now they caught my attention and they were breathtaking. Although similar in appearance, they were not identical. Tane had short, dark hair, cropped close to his head and Matiu had long, chocolate-brown dreadlocks. They were an exotic mix of island—maybe Hawaiian or Maori?—and something western. It was difficult to tell because they didn't talk much. Both powerfully built, their sculpted arms were covered in tattoos, obviously done by a master because the ink was like nothing I had ever seen before.

Alongside me was Luke. He was silent and vigilant, doing his best to hurry us along. But between the bulky, bullet-proof jacket I was now wearing and carrying Lily, who had her arms and legs wrapped tightly around me, I was finding it difficult to manage. By the time we hit the second floor Luke holstered his gun and stepped in front of me. Without any discussion, he gently pried Lily from my arms, held her easily against him and moved ahead. She seemed as startled as

I was, but after staring solemnly at him she rested her head against his shoulder and curled her arm around his neck.

We hit the basement and three black Ford Expeditions were lined up waiting for us. A dark figure stepped out from behind the front vehicle and for a split second I couldn't breathe.

"Mira!" Gray called. "Ride shotgun."

Okay then, I guess she's part of the team.

The slight woman dressed head to toe in black leather, hair sleeked back and confidently wielding a very big gun, nodded. Instead of walking around to the passenger door, she did an acrobatic one-handed move that took her over the SUV's hood. I gasped as she landed like a cat and smoothly climbed into the vehicle. She was like Batman's exotic side-kick!

Lily and I traveled with Luke. Lily was strapped into the small middle seat at the back, with me next to her, behind the passenger seat. Luke drove up front, alone. Mostly he was silent, his concentration alert to our surroundings. Every so often, he murmured into a blue-tooth device that connected him with the rest of his team. He did this so quietly that I couldn't make out what was being said.

We moved in convoy along FDR Drive and I soon caught glimpses of the East River. It suddenly occurred to me that I had no idea where Luke lived. *Damn.* I was reluctant to break the tense silence but I wanted to know where we were going. Leaning forward, I caught Luke's attention. "Um, where do you live?"

"Bay Ridge."

"Brooklyn?"

"Yeah."

"Isn't that where they filmed Saturday Night Fever?"

"Babe," he drawled. "We prefer to be known for our views of the Verrazano Bridge and Statue of Liberty, than John Travolta strutting his stuff to *Stayin' Alive*."

I quickly dipped my head to hide my smile. *Darn. I forgot how funny he could be.*

I was also stunned. *Luke lived in Bay Ridge.* I couldn't picture him in suburbia. A bachelor pad maybe. Or army barracks!

We crossed under Manhattan Bridge and Lily moved closer to me, finally taking an interest in the view from my window. "Would it be a problem to go over the Brooklyn Bridge?" I called to Luke. "It's nicer for Lily than the Tunnel."

His eyes briefly met mine in the rear-view mirror and I chose to ignore the weird spark that ignited somewhere inside my traitorous body. "Shouldn't be a problem," he said, and muttered into his mic, probably to alert the rest of the team.

Nearly thirty minutes later we pulled up to a lovely Victorian-style home. It had a wood facade, a steeply-pitched slate roof and was three stories high. A huge cutaway bay window looked out the front from the ground floor.

The intricate gabling and ornate moldings found in a lot of Victorian-style homes was absent, leaving only clean lines enhanced by an elegant dove-grey wash. All offset by crisp, white trim and window panes. The house shouted contemporary good taste.

It also shouted family.

"Katya!" Luke's exasperated voice interrupted my

distracted reverie.

"What?"

"You with me here?"

"Of course."

"I said Gray and I are gonna check my house. The twins will cover you. Stay put until I come get you."

"Oh."

"Yeah?" He pushed, clearly impatient with me.

"Okay. Yeah!" I repeated back at him.

Jeez! Luke had a million different ways of saying 'yeah'. Once, I had found it sexy. Now it annoyed me. *What right does he have to be irritated with me?* In the course of a morning, I had been caught in a hail of gunfire, my best friend shot, my daughter taken, and my worst nightmare of a Russian-drug-psycho appeared to be back in my life. Not to mention I had just inherited a ridiculous fortune.

And the icing on the cake? The man who had shut himself out of my heart five years ago was suddenly back in my life and giving me orders.

Jeez! Give me a break. I was entitled to be just a little bit out of it. *Wasn't I?*

****

Katya

Between the jet lag and the morning's trauma, Lily was shattered. As soon as he closed the front door, Luke noticed her clinging to my side and subtly suggested she take a rest. I gratefully agreed. Fear and exhaustion were swamping my baby-girl. She needed a bath, some hot milk and a long nap, which wouldn't happen until she felt safe again.

Luke wanted to put us in his bedroom but I flatly refused. There was no way I could cope with sleeping in his bed. We had a silent stare-down, which I won, and he ensconced us in a guest room on the same floor.

It took over an hour to settle Lily. I finally slipped from the bedroom, leaving the door ajar so I could hear her if she woke.

It was time to confront Luke.

I made my way downstairs, taking in the house as I went. There were hardwood floors throughout and the high ceilings and huge windows gave his home a light and airy vibe.

I found him downstairs in the kitchen. It was family-sized and recently renovated, with top-of-the-line appliances, custom-wood cabinets and quartz counter-tops. Luke was at the island, busy with what looked like the fixings for sandwiches. He had shed the bullet-proof jacket and visible weaponry, but was still dressed in black cargo pants and a tight black Henley, long sleeves pushed up to his elbows. I couldn't ignore how the fabric clung to his ripped physique.

He briefly looked up at me. "She asleep?"

I nodded.

"You want a sandwich?" He looked back down, continuing to slice cheese.

"Okay," I said, distracted by the muscles that roped down his forearms. He had long, strong fingers, scarred knuckles. I shuddered, a fleeting memory of calloused hands stroking my body.

Dammit! Remember who this man is. The damage he's done to you.

I shook off the seductive haze. "Who are you?" I asked determinedly.

"Is she mine?"

"Who was Michael?"

"Am I Lily's father?"

"Lily doesn't have a father!" I shouted vehemently. "Who is Luke? Is *that* even your real name?"

He put down the knife and leaned both hands on the counter-top. As he bent his head I could see a muscle jumping near his unshaven jawline. Except for his hands, which repeatedly stiffened then relaxed, he remained still. I held my breath, unnerved by the ringing silence. When he finally looked up, infinite blue pierced through me like the finest needle drawing blood. I knew in that moment that nothing had changed, this man would always affect me like no other.

"Breathe, Katya," he sighed. "We'll play this your way. If nothing else, you've earned at least that from me. Why don't you sit?" He nodded at the bar-stools alongside the island.

I quickly slipped onto a seat, not wanting to risk he'd change his mind. Leaning lightly against the island, I clasped my elbows and waited.

"Gray and I were recruited into a special task force straight out of the marines," he said quietly. "The purpose of the unit was to take down the country's worst criminals, especially those that believed they were untouchable. At the time I met you, our unit had been attached to the DEA for over a year. Gray and I were sent to New Orleans to recover the memory stick you took from your father."

It was a relief to learn he was one of the good guys, but it didn't warm me. Instead, bitterness leaked into my veins. He was selfish. Using my vulnerability, stampeding over my hopes and dreams, all in pursuit of his mission.

Luke continued his explanation, but I struggled to

contain the depth of my resentment.

"We were all over the Russian drug-ring but we couldn't get a foothold. Finally, months of back-breaking surveillance revealed that your father was involved, that he was the main transporter, and possibly the way in to take them all down. But your father was smart. He ran Lightning Transport as a legitimate business and he rarely put a foot wrong."

He crossed to the refrigerator and pulled out a Tupperware of lunch meats. I sat motionless as he moved back to the island, reached for the bread and started to spread butter. "Then we got lucky. One of our techs managed to secure a reverse tap on Nicu's phone. When activated, it behaved like a normal bug and we could listen in. We had to be careful how we used it, though. He swept his office regularly, and would have found it if we'd activated it during a sweep. The night you ran," he looked across at me, "we activated it hoping to pick up chatter between him and Arkady Boykov. Instead, we heard Nicu giving urgent instructions to Petrov to find you and recover his memory stick."

My throat tightened. I took that memory stick to keep me safe from my father. It seemed cruelly ironic that it had led to a far worse betrayal.

"Ham and cheese okay?"

I nodded, not yet trusting myself to speak.

"Mayo?"

I swallowed awkwardly, feeling trapped. His intense, questioning gaze asked me so much more than which sandwich fixings I was partial to. Slowly releasing a pent-up breath, I nodded again. His lips briefly twitched before he turned away to fetch the mayonnaise.

Nothing further was said as he finished up and handed me a plate with my sandwich. "Soda? Coffee?"

"Water's fine."

He fetched me a glass of water and sat down, leaving one bar-stool between us. The space allowed for a silent truce and we started to eat. I managed only half a sandwich, preoccupied with what to say next. Luke wolfed down his food, his appetite not hindered in any noticeable way.

I hesitantly planned my approach like I was standing on the edge of a mine-field. And once again my dithering gave him the opportunity to jump in first.

"It wasn't like you think, you know." He stood up and grabbed our plates.

What?

I flinched as he slammed them back down onto the table and looked at me. "I never planned to sleep with you."

Sleep with me?

I forced myself to maintain eye contact, but pain lanced through me. I hated him more at this moment than I ever had before. He had no idea how he had broken me and I needed to keep it that way. It had taken me too long to knit the pieces of myself back together. I would be a crazy person to ever let him close to my heart again.

"Then what exactly did you plan?" I was careful to keep my trembling hands under the table. He must have heard something in my voice because he stilled and studied me closely. I gripped my hands together, determined to maintain my outward calm.

"The *plan,*" he continued with emphasis, "was to

get friendly, wait for an opportunity to get you off guard and lift the memory stick. But you're *you*, so totally fucking addictive." He leaned closer and lifted his hand. I went rigid as his thumb brushed my lips, light as a feather. "The minute I saw you covered in sugar, I knew I was deep in it. So deep I was never getting out."

"Never getting out?" I scoffed, jerking away from his touch. "Bull! You were out the very next day."

"Was I?"

"Yes! Mission accomplished and you were out of there. Just explain one thing," I asked bitterly. "Why did you have to turn the screws, beg me to meet you in New York a year later. Tell me, what asshole does that?"

"Dammit, it wasn't like that!"

"I was there and it was exactly like that."

He ran both hands roughly through his hair. It was shorter, I noticed, and then turned away in irritation because I missed his ponytail.

His phone rang, a discordant note adding to the strained silence.

"Yeah," he murmured, answering. "One second." He walked out the kitchen.

I flopped back in my chair and pressed my hands to my churning stomach.

Well. That didn't go as smoothly as I would have hoped.

I took several steadying breaths and rolled my shoulders in an effort to ease the rising panic. Like my daughter, I needed a hot bath and a nap.

What's taking him so long? My head drooped and I battled to fight off the sudden heaviness in my body. I was so goddamned tired.

Luke came back in, pocketing his phone. "That was King. Your friend is out of surgery. She's critical but stable."

Relief washed through me. "Oh, thank God!" I was blinking back tears. Luke stepped closer, his warmth and strength a siren song to my senses. *Please hold me.* I gripped my forearms to stop myself from reaching out to him. "You're sure Dani's okay?" I breathed, my throat thick.

"Yes, for now at least."

"Good. Okay, that's good."

"Yeah, it's good," he agreed. "Look, why don't you go up and join Lily? Get some shut-eye. I'll wake you when the police arrive. King's arranged for them to be here around five o'clock to take your statement."

I nodded. My head was a jumbled mess. I needed time alone to regroup.

"I also asked him to arrange for a trauma counselor for Lily. It's a good idea for her to see somebody."

Why hadn't I already thought of that? "Thanks, that's important. Can we arrange it for tomorrow?"

"Already sorted. Counselor will be at our offices around midday. You'll meet with her first and decide how you want to proceed."

He was being bossy again but I didn't have the energy to point it out. *Or the right.* I scolded myself. At least he was thinking about Lily's welfare, which was more than I was doing.

I rose to leave. "I need the details for the hospital," I said quietly. "I have to phone Dani's parents and they'll want to know where she is, who to call."

"Go on upstairs, I'll have King text everything to

you."

"Okay, thanks."

I moved across to the door but hesitated and turned back to him. "You already know she's yours, don't you?"

"Yes."

There was so much to say, but he seemed to understand this wasn't the time. "Go on up. We'll talk more later, yeah?"

I nodded.

"Katya, it's gonna be okay."

Was it?

"I know," I said evenly, "it always is." *Eventually.*

****

Katya

I curled up on a small chair by the window in our room. Lily was still sleeping. I wanted to join her, but I was too strung out to close my eyes, even though every muscle in my body ached. I hugged my knees to my chest.

God! Will this day never end?

The madness of the morning swirled around in my brain and fatigue bit deep, making it impossible to focus on what needed to be done.

My phone call with Carmen had been heart-wrenching. There were tears and hysteria. Carmen and Antonio were beside themselves with worry over Dani, but they were also concerned for Lily and myself. They were busy making flight arrangements to New York so they could be here without delay. Carmen also insisted on contacting Hector, wanting him in New York to ensure my safety and Lily's. I wanted him here too. Then I wouldn't have to stay with Luke.

God! Luke. I looked at him and all I could see was memories of my time with Michael.

'Once burnt, twice shy,' goes the cautionary idiom. But me? I was already burned twice by Luke. How much more suffering would I force myself to endure before the wisdom sunk in? If I wasn't careful, I was going to go up in flames. *Whoosh! Totally incinerated.*

Agitated by my wild imaginings, I got up and went over to my purse. I rummaged through it until I found what I wanted and then smoothed it out reverently between my fingers. The leather was supple and soft after so many years. Then, like countless times before, I wrapped it methodically around my wrist.

Michael's leather hair-cord.

Yes, I kept it. It was a memento that evoked the beauty of Michael before he betrayed me, but also a torturous talisman that reminded me never to let my guard down again. Never to let another man use me. Discard me. Break me.

With the cord wrapped around my wrist, I curled up next to Lily, her small body sheltered by mine. Her light breaths acted as a balm on my frantic nerves and I drifted off.

On the edge of sleep, I heard the door click open. I held my breath but he didn't come in. I kept perfectly still, waiting until I heard the door close.

Before long, I mercifully succumbed to a deep sleep.

****

Close to Midnight
Luke

Dammit!

Luke put the phone down from King and took a

129

slow sip of bourbon. It was close to midnight. The house was quiet and Katya and Lily were asleep. He decided not to disturb Katya with the news about Dani, even though he risked her wrath in the morning. King reported that Dani was not good but there was nothing Katya could do about it right now and he would rather she sleep.

She had managed to get some rest this afternoon but when he woke her to meet with the detectives, she had been distracted and jumpy, her beautiful eyes still haunted with signs of fear. When he considered the day she had lived through, he was not surprised to see her temporarily knocked sideways.

She had also been uncharacteristically placid when he suggested Lily join him in the kitchen, giving her privacy while she gave her statement to the police. Afterward they had eaten a pasta dinner at the kitchen island, just the three of them. Katya was subdued, quietly urging Lily to eat, while hardly making a dent in her own food.

And Lily? She was still quiet, but her natural curiosity was beginning to emerge. She hadn't yet found the courage to ask him who he was, but the question was there in her blue gaze, the mirror image of his own. It was enough to keep him awake, pacing the windows, an emptiness in the pit of his stomach.

All his instincts were screaming: this was the calm before the storm.

"Hunter."

His adrenaline spiked as he spun around. *Fuck!* He let out a slow breath and watched stonily as Matiu loped across the room. *When did he enter the house?* It was fucking bizarre how the 'Island Twins' could materialize out of thin air. Nobody else had the skill to catch him off guard quite like they did.

"Yeah," he said, keeping his tone neutral.

"King sent a message. Said he gave you an update on the woman."

Luke met Matiu's topaz stare. It looked right through him like a fucking cat's, but he knew him well enough to know that the man was uptight about something. "She's not good." He tipped back his glass to finish the last of his drink. "Internal bleeding. They've taken her back into surgery."

Matiu nodded without blinking. "I'll call Mira. She'll take the rest of the night shift with my brother."

Luke watched him slip silently out the front door.

He shook his head and was about to move to bolt the door when Tane nudged it open and entered quietly.

The brothers were like fucking panthers.

"What's up with your twin?" he asked irritably.

"My brother's spirit awakens," Tane said enigmatically.

"For Katya's friend, Dani?"

Tane shrugged and drifted over to the bay window.

"She's in bad shape," Luke murmured. "What if she dies?"

"She won't die," Tane said confidently. "The fates would not be so cruel as to take another chosen one from my brother."

Matiu had lost somebody? Luke had no idea what 'chosen one' Tane was referring to but he knew better than to ask. "The woman is shot to shit. The last thing she needs is to be stalked by your twin."

"You should focus on your own woman, Hunter." Tane turned to stare him down. "You have a lot to learn about *her* needs. Leave me to take care of my brother."

Fuck. The man wasn't wrong. He had a lot of work to do if he was going to repair the damage he had wrought. Not just with Katya, but with Lily as well.

Christ! Lily. She was pure sunshine, even shock and fear couldn't dampen the beauty of his daughter.

Preoccupied, he didn't notice Tane retreat from the house.

Chapter Eight
Skank On Your Six

Luke's House, Bay Ridge, Brooklyn
Katya

I jerked awake, my heart pounding. The echo of bullets reverberated in my head and I lay rigid and alert. Slowly, my nightmare faded and I shivered, my body coated in cold sweat. A sob welled up and my throat thickened. I bit down hard on my lip: *I will not cry, dammit.*

Lily stirred and I gripped the duvet, forcing myself to breathe quietly. It was still dark, maybe around four-thirty. It wasn't unusual for me to be awake before dawn. Whether from stress or just loneliness, I don't know, but over the years I was frequently wrenched from sleep by panic. I learned to breathe through it. I also discovered a good antidote: running.

I needed to run now.

I slipped from the bed and carefully tucked the duvet around Lily. Pulling on jeans and a sweater, I decided to fetch a glass of water and investigate the feasibility of bypassing Luke's security.

I made it to the kitchen with ease, thankful that Luke had not turned off all the lights. I found a glass on the draining board next to the sink, and reached to fill it with tap water. My mouth was dry and I noticed a small tremor in my hands. *C'mon, girl, shake it off.*

133

"Can't sleep?"

His husky voice didn't surprise me, I had half expected him to hear me as I tip-toed around his house. I examined his reflection in the window above the sink and continued to empty my water glass. My mind was strangely blank and I put off turning around to look directly at him. He came closer and stopped by the sink. He was so close I could feel his body heat against me, and still I didn't look away from his reflection. He gently pulled the empty glass from my hand and my gaze dropped as he refilled it from the tap. Mesmerized, I followed its journey to his mouth and watched the tendons in his neck ripple as he drank. My lips tingled at the strange intimacy and I swallowed as warmth crept through me.

"You okay?" He placed the glass in the sink and looked at me.

I nodded and swallowed again. "I want to go for a run." My jaw clenched. *I sounded so damn timid.* Irritated, I lifted my chin and stared at him. He showed no reaction. He had several days' growth on his square jaw. Instead of looking unkempt, it gave him a hardened, edgy appearance that only added to his appeal.

"Why didn't you reach out to me when you were pregnant?"

Pow! That came out of left field. I backed away towards the island.

"Or at least when Lily was born?"

"How was I supposed to find you?" My body stiffened in resentment. I wasn't ready to have this conversation. *Dammit. He had no right to ambush me like this!*

"I left you with a contact number."

"And you think I kept that?" I said scornfully. "I left it on the floor, exactly where it belonged."

"Then why didn't you ask your father?" he growled.

Yes. He actually growled.

"When I took that memory stick, you had to have known there was a good possibility your father knew who I was? Where I was?"

"You didn't take it, you stole it!" I cried and stalked back to him. "And why would I contact my father when I knew exactly where you would be three months after Lily was born? After all, it was *you*," I pointed accusingly at his chest, "who begged me to meet you in New York on the thirty-first of March? Wasn't it?"

His lips tightened and he gripped the edge of the counter-top, but he didn't say a word.

"I came to New York you know. I came and I waited." I swallowed rapidly to clear my clogged throat. "It was raining, freezing, but I waited at that damn statue for over an hour, convinced you would come." I folded my arms and met his shuttered gaze. "But you didn't come, did you?" My voice thickened. "And I finally understood that everything between us had been a lie. Everything!"

"Lily isn't a lie!"

"No she isn't. But understand this," I hissed. "You might have had a part in making her, but that's all you get to have. You made a choice, and it definitely wasn't us!" My throat hurt as I forced air from my tight chest. I would not let this man break me ever again.

He turned away to face out the window. There was

silence except for my labored breaths.

He had to say something, didn't he?

After what seemed an interminable time, he muttered something.

"What?"

"I was there you know, at Union Square that day."

"What?" I whispered.

"I watched you as you waited for me." He turned and met my surprised scrutiny. "I watched you cry and I watched you walk away."

I struggled to compute what he was saying. Hurt bubbled deep inside and spread like toxic waste. "Why?" I whispered brokenly.

"I was deep undercover with Lightening Transport. We were so close to taking down your father, the Boykovs and all the other assholes he transported for. That was the mission, and I had to prioritize it."

"Why?" I cried.

He flinched and looked oddly startled by my question. Then he turned to stare out the window again. I waited but it seemed he wasn't going to answer. And suddenly I didn't want to hear what he had to say.

"I need to run. Can you make that happen for me?" I asked evenly.

"Go and change into your gear and I'll run with you. I'll bring Mira inside to keep an eye on Lily."

"Mira?"

"Yeah." He turned to face me and I noted absently that he sounded tired. "She and Tane are outside, maintaining perimeter security."

"Oh. Bat-woman."

"What?"

"Bat-woman. I saw her in the hotel basement, by

the SUV."

"Yeah, and—"

"Well, she, uh, she did that one-handed thingy over the car…"

"Mmm, and—" His mouth twitched.

No, no, no! Not that damn smile.

"She, ah… Oh, never mind. I'm going to go change."

"Yeah, babe, why don't you go do that?"

****

Katya

Our dawn run was an unexpected solace.

Luke led us down to the Shore Parkway, across a pedestrian walkway and onto the Shore Promenade that runs along the water's edge. We didn't talk as we started out towards the Verrazano-Narrows Bridge, its pretty lights a beacon in the distance. The water was calm except for the occasional wave that lapped against the rocks. We ran side by side, our breaths in concert with each other, a strange familiarity between us. When we reached the bridge, we took a short rest and Luke explained to me that Dani had gone back into surgery. He said King called and she was now in recovery, but he didn't know anything further. He had arranged for us to visit her after breakfast.

The route back was just as beautiful. The night-lights of the Manhattan skyline slowly turning golden under the rising sun. Our peaceful truce continued and we returned to Luke's house to find Lily awake. She was in her pajamas and chatting with Mira in the kitchen.

I was still unsure what to make of Mira. She was like a sprite, small but full of suppressed energy. When

Luke called her into the house earlier, she had barely acknowledged me.

Now, she sat on the island counter in animated conversation with Lily and didn't seem to notice that Luke and I had returned.

"Mommy!"

Yay! At least I'm not invisible to my gorgeous daughter.

"Good morning, sweetheart." I leaned over and kissed Lily on her head.

"Mira says that Mr. Luke makes the best pancakes in the world."

"That's Miss Mira to you young lady," I gently rebuked. "And don't forget to say good morning to Mr. Hunter."

"Morning Mr. Hunter," Lily piped, completely unfazed.

"My name's Luke, sunshine," he replied and passed me a glass of water.

Before I could correct him, Lily giggled and did it for me. "I'll get in trouble. Mommy says I have to call big people and strangers, mister and missus."

"Is that so?" Luke leaned on the island to stare at Lily who was perched on a bar-stool. His eyes briefly lifted to me and then he looked back at Lily. "How about we make a deal and settle on Mr. Luke?"

Lily turned to me, seeking permission.

Oh! With Luke standing behind her, the likeness between them was heart-stopping. I quickly lifted my glass to mask my consternation. The silence stretched uncomfortably while I took a gulp and lowered my glass again. "Sure, um, that's fine." I forced a smile.

"Good, that's sorted so why don't you go shower

and Lily and I will make pancakes," Luke said.

"Love your pancakes, Hunt, but I'm off," Mira said, hopping off the counter. "Gray's on his way down and Tane is still outside. See ya later, kid." And with a short wave to Lily she was gone.

Pfft! What am I? Invisible?

"Shower, babe."

"What?"

"Go shower. I'll feed Lily."

The room faded and all I could see was Luke and Lily. It was suddenly too much to bear, so I did the only thing I could think of: I went off to shower.

****

Two hours later we arrived at the New York-Presbyterian Hospital to visit Dani.

We had been delayed by traffic, but I didn't mind. I was desperate to see Dani but I was also wracked with guilt. Yesterday's violence was still being unraveled, but I knew one thing for sure: in the eyes of the law, my name was Molina, but in the eyes of the world, I would always be a Dalca. This inescapable fact got Dani shot. Luke told me it was definitely Lev Boykov's thugs at my hotel. This, and the knowledge that Grigori Petrov turned up on my father's instruction, screamed to me that six years was not nearly long enough to separate myself from my father's filth.

My body was tight with trepidation as we walked into the hospital. Luke was beside me and Lily was clinging to my hand. Gray an ever-present shadow behind us.

"When do I meet with the counselor," I asked him quietly.

"She's coming to HQ at noon."

"HQ?"

"King Security's head office. It's just over the Manhattan Bridge, in DUMBO. I'll take you and Lily there when we're finished here."

"Okay," I agreed. "What information do you have about Lev and my father?"

"Relax, Katya. I'll get an update at HQ and then brief you in. Just focus on Dani for now."

HQ? Brief me in? Jeez. He sounded like a sergeant major preparing for battle. But he was spot-on about Dani. I did need to focus because I owed her my full attention.

We found King in the family waiting area of the ICU wing. He greeted us cordially and immediately took control.

"Gray, why don't you take Lily and show her the vending machine. She can have a soda while I bring Katya up to speed on Dani."

"Yes, *Kemosabe!*" Gray quipped with a wicked salute, and then bent down to speak to Lily. "Come on, sunshine. You wanna come get a soda with me?"

Lily shook her head and looked up at me with pleading eyes. "Where's Auntie Dani?"

I crouched down in front of her and took both her hands in mine. "Auntie Dani is hurt really bad, baby-girl. But the doctors are taking very good care of her."

"You said I could visit!" Lily stomped her feet in agitation.

"And you will, I promise." I lifted her small hands to kiss her palms. "But first I have to speak with Mr. Kingsley and then visit Dani on my own. After, I promise, you'll visit with Auntie Dani and give her a special get-better kiss. Okay?"

Lily nodded reluctantly, but her eyes had darkened.

"Okay, sweetheart. Now off you go with Mr. Gray."

"Uncle Gray."

"Sorry?"

"He's Uncle Gray. He said so," she said belligerently.

I looked at Gray and he shrugged, his eyes laughing at me. I wasn't going to win this battle.

"Okay then, off you go with *Uncle* Gray."

Gray led Lily out, her much smaller hand tucked into his. It seemed my daughter had a new best friend.

"She's not going to be able to visit with Dani."

"Excuse me?" I turned to King who was looming over me. He was dressed all in black. Black designer jeans, a black shirt that molded to his powerfully-built torso and a black, obviously expensive, tailored jacket. Hands on hips, his face was set, uncompromising. *Damn, this man irked me.*

"She's in critical care. Only immediate family allowed, definitely no kids. I've managed to get you access—"

"That's not going to work," I interrupted. "Lily has to see Dani. She has to see her alive—"

"And she will, babe, don't worry." Luke stepped closer and rested his hand on my lower back. "King will make it happen, won't you?" He locked eyes with his boss.

I held my breath as the two of them had a silent showdown, then King sighed and nodded.

My relief was short-lived when King turned back to me. "I was with Dani's surgeon earlier, you ready to hear what he had to say?"

I nodded and leaned back into Luke's hand that was a hot brand on my lower back. I didn't care if I was being weak, his touch gave me the strength I needed to hear King out.

"She took two bullets to the chest," King said steadily, his moss-green eyes narrowed on me. "The first was a perforating trauma. That means that although the bullet damaged her lung, it passed through and exited her body. They've repaired the damage and re-inflated her lung. She's going to be left with some scarring, but no permanent damage."

I nodded again and wrapped my arms tightly around myself. *Oh God, Dani. I'm so sorry.*

"Okay then," King said quietly. His close scrutiny was no longer overbearing, it had softened and I found it oddly encouraging. "The damage came with the second bullet. This one lodged in her diaphragm but a tiny piece sheared off and nicked her heart which caused massive bleeding."

My hands flew up to cover my mouth but I couldn't stop a cry of despair. Luke pulled me against his body and his arms wrapped around my waist. I gripped his forearms but instead of pushing them away, I dug my fingers in and clung on.

"They managed to contain the bleeding and remove the bullet. But last night she started to bleed again. They took her back into surgery and found another small piece of shrapnel. They've stabilized her but she hasn't regained consciousness." King looked up and something passed between him and Luke. Then he continued. "Don't get a fright when you go in to see her. She's still intubated and she has a chest drain. Both are helping to keep her comfortable and ensure her lung has time to heal."

"You say she's still unconscious," I whispered. "When will she wake up?"

"They don't know."

****

I entered Dani's cubicle and had to still the urge to vomit. She was lying there, heartbreakingly still, a machine breathing for her and a multitude of tubes and drips hooked into her beautiful body. Dry heaves wracked my body and I clung to her bed frame, swallowing back a scream that threatened to tear me apart.

It took several moments before I trusted myself to move closer. I was still breathing roughly but I needed to touch her, talk to her. The constant beep of monitors that tracked her pulse and oxygen levels and goodness knows what else were claustrophobic and made it difficult to think.

"Here, use this."

My heart stuttered and I turned. *Matiu? Why is he here?*

"She has blood on her. Use this to wipe it away." He handed me a damp towel.

"I, uh, thanks." I took the towel from him. "Why are you here?"

Topaz eyes rimmed with dark-brown considered me enigmatically. He had high, angular cheekbones and full sensual lips that only added to his beauty. Like his brother, he had an otherworldly quality about him. And he didn't seem to like being questioned.

"Your little girl, when she visits, she must not see blood."

I turned to Dani and moved in closer. Her hair was

encrusted with dried blood. "You're right, Lily mustn't see any more blood on Dani." There was no answer and I looked over my shoulder. He had vanished.

My hand shook as I used the damp towel to rub gently at the congealed blood in Dani's thick auburn hair. She would hate it if she knew she had frightened Lily. Once the blood was gone, I used a clean section of the towel to bathe her dry mouth. "Hey, Dani girl," I whispered in her ear and dabbed at the bloody crack in her lip, probably caused by the tube stuck down her throat. "You're going to be fine, you hear." I couldn't stop the tears as I stroked her limp hand. "Your mom and dad are coming soon, and Hector. You have to fight, Dani, please girlfriend, fight hard."

A short while later Luke came in with Lily in his arms. When she saw Dani she looked confused and clung closer to him. But I spoke to her reassuringly and told her Dani was sleeping so that she could get better. Luke held her steady so that she could kiss Dani on the cheek and then we left.

Gray was in the waiting area when we came out and he swung Lily up into the air making her giggle. It seemed like it had taken no time at all for the Texas charmer to bond with my baby-girl.

"Skank on your six, brother," he warned Luke.

What? He called me a skank!

I sucked in a breath, ready to give him a mouthful, but before I could get a word out, Luke turned and pushed me behind him.

"Call Matiu to bring the vehicles. Take Lily and we'll meet you out front," he snapped at Gray.

"What are you doing?" I said, shoving at Luke. He ignored me but I ducked around his huge bicep and was once again struck dumb when a stunning woman stopped alongside us. She was tall, very slim and her long blonde hair reached nearly to her hips.

"Luke," she greeted tentatively and I immediately knew she was Eastern European, probably Russian.

"Anna," he said curtly.

Her arctic-blue eyes shifted to me. "You must be Katya?" She raised a perfectly arched eyebrow.

"Why are you here, Anna?" Luke asked impatiently and reached for my hand.

"I have a message for Katya, from Nicu."

I involuntarily squeezed Luke's hand and then pulled away.

"Please, Katya, I know you don't know me but I promised your father I would give you his message."

She really was beautiful. And skanky! Too much make-up. *I was such a bitch.* And she was obviously nervous of Luke so I took pity on her.

"Anna, is it?" I said.

"Yes. Anna Kirilova." She lifted her hand to shake mine. Her hand was cool, slack.

"What is the message?"

"Your father says he needs to meet with you urgently. It's important you make arrangements to go and visit with him."

"I'm sorry Anna but that's not going to happen," I said firmly. "The only thing my father brings into my life is violence and ugliness. You can tell him that I have no interest in him or in anything that he sends me."

Her hands fluttered, and I knew she wanted to say more. But I wasn't interested.

"I'll see you in the front," I said to Luke and before

he could answer, I stepped around Anna and walked quickly away.

I wanted nothing to do with my father.

And the dangerous parcel he had delivered to me? I wanted nothing to do with that either.

I had a strong suspicion the timing of this explosive mess was not a coincidence.

****

Katya

Luke and I drove alone. Lily insisted she was traveling with Gray and Tane, and clambered into their SUV before anybody could stop her. I didn't want to argue with Lily. She was still processing the scare of seeing Dani unconscious, and Gray was a safe distraction for her. My distraction was my confrontation with Anna. I asked Luke about the beautiful—but skanky—Russian. All he would say was she worked with Nicu when he was undercover. A tense silence filled the vehicle and for the rest of our drive I mulled over how Anna fitted into the picture.

There had been a weird vibe between Luke and Anna that I couldn't let go of.

Had he used Anna the same way he used me?

What could she have had that he needed?

Maybe he just liked her!

We pulled into the underground parking at King Security and Luke parked the SUV in line with several other huge black Ford Expeditions. It appeared King Security had its own fleet.

Unable to stop myself, I blurted out. "You were with Anna when you were undercover with my father, weren't you?"

Luke pulled the keys from the ignition. In the

deafening silence I didn't think he was going to answer. Then he turned to me and bit out. "Yes!"

Wow! I didn't expect him to be so honest. I sat back and folded my arms, tight. *Damn, his answer hurt me.* "So you make a habit of lying to your women? Being with them while you're pretending to be someone you're not? Is that your thing?"

"She wasn't *my* woman," Luke growled. "She was just *a* woman. She was there, I was there. It was never deep and it sure as hell wasn't forever. Then it was over, and I made certain she was clear of the investigation. That was it." He leaned towards me and said impatiently, "That tell you what you want to know?"

"Not even close. You made love to her didn't you?"

"Hell no!" Luke snarled. "I fucked her. Like I have all the other women in my life. There's only one woman I ever made love to Katya. And that was you."

I went rigid, stunned into silence. Luke turned to open his car door. "You didn't make love to me. Michael did," I whispered.

He quickly turned back and leaned in close, right up to my face. His breath smelled lightly of coffee. I stopped breathing when his inky gaze drifted from my eyes to my mouth then back again. I felt cornered but also strangely alive. Then in his rough, *oh so sexy* voice, he replied, "You can wish that as hard as you want, sweetheart, but it was me, Luke, sliding through your innocence, taking everything you had to give. And it was my cock driving you to come, baby. Over and over again!" He stared at me a moment longer, then climbed out of the car, slamming the door closed.

Chapter Nine
Magic Princess

King Security Head Quarters, DUMBO, Brooklyn
Katya

In the elevator Luke was non-communicative. I guessed he was nurturing his anger over my accusation. I gripped my purse to stop me fidgeting and wondered if my stomach was flip-flopping because of anger, fear or excitement. Maybe all three? The doors opened to the first floor and we stepped out into the plush reception of King Security. A man stepped from behind a desk and came forward to greet us.

Whoa! He looked like he had just finished a GQ photo shoot. Dressed in a black and charcoal-gray suit, shirt and tie, he was so perfectly coordinated that if Dani were here, she would swoon with delight. He was slim, medium height, with flawless, elegant features, dark eyes and coiffed black hair, every strand tamed to within an inch of its life.

"Luke," he greeted but his curious gaze was pinned on me.

"Blake." Luke nodded curtly at him.

"And you must be Miss Molina." He smiled, totally ignoring Luke as he held his hand out to me.

"Um, yes, Katya," I corrected him and shook his hand which was cool to the touch but unexpectedly calloused.

"Blake Lee, Mr. Kingsley's assistant and general help-mate." He looked back and forth between both of us. "Aren't you just perfect? Now I see what has our Luke all strung out."

"Chrissake," Luke muttered irritably. "Where's King?"

Blake switched seamlessly into professional mode. "They're waiting for you in the war room. Everybody's arrived except Grayson and Tane, who called to say they've stopped for ice-cream with Lily." He stared Luke down and continued in his precise, cultivated voice. "The therapist Eva recommended for Lily is also here. I've put her in the small meeting room."

Impressive! Mr. GQ had changed into the perfect Man Friday. And he wasn't at all fazed by Luke's bad attitude.

"Good," Luke said grudgingly. "Show Katya to the meeting room. When Gray and Tane arrive, send them to join us and take care of Lily while Katya's with the therapist." He turned and gave me a measured look which I couldn't even begin to read. "When you're finished, stay with Blake. I need to get an intel update from King. I'll brief you after, let you know how we're going to proceed."

My jaw dropped as I watched him turn and stride away.

"Mmm, Studley Do-Right he isn't," Blake sighed dramatically. "Our Luke can be terribly bossy but an eyeful of that tight, sexy butt helps make up for it, don't you agree?"

I continued to gape, only now it was at Blake who stood, hands clasped together and eyes glued to Luke as he disappeared down the corridor.

"Now, Magic Princess." He turned gleaming eyes to me. "Let's take you to meet with the therapist before your Prince Charming summons you. Yes?"

He was flawlessly urbane and modish, but he also had a peculiar lethal quality about him. I was smitten and one hundred percent intrigued by him. "Magic Princess?"

"Your potent magic has our Cool Hand Luke in a rare emotional tizz," he explained, and nudged me towards the corridor Luke had disappeared down. "And sweetie, you are so beautiful that you must have royal blood flowing through your veins. *Voila!* Magic Princess!"

****

An hour later I was still stuck in the gym with Blake and Lily. I paced restlessly while I waited for Luke to summon me to the ominous sounding 'war room'. I had already met with the trauma specialist, Judith Crawford. She was kind but also firm. She gave me clear pointers on what to watch out for with Lily and explained she would like a session with her in the next two days. She also intimated I might want some counseling myself but I demurred. Right now, I wasn't keen on analyzing the emotional tornado wreaking havoc in my head.

I finished with the counselor and joined Blake, who was entertaining Lily in the gym. It was an incredible space. Taking up the entire third floor, the exposed face-brick room was spacious and contemporary, like the rest of the building. The length of the gym faced the East River through a wall of floor-to-ceiling, one-way sash windows—we could see out but nobody could see in. State-of-the-art circuit training and weight equipment filled a third of the floor-space in front of a mirrored wall and some sort of complicated roping mechanism was rigged to the ceiling rafters. The center of the room was covered in thick matting. I asked Blake what this was for and he absently said that it was where the alpha agents did their stuff. We were seated on the other side of the room, where two treadmills, two spinning bikes and a rowing machine were arranged along the windows to enjoy the view.

Lily was playing in front of the mirror on the far side of the room and Blake and I were in the small area opposite the cardio equipment. It was furnished with a black leather couch and a unit set up against the wall with a water dispenser and coffee machine. Blake mysteriously referred to it as the best 'waiting-room' in the house.

I had just put the phone down to Carmen. She and Antonio had landed at LaGuardia and they were going straight through to the hospital to see Dani. Hector, Carmen told me, had arrived before them and was already en route to the hospital. I promised I would meet them there as soon as I could get away.

"I'm going to run downstairs and find Luke. I need to tell him about Dani's parents."

"Not a good idea, princess. Play with Lily and I'll arrange for hot chocolate to be sent across to us."

Blake's attempt to placate me was annoying. "Not to ruin your day Blake, but I don't *want* hot chocolate—"

"I said play with Lily, sweetkins, not play the bitch." His tone was perfectly nice but his glittering onyx eyes were narrowed and definitely not nice. I stared at him in bewilderment. How was I supposed to respond to *that?* "Look, Katya," he said more reasonably. "I know you and Luke have your issues, but now is the time to trust him. He's very good at his job, and with the stakes being as high as they are—" He paused and slid his eyes pointedly to Lily. "He has more incentive now to do it better than he ever has before."

Trust Luke? A heated tingling started in my chest. I did trust Luke. I trusted him with Lily's safety and maybe my own. But I didn't trust him with anything else.

Of course I didn't say this to Blake. He leaned closer to me. "Thane Kingsley operates the best security team in the business—"

"That he may do," I interrupted. "But I don't know him. And I really don't know Luke either." *Enough.* Blake may be flawless and possibly deadly, but I'd had more than my fill of being bossed around by male testosterone. "Please keep an eye on Lily for me." With that, I turned on my heel and stalked out of the gym before he had a chance to cajole me any further.

****

"Does Katya know about Nicu's cache? Or have any idea of its location?"

King's questions stopped me in my tracks and I sucked in a sharp breath. The door to what I thought was the 'war room' was ajar and before I could make my presence known, Luke answered him.

"I don't know. From what I can tell, she's still estranged from her father. She was seriously pissed when she got the message he wanted to meet with her."

"Can you talk her into a meeting with him?" King asked. "If we can find his cache and connect Nicu and

Lev to it, we can finally put those fuckers down."

"And Nicu would get twenty years instead of eight."

Luke's emphatic statement ripped through me. *Oh my God! He's still on mission!*

I leaned against the wall to stave off a sudden lightheadedness. *When was I going to learn?* Luke's priority was never going to be Lily or me. It would always be the mission.

I backed carefully away from the door. It was time to leave.

As I moved quickly down the corridor, a woman stepped out from a side office.

"Hello? Can I help you?" Her husky voice was a perfect match to her luscious appearance. She was a dead ringer for Scarlett Johansson.

For goodness sake. Is anybody in this building just a Plain Jane or Ordinary Joe?

"No thanks, I'm fine," I lied, and hurried past her.

I needed to fetch Lily and get far away from this place.

Far enough away so I could think clearly, where Luke's betrayals would no longer matter to me.

****

Luke

"Forget it King, that's not gonna happen," Luke insisted.

"What? Finding that cache? Making sure Nicu gets the sentence he deserves?"

"Forget that! Our only focus is to protect Katya and Lily. I won't let you use Katya to take down Lev."

"Asking her to talk to Nicu does not put her at risk," King reasoned.

"Maybe not, but it does put her in a difficult position. And it opens her up to further hurt. That's just not gonna happen."

"Bloody hell, Luke. You know as well as I do that we need to take down Lev to make her safe."

Eva pushed into the room but Luke ignored her, his focus on King. "Yes, but we accomplish that without Katya's input. And without extending Nicu's sentence." He got to his feet and surveyed the room, meeting the questioning scrutiny of each team member. It was critical they clearly understood him. "I will not betray my woman and child again. Either you're all on board with this or I'm out."

"I just saw *your woman* hurrying down the corridor," Eva quipped.

"Fuck! I thought Blake had her."

"Apparently not. And whatever she heard did not make her happy."

Luke grabbed his phone and took off for the gym.

Like he thought earlier, the storm was approaching and things were starting to spin out of control. *Shit!* The storm had hit the minute he looked into Lily's eyes. The realization he had a daughter flipped his whole world on its axis. He promised himself long ago he would always be there for his family, especially for any child of his. *But where was he when Lily was born?* He had ignored his gut and put his mission before his woman. Twice! And look where that got him.

Katya and Lily had paid enough!

Dammit! Why hadn't Katya hung around long enough to hear the good stuff?

He was due a break for fuck's sake.

****

Katya

I hurried into the gym. Lily was swinging from a rope while Blake spotted for her.

"Lily, we're going. Now please!"

"No, Mommy," she sang out. "Look, I'm a monkey."

Before I could answer Luke stormed inside.

"Look, Mr. Luke, I'm a monkey," Lily squealed and promptly swung upside down.

My hand flew to my chest, but Blake moved closer, his arms reaching to catch her if she fell.

"We need to talk, *now!*" Luke growled, his fingers closing around my upper arm. "Blake! We're going to be downstairs for a while. Keep an eye on our monkey, yeah?"

"No problem, take your time." Blake waved his hand airily.

Traitor!

Luckily for Luke, he let go of my arm as soon as we exited the gym. I didn't want to talk with him but I knew we had to have it out. And we couldn't do that in front of Lily.

I let him guide me back to the meeting room where I met with the counselor earlier. Rage, and a whole lot of hurt, boiled up inside me.

Luke closed the door firmly behind us and stalked over to me. Fury poured off him, from his stiffly held body to his pissed off scowl and ink-darkened eyes.

Yikes! I backed up until I was practically sitting on the table. He kept advancing until he loomed over me.

"Stop!" I cried, putting my hand up against his chest.

He just stood there. Hands on his hips and huge

shoulders rolling forward to dwarf me.

"What are you doing, Luke?" *Dammit!* I was squeaking like a mouse.

His eyes drifted over my face and I was suddenly keenly aware that I was still touching his hard chest. Like he read my mind, his hand came up and covered mine. I was so goddamn angry with him, but his heat still seared through me.

"What are *you* doing, Katya? Lurking outside doors isn't very ladylike."

His sarcasm fed my anger. "Who said I was a lady?" I sneered. "And anyway, I wasn't lurking. I was coming to find you. Then I heard you discussing me, talking about my father—"

"And you picked up the complete wrong end of the stick."

"Really? So you aren't still on a mission?" I said contemptuously. "You really have no interest in taking down Lev or in destroying my father more than you have already?"

"No. And if you hung around a little longer or actually came inside the damn room you would have heard me say that."

"Say what?"

His body relaxed and the tight lines on his face smoothed out. I tried to pull my hand away but he caught it between both of his. "Nobody is going to hurt you or Lily," he said evenly. "And if you stayed and listened, you would have heard me tell King and the team that our only priority is your security."

"Why should I believe you? You've betrayed me more than once to take my father down."

"Dammit, Katya, I didn't betray you. I made

decisions based on the priorities and information I had at the time"

"That's right! A decision that succeeded in incarcerating my father. But it lost you your daughter. Was it worth it?"

"No!" He said emphatically.

"So what's changed? Why should I believe you this time?"

"Because I'm asking you to!"

He dropped my hand and stepped back, running his hands through his hair. He was clearly frustrated, whether with me or with the situation, I wasn't sure.

"You know, five years ago, my decision not to meet you wasn't based entirely on your father's case. It was also to keep you safe. We knew there would be violence when we took Nicu and the drug crews down, and I didn't want that spilling into your life."

"Now you sound just like my father." Weariness tugged at me. "Always focused on my physical safety, to hell with my heart or my soul."

He remained silent, his beautiful eyes thoughtful as he scrutinized me. I was grateful the table was supporting most of my weight. My legs teetered as the rage slowly drained from me.

After several quiet moments, he started to speak again. "Lev is trying to re-establish himself in the drug trade here in New York. For some reason, he thinks you can help him with this. Do you know why?"

"No." I was careful to keep my tone steady.

He looked at me enigmatically then nodded. "It was the DEA that tipped us off Lev was after you. They've had wire-taps on him. They picked up a call from a woman who told him where you were staying."

I sucked in a breath. "What woman?"

"No idea. We're waiting for a copy of the recording."

I nodded. "Why would the DEA call King Security about me?"

"I still have friends there. They knew to give me a heads up if your name ever came up." He folded his arms, his voice steady, giving nothing away. "Your name came up, they called me. They couldn't activate a unit fast enough and they know what our team is capable of, so they trusted us to get you clear."

"Dani didn't get clear," I whispered.

"I know. But if we didn't get that tip-off it would have been so much worse."

I nodded and clung to the table edge. He was right. *What if they had hurt Lily? Or taken her?*

I blinked away that awful image and paid attention to what he was saying.

"Lev has dumped his phone and disappeared. We're looking for him and so is the DEA." He paused and his expression hardened. "But until we find him, you're going to have to trust me to keep you and Lily safe."

"Why? I hardly know you and I don't know your team."

"I get that but you don't have a choice. You may be willing to risk your own safety but if you want to keep Lily safe, you're going to have to trust me."

"You're wrong. I do have a choice. Hector's arrived in New York and he'll take care of us."

He went rigid and the air stilled, like the quiet of a jungle when a predator is close. "Who the fuck is Hector?"

I steadfastly ignored the deadly vibes he was emitting. "He's Dani's brother and he's more than capable of keeping us safe."

"If you think I'm letting a stranger take care of Lily's security," Luke snarled. "Or yours for that matter, then you're out of your fucking mind."

"You're not making any sense," I reasoned. "Hector's not a stranger. He's been there for us these past six years, unlike you—"

"Jesus fuck, enough! Don't you think I regret that?" He impatiently combed his fingers through his hair. "I didn't know about Lily. And even though I screwed up with you, I thought I had it in hand, that I had the resources to find you." Restlessly, he stepped closer to me. "Tell me something, how did you disappear so thoroughly?"

I lifted my chin and stared mutely at him. *Damn him, it was none of his business.*

Our standoff continued until he unexpectedly shook his head, his lips twitching. "Jesus Christ! You're a pain in my ass."

My eyes widened but I breathed a silent sigh of relief as the tension between us dissipated.

Then he surprised me again when he reached out and cupped my jaw. "The team is waiting to talk to you and King wants you briefed." His thumb lightly brushed my cheekbone. "Come on, babe. It won't hurt you to listen."

Jeez, I'm such a sucker!

Were midnight-blue eyes and a husky 'babe' all it took?

Apparently yes.

Because I let him lead me out of that room and

upstairs to the war room.

****

Katya

"Mira, any update on the tipster?"

"Nope, waiting on the wire transfer."

"Where are we on Lev's KAs?"

King continued firing questions at Mira who was glued to her laptop. Today she was wearing form-fitting, blue-brown-yellow camouflage shorts, matched with a cool white T-shirt covered in Asian symbols that hung off one shoulder. A glossy red peak partially covered her jet black hair, which was slicked back against her head. And her striking make-up consisted of cobalt-blue eyeshadow, thick black mascara and eyeliner and golden-yellow lip gloss. She looked fabulous!

"UTL," she responded without looking up. "Eva needs to work on the GSW vic."

I sat at one end of the long table as the conversation swirled around me. Well it wasn't really a conversation per se, rather a brainstorming session using an indecipherable short-hand. I didn't mind that I was excluded. I was preoccupied trying to process the brief King had just delivered to me about my father's take down four years ago.

King said Luke's undercover mission was only a partial success because when the final take down happened, which was during a huge drug and cash transfer, it was, in Marine-speak, FUBAR: Fucked Up Beyond All Recognition!

Arkady Boykov was caught in the crossfire and shot dead. His son, Lev, disappeared. And somehow my father did a Houdini with the cash. So the cops were left with only the drugs, which they couldn't connect to my father. The only evidence they had was what Luke put together while he was undercover. That wasn't enough for a maximum drug penalty, which was why he received what they considered a too short sentence of just eight years.

Papa! I looked down at my hands hidden under the table and weighed them in the air. They were trembling and I quickly closed them into fists. I knew he was guilty, but deep down in that secret place inside me where I cried out for my father, I couldn't stop the tiny pulse of relief that he didn't get a life sentence.

Needing a distraction, I looked around the room.

Luke and Gray were sitting on the other end of the table in animated discussion with Matiu and Tane. King told me that soon after my father's case was closed, Luke and Gray left law enforcement to join his security company. *Why*? Luke had seemed so dedicated to his mission. *Jeez, that was putting it mildly!*

Mira was tapping away at her laptop, King bent over her shoulder focused on whatever she was doing.

My mind drifted and I idly wondered if the blonde bombshell I bumped into earlier formed part of this team.

"Katya!"

"Sorry?" King's sharp call pulled me from my jumbled thoughts.

"Both Grigori Petrov and Anna Kirilova have passed you a message from your father." King's penetrating stare and creased brow made it clear he was asking a question.

"Yes." I crossed my arms. "So?"

"They both said he wants to meet with you

urgently—"

I calmly met his gaze. But my heart started to pound and I struggled to hear his next question.

"What does he want to talk to you about?"

It sounded like an accusation.

"How would I know?" I replied evenly.

"Has your father been in contact with you at all in the last six years?"

My head tilted as I continued to stare him down. He was like a black panther, beautiful to look at but terrifyingly dangerous.

"King," Luke murmured. It sounded like a warning.

I reflexively wet my lips before I finally answered, still without breaking eye-contact. "No."

"I told you about the cache that the DEA believe Nicolae has secreted away—"

I could see he was waiting for my acknowledgment so I nodded.

"We believe Lev Boykov wants that cache to re-establish himself in the drug hierarchy here in New York. And for some reason, he thinks kidnapping you and Lily will gain him access to that money."

Well, shit!

"If you know where that cache is Katya, for your own safety and Lily's, you need to come clean," King said.

"Babe—"

I turned to Luke. He approached and pulled the chair out next to me. My breath hitched as he sat down and swung my chair around to face him. Then he leaned forward and clasped his hands, resting his arms on his knees.

"Any knowledge of that cache is dangerous to you. If you know anything about it, nobody can know. Not even the DEA."

For a moment I lost myself in his eyes. Bottomless oceans of glittering blue.

I blinked, furious with myself. With him. With all of them!

Who the hell do they think they are to sit here and accuse me?

"I have no idea what you *and him*," I nodded angrily at King, "are talking about." Luke was right. Any information relating to my father's secret cache was dangerous, and I had no intention of telling anybody what I knew. Including Luke.

"He's been watching you for years, Katya. Why would he do that?" Luke asked quietly.

"I don't know." I said frustrated. "You heard Grigori, he's my father!"

Luke looked down at his clenched hands then back up at me. "The only person we're going to get answers from is Nicu. You need to think about meeting with him."

"No!"

"Katya," King intervened. "We're all looking for Lev, but even when we find him, the police might not have enough to hold him."

"What do you mean?" My mind raced. Lev was a horror show all on his own. Lily and I would never be safe while he was free.

"The shooter that tried to kidnap you from the hotel, he's the only witness we have that Lev gave the order for the hit on you. He's still in surgery but when he comes out, if he doesn't talk, we've got nothing."

"I still don't understand." I turned to Luke searchingly. "How can my father help with this?"

"Firstly, he might have a good idea where we can locate Lev." He leaned closer and wrapped his hands around mine. "Also, what I know of Nicu from working with him, he always had contingency plans upon contingency plans. It's likely he has enough intel on Lev to bury him."

My chest ached and energy leached from me. I was cold, except for my hands still held captive in Luke's much larger ones. "I need to go to Lily," I whispered.

He stared at me and his hands tightened. Did he know I was drowning?

My father.

Dani.

Lev.

My father. *Shit!* My father!

And Luke!

All I could see was Luke. And as much as I wanted to run far from him, I also longed to be enfolded in his warmth.

"How about I take you and Lily for lunch? Yeah?"

Yes please!

I kept my head bowed and nodded, blinking away a film of hot tears.

Chapter Ten
Hombre de Acción (Man of Action)

Luke

Luke watched Katya in his periphery vision. She was scrunched up against the passenger seat door, staring out of the window. He gripped the steering wheel, and had to clench his teeth to keep from swearing out loud. It jacked him up to know she obviously wanted to be as far away from him as she could get.

Things hadn't been much better at lunch. He had taken them to his favorite diner around the corner and thank Christ for Lily who had clearly shaken off her shyness around him. In between demolishing a hamburger and fries, she chattered non-stop. He found himself increasingly helpless to resist her brightness that pierced through layers of self-protective shell. The girl was pure sunshine.

But Katya? *Damn.* She had totally shut him out. Her violet eyes were shuttered as she picked at her chicken salad. She made an effort to engage with Lily, nodding and smiling at all the appropriate points, but it was easy to see she was barely present.

After lunch, they dropped Lily back at King HQ. She didn't argue about being left behind with Blake and Mira. He'd snorted when Katya asked if Lily would be safe with them. *Hell.* They were more lethal than the

Secret Service.

Now, they were en route to the hospital with Gray following close behind for added security. They were going to meet up with Dani's parents and brother, Hector.

Hector. The great fucking protector!

When Katya brought his name up, he immediately had Mira look into him. She was a wizard on the laptop, nobody could hide from her forever. Except for Katya of course. Ever since Mira joined them nearly two years ago, she had been trying to find Katya for him. Without success.

But it hadn't taken her long to root out Hector. The man was a Senior Inspector US Marshal with Witness Protection. *Christ!* His woman had found herself a bone-fide hero who disappeared her so thoroughly even the best hacker he knew couldn't unearth her whereabouts.

He slanted another look at her and grunted in frustration. He'd be damned if he allow this silence between them to continue. "What brought you back to New York?"

She remained quiet and he rubbed his jaw where it ached from being clenched. Just when he thought she was going to ignore him she looked away from the window.

"I, uh, had to see my family lawyer about a personal matter." She nervously combed her fingers through her hair. "And anyways, I've been promising Lily to show her where I grew up and now seemed a good time."

"You never followed your father's trial?"

"No." She shook her head. "Hector offered to keep

me informed, but I refused. I wasn't interested."

His hands gripped the steering wheel again and he bit out, "Tell me about Hector."

She finally turned to glare at him. "What about him?"

She sounded so damn defensive!

"Are the two of you together?" He held his breath. The thought of Katya giving her loyalty to the other man was so obscene to him he had to swallow back a wave of nausea. The hurt cut clean through to his core.

"Not that it's any of your business, but no. Hector's like family to me."

Their arrival at the hospital stalled his response. She should be grateful because she wouldn't like what he had to say about her supposed 'family' relationship with the US Marshal!

Gray accompanied them to the ICU Unit. Katya walked between them, but kept her eyes glued forward. She was coolly elegant in dark jeans, a pale-blue shirt and tailored navy blazer. He couldn't stop falling a half step back to enjoy her perfect heart-shaped ass in the form-fitting jeans. She was wearing high wedges, which only accentuated her sexy walk. A picture of black Gucci boots with killer heels flashed into his mind. *Fuck!* It wouldn't do to arrive in the ICU with a boner.

He needn't have worried. As soon as they hit the ICU, Katya raced ahead, right into the welcoming arms of the Molina family. A broad-shouldered Hispanic man with an air of authority stepped forward to put an arm around his woman. Hector. Well, that put paid to his fleeting fantasy.

"So that's Hector Molina, US Marshal," Gray

murmured sardonically.

Luke nodded. Katya settled quickly amongst the family, and he had the sense if he didn't break through her defenses soon, he was going to lose her again.

And maybe this time it would be for good.

Katya repeatedly tried to apologize to the Molinas for her part in Dani getting shot. Luke's tension eased when they refused to accept she was to blame, and instead, comforted her like a favored daughter. He stepped forward to be introduced and felt a tingling warmth when she didn't hesitate to include the surprising news that he was Lily's father. They shook his hand politely and said little. He swallowed his laughter when he saw the curiosity burning in their eyes. He had no doubt when Katya was alone with them she was going to be ambushed with questions. After much crying and hugging, Katya agreed to accompany Carmen and Antonio to Dani's bedside.

Hector immediately approached him to request they speak privately. He left Gray as watchdog and joined Hector by the coffee machine. Both remained silent while they poured coffee and then, with mutual head nods, moved down the corridor and outside into a small courtyard.

They sipped their coffee and took time to size each other up.

Luke wanted to pump his fist like a teenager when Hector broke the silence first. "She looks a little fragile, *hombre*, how is she doing? And Lily?"

"She's holding her own, considering—" Luke took a final chug of coffee. "Lily's good too."

"I read the police report. Any update on Lev Boykov?"

"He's in the wind."

"Nicu?"

Luke studied him. The bastard was making no bones about the fact that he was completely in the loop where Katya was concerned. "She won't see him."

Hector nodded. "Can you convince her otherwise?"

"Maybe." Luke tapped his coffee cup against his leg. "Tell me something, Molina. How did you keep Nicu away from her? He knew where she was. What deal did you make?"

Hector contemplated him as he finished his coffee. He may be shorter than him, but Luke knew the man was no pushover. In a fight, he would be a worthy adversary.

He forced even breaths while he waited for Hector's response. He was nearly out of patience when the man finally spoke. "I agreed to keep her safe."

"What else?"

Hector raised his brow at Luke's curt question. "I also agreed to send regular updates, so long as he kept his distance."

"She never knew?"

"No, she wouldn't have stayed if she knew. It was the only way to keep her safe," Hector insisted. "Nicu wanted her out of New York, but he also wanted her in a secure place. I wanted her safe but also to have time to be her own person." He shrugged. "As long as he kept to his half of the bargain, Katya would have a chance to be happy."

"Did he know about Lily?"

"Yes. I sent him photos."

Luke crumpled his paper coffee cup. *Nicu knew Katya had a child!* Did the bastard know Luke was the father? *That piece of shit!* He'd put money on it he knew.

"Calm, *hombre*," Hector said quietly. "Nicu might have done bad things in his life, but he is not an evil man. He would do anything to keep violence away from his daughter."

Luke didn't feel calm. He wanted to punch the wall. *Fuck!* He wanted to beat the shit out of Nicu!

Instead, he met Hector's concerned gaze and smiled tightly. "What are you to Katya?"

There was no doubt the man knew exactly what he was asking.

"I am her brother," he said steadily, "or as good as."

"Do you want more?"

"If Katya wanted more she would ask for more."

Luke could see Hector wasn't going to be pushed any further, but he braced himself to ask one more question. "I think she might run again. Will you help her if she does?"

"You know who I work for?" Hector queried.

"Yes."

"Then you know if I help Katya and Lily disappear, you will never find them."

"Jesus fuck! I think you proved that already, *hombre!*"

"I have no doubt."

Nostrils flaring, they squared up to each other.

Both angry.

Both born protectors.

Hector slowly softened his stance. His eyes drifted before coming back to rest on Luke. It appeared he had made a decision.

It better be the right fucking one!

"It is time for Katya to stop running," he said. "The question is whether you can give her something to hold on to. Something to believe in." Hector's intelligent scrutiny didn't waver. "Are you man enough to step up? To be there, this time around?"

Luke's body tensed but he swallowed back the fury. *Shit!* He deserved Hector's skepticism. After all, the man had been there for Katya and Lily when he hadn't been.

"She's going to come to you, ask you to protect her again," Luke said. "I need you to back off. If I'm going to heal Katya's wounds I need time." He waited, his body strung tight.

Then Hector nodded firmly. "Good. *Hombre de acción.* Man of action. *Si,* she will need this," he encouraged. "Katya's heart is locked behind a thick shell. For you to succeed you will need to be bold."

Luke snorted. *Well, halle-fucking-lujah!*

It was about time the tide changed in his favor.

****

Katya

I squeezed Carmen's hand as Dani eyes fluttered open.

"Good girl, Dani. Open those beautiful eyes for your mama," Carmen coaxed.

I was amazed at her huge improvement since the morning. The doctors reported her breathing had eased as soon as she awakened earlier, and they had removed her breathing tube.

"C'mon, Dani girl. You can do it," I pleaded.

Her eyes fluttered again and then she did it. Her twinkling, coffee-brown eyes blinked and stayed open.

I couldn't stop my smile as I leaned closer to her. "Hey there, sleepyhead."

"Hey," she croaked.

Carmen quickly reached for a cup of water and I stroked Dani's arm as she sucked weakly from the straw.

"*Te amo mi hija hermosa*," Carmen whispered and gently kissed Dani's brow.

I love you my beautiful daughter.

I wiped away tears as Carmen straightened. "They're happy tears," I laughed. "I promise."

Dani was struggling to stay awake. Only two visitors at a time were allowed in the ICU, so I crept out to give Antonio a moment with her.

I stood against the wall and waited, hoping for another quick visit. I must have looked like a crazy woman because I was beaming ear to ear and kept waving my arms in silent victory. *Go Dani!*

Antonio came out and smiled when he saw me. I hugged him tight when I saw the trail of tears on his cheeks. "She's awake now, *Tío* Tony, she's going to be okay," I whispered into his neck.

"*Si*," he nodded and gently pushed me back. "She asks for you again."

I hurried back inside. Carmen was holding Dani's hand and smiling down at her. "I told her what happened. She knows Lily is safe."

I clung to Dani's other hand. "You saved her life, Dani. I can never repay you," I said fiercely.

A weak smile brightened her wan face. I couldn't hear what she was trying to say, so I bent closer.

"Luke?" she murmured and raised an eyebrow.

I looked at Carmen. "You told!"

"*Si*, of course," she drawled.

Dani whispered something and I bent closer again. "What, honey?"

"Is he hot?"

"Oh yes!" Carmen sighed dramatically. "He is big and beautiful, like Thor!"

My jaw dropped. I wanted to deny Carmen's assertion but what could I say?

He *was* big.

He *was* beautiful.

And he really did look like Thor.

I scowled at Carmen and then looked back down at Dani. Her eyes were closed but there was a small smile on her face.

Hmph!

****

Katya

I was staring out the car window again with too much time to think. It was early evening, and Luke and I were heading back to Bay Ridge.

I pressed my lips together to stop them trembling. My elation at seeing Dani awake had been replaced with a simmering anger. Hector left me in the lurch, insisting I stay with Luke. I protested, but gave in when he pleaded with me to go so he could focus on caring for Dani and their parents. I felt bad for behaving like a selfish bitch, but did an immediate about turn when he suggested staying with Luke would give us both some time to be together.

Yes. He said *together!* He said it wasn't just important for me but also for Lily.

I told him I had already given Luke a chance, five years ago, and he failed, monumentally! Hector just gave me one of his bottomless stares and said, '*Chiquita*, life is not so simple. You of all people should know this, *si*?'

I had no meaningful reply to that.

So here I was, trapped alone in a car with Luke.

And he was ignoring me.

My fingers tapped nervously on my thighs. *How can he act like this? Like he hasn't done anything wrong.*

Deep inside me, I felt something crack. A trickle of grief and pain leaked out.

Flattening my hands, I rubbed them against my jeans. *Dammit.* I thought I let go of this anguish years ago. *What the hell is going on?*

"How long are you going to keep ignoring me?" Luke demanded.

"What?"

"We've spent plenty of time in the car today, alone, but you've barely said a word." I flinched as he slapped the steering wheel. "For *Chrissakes,* Katya, you won't even say my name!"

Who the hell does he think he is? Throwing accusations at me?

"Because I don't know who Luke is!" I said in frustration. "To me you're Michael. A man who smiled at me over sugar beignets and took my breath away." My chest constricted. "Michael held his hand out to me and when I took it, I felt something beautiful. He charmed me into spending one perfect evening with him. And then one perfect night."

Luke was silent. His nostrils flared and I watched the tendons in his neck tighten. "Not another word," he snarled.

What?

"I mean it, Katya. You don't get to say shit like that while I'm driving."

Oh! I sucked in a breath as he pulled into a side street in Sunset Park.

He turned off the ignition, loosened his seatbelt and turned to fully face me. His eyes were smoldering but I didn't care. I was too focused on what I needed to say. "I went to sleep with *Michael*, wrapped up in his warmth and when I woke up, for one perfect moment, I felt safe and filled to the brim with so much beauty."

My body was trembling so hard, I wrapped my arms around my waist to help brace myself. I had to finish. "When I opened my eyes there was a different Michael. He looked deep into my soul and *lied* to me, *stole* from me." I leaned closer to him. "*He* made promises he knew he wouldn't keep. And then he left." I angrily rubbed away a stray tear. "He took my security, my warmth and worst of all, he took all that beauty and turned it to *nothing*."

Luke's eyes flared, so intense they were nearly black. The silence screamed between us, but I didn't want to hear anything from him. My head was filled with bitter memories and I wanted him to hurt as much as I did. "Michael begged me to meet him a year later and then he betrayed me again! He's the man who stole my dream of the beautiful family we had the promise to be. And he's the man who stole my daughter's father away."

Luke's nostrils flared but he didn't interrupt. I leaned even closer. "*Luke?* I don't know who Luke is. He's a stranger to me."

A myriad of expressions moved across Luke's

face, too quickly for me to read. Then, amazingly, his body relaxed and his mouth, that beautiful sensual mouth, tipped into a small smile. "Baby," he murmured huskily, "that's why we need some alone time. Just you and me. Katya and Luke." His hand lifted to slide around the back of my stiff neck. "And just so you know, sweetheart, New Orleans? That was all Luke."

I remained frozen as his fingers combed through my hair. "A man can be more than one thing at any one time, Katya. It doesn't mean he's good or bad. It just means he's dealing with the hand he's been dealt. And sometimes, baby, life deals a really raw hand." He moved his hand from my hair to cup my jaw.

As much as I hated to admit it, it felt good.

"I'll apologize to you as many times as you need. But you have to understand that no matter how many times you shove my mistakes in my face, nothing you can say will ever be as harsh as what I say to myself." His thumb brushed my mouth and I felt myself begin to thaw as he admitted. "I can never make up the time I've lost with you, with Lily. All I can do is move forward and make sure I never let you down like that again."

****

Luke

He's the man who stole my dream of the beautiful family we had the promise to be.

Katya's soul destroying words distracted Luke from the game, a repeat from Sunday against the Red Sox.

Fuck! His woman had a way with words that cut right to the bone.

He took a swallow of chilled beer and closed his eyes. *Damn.* Her words also revealed how deeply their brief time together had marked her. *He was a lucky bastard.* Somehow, he had managed to burrow into her heart. Now all he had to do was cling on like a stubborn burr while he convinced her to give him another chance.

He'd taken the first step by persuading her to have dinner with him tonight. Alone. Even though she had endured two grueling days, she still needed to eat and he'd ruthlessly used this argument against her when she insisted she was too tired. They needed quality time together and they needed it now. He had an inkling she gave in because she was too tired to argue. He didn't care, he'd make it worth her while.

Movement at the door to his basement den caught his attention.

"Hey there, sunshine," he called to Lily who was hovering outside the door. "You looking for me?"

She nodded. Taking his smile as permission, she skipped into the room.

"Your mom still getting dressed?"

"Yup!" she piped, and clambered onto the couch next to him.

"What's that you got there?"

She thrust a bottle of glittery pink nail polish into his face. "Uncle Gray said I can paint you."

"He said that, huh?"

His daughter beamed at him and bobbed her head. From what he'd noticed, she was into everything that sparkled. Even now, she wore a white T-shirt with a large sequined heart covering the front.

"Well, sweetheart, did your mom tell you I'm taking her out for dinner?"

"Uh-huh," she nodded.

"You think she'll like it if I'm wearing pink polish?" He gave her a mock frown.

Lily giggled and rocked on her knees.

"Yeah, I don't think so either," he said. "But Gray and Mira are gonna take care of you while we're out, so you have permission to paint Gray's nails. What do you think of that?"

"Goody," she agreed.

"Yeah, goody," he smiled and warmth crashed through him. Lily had that effect on him.

Then she proceeded to rock his world.

"Are you my daddy?" Innocent blue eyes stared curiously at him.

"Why do say that, sunshine?"

"Cos you look like me."

"You think so, huh?"

"Mm-hmm," she nodded wisely.

"Well, smarty-pants, I think it's *you* who look like me." Luke tickled her under her chin. She giggled and tried to pull his finger away. "Would you like it if I was your daddy?" He held his breath when his daughter stilled. Her face turned serious as she thought about his question.

"Y-yes," she faltered, "but Uncle Gray might get mad."

What?

"Why's that, sweetheart?"

"Cos he said he's my favorite!" Lily confessed.

My daughter really had a thing for Gray.

"Well, sunshine, he's most definitely your favorite uncle," I agreed. "But what do you say about me being your favorite daddy?"

Lily smiled and nodded vigorously. That worked

for her.

Thank Christ!

Beat that Gray, you charming bastard.

He grinned back at Lily as the tension bled from him. In its wake, an unfamiliar lightness.

Fuck! Whatever.

He was a dad, everything else seemed inconsequential.

"Come on, sunshine, let's go and see if your mom is ready."

****

Katya

It had taken me forever to make a decision on what to wear. And I was further thrown when Lily dashed inside and jumped onto the bed, singing out that Luke was her favorite daddy. *What*? Before I had time to question her, she jumped off the bed and skipped back out the room. I was flabbergasted. Why would Luke admit to being her father without first consulting with me?

I dressed quickly, deciding to stay with my dark jeans. I threw on an ultra-thin black cashmere sweater with loose neck and tight sleeves. Then I grabbed my strappy, black heels and went in search of Luke.

It didn't take me long to find him, he was lurking right outside my room. He maneuvered me back inside and before I could say a word, recounted what had happened between him and Lily. "She asked me straight out if I was her father and I refused to lie to her," he said.

I sat back on the bed and took a moment to gather myself by doing up the straps on my sandals. Instead of being furious, I felt weirdly giddy. *I was glad she knew.*

And more importantly, Lily was happy.

****

It was just after eight o'clock when Luke guided me into *Petit Oven*, a small French bistro on Bay Ridge Avenue. Butterflies nestled in my stomach and I kept having to rub clammy palms against my jeans. I couldn't tell if I was suffering from nerves or excitement. I was trapped on an emotional seesaw and my control seemed sporadic at best.

I looked around and immediately liked the restaurant's intimate elegance. Luke said it was a hidden gem, known for its excellent fresh-produce menu and top notch wine list. We settled and he ordered a bottle of Bordeaux. Like any normal couple, we discussed our food choices, but my heart was beating so loud I could barely hear him. And I didn't think *that* was normal!

"You ready, babe?" It was like he was talking through bad cell phone reception.

I nodded and took a steadying breath.

The waitress came and we gave our order. I chose a slaw to start, made up of Brussels sprouts, cranberries, feta, olives and lemon, and Luke went with homemade fettuccine with creamy sauce and bacon. For mains I selected the duck confit and Luke settled on the fried chicken with bitter greens and mashed potato.

Yum. I hadn't eaten much during the day and I was hungry.

The waitress topped up our wine glasses and then we were alone again.

"Why do you live in Bay Ridge?" I was curious why he had chosen to live in a small family neighborhood, so far from Manhattan. In many ways, it reminded me of Harrison.

Luke shrugged. "I had a girlfriend in college who came from here. I liked it. I decided then one day I would live here." He took a sip of wine and fiddled with his glass. "I always wanted my own home, a place where I could safely bring up a family."

I was riveted and eager to know more. "Where did you grow up?"

"I was born in LA," he replied, "but I spent my teen years in New Jersey."

"Your parents—"

"They're dead."

"I'm sorry, Luke." His terseness stung. "I didn't mean to pry."

"Yeah, you did," he said softly. "And it's okay. It's good you want to know more. But my early childhood is a crap story. Not something for a second date."

"Okay," I murmured. "But isn't this our *first* date?"

"You forget about *Cochon?*" I swallowed. He quirked his brow at me. "Roast pork and jalapeño tequila?"

"No!" *How could I forget?* My skin tingled. Every moment of that night was emblazoned on my brain.

"It *was* good wasn't it?" he said huskily.

"It was great," I quipped. "Right up until you stole out the door!"

Shit! Did Luke just flinch?

He remained silent and took another sip of wine.

Oh God, I'm such a bitch.

"I'm sorry, that was really bitchy," I whispered.

He reached out and slipped his hand over mine. Warmth. *Jeez,* his body always radiated such warmth.

"Relax, babe, I've got a thick skin. I can take a few

knocks."

"Okay." It wasn't okay. He had explained himself, he had apologized, over and over. What was it going to take to rout out my bitterness?

I was rescued from further awkwardness by the waitress who arrived to serve our starters.

Peeping across at Luke, I nibbled on cranberries and feta. He plowed into creamy fettuccini, seeming unfazed by my bitchy slip. So I decided to shrug it off as well.

"I love your house. The renovations are fantastic, very contemporary."

He looked up and smiled. "I'm glad you like it. It's been a lot of work but worth it, I think."

I breathed a little easier. "When did you buy it?"

"A couple of years ago. I got a generous joining bonus from King. Used it for the down-payment."

He lifted another fork of pasta to his mouth and my eyes drifted down to his broad chest. He was wearing a black silky T-shirt that did nothing to hide his powerful frame. It must take a lot of food to feed all those muscles.

"Babe?"

"What?" I looked up. His eyes had darkened and— *Oh Lordy!* There was that killer, lazy smile.

"Want to tell me what you're thinking?"

"About your house." I quickly bent over my slaw. "Um, Lily says that Gray lives upstairs."

"Yeah." I had the feeling he let me off the hook. "He rents the top floor which we fixed up into a studio apartment."

"How come he's not with anybody?"

"A woman you mean?"

I nodded and sipped my wine. Gray was hunk material and charming as all get out. *Why was he alone?*

"It's complicated. And it's his story to tell," he said quietly. "Gray might seem sociable but he's actually not much of a joiner." He pushed his empty plate aside. "There are few people that he really trusts. I'm lucky to be one of them."

"What about his family?" I asked, curious.

"He's estranged from them."

"How come?"

The waitress arrived to clear our plates and he didn't answer.

When she left, he leaned forward and said gently, "Babe, if you want to know more about Gray, you have to ask *him*. Yeah?"

Darn-it. This was his best friend and I was being too pushy.

"Yeah," I agreed quietly.

"I like having him around and he seems to like being around."

"Okay."

Luke remained leaning forward. The air between us thickened as we sipped our wine. My skin prickled. The wine's full-bodied richness coated my tongue. *Mmm.* I wanted to lean a little closer and cover his mouth with mine. Did he taste as good as I remembered? *Oh yes.* I knew without a doubt he absolutely did.

I licked my lips and greedily took another sip of wine.

"You want to kiss me, babe?"

I forced my eyes from his sensual lips and was

183

immediately trapped by his wicked stare.

"You keep looking at my mouth and licking your lips," he drawled.

"No I don't!" I wet my bottom lip again. *Shit!*

His eyes darkened and the butterflies nestling in my stomach lifted off in a frenzy.

No. Yes. No! I jerked back in my seat.

He burst out laughing and for some crazy reason I giggled.

"All you have to do is ask." He smiled at me. "But if you keep on at your lips like that, I might lose control and just take what I want, yeah?"

I gulped. *That wasn't a question!*

Choosing not to embarrass me further, he changed the subject. "Tell me something about Lily."

"What would you like to know?"

"How did you decide on her name?"

"Do you like it?" I stilled.

"Yeah I do, a lot. It's perfect for her. She's as pretty as a flower and she just bursts with sunshine."

Breathing again, I smiled. "She is pretty awesome, even if I say so myself."

"And you can, babe. You've done an amazing job with her."

I knew he meant it, and flushed with pleasure.

Reaching for some water, I let the coolness soothe my throat. Then I told him why I named our daughter Lily. I described the lily fields and the sanctuary the Molina Family had provided for me. I tried to paint a picture of the life I had built in San Diego. He listened intently and I only tapered off when our main course arrived.

Then I happily bit into crispy duck skin smothered

in red-currant sauce.

"You were right, Luke, when you said this place is a hidden gem. It's amazing."

He ignored my comment and abruptly lay down his knife and fork. "Why did you never marry?"

I blinked rapidly, disconcerted by his unexpected question. My stomach rebelled against the rich food. I didn't want to answer him, but he'd find out at some point. "I got engaged about eighteen months ago but it didn't work out."

Nothing changed in his demeanor, but the hair on the back of my neck stood on end.

"Who was it? Hector?"

What?

"No!" I spluttered. "Of course not! He's like my brother."

Luke bent forward and now every hair on my body stood on end. "He's not your brother, Katya, and you know it."

"What are you saying?"

"The way that man looks at you, he's definitely not your brother."

"You're crazy," I hissed.

But he wasn't. I just refused to admit it.

Hector was my benevolent protector. He wasn't always at the farm, but he made it clear he would be there whenever I needed him. He came around more often after Lily was born. In his subtle way, he intimated he liked me. I mean, *liked* me. But at that time, Michael still loomed large. I dreamed of him regularly and it was difficult not to hope with every ounce of my being, that we had a future together. I was a different woman after I returned from New York. It took me a long time before I started dating. I never entertained the idea of exploring a relationship with Hector. He was Dani's brother. What if it all went wrong? Hector, being the cool alpha-hotness that he was, took my rejection in his stride and never let it affect how he treated me.

"So if not Hector, who?" Luke demanded.

"Don't interrogate me!"

He didn't back off, but his posture eased and he lowered his chin.

Is that alpha-speak for sorry?

I shrugged impatiently. "His name is Tim, he's the brother of a friend of mine. A friend of Dani's really. He's a hotel manager. He was really nice. And he was good to Lily too."

After New York, and two years of Dani pestering me, I eventually began to date. I wasn't very good at it but Dani kept on at me. The first time I made love with another man, I went home and cried all night. Not that the sex was bad. It was really nice, actually. But it was a far cry from the explosive passion I'd had with Michael. It was better that way, I convinced myself. There was less risk my heart would be shattered again.

"So why didn't you tie the knot?"

Because I was gone for some asshole who wouldn't get out of my head.

"I woke up one morning and I just knew he wasn't right for me."

"What do you mean, not right?" He persisted.

"There was no *one* thing, it just wasn't right," I said stubbornly.

Luke nodded and sat back. "You want anything for dessert?"

I shook my head and relief swept through me when he called for the tab.

I didn't tell him that the morning I woke up and decided to end things with Tim was the thirty-first of March. Like countless times before, I walked out to the ridge to watch the sunrise and in that fleeting moment when the sky turned to crimson, I pried open the secret place buried deep inside my soul. And finally accepted nobody could ever replace the man who stole my heart in New Orleans.

To give myself to somebody else without loving them would be to betray them.

And I couldn't live with myself if I did that.

****

Katya

I waited in the hallway while Luke locked up behind Mira. Lily was asleep and Gray had disappeared upstairs.

The drive home was short, giving us little opportunity to talk. Luke had been quiet. The mood between us wasn't tense, but it wasn't exactly comfortable. I was dead on my feet, but I wanted to smooth things out with him before I went to sleep.

I studied his face as he came over to me. His expression was difficult to read. If it wasn't for the sparks shooting from his heated gaze, I'd swear he was indifferent to me. He didn't stop until he was right in front of me and my breath hitched as he lifted one hand to tuck my hair behind my ear.

"Go on upstairs, babe. You need to get some sleep." His rich, low voice awakened my drowsy butterflies.

"Why are you angry with me?"

"I'm not angry with you."

"But you were."

"No, I wasn't," he insisted.

I searched his eyes and found only truth.

"Come here, baby." His arms wrapped around me and pulled my body flush against his length. I turned my head to rest my cheek against his chest. His musky scent soaked into my pores, spreading a heavenly warmth in its wake and I curled my fists into his side, clinging to his T-shirt.

He bent down and murmured in my ear. "I wasn't angry with you. I was pissed at myself."

"Why?" I whispered and cuddled closer.

"It's been six years. My brain tells me you've got to have had a life without me. But my heart is taking time to catch up."

My breath caught. *His heart?*

"Hearing you talk about other men reminded me how badly I fucked up." The bleakness in his voice made me look up at him. He returned my stare and his mouth twitched. "You gonna give me a goodnight kiss?"

His mouth was smiling, but there was a starkness in his eyes I hadn't seen before and I wanted it gone. Reaching up on tiptoes, I cupped his face and pressed my mouth to his.

His lips parted and I slipped my tongue inside his mouth and touched it to the tip of his. He groaned and his hand immediately moved up to support my neck. His mouth slanted and he deepened the kiss. *Oh yes!* Years of pent up need exploded inside me and I buried my hands into his hair to pull him closer and greedily take my fill.

It was like drinking in molten heat. And I was an addict. The more I tasted, the more I wanted.

Our tongues danced and then, like he had so many years before, he caught my lower lip between his teeth and bit down. I sagged against him and his mouth lowered to glide beneath my jaw and settle over my pulse. He sucked gently and its frantic beating skipped into overdrive.

"Luke!"

He lifted his head and tucked my head into his neck.

And there he held me until our erratic breathing slowly returned to some semblance of normal. After a while, he eased me away and cradled my face. "Go on upstairs. You need to sleep. And I need to speak with King."

I searched his eyes and was pleased to see the shadows were gone. "Okay," I nodded. "Thanks for dinner, it really was good."

"Glad you liked it, babe. I did too." He leaned in and brushed his mouth against mine. "I liked hearing about Lily."

"Good, um that's good." My mind raced. *Oh Lordy.* I'd kissed Luke. And I wanted to do it again.

He dropped his hands but didn't move.

"Night," I whispered and backed away slowly. Then I whipped around and ran up the stairs.

Minutes later, I eased back the duvet and slipped into bed. Lily was sleeping, but her eyes fluttered open when I leaned over to drop a kiss on her brow.

"Mommy?"

"Hi, baby-girl," I whispered. "Go back to sleep."

But she turned and snuggled into me. "Are we

going to live with Daddy now?"

Crap! My chest tightened and I pulled her into me. "Do you want to live with Daddy?"

I didn't think she would answer but then she muttered, "Daddy's all alone."

What?

I leaned closer and she tilted her head to stare sleepily at me. "Daddy needs a family, Mommy. And we need a daddy."

She mumbled something else I couldn't hear and I watched her fall back to sleep.

My stomach fluttered, but this time it wasn't with fear or excitement.

It was with an unfamiliar ray of hope.

Smiling, I drifted off to join my daughter in a deep sleep.

Chapter Eleven
A Bourbon Kinda Girl

Katya

I woke up alone. It was dead quiet and I stretched drowsily before snuggling back into the duvet. Such moments of solitude were a rare treat. I'd slept so deeply, I hadn't even heard Lily leave the bed.

Mmm. Awareness crept in and I smiled. It was good to feel vaguely human again. My hand drifted up to cup my breast and I closed my eyes and lightly tweaked my nipple.

Luke!

His potent image filled my head, sending a heady warmth blossoming through my body.

Oh Lordy, that man can kiss!

What was it about him that had me in an endless tailspin? I rolled to my back and let my other hand glide down between my legs. Even now, the mere thought of being pinned down by those tractor beam eyes was making me wet.

"Aaah!"

The deep moan escaped before I could clamp my mouth shut and I quickly slid my hand away. *What am I going to do now?* An image of Dani bleeding in that damn hotel room invaded my mind.

Hell!

Life could turn on a dime. I didn't want to look

back in a year and wish I'd been brave enough to reach out and grab what I desired more than anything else in the world.

I brushed my fingers against my aching breasts. Luke made me feel alive and safe and so damn hungry for him I wanted to scream. Rolling into a tight ball, I fisted my hair. Because he also made my pulse race and it wasn't from desire, but terror. I trusted him to keep us safe from flying bullets, but I didn't trust him with my heart.

No. Not at all.

Aargh! My very own 'Thor' was giving me a whopping headache.

I threw back the covers and leaped from the bed, heading for the shower. I needed to stop thinking and get moving.

Twenty minutes later I hurried down the stairs. I'd thrown on some yoga pants and my favorite T—a Johnny Cupcakes Dani bought me from LA: it was purple-rush—*their* color description—with a bright orange cupcake at my chest, gradating down to pink crossbones positioned strategically under my boobs. My freshly-washed hair was still wet and I had twisted it up with a hair-stick to keep it on top of my head. It was dripping, but with all the craziness swirling around in my head, I didn't feel like taking the time to dry it.

My bare feet were silent on the hall floor. I heard giggles from the kitchen and a deep voice murmuring.

Luke and Lily.

Pausing at the kitchen door, I had to support myself against the frame. *Such beauty!* Lily was sitting on the counter next to a steaming waffle-maker manned by Luke. She was bent double with laughter as she tried to swipe at Luke, who kept dabbing her nose with batter. He was teasing her, but my ears were ringing so I couldn't make out what he was saying.

His head turned and he smiled at me. Not his lazy, sexy smile, a full-blown grin that hollered joy.

"Mommy, look, waffles!" Lily screeched.

But I couldn't take my eyes off Luke.

His faded jeans were old and torn and he wasn't wearing a belt, so they hung precariously on his hips. A washed-out blue Henley stretched over his chest and biceps, doing nothing to mask the sheer strength of his physique.

Tingles rippled through me and I bit my lip as heat flooded my chest.

He ambled over and stopped right in front of me. *Oh Lordy!* He was barefoot.

"Hey, babe, you finally awake?" His smile settled into a sexy twitch and I stared, mesmerized, as he lifted his hand to cup my cheek. "Love it when you blush like this," he murmured and his thumb brushed my cheekbone.

I leaned harder against the door frame, bending a thigh to try and stop the needy quiver that had started up between my legs. "Um, hi," I stuttered. My mind was blank like I had the worst stage-fright. I licked my lips while I tried and come up with something, anything.

Ring!

I was saved by the bell. Literally.

Luke leaned in and spoke into my ear, "Take care of the waffles, babe, while I get the door."

Then he moved around me and was gone.

I closed my eyes and gripped the door frame.

"Mommy?" Lily called uncertainly.

Get a grip, girl.

I pushed upright and took a deep breath. "Morning, baby-girl," I chirped over-brightly, and walked over to her to kiss her head. Checking the waffles, I nattered with my daughter and refused to think about anything else except sweet waffle batter, syrup and coffee. *Yes!* Coffee.

"Hey, flower." Mira brushed past me to jump up onto the counter next to Lily and lightly nudge her shoulder.

"Hey, MeeMee," Lily giggled.

They sat there, swinging their legs in concert and I sighed, deciding not to correct Lily. Mira might make an art of ignoring me but she clearly liked my daughter. And since it seemed she was Lily's designated protector, I didn't want to mess with that. It was also crystal clear Mira was a free spirit, my mommy rules about respecting adults would doubtfully register on her 'something to bother about' meter.

I made coffee and surreptitiously studied Mira. She was my height, around five foot three, but she was much leaner and exuded a spiky aura that screamed 'hands-off!' Her golden skin and raven, angular-shaped eyes hinted at an Asian heritage. She had an audacious sense of style that added an edge to her exotic beauty. Today she was wearing gold lamé leggings, a tight black tank and a knee-length, synthetic leopard-print jacket. Her hair was pulled up into an intricate twist, revealing lips and eyes painted gold. This mind-blowing ensemble was finished off with kick-ass, black combat boots.

"Katya." I turned at Luke's call from the doorway.

He was frowning and my skin prickled. Laughing, teasing Luke was gone.

"Come here a second, babe. I need to talk to you."

It wasn't a request. I looked at Lily and then my eyes slid to Mira.

"Go," she said.

I hesitated and put down my coffee. Goosebumps spread down my arms and I shivered.

"Katya, it's important," Mira said quietly. "Go with him. I'll watch over Lily."

I searched her dark eyes and saw only a direct honesty that I weirdly trusted. "Stay with Mira, baby-girl." I followed Luke into the living room.

The last time I was in Luke's living room was after I gave my police statement and I had been too distracted to take notice of the room's decor. Now, with my senses amped up, I couldn't help noticing the cozy, classy decor. The room centered around a wood-burning fireplace set into a stone wall. The remaining walls were painted a pale mushroom color that blended warmly with the parquet wood floors. Large, framed photographs hung on the walls: unusual landscapes, still lifes and fascinating portraits. They were extraordinarily good. The oversize chocolate-brown sofa made a masculine statement that was softened by a burnt-orange and terracotta rug covering most of the floorspace. A pair of comfy chairs upholstered in a contemporary abstract design sat perpendicular to the couch.

"Let's sit," Luke said.

"No."

"Katya—"

"I don't want to sit!"

Luke put his hands on his hips and stared down, blowing out his cheeks.

I cupped my elbows and forced myself to stand still. "Luke, just say whatever you need to s-say." My voice cracked and Luke looked up.

"Okay." He sat against the back of the couch and searched my face. "You're not gonna like this, but it needs to happen so I've gone ahead and sorted it."

"What?" I whispered.

"Gray and Mira are going to take Lily sight-seeing today," he said steadily, "while you and I take a trip to Sing Sing."

"No!"

"Yes," he insisted calmly.

"I am *not* going to see my father!" I hissed.

"Katya, you need to calm down and think clearly. Nicu is the best chance we have of finding Lev quickly and he might be able to give us what we need to put him away."

"How dare you plan this without asking me?" Acid coated my throat and I swallowed, forcing down the bitter taste.

"Because I knew you would refuse."

"Then why did you do it?"

"Because, babe, it's the best way I know to keep you and Lily safe. Lev is off the grid and it's taking too long to track him down."

I blinked back tears. *Dammit.* Everything he said sounded reasonable, so why did it reek of betrayal?

"I'll go back to San Diego," I said. "We'll be safe there."

Luke shot upright and loomed over me. "Lev has you in his sights, Katya. Do you really think you'll be safe in San Diego? Anywhere, for that matter? Fuck!" He jumped up and paced away, running his hand roughly through his hair. Clearly agitated, he stopped and turned back to me. "It's time to stop running."

"Dammit, Luke, this is not my life. It's not Lily's life. I won't let it be!"

"If we can get Lev, his crew will scatter. Please, babe, give me the time to put him down."

I met his penetrating gaze and my stomach churned. Drops from my wet hair trickled down my neck. He stepped closer and I hugged myself tighter.

"We put him down, then you can decide where home is." He hand lifted and curled around my damp nape. "If it's Encinitas, San Diego, then I guess I'll learn to like flowers and the beach," he said huskily.

My eyes widened. "What?"

"What were you planning, babe? To leave with Lily, return to San Diego without me?" He said it mildly but it still sounded like an accusation.

"I haven't really thought about it," I lied.

He squeezed my neck and paced away again. "Well, I have and it's *not* happening." He lifted a hand in protest. "I'm not watching you walk away from me again, Katya. Not again! It's just not happening."

My chest constricted at the rawness in his voice and I squeezed my eyes shut. *What the bejeezus is happening here?*

"Breathe, baby."

My whole body tingled.

He was close.

Too close.

So close I could smell the coffee on his breath as it lightly brushed my lips.

I opened my eyes and was immediately mesmerized by midnight-blue. "I want my waffles," I whispered.

"Christ, you're cute," he murmured.

I lifted my head to close the gap between our lips but he snorted and stepped back.

"No time, baby. You've got twenty minutes to get sorted."

"But—"

"I'll send your waffles up with Lily. Now move your ass or I'll carry you up myself," he threatened, hands on hips. "And if I do, Katya, make no mistake, I'm gonna spank that gorgeous ass."

What?

My stomach flip-flopped and heat zinged between my legs. "You can't—" I spluttered.

"I damn well can!"

"I want my coffee too," I hissed, putting *my* hands on *my* hips.

"Go! Now!" He pointed towards the stairs. Then, without waiting for me to move, he turned and strode back to the kitchen.

For a split second I was frozen except for my hammering heart. *Freaking hell!*

I didn't know what else to do except head upstairs and get myself sorted. I stomped into the hallway and came up short when I saw Gray. His arms were folded and he was leaning against the wall at the bottom of the staircase. Grinning!

"What are you looking at?" I snarked.

He raised his eyebrows deliberately. "Darlin'," he drawled and without saying anything further, his laughing eyes dropped to my breasts. I looked down and realized my T-shirt was wet from my dripping hair. My now-pebbled nipples and thirty-two Cs were on show for all to see.

"Go away!" I hissed and stalked past him up the stairs. I didn't hear him move, so I stopped and turned back to glare at him. *Damn him!* His head was cocked and he was blatantly fixated on my ass.

"Stop staring, you pervert!"

He burst out laughing.

"Gray, get your ass in here," Luke called.

I stuck my tongue out at him and ran the rest of the way up the stairs.

****

Katya

Sing Sing!

Oh my God!

I was going to Sing Sing Correctional Facility. To visit my father!

Sing Sing, where all the really bad—I mean the worst of the worst!—criminals were sent. Weren't they?

Luke was sticking to the freeway and he was pushing the speed limit. He said the drive was fifty miles and would take us around ninety minutes. But we were flying along, leaving the city traffic behind and closing in on our destination much too quickly. My hands were trembling so I curled them into fists and tucked them into my pashmina. It didn't warm me and a cold shiver ran down my spine.

Crap!

We were definitely traveling much too fast. I ached to beg Luke to slam on the brakes and turn the vehicle around. I wasn't ready to see my father in a prison jumpsuit, locked up in one of the worst prisons in the state!

"Why is he in Sing Sing? He's not a violent criminal," I asked Luke. My chest constricted. *Shit!* "He isn't, is he?" I wasn't asking, I was pleading.

"Hush." Luke reached for my hand and briefly glanced down when he found it tangled up in my pashmina. "Give me your hand, baby," he ordered gently.

"Luke—"

"Hand, babe, now."

I unwound the shawl and let his much larger hand wrap around my trembling one. He placed it on his thigh and covered it with his own. The miles raced by. He still didn't answer me. But my hand, trapped between his rock-hard thigh and warm stroking fingers, felt like it was infused with calming balm. Slowly, the crazy turbulence that consumed my heart and brain quieted.

Much too soon, we pulled into the prison parking lot. My earlier dread had dissipated and I was left with a dull numbness that separated me from a reality I was never going to be ready for. Luke came around and helped me out of the vehicle. Incongruously, the view of the Hudson River was spectacular, but I shuddered as I stared up at imposing concrete walls, regularly interrupted by tall, heavily guarded towers.

To be locked up in there with no way out! Hell on earth.

We entered through a small gatehouse. Luke said King had worked his magic and smoothed our access but the check-in procedure was still lengthy and intimidating.

Rigid paperwork and identity checks.

Bag search.

Body search. And not just a metal detector but an actual pat-down.

Finally, we were given the green light and two prison guards were assigned to take us to a specially assigned visitor's room. They led us through a heavily guarded entrance and I knew we had left freedom in our wake when the steel gate slammed shut.

Behind us.

Following a maze of snaking corridors, we moved deeper into the prison, our progress repeatedly broken by buzzing locks and slamming gates. The walls were grimy and pitted. And solid! Yellow traffic lines were painted down the middle of most of the hallways, sometimes they faded but inevitably they returned. Each time we entered a new section, a loud buzzer opened the gate and once we had passed through, it clanged closed behind us. The sound resonated, curling down my spine until their accumulation finally penetrated my cloak of numbness and I started to shake uncontrollably.

We arrived in another drab corridor and the guards stopped us outside a door marked B126. "This is it," one of them said, pointing at the door. "We'll bring him in when you're seated."

"Give us a sec, yeah?" Luke said to the guard. Catching my hand, he led me a few steps away, crowding me against the wall. "Deep breaths, baby."

I couldn't stop shaking and grabbed onto his shirt, curling my fingers into the fabric. He immediately wrapped an arm around me and cupped my head in his hand, pulling me into his warmth and waiting patiently while I forced air into my lungs. I was trembling like a newborn. I shamelessly drew on his strength, filling my senses with his unique scent to dampen the smell of despair that permeated this god-awful place.

"You ready?"

I shook my head *'no'*. "I guess."

"That's my girl," he encouraged.

Taking a final deep breath, I pushed against him and looked back at door B126. "You'll come in with me?" I whispered.

"No, babe. That's not the best idea."

My pulse jerked and sped up. "Why?"

"You've gotta know, baby, I'm not his favorite person. There's more chance of him cooperating if you speak with him alone. You understand?"

He stepped back and I stared into his eyes. They were glinting and stunningly blue. My very own Achilles heel.

Taking my silence as compliance, he carried on. "But, Katya," he said urgently. "It's important you get him to agree to speak with me after, alone."

"It's time," the guard called.

I looked from the guard back to Luke and nodded. With each carefully drawn breath, I slowly disengaged from Luke. "I'll be fine." I turned away, moving purposefully towards the guard.

I entered B126 and the door closed behind me.

It was a small room, gloomy and dank. And cold. *There's no heating in Sing Sing, Papa!*

A steel gate dominated one wall. Another guard waited there, I guessed it lead to the prison cells. Through a small window in the opposite wall I could just glimpse the edge of a guard tower. A small steel table was riveted to the floor in the middle of the room, two plastic chairs facing each other across it.

"You need to be seated, ma'am," the guard said.

I moved to the small table and pulled back a chair. I was about to sit when I heard a now familiar buzzing and then a slamming gate. My father!

He was in the corridor but my view was blocked by the guard.

"Please, ma'am, sit down."

I dropped into the plastic chair and gripped the table. My heart was pounding and black spots hovered in my vision.

Dammit, girl, don't you pass out.

I gripped the table even harder. It took everything I had to keep myself seated. At that moment, I would have given anything to leap up and flee the small, depressing room.

I'm not ready for this!

"Hello, Katya."

My father's familiar voice sliced through me. My skin went clammy and sweat broke out on my upper lip. I squeezed my eyes shut.

'Catch me, Papa,' I squealed and jumped from the pool's edge right into his arms.

"Katya, please look at me."

His deep voice pulled me back to the present. Pushing away the disconcerting memory, I looked up to meet his narrowed eyes.

My eyes.

Lily had her father's eyes.

Please God, whenever Lily looks into Luke's eyes, may she only be proud of him, may she only feel loved by him.

I blinked and focused on my father. He was dressed in dull-green prison-issue trousers with a matching shirt over a white T-shirt. His hair and beard were neatly groomed, but peppered with more grey than I remembered. He angled his head and I braced myself.

"You look good," he said.

"You wanted to speak with me." I leaned back and folded my arms. "So I'm here. What did you want to talk about?"

"How is Lily?"

"Why? From what I understand, you already know everything about us."

"You are my daughter, of course I know." He glared at me. "Why do you look so shocked? Six years ago, Grigori only just missed you in New Orleans but I knew where you would run to." He reached toward me and said hoarsely, "Katya, *prinţesa mea*, I never lost you."

"Don't call me that!" I cried, rearing back.

His brow knitted and he blinked slowly before continuing. "I knew you would go to your friend, Daniela Molina. She was the only one you trusted."

"How did you know about Dani?"

"Katya," he sighed, "she was your closest friend, of course I knew."

"But I never brought her home. You didn't even meet her."

He didn't reply but his fingers drummed the table and he studied me.

"I don't understand," I said, sharply. "Luke brought you the memory stick. Why did you care where I went after New Orleans? For God's sake! You were going to marry me off to that psychopathic drug dealer.

How can you pretend you cared?"

"Never!" His hand smacked down on the table. My body jerked in surprise at his unexpected display of anger. "I would never have allowed that Russian snake to touch a hair on your head!"

Such lies! My head spun in disbelief. "I heard you!"

"What do you mean?"

"I heard you make that deal with Arkady Boykov. I was there, in the library. I heard you shake on it!" I glared at him accusingly.

"Katya," he implored, leaning forward, his hands splayed flat on the table. "I was playing Arkady. He was getting ready to make a dangerous push into my business and I needed time to strategize." His eyes bored into mine and I drew back into my chair. He frowned and slowly sat back too. "But then you did it for me. When you ran, everything fell into place. You would be safe with the Molinas, far away from the Boykovs, and I would have time to consolidate my business."

"You thought everything fell neatly into place?" I was stunned. And sickened. *God! I had been so terrified.* My throat clogged as memories bombarded me. "You didn't care that I was gone?"

"Yes, I cared," he said angrily.

"But you cared about the memory stick more."

"What makes you think that?" He scowled at me. "That memory stick was more dangerous to you than it ever was to me. For goodness sake, Katya, you are my family. My daughter! When I stood over the graves of your mother and Uncle Alexi, I swore that nobody would ever hurt my family again."

"You don't think being left all alone hurt?"

He stiffened and his face went blank. My question was a reverberation in the widening chasm between us. And deep inside me, my carefully guarded box of pain, fractured.

"Mom died and you left me *alone*." I swallowed back the anguish. "We buried her and Uncle Alexi and then you sent me away."

"It wasn't like that!" he roared, leaping to his feet.

"Sit down!" The guard ordered, rushing to my father. "Now, Dalca, or I'll cuff you to the table."

My father remained standing, both arms braced on the table, breathing heavily. Then he slowly sat down again.

I was stunned.

Shit!

My father was not a demonstrative man. I had never seen him lose control.

"Then how was it father?" I asked, less sure of myself. "How did I end up staying with mom's parents for so long?"

"The Langworths wouldn't let you go. It took me time to get you back."

What? My mind raced. "What do you mean?"

"I sent you to them after Silvia and Alexi were killed." He ran his hand through his hair, leaving it disturbingly disheveled.

My stomach clenched.

"I needed you safe while I tracked down their killers. But when I came to collect you, bring you home, your grandmother wouldn't let me on the property. They blocked me with an emergency interdict while they went after custody," he said.

"What? I don't remember that."

"You were young, Katya. And you were still in shock. It took me another four months to get you back."

"I thought you abandoned me." My hands fluttered under the table. "I thought you didn't want me."

My father winced and I easily recognized the anguish burning in his eyes.

"How could you think that?"

"Because you were different after you bought me home." My throat burned at the bitter memory. "It was like my Papa died with Mama and Uncle Alexi. And all that remained was a cold, angry man who didn't love me anymore." I lifted my chin and stared him down. "I called him Father."

He closed his eyes.

I waited. And then I'd had enough. "Father—"

"I was grieving!" The endless pain in his voice echoed through the room. "Every time I looked at your face I saw my failure, my guilt." He sagged back in his chair and looked at me. "I didn't handle it very well."

I felt like I was being sucked into a vortex. My past colliding with my present. I scrambled to find something to hang on to. Everything I believed in was disintegrating.

Papa?

"Katya?"

I shook my head and grabbed hold of the question I was burning to ask. "Your secret stash? Why did you send me that information? *Damn you!* That's why Lev is hunting me. That's why Dani got shot." My voice cracked "Tell me, father, if you care so much, why would you put Lily and me at risk like that?"

"That was never meant to happen. I don't know

how Lev found out you were even in New York. Katya—" He leaned forward, and lowered his voice. "You do not tell anybody about what you know, do you understand? I sent it to you as an insurance policy, in case something happened to me."

"Are you insane? Do you think I will ever touch *that* money? No matter how desperate, I would *never* touch a cent of your filthy, dirty money!"

"When you're like this, all fired up, you look just like your mother."

What? My muscles locked. He never spoke about my mother.

"My eyes and hair, but everything else is all Silvia." He smiled enigmatically.

I grappled to reconcile this stranger, this man who displayed so much emotion, with the man I called Father.

No! I jerked to my feet, my chair scraping against the concrete floor. I refused to let him manipulate me. "What do you want from me?"

He remained seated. My fingernails cut into my palms. "What do I want?" An odd expression sliced across his face. "I want you to be happy. To be safe."

Oh my God! That expression on his face was grief. Heat prickled and I blinked back tears. Everything was unraveling.

I need to get the hell out of here!

Away from this man who had barely spoken to me since I was ten years old.

A man who had shut me out of his heart and left me in a world void of family.

He lifted a hand, reaching for me.

No more.

"No!" I croaked, holding up my hand to stop him. The walls were closing in and I had to get out. "Luke says you can help him find Lev. He says Lily and I won't be safe until Lev is locked up. Will you help him?" I whispered hoarsely.

"He's here?"

I nodded jerkily.

"Send him in."

And without another word, I turned away. The door loomed and I banged on it desperately. "Open!"

It unlocked and I slipped out. As soon as it closed, I bent over and clutched my thighs, hauling in deep breaths.

"Babe?" Luke's concern was palpable and I felt his warm hand settle on my back. "Talk to me, baby. You okay?"

I slowly straightened and looked into his worried face. "No," I said.

He tugged me into his arms and I sank gratefully against his warmth.

"What happened?" he murmured against my head.

"Nothing. Everything." I clung to him. "I don't know."

His arms tightened and he rocked me gently.

"He said he'll see you," I whispered into his chest.

He slowly let me go, his hands coming up to cup my cheeks. "You gonna be okay?" He looked searchingly at me.

"I don't know."

His mouth quirked. "You're gonna be okay."

My heart lurched, in a good way, as he pulled me flush against his body and murmured in my ear. "I'm going in. Sit tight, I won't be long and then we'll be outta here."

****

Luke

Luke entered the room and immediately zeroed in on Nicu seated at the table. Their eyes locked as he walked forward and dropped into the chair. Nicu sat, stiff and upright, his hands flat on the table. The room was poorly lit, his face shadowed by the sun trying to penetrate the small window behind him. Tense silence stretched between them and Luke wondered how the bastard felt about seeing him again. The last time they occupied the same space, Nicu was being led away in handcuffs.

Fuck it! After witnessing Katya's distress, he really didn't give a damn. He was here for answers and it was time to get on with it.

"What's she like?" Nicu's abrupt question rocked him.

"Who? Katya?"

"Lily!" he snapped.

Jesus, the guy has nerve!

His question was like a match to the hate burning inside Luke and bile shot up and coated his throat. *Bastard, sitting there like the fucking godfather!* He had kept Lily from him.

Leaning forward, he jabbed his finger at Nicu "You knew I was her father! Why the fuck would you keep that from me? Why would you do that to Katya? To Lily?"

"Sir, you need to calm down," the guard ordered.

Luke's eyes flickered to him then returned to Nicu.

"I guessed, but I didn't know for sure," Nicu replied, his voice remote.

Taking a deep breath, Luke sat back and studied Nicu, looking for some crack in his demeanor. *Fuck! He had to try and rein it in.* Raging at this man would not get him the answers he needed. "What are you saying?" he asked with more control.

"I knew you recovered the memory stick from Katya. I just wasn't sure how you got it." His penetrating stare didn't waver. "My best hope was that you charmed her. Did you *seduce* her? I couldn't be sure."

Luke stilled at the small inflection in Nicu's voice. He glanced down. Nicu's fingers were curled into tight fists. *Maybe he isn't the only one reining it in?*

"She disappeared for several weeks after New Orleans but I knew where she was going." Nicu's voice was smooth again. "Once she settled with the Molina family, I had somebody keep an eye on her and left her alone." He seemed to become aware of his clenched hands and relaxed them, turning them over to study his nails. "It was safer for her to be away from me. The Boykovs had become unpredictable and the DEA was sniffing around more than normal." He glared pointedly at Luke.

"So why did you let me in, trust me?"

"I didn't. Not really. I was curious about you. If you were what you said you were, you had value to a man like me. But I couldn't make up my mind whether to trust you or not. That changed after Katya came back to New York."

"Why? What happened?" Luke growled impatiently.

"Three months after Lily was born, Katya came back to New York." He stared at Luke intently. "But then you knew that, didn't you? Grigori was there, watching over her. He told me she waited in Union Square for over an hour. Crying. Grigori didn't see you. But I know you. *You were there!*" he sneered.

Luke hands tightened on the table edge.

Nicu continued, relentless. "When she finally walked away, you sent a man after her. Grigori stopped him."

"All this time, you've known where she was. That she was a mother, alone. And you didn't tell me?" Luke knew if he let go of the table he would beat the bastard's smug face into a bloody pulp.

"Why would I tell you?" Nicu mocked. "Why would you *want* me to?" His question hung between them, then he waved dismissively. "You put *your job* first. You put *yourself* first. You seduced my daughter. Then you abandoned her. *Twice*. For what?" His voice rose and Luke felt bile in his throat again. "For your job? For the good of mankind? To put me in a cage?" Nicu clasped his hands together and took a deep breath, visibly steadying himself. "Katya deserves better. She deserves a man who puts her first! *Always first!*"

"Yes, goddammit she does!" Luke exploded, flying to his feet. He gripped the table with all his strength. "You think I don't know that? You think I don't know I made a mistake? The biggest fucking mistake of my life!" He shoved off from the table, knocking over his chair. He couldn't seem to contain the heat coursing through him.

Rage? Guilt?

"Sir, sit down!" The guard ordered.

Ignoring the order, Luke paced towards the far wall and slapped his hand uselessly against the hard stone.

"Sir!"

Luke turned his head and glared at the guard and was relieved when he shrank bank against the steel bars. Turning back to the stone, he braced himself against the wall and forced air into his constricted chest. As much as he wanted to hate Nicu, he hated himself more. "Yes," he admitted, "I watched her waiting for me. In New Orleans, *I* made her promise to meet me a year later." He spun round to glare at Nicu. "*I* watched her cry," he bit out, punching his chest. "And *I* watched her walk away." He rubbed his hand over his heart. "My gut was screaming at me to go after her, but I was focused on *you*." Taking a ragged breath, he stared at Nicu. "That's how I'm built. Put the mission first, above all else."

Nicu was silent but his eyes never left Luke.

Swallowing hard to relieve his burning throat, Luke moved back and righted his chair. He sat down and met Nicu's unflinching gaze. "I sent my partner after her to keep track of where she was going. I convinced myself that I could fix what I had broken. When the job with you was finished, I planned to go back and find her."

"So how did that work out for you?" Nicu's voice was sardonic, his face as bland as ever.

Luke winced but refused to get into a stare down with Nicu. He wasn't convinced he would win. Instead, he pushed on with what he needed to know. "Why *did* you trust me after Katya left New York?"

Nicu's answer was frank. "Because any man who could be that cold was a man I could trust with my business."

Shit!

Luke recoiled. *Was he really that cold?* An image of Lily's laughing face flickered. Give that girl a waffle and her smile lit up the entire fucking world.

Easing forward, he rested his arms loosely on the table.

If he had been that cold, he sure as fuck wasn't anymore.

They contemplated each other and the room seemed to cool. The fury had burned itself out. For now. Nicu sat forward. "What do you want, Luke?"

"I need to know where Lev is. He's too focused on Katya and Lily. For their safety, he has to be taken out of the picture."

"Give me a few hours. Grigori will contact you. Anything else?" He prompted.

"Do you have anything on him? Anything we can use that will make the DA's life easier?"

"No."

Luke studied him. Not as the powerful gangster he had succeeded in taking down, but as his woman's father. The prison garb did nothing to detract from his aura. He was a man others took notice of. His presence demanded respect when he entered a room. *Fuck.* The man had accused him of being a first-grade asshole and he couldn't really fault his logic. Nicu had done what most fathers would have done, protected his daughter as best he thought fit.

Shit. Luke knew it was time to suck it up and be the man he wanted to be. Flattening his hands on the table, he leaned closer to Nicu and trapped his violet gaze. "You have my word I'll never let Katya or Lily down again," he vowed quietly. "For as long as I live, I will put them first, no matter what."

Nicu blinked and time seemed to stop.

Then his mouth twitched. "Well, that's a start," he said.

Christ! Luke felt like he had just climbed the Empire State Building, without ropes!

He nodded firmly at Nicu and stood to leave. "One more thing," he said. "Why did you send Anna to contact Katya? You knew Anna and I had been together. Why would you send her to speak with Katya?"

"It didn't occur to me that it was a problem." Nicu's brow furrowed. "I haven't spoken much with Anna since I got arrested, but I needed someone to contact Katya. She's done favors for me before. Why the concern?"

"A woman told Lev about Katya's arrival in New York. We got the intel they planned to take her but we don't know who the bitch is. It could be the same person who alerted Arkady six years ago that Katya was on the run with information that could cripple him." He regarded Nicu carefully. "Do you trust Anna?"

Nicu answered thoughtfully. "I've never completely trusted her. She was always Arkady's pet."

"And Lev's?" Luke questioned with a raised brow.

Nicu nodded and replied vehemently. "Find her and you'll find Lev. She always was an ambitious whore!"

Luke tipped his chin at Nicu and didn't delay. He exited the cold, gray room, eager to return to Katya.

He had a desperate need to feel her warmth and softness in his arms.

****

Katya

I was huddled against the wall in the bleak hallway when Luke stepped out of B126. He glanced quickly around and then his gaze landed on me. I was shivering, the tremors coming from deep inside me. He moved towards me.

God, he's beautiful.

His extraordinary eyes had turned so dark they were nearly black. Caught up in their liquid intensity, I didn't realize he was up against me until I was engulfed in his arms. He tucked my head into his chest, his large hand combing through my hair. His other arm wrapped tightly around my back and he held me. His warmth seeped through my clothes and I loosened my arms and slid them around him, curling my hands around his shoulders. And then I hung on and breathed him in.

There was an insistent cough from the direction of the exit gate. Looking up, I saw the guard shuffling impatiently. I smiled up at Luke and whispered, "I think he wants us to go."

Luke's hand slid from behind my head to cup my cheek. His thumb moved gently across my lips and he muttered, "Yeah, let's get outta this hellhole." Sliding his hand down my arm, he threaded his fingers through mine and led me out.

He didn't let go. Even when the last gate clanged shut behind us and we stepped out into the noon sun, his hand was still curled around mine. But as soon as we were outside, his stride lengthened and I had to skip to keep up. I didn't mind, I was as eager to leave as he was. We neared his SUV and he tugged me closer, letting my hand go to wrap his arm around my shoulders.

"We need a drink, babe. It's tequila time." He winked down at me.

My lips quivered, wanting to smile. I squinted back at him. "Uh, Luke. I don't really like tequila. I'm more of a bourbon kinda girl." I bit my lip. "Is that okay?"

His head tipped back and he burst out laughing. He still held me close and I felt his laugh rumble through me. Turning me to fully face him, he combed his hands through my hair, and then cradled my face. Urging me upwards, he forced me to lean against his hard body, up on my tiptoes. His mouth hovered right up against mine. "Bourbon's good, babe," he said huskily. "Bourbon's real good."

Then his hands smoothed back to tighten in my hair and his lips covered mine. His tongue sank into my mouth and curled playfully around mine, before sucking it back into his mouth. My body bucked and reality faded as heat inflamed me. I pressed hungrily closer to him, pushing against his delicious hardness. My fingers dug into his shoulders and he groaned into my mouth.

"Christ!" He lifted his head and pulled roughly on my hair. His breath filled the space between us. I forced my eyes open. I loved his intensity. "Bourbon's calling, babe, let's go," he muttered against my lips.

Fifteen minutes later, we pulled up outside a liquor depot and Luke switched the ignition off.

"Where's the bar?" I looked around, seeing nothing that vaguely resembled an acceptable drinking hole.

One foot already out the car, Luke turned back to me. "No bar, baby. I'm getting a bottle and we're checking into a motel."

"W-what?" I spluttered.

Leaning intently towards me, Luke's gaze locked on my face. "I need *you,* Katya. Not sitting across from you in some sleazy bar, tossing back bourbon. I need to be naked with *you,* buried inside *you.* I need to feel your fucking gorgeous hair sliding over my skin as my cock sinks into your hot, wet mouth."

I sat frozen.

Oh my God!

I could actually feel my body igniting, tingles flaring up, *everywhere!*

"You have a problem with that, Katya?" Luke demanded.

My jaw locked open and I gaped at him.

On no! I'm gawping like a goldfish.

I snapped my mouth shut and swallowed. And swallowed again.

Luke continued to lean right into my space, his eyes roving from my shocked gaze to my suddenly dry lips. *Yikes!* He wasn't going to move until I gave him some sort of response. I blinked to clear my befuddled brain and wet my lips. His eyes darkened to liquid black.

Oh man!

Rubbing my suddenly damp palms on my jeans, I managed to get a semblance of an answer together. "Umm. No, no problem, Luke. I'm uh, umm, I'm fine with that."

He stared darkly at me for a moment longer, then, his lips twitched and he said gently, "That's good, baby, that's good that you're fine with that. Now, while I'm buying bourbon why don't you give Lily a ring and check in with her. Let Mira know we'll be back by nine tonight. Okay?"

"Okay."

I'm such a sap!

At that moment he could have asked me anything and I would have said 'okay!'

What was with that?

Chapter Twelve
The Memory of Me Tattooed Against His Heart

Red Cherry Inn, Yonkers
Luke

Luke pushed the motel-room door open and held it back for Katya to enter.

The Red Cherry Inn.

Relief had swamped him when he spotted the giant red cherry sign off Saw Mills River Road. With the taste of Katya still on his tongue, it sat like a beacon, calling to his hungry need.

He didn't look at her as he stalked inside, giving the room a quick once over. It was a decent size. Clean enough. Pleasant earth tones with cornflower-blue highlights. The air-conditioning worked.

Fuck. He really didn't give a shit.

The only thing that mattered was the piece of furniture dominating the room. A king size bed. *Thank Christ!* And bonus—there was a solid headboard with room enough to curl your fingers underneath and hold on tight!

He put the bourbon on the small dressing table and opened the brown paper bag to fish out the condoms he had purchased.

Right now, he didn't have a need for bourbon.

Shrugging off his jacket, he dropped it on the cheap stool and tossed the long strip of condoms on the bed.

Katya hadn't moved from the door.

"Jacket off, baby."

Her breath quickened and she backed up against the door.

So fucking beautiful!

She slipped off her jacket and let it fall to the floor. His eyes ate her up as he slowly closed the gap between them. She had cut her hair since New Orleans, but it was still long, well below her bra strap. Thick. Glossy. A cascade of black velvet. *Jesus*, he always had the compulsion to stroke his hands through the silky strands. Her eyes were wide. Endless pools of violet beauty surrounded by those long, lush lashes.

Fuck! His dick hardened and his balls tightened. She was holding her breath again. He loved how she did that. Whenever she was surprised. Or overwhelmed. She'd hang on to her breath, like if she let it go, her whole world would fall apart.

"Breathe, baby. And toe your shoes off."

She exhaled in a puff and her tongue peeked out to lick her lips. *Jesus fuck.* His cock twitched as she nibbled on her lower lip.

"Shoes, baby. Now!"

He couldn't stop the growl that rumbled from his throat. Her hands flattened against the door for balance and she toed off her shoes. He kept her pinned with his gaze and watched as her pupils dilated, eating up some of that gorgeous violet. Her lips parted and her breath quickened.

"Luke—"

Her husky voice was filled with so much need nothing could stop him taking that final step and enclosing her in his arms. His mouth slammed down on hers, smothering her plea into a whimper and he greedily swallowed.

Easy, you prick.

Her hands pressed against his chest and he felt her pull back. Sensing her surprise, he tried to be gentle. She deserved no less from him.

Tender, slow kisses.

Warmth and reverent.

She made a soft groan that caused the bottom of his spine to tingle and her hands stopped pushing. Instead, her fingers curled into his shirt and pulled him closer. Her mouth opened, surrendering to the insistence of his tongue. He buried his fingers into her silken mass and his tongue began to entwine with hers.

So much fucking beauty.

He fisted his hand and tilted her head. He couldn't do slow. He needed to plunder her mouth, deeper and deeper. Because, at this moment, there was no gentle or tender or slow.

There was only hunger. Heat. Need.

A need that burned so hot, if it wasn't satisfied, he would explode. He was driven to devour this woman. Without the guilt of betrayal. Or the sorrow of past mistakes.

Just Luke and Katya.

Man and woman.

She returned his kiss with wanton abandon, her need as desperate and greedy as his own. Soft, pouting lips moved sensually beneath his, her tongue swirling and entwining, licking and teasing.

It wasn't enough.

He pushed her against the door, using his hips to

keep her in place.

"Undo the blouse, baby." He pulled his shirt over his head, not wanting to miss a moment of her slow reveal. Her hair was mussed, her lips wet from his kisses. "If you don't hurry, I'm gonna tear it off."

Fuck! He was growling like an animal.

But he needed more of her. Six years he had spent dreaming of her. Her luscious, sexy body. Her softness. Her wet heat. The tightness of her cunt as it closed around his cock. The trust in her eyes when he pushed through her innocence. He squeezed his eyes closed.

Shit! How many times had he jacked off to the memory of making love to her?

Her hands clutched his shoulders. "Luke?"

He opened his eyes, the uncertainty in her voice piercing through his sexual haze. Her blouse was hanging open, her gorgeous tits enclosed in white lace, peeking out. "Come here, beautiful." He lifted her against the door and moved his thigh between her legs, pressing it up against her jean-clad pussy. Her mouth gasped open and her hands shot up around his neck and into his hair. "Ride me, baby," he groaned and lifted her closer. The heat from between her legs started to burn through his jeans. He tightened his arm around her and used the other one to hook under her knee and pull her leg up around his hips. And then he started to grind against her cunt. Her body undulated and she yanked his hair, forcing his head down as her tongue sank into his mouth.

Jesus Christ! She was like molten steel burning through him. Wild. Searing. His cock raged and he gripped her hips, forcing her to ride him quicker. Harder.

She tore her lips away and gasped into his mouth. "Luke! Oh God—"

"That's it, Katya. Burn for me." Pain tore at his skull as her body convulsed and his hand shot up to cushion the back of her head as she slammed back against the door.

Fuck, yeah!

Her eyes closed and her body trembled. He leaned down to lick at the small droplets of sweat trickling down her cleavage. "You want to let go of my hair, baby?" She shuddered and he grinned, easing her to the floor. Untangling her hands, she fell back against the door and shook the hair from her eyes. She looked at him from beneath her lashes, her eyes darker than he'd ever seen them. The tip of her tongue flicked out and licked her upper lip.

Fuck!

He fought back another growl as she lifted one shoulder and let her blouse slide off. Then she did the same to the other side and slowly, so fucking slowly, let it ease down her back and drop at their feet.

His dick jumped and began to pulse against his zipper. "I need more of you," he rasped and moved to pick her up, but she evaded him and slithered down against the door, onto her knees.

Oh, Christ!

Her hands darted to his belt and she pulled at the buckle. "I need you too, Luke. Oh God, I need you so bad."

"Ah, hell."

His belt gave way and she made quick work of his button and started to lower his zipper. Then she stopped. "Luke?" Her sultry eyes were pleading. He leaned down and gently threaded his fingers through her hair, combing it back from her face. His thumb brushed her pouting lips.

How many times had he dreamed of this? Dreamed of sinking his length into her pouting mouth?

"Whatever you need, baby. Take whatever you need." She smiled and her tongue flicked again. Like a fucking cat. "But if you keep licking your lips like that, I won't be responsible for what I do." Warmth tingled through his chest as she scowled up at him. "Keep your eyes on what you're doing!" She was lowering his zipper.

"Stop being bossy." Her snipe turned to a purr as she parted his jeans and released his fully engorged length. He bent down and shoved his jeans down his hips. "No!" She pushed at his hands. "It's my turn."

"Fuck!" He was used to taking control. *Dammit.* He liked taking control.

"Please, Luke."

Her lips were hovering over his aching dick and he could feel her breath puff against its sensitive head. Her hands also hovered, but they didn't touch.

"Christ!" He shuddered and arched over her, flattening his hands against the door, hoping the cheap wood would bear his weight. She waited a moment, motionless. And then her hands settled on his thighs and she leaned closer, her eyes tipping to his. He stopped breathing when her tongue came out and she delicately licked at the drops coating the top of his cock. "Fuck! Fuck!" He breathed. And then, like she lost patience with the tease, she parted her lips and the head of his cock sank into her scorching mouth. "Jesus fuck!" The pleasure was agonizing. It flashed through his body, drew his balls tight and made his cock so fucking hard, he could no longer distinguish between pleasure and pain. Her sharp nails dug into his thighs and she lifted higher on her knees to take him deeper.

"Katya, baby—" He struggled to keep his hands flat against the door. He wanted to fist her hair and force her head where he wanted it. But the memory of her plea for control, the depth of feeling glistening in her eyes, staid him.

And she sucked.

He was large and so fucking hard, but she sucked his cock as deep as she could. She wrapped a hand around his shaft, stroking and squeezing him while her mouth continued to suck. Her tongue constantly moving, laving, darting around the head and underneath.

Tonguing and sucking.

Jesus, the pleasure!

Her other hand slipped between his legs and cupped his balls, gently caressing them.

"Lick them, baby," he ordered hoarsely. "Lick my balls."

She hesitated at his request and her eyes lifted to him, languorous and filled with heat.

"Please, baby."

She dropped her head and her tongue darted out.

"Fuck, yeah!" He flexed his hips and there was no way he could stop his hand moving to hold her head when she used her fingers to gently push, first one sac and then the other, into her mouth. She sucked and licked and swirled her tongue. Sensation raced through his body, weakening his legs and sizzling down his spine.

Holy shit! He couldn't ever remember being this turned on. "That's it, baby. So fucking beautiful."

Her mouth returned to his cock, her tongue licking from root to head. Then she moaned and swallowed down his turgid thickness. *Shit!* He nearly erupted. Gripping her hair, his hips began to thrust.

Jesus Christ! Fucking her mouth was pure ecstasy.

He could feel the pressure building and knew he wasn't going to be able to hold back.

Dammit! He didn't want to come like this.

"Baby!" He tightened his hold on her hair and eased her back. "Not like this, beautiful baby."

Her eyes, dilated from desire, tested his control and his gaze dropped to her lips. Swollen and wet from his cock. So fucking tempting but he didn't want to come in her mouth. He leaned down, slipped his hands under her armpits and pulled her to her feet. Lifting her up, one arm circling her waist, the other tucked under her knees, he moved towards the bed. "Baby, as much as I love your mouth. This first time I come—" He tossed her on the bed. "I want to be buried inside you." He grinned as she bounced, her hair flying everywhere.

"Luke!"

Before she could scramble away, he grabbed her ankles and pulled her to the edge of the bed. He made quick work of her jeans and panties, tossing them to the floor, and stood up. She crawled backwards until she was up against the pillows, panting.

"Bra, baby." He got rid of his boots and kicked off his jeans. Katya's eyes were wide, glued to his body. And she hadn't moved to do as he asked. "Come on, baby, let me see those gorgeous breasts." He expected her to hesitate but she didn't. She arched up and her hands went behind her back, quickly undoing her bra. She tossed it aside and then settled back, her hands coming up to cup her breasts.

Christ!

His cock throbbed. "The most beautiful tits I've ever seen," he groaned and climbed onto the bed, reaching for her ankles. "Soon, I'm going to suck on those until you scream for mercy." He smiled wickedly and spread her legs.

"What are you doing?" She kicked against him. Her breathiness made him smile. He tightened his hold and forced her legs wide, settling down between them.

The sweetest cunt he had ever tasted lay open before him. Plump, glistening folds, surrounded by downy, soft silk. His balls tightened at the sight of tiny pearls of cream clinging to her curls. "First, baby, before I fuck you, I'm going to taste you." He angled his shoulders to hold her legs wide, then leaned in and savored his first lick.

Oh yeah! Just like he remembered.

Sweet. Heady. Delicious.

Totally fucking addictive! Katya.

****

Katya

My fingers curled into the bedding as hunger consumed Luke's face and ignited a matching hunger deep inside me.

"Do you want me, Katya?"

He was beautiful. The ultimate predator, set to pounce. Powerful. Potent. Lust blazed in his midnight eyes, his full lips twisting sensually.

My heart skipped and then started to thrash as the tenuous hold on my control broke.

So goddamn beautiful!

Whenever I was with Luke, need consumed me. But with the need, came memories and they weren't all good. They were tainted with pain and betrayal, tears and an emptiness so shocking it terrified me to expose myself to him again.

Memories be damned.

The touch of his tongue on my hot core. The taste of his essence in my mouth.

Memories be damned!

Today. There was only the Need.

"Luke!" I reached for his head, desperate to pull him closer.

"Answer me, baby. Do you want me?" His wicked smile connected directly with my throbbing pussy as he easily dodged my searching hands.

Yes, Goddammit! I want. I ache with wanting. Even the violent chaos of the last few days had not stopped me aching for him.

"Yes! Oh God, Luke, I want you."

"Then stay open for me, baby. I'm tired of fisting my dick to the memory of your taste and I'll be damned if I'll wait any longer. I want the real fucking thing."

My breath caught at his blunt words and my brain scrambled to unravel them. His head lowered. His tongue licked. And my brain scrambled all over again as his hands closed over my inner thighs and stretched me even wider. His thumbs opened me up to his ravenous tongue and every nerve in my body ignited. Like a match to kindling, his hunger burned me up. I was awakening from six years of loneliness. Primal need scorched through me and I clawed at the bedding, writhing against his tongue.

"Oh yes, Luke. Yesss."

His mouth was hot and hungry. His tongue probing at my heat. He was taking what he wanted. This wasn't the gentle lover who coaxed me to orgasm, mindful of my lack of experience. This was an alpha predator, taking what belonged to him.

He eased back, his skilled tongue invading my sensitive folds. Sucking and licking. Constantly circling but never touching my begging clit.

Oh God, please!

His tongue flicked and my hips surged.

"Easy, baby."

With casual strength, he held me down and continued to feast. Circling my engorged nub, he never let up. It was like an electric storm lashing at me. Brutal and Insatiable. Beautiful and Irresistible.

I was on fire.

His hands dropped to slip beneath my ass. He lifted me to his mouth and started to lick his way down my crease. Rich cream seeped from my core and I could feel him lap it up as his mouth moved down. Down.

Oh God!

His reached that dark, secret place that nobody else had ever touched and his tongue circled.

"Luke!"

Threads of liquid heat started to spread. Connect. Duplicate.

I was aflame. Burning alive.

His tongue probed. Lashed. And then he was licking back along my slit until he latched onto my clit and began to suck.

Harder. Softer. Teasing.

A wave was building. The storm gathering. I thrust

against his mouth and tugged at his hair.

More. I needed more!

"You want my fingers, baby?"

His guttural voice sang against my senses and I shuddered.

"Please, Luke. I'm so close. Ple-eease!"

His fingers penetrated me and I squirmed against him. "Yes! More!" He answered my demand and gave me the fullness I was desperate for.

His fingers pumped. His tongue danced.

Electricity ignited and the storm broke. Wicked, greedy wildfire swept through me and nothing mattered. Only Luke. More of his tongue. More of his fingers.

"More. More. More." My desperate cries reverberated and I realized I was chanting aloud. "Luke. Luke. Luke." Only he could give me what I craved.

"Come for me, baby." His fingers curled, stroking deep inside me and then he gently bit down, catching my throbbing clit between his teeth.

Carnal sensation exploded through my body.

And I screamed.

And screamed.

Luke stroked and licked, petted and kissed, reverently bringing me down. My legs were trembling. *Jeez!* My whole body was trembling.

A wrapper tore and my chin dipped. Burning midnight riveted me in place until he jerked upright and I nearly swallowed my tongue when he sheathed his huge erection in the condom. I was still sprawled flat on the bed, spasms rippling through me from the hottest, most mind-blowing orgasm of my life. But nerves started to re-ignite as Luke came over me and slowly lowered himself.

Heat. Oh God. So much heat. Surrounding me. Enveloping me.

My eyes blurred and suddenly I was crying.

"Shh, baby, I've got you." His lips feathered against my cheeks.

Luke!

My arms curled around his neck. *I needed him. God! I've needed him for so long.*

Velvet lips glided to catch a tear that escaped from the corner of my eye and then his warm breath brushed against my ear. "Don't cry, baby."

"Please, Luke," I sobbed. "Please, I need you."

"I need you too, baby. *Christ*, beautiful, I'm burning up for you."

His weight was on his arms and he shifted, one arm snaking down to guide himself into me. "Tilt for me, baby."

Oh Lord! His guttural demands were so damn sexy!

My muscles were jelly but I found the strength to slide my legs around his hips and tilt up to meet his pulsing hardness. He hovered at my entrance, nudging, tempting, but not entering. Creamy warmth spilled from me and that voracious need began to throb.

Dammit! I lunged up and nipped his neck.

"Fuck!" He reared back, his arms ramrod straight. Biceps bulging. "You bit me!"

"You're teasing me." I used his neck as leverage to hold me up as I let my mouth drift across his chest and to his straining bicep. "I don't remember this." My lips traced the intricate artwork of a tattoo that traveled down the inside of his left bicep. Purple violets with dark green leaves and twirling black stems. The design was detailed, complicated, beautiful.

"Violets. Like your eyes."

My heart stopped. "What?"

"Babe, you want to talk or you want to fuck?"

His demanding thickness nudged my entrance and lust burned in his eyes. "Fuck, Luke. I want to fuck." I arched up, inviting him to slide his cock inside me.

"Jesus, baby! So fucking tight."

My heart started to pound as he slowly worked his hard, searing length into me, inch by beautiful inch.

Delicious.

Deeper. Deeper.

My nails raked his back.

"Fuck, yes!" His arms lowered and his powerful body was suddenly close. Breathtakingly close. My neck tingled as his warm lips settled over my pulse, light stubble rasping my neck. "Christ! Just as tight as I remember. And so fucking hot and wet."

I loved his dirty mouth!

He glided out, just his tip rubbing against my tender folds. "Luke, honey? Ohh—" I groaned as he thrust hard, his rigid length burying deep and his balls slapping against my damp thighs. Deep inside, I contracted and bucked against him. "Yes! More, Luke, more."

He grunted and his hips flexed. Slamming into me. Once. Twice. And then he began to fuck me hard. I clung to him as our bodies glided together. Slick. Hot. Frantic.

Just when I thought it couldn't get any better, Luke's hand slipped under me and clamped onto my ass. *Oh Lord!* He tilted my body, lifting me to him and continued to thrust. Harder. Faster. Deeper. Our eyes connected and the frisson of awareness was so powerful that my vision blurred and I started to weep.

"Jesus fuck!" His mouth hovered over mine and he licked my lips. "I'm not going to last, baby." His tongue briefly played with mine and our hot, rasping breaths mingled. "Not this first time." His nostrils flared, eyes liquid black, droplets of sweat beading his brow.

Holy cow! I released his neck and framed his beautiful face.

Luke!

This man could eat me alive. "It's okay, honey. Let go."

"You first, baby. Always, you first." His voice was husky but unyielding.

My legs tightened, my hands returning to dig into his back. His hips flexed and need ignited through my veins. "Harder, Luke." I needed him to take me.

Harder. Faster. Deeper.

His hand left my ass and snatched a pillow, thrusting it beneath my hips. I grabbed his hair, my body bucking wildly as his turgid flesh stretched me. Burned me. He sucked in his abs and I stared down between our dripping bodies. Mesmerized. His gorgeous cock coated in my juices, plunging through my soaking folds. His fingers tweaked my nipple and my head jerked up.

"You need to get there, Katya, now!" His hand smoothed down my side, between our bodies and I gasped as his thumb landed on my throbbing clit.

Harder. Faster. Deeper.

My insides clenched and I was coming.

Oh God!

So much pleasure. Building, swirling. "Luke!" A scream ripped from my throat and I fractured. Like a brilliant crystal hit by a ray of sunlight, I fractured into a million different colors.

But I wasn't lost. I knew exactly where I was. Where I wanted to be.

Sheltered in Luke's arms.

His shoulders bunched and he moved his knees, digging in for better purchase. Then he began to fuck me with fast, furious strokes. I curled my limbs around him, wrapping him up tight. His body bucked and thrust until, with a final strangled groan, he buried himself full length and spasmed, spilling himself deep inside me.

And for one insane moment, I wished he wasn't sheathed. I yearned for there to be nothing between us.

His weight settled and my chest compressed. I stroked my hand down his spine, enjoying his weight pressing down on me. I liked that, for a short moment, the force of our lovemaking had robbed him of strength.

Our breathing slowed and I continued to caress his damp flesh.

It felt like an age but all too soon, Luke lifted his head and mumbled into my neck. "Jesus Christ, baby. You're gonna be the death of me." His weight lifted and he gently eased away, rolling to his side. His hand glided down to cup my breast. "Give me a moment, babe and then I'm going to feast on these." He lowered his head and his mouth settled over my nipple, gently licking.

Zing! My nipple hardened and an electric spark sizzled to my swollen clit. "Honey, I can't," I moaned and threaded my fingers through his hair, pulling lightly.

He gave one last, wet lick and raised his eyes, his lips twitching. "You fucked out, baby?"

I scowled, and he chuckled, falling back to his side, elbow bent, head resting on his hand. The purple flowers winked, catching my attention.

Violets. He had called them violets, like my eyes.

I rolled to face him, resting my head on a pillow. My fingers drifted to his bicep. Stroked. His muscle rippled and the flowers moved, like they were alive.

"What did you mean, violets like my eyes?"

Luke breathed deeply and tucked my hair behind my ear. "No matter what you thought, baby, it was never wham, bam, thank you ma'am." He cupped my cheek and his thumb gently brushed my lips. "At least not for me, it wasn't."

My stomach knotted at the intensity in his eyes and I looked away, staring at his tattoo. "What does it mean?"

"It means I never forgot you, Katya. Never. The violets are for your eyes, the black stems for your long fucking lashes. And baby, it's inked on my left arm, so that it rests right up against my heart."

Oh my God. Luke has the memory of me tattooed against his heart!

My pulse raced and I couldn't breathe. Luke's arm circled my waist and he pulled me to him, folding me against his length.

"I don't know what to do with this?" I whispered, my voice hoarse.

"You don't have to do anything with it, babe. It wasn't for you, it was for me."

He was wrong.

Another tiny fissure deep inside me cracked.

Luke never forgot me.

I snuggled against him, his heartbeat a reassuring anchor beneath my hand.

****

Two hours later.

Katya

Luke's chest rumbled against my cheek. "Tell me about your father. What happened at the prison?"

I was lying on my side, flush with Luke's naked, damp body, my head resting against his chiseled pec. I was also damp. We had just shared a shower. An interesting feat because the shower was in the bath, which was smaller than average, and only had a ratty curtain to protect the bathroom from flooding. Luke had only half risen to the challenge. *Oops!* He had only *half* risen to the challenge because after our shower, when we stepped out from the bath, the floor was soaked.

But Lordy. He had risen in every other way!

My muscles still quivered and I idly caressed my fingers along my inner thighs where Luke's stubble had lightly abraded my skin.

"Babe?" Luke pulled my attention back to him.

I shifted and looked up at him. "It's difficult to explain."

"Try," he urged. I was reluctant to revisit that awful room and Luke must have felt me stiffen. "Don't tense up on me, baby, there's no pressure to tell me anything you don't want to tell. Yeah?"

"Okay." I searched his warm gaze and then relaxed down against his beautiful body. He tucked me tighter and his hand drifted, feather-light, down my spine and settled on my ass. *Nice.* I bent my knee to rest my leg on his and lightly trailed my fingers across his abs. "To understand the tale of Nicolae and Katya, you have to start at the beginning," I murmured.

He cupped my chin and gently tilted my face up, then he did a small ab-curl and brushed my lips with his. "So start at the beginning," he said.

And so I did.

I told him about my storybook childhood.

About a young, ambitious Romanian immigrant called Nicolae, who fell in love with a Westchester heiress, Silvia. Despite her parent's concerns, they married and lived in Manhattan until they had a daughter, Katya. Silvia convinced her indulgent husband to move to Stirling Ridge in Westchester, because she wanted her daughter to grow up like she had. Safe and loved.

"And I did," I whispered. "My early childhood was so beautiful sometimes I think I made it up."

I told him how my father used to look at my mother. "Like she was the most beautiful creature he'd ever seen. Sometimes, she'd be walking by and he'd just pull her into his arms and kiss her. She'd laugh and giggle and tell him off. Even though I was a little girl, I knew she loved it. Loved him."

"And you?" Luke combed his fingers through my hair. I loved it when he did that, it was sexy and comforting and so much more.

"My childhood was all about my father." I angled my head so I could look at him. "Don't get me wrong, I loved my mother. Adored her. Lily's a lot like her, trailing sunshine everywhere she goes."

Shifting, I sprawled across his chest, resting my head on my hand so I could meet his eyes. "But my papa? He was my whole world. With him I was fearless."

Memories swamped me, like I'd turned on a faucet: sitting on his shoulders while he laughed with his friends, jumping into his arms when we played in the pool, Papa tucking me into bed and reading endless bedtime stories to me, teaching me how to eat with chopsticks. Laughing and loving and always feeling safe.

My fingers curled into Luke's bicep. Even now, twenty years later, I struggled to reconcile my father: cold and formidable, with the man I ran to as a child for shelter and love.

"So what happened, baby?"

I lifted my head and met his searching gaze. "When I was ten years old my mother and Uncle Alexi were murdered." I held my breath and waited for Luke to say something but he didn't. He just held me tighter and continued to stroke my hair. Letting my head rest back down on my hand, I absorbed his warmth and slowly matched my erratic breathing to his steady heartbeat. "I was in the car with them. We were on our way home. Somebody attached an explosive device to the car's breaking system and when it blew, the car crashed. I was okay, but mom and Alexi died."

Luke's hand tightened in my hair. "I read Nicu's file. The police investigated but never found who was responsible—"

"My *father* was responsible!" I cried. "I didn't understand at the time, I was too young. But eventually I got it. His business spilled into our life. It ripped my family apart." I closed my eyes and breathed deeply. "He sent me away to my grandparents so he could track down the killers."

"And?"

"He must have been successful because eventually he brought me home again." I chose not to tell what my father had told me, that my grandparents had prevented him from bringing me home sooner. I still needed time to process that. "But it wasn't the same," I explained. "*He* wasn't the same. It was like papa had died with my mom and this stranger took his place. He stopped smiling. *God*, he could hardly look at me. And all the time, we were surrounded by security. He only cared that I was safe and in his control. And it got worse as I got older. If he even sensed I was out of his control, he would go crazy."

"Did you talk to him about it?" Luke asked gently.

I shook my head and my chest tightened.

Every time I looked at your face I saw my failure, my guilt.

My vision blurred.

"Babe?"

"I look like my mom," I whispered. "Today, he blamed his grief." I blinked away a tear. "I think when he looks at me he sees my mom. And he remembers."

Luke reached up to wipe away another tear but more kept falling.

"C'mere, baby," he urged and rolled to his side, gathering me close.

I didn't sob. Too much time had passed for that. But I did weep bitter tears, despairing that the gulf between my father and myself had become insurmountable.

Luke held me for some time, and then he untangled himself and went to fetch the bourbon.

"Drink up," he ordered, passing me a cheap glass with a large measure. I sat up and took it, enjoying the burn and the sweet heat it left as it went down. I propped myself against the headboard and held my glass out for a refill. And after taking another gulp, I settled back and recounted the rest of my story, including why I ran from my home six years ago.

"Why did you come back?" Luke asked when I'd finished. "You said it was a personal matter."

Yikes! How do I tell him I'm rich?

"My mother's side of the family was pretty well off," I said tentatively. "Um, actually, they were really loaded. My great-grandfather left a complicated will which only allows direct descendants to inherit on their thirtieth birthdays." I took another sip of bourbon.

"You just turned thirty, so you came here to sign for your inheritance. Yeah?"

"Yeah."

We were lying side by side against the headboard. Luke turned and grinned. "So my baby's loaded now?"

"Um, yeah, kinda," I stammered.

My baby! It still made my insides melt.

Luke leaned over and took the glass from my hand, placing it on the bedside table. I slipped an arm around his neck, lifting my body to slide erotically against his. I was addicted to his heat. He was like my own powerful magnet, impossible to resist. Holding me with one arm, he pulled the pillows away and settled me flat on the mattress.

"So, how many millions you got?" He teased, giving me more of his weight.

"One-hundred and fifty-eight." I lifted my head to cover his leaping pulse with my tongue.

"What!" He roared, his arms stretching rigid, and his ripped body suspended over me.

Yum!

Straining biceps and his sculpted chest was just too delicious to resist. I reached to caress the light covering of blond hair. "Katya!" He panted.

My stomach flip-flopped and tingles raced down between my legs.

Luke was panting.

My hands glided up to lock around his neck and I arched up until his breaths puffed against my face. "It's only money, honey," I whispered huskily and then I kissed him.

He let me hang there, laving my tongue along his sensual lips and then he groaned and lowered us both back to the bed. He lifted his head and I was instantly wet as his eyes smoldered down at me. "Only money?" His voice was hoarse, his brows drawn together.

"Mmm," I muttered, focused on his mouth. "Luke, I want more," I whined, trying to pull his head closer.

"Shit, babe, you can have as much as you want, but you need to give me a sec here," and he rolled over to his back.

Damn.

A not so good tingle curled down my spine. I leaned up on one arm and looked at him. "Do you hate it that I'm rich?"

"Christ!" He rubbed his face, and then pulled me until I was sprawled over him again. Stroking my hair back, he cupped my face. "I don't hate it that you're rich, baby. You just shocked the shit outta me." He dipped his head and brushed my mouth with his.

I softened against him, crossing my arms on his

chest to rest my chin on my hands. "There's something else."

"What? You inherit a title too?"

"No!" I smiled and slapped his chest. "I got a letter from my grandmother, Mary Langworth."

"Yeah. Is that unusual?"

The touch of his slightly, roughened hands as they stroked my back, made me tingle but it was also deeply soothing. "I guess, since I haven't seen or spoken with her in over twenty years."

"Really?"

I nodded. "That's a story for another day."

He pulled my hair gently. "So what does she want?"

I shrugged. "Me to call her. She wants to heal the breach between us."

"So call her," Luke said.

"It's been a long time, maybe too long," I hedged.

"Call her, babe. She's family. It's never too late."

I studied his face. Impossibly handsome: wide-set stunning eyes, now more beautiful because of the concern that filled them, sensual lips that I constantly wanted to devour, chiseled jaw covered in stubble that even now, I could feel the effect of between my legs. But there was so much more to Luke than what you saw on the outside. He had an honor and morality, I was coming to learn, that was as deeply woven into his being as his military training and discipline.

I wanted to believe he was right, that breaches could be fixed, betrayals forgiven.

I moved onto my knees and straddled him. "It's your turn." I braced my hands on his pecs. "I want to know about little Luke."

"Shit no." He stroked his hands up my sides. "That's *definitely* a story for later."

I sat back, careful to avoid his growing hard-on. "You said that last time," I said, a sense of disquiet creeping in.

"What?" I could see he was confused.

"The last time I asked about your childhood, you said you would tell me later."

"Now's not later, babe."

"So when is later, Luke?"

I stared down at him, refusing to look away. Something passed through his eyes but before I could interpret it, he curled up and lifting me off him, rolled right out of the bed.

"Luke!" Dismay sent icicles racing down my spine.

He reached down and hoisted me into his arms, carrying me over to the reading chair by the window. He sat down and planted me on his lap.

"What are you doing?" I gasped

"I told you, this isn't a bedtime story."

"We're naked!" I spluttered, curling my knees into his chest.

"You want to hear my story, I get to choose how I wanna tell it." His tone was light but shadows haunted his eyes. My heart lurched and I bit my lip.

I was forcing him to talk about his childhood and he really didn't want to.

"Luke, honey." I slid my hand up to cradle his face. "I don't need to know if it hurts so much. Really."

He hugged me tighter. I swallowed past the lump in my throat and urged his head down. Velvet lips settled over mine and then he slanted his head and tangled his fist into my hair.

And we kissed.

It was gentle and wet and meant to comfort but as our tongues lazily stroked against each other, heat unfurled in my belly and I pressed closer.

He gently bit my bottom lip and eased back.

"You really wanna hear about young Luke?" he murmured.

I nodded. "Only if you're okay to tell me," I whispered, licking his taste from my lips.

He rested back against the chair, tucked me against his chest and sighed deeply as he began his story.

It started with his father, Carson Hunter, the youngest son of a middle class family from Clifton, New Jersey. Over-indulged by his parents and older siblings and too handsome for his own good, Carson led an easy life until he turned nineteen. Fresh out of drama school where he had displayed zero talent, he wanted to act in the movies. His parents balked at supporting this ambition, "but my father wasn't used to the word 'no', so he stole cash from his folks and took off anyway, landing his stupid ass in Hollywood," Luke said. "He picked up some bit parts that didn't cut it and kept calling New Jersey for more dough. For once they didn't indulge him so he did what he always did. He took the easy road which ended up being a dead-end." Luke explained bitterly.

Carson started dabbling in drugs.

"Then he met my mother and that was just a tragedy waiting to happen."

Emma Hall was a lost soul he told me. Beautiful. Fragile. Blonde. Fresh out of the foster system, she'd had few breaks in life and was looking for a lifeline.

"*Christ.* She thought she found it with my father,

so she hitched her star to his. They got pregnant but the prick wouldn't marry her. Not that he had much to offer." Luke dropped his head to look at me. "When she delivered me, she was so strung out and fragile we *both* nearly bought it." I stretched up and brushed his lips with mine. He smiled but he looked sad as he rested his head back against the chair. "So there we were. Living in a hovel in East Hollywood, sick mother, sick baby and my idiot father still doesn't call his family. Doesn't even tell them that he's a father."

My chest ached. I tucked my head into Luke's neck and stroked his nape.

"My father caught a break—if you can call porn movies a break—and moved us all to Pacoima in the San Fernando Valley. *Fuck.* Home of the porn movie industry, at least at *that* time, and a cesspool for drugs." I held him tighter as he recounted how Carson's movie aspirations failed, how he landed up lurking around the fringes of the studios, running errands and dealing drugs. "And my mother. She kept dreaming of the big break but with each fucking rejection, she downed more vodka and smoked more dope."

"And you, honey? Who looked after you?"

"My first memories are when I was around five and my father moved us all into this shit-hole flat in Van Nuys. It had one room and my father, being the pig he was, had no problem going down on my ma while I was on the couch."

"Luke!" I cried involuntarily.

"She would try to hold him off until I was asleep, but even then, they were so fucking loud I would wake up anyway. I stayed quiet, because if I made a scene or my mother did, he'd go ape-shit."

"He hit you?"

"Sometimes. But I was a fast learner and learned to steer clear."

"Oh, Luke," I whispered. "I'm sorry."

"Told you it was a shit story, babe."

"I know, honey, but you've started now and I need to hear the rest."

He nodded. "I didn't know at the time, but my father had convinced my ma that she would be the perfect porn star."

I squeezed my eyes closed and listened as he talked.

If he can tell it, I can take it.

He told me how their drug addiction spiraled. Most days he would come home from school to find the flat filled with seedy layabouts, his parents high or drunk or both. "I hung out on the streets. There was this guy, Morrie, he owned the corner grocery. I'd help him with packing shelves and he'd let me hang in his back room. I could study and sometimes he'd feed me." He paused and I looked up to see his eyes closed.

"Luke?"

His eyes opened and my throat thickened. He looked so damn haunted.

"When I was nine, my father got arrested for dealing coke. He got caught up in a police raid at the studios and the stupid bastard refused to roll on his supplier, so they locked his ass up. He got 10-99 with a mandatory minimum of ten years. *Fuck.* It wasn't that he helped much, but alone with my ma? We had no chance."

He ran his hand through his hair and sighed. "We never left that shit-hole. His crap friends would come over but now my ma would lock me outside. For hours. Later, I cottoned on that she was whoring herself to them. Probably for next to nothing, just enough to score what she needed to make it through the day."

I remained silent as he told me how he learned to look after himself. Newspaper deliveries and packing shelves at the grocer was the difference between eating and starving. "I kinda fell between the cracks. It was really all about survival. I learned to keep my nose clean. I was big for my age and I think I had cultivated a mean look that kept the gangbangers from giving me a go. Luckily, I wasn't a stupid kid. School was an escape, and I realized it was my only way out, so I worked hard at it."

He shifted me and stroked his hand down my back. "I tried to help my ma. Even managed to get her to a local walk-in rehab center. And for three years she worked at it, but she could never stay off the junk. I knew she loved me. When she was clean she tried really hard to be a mother but she just wasn't cut out for this world. And not without somebody looking out for her."

He reached for my hand and linked his fingers with mine, absently running his thumb over my palm. "*Shit, babe, I tried.*" Anguish wove through his voice. "I really tried, but I was just too fucking young to be much help. Towards the end it got really rough. She would come home in the early hours, really banged up. Stoned out of her head. Some days I don't think she even knew who I was."

I blinked away a tear as he flattened my hand against his chest, right over his heart. "There was a local community center that offered free activities for kids who couldn't afford the fees. Meant to reduce juvenile delinquency," he said. "I started to spend a lot of time there, boxing. The trainers tried to get me to talk, but I was a loner. Preferred it that way. I was also shit scared that somebody would get nosy, call child services."

"Wouldn't that have been a good thing?" I asked tentatively.

"She was my mother!" Luke said sharply. "My father left her to face it alone. I sure as shit wasn't going to." His face was tight and he took a deep breath. "*Jesus fuck!* I couldn't protect her. I've never felt so helpless in my life."

His pain cut clean through me. I could do nothing but cling to him as he told me how she died.

In a sleazy motel.

Lying next to a man who they said was her john.

Both dead from a bad dose of crack.

Luke was twelve years old.

"That's enough, Luke, you don't have to tell me anymore," I said huskily, my throat thick with unshed tears.

"No, babe, let's finish this," he said firmly. "I want it done. Then we never have to talk about it again. Yeah?"

"Yeah," I whispered.

They put Luke in temporary foster care. A week later they took him to visit his father in prison.

"The bastard tried to hug me but I pulled away. I didn't want his hands on me. I stared at him and *Christ*, babe, I looked just like him. But all I saw was my mother, stoned on the couch, saliva drooling from her mouth." Luke's face twisted and my stomach convulsed. *I hated seeing him in this much pain.* "He said some shit about loving me, loving my ma, and that he was sorry. *Sorry? Jesus!*"

I wriggled from his hold and went to fetch the bourbon. Filling both glasses, I walked back and climbed into his lap. He took a glass and wrapped his other arm around me. There was no awkwardness in our nudity, only a beautiful intimacy. I stroked his chest and he dipped his head to lightly brush my lips with his, then he carried on.

"He bragged on and on about how he had arranged for me to go to New Jersey, his brothers were going to take me in. I guess I was too slow to respond because he began to lecture me that I should be grateful I had good family to take care of me. *Fuck!*" He gulped back a mouthful of the booze. Wincing slightly, he continued. "I just lost it. Ranted at him that he had destroyed our family. Screamed shit like 'why did he hate us so much,' 'why didn't he look after us,' 'it was his fault that my ma was dead.' *Hell.* I told him he might as well have killed her himself. He just stood there and said nothing. Jesus, babe—" He sighed, combing his fingers through my hair. "I was filled with so much rage. The last words I screamed at him were that I hated him. That I'd always hate him and I would never forgive him for being such a bastard father."

He finished his drink and leaned down to place the glass on the floor. "I never spoke to him again. He wrote me for a while but I refused to read the letters. When I was on my first tour in Afghanistan, I got a telegram informing me he had died." He shrugged. "Apparently he caught pneumonia and there were complications. When I read about his death I felt nothing. Absolutely nothing."

"I'm so sorry, honey," I whispered helplessly.

"Don't be. The only good thing he ever did was to call his brothers to take me in. That saved my life."

I finished my drink, using the burn to try and wash away the bitter taste in my mouth. Looking up at Luke, I lifted a hand to gently cup his face. "Was it better for you in New Jersey?" I held my breath, dreading his answer.

"Yeah, babe, it was." He bent to kiss me gently. "They taught me about family and love and security. But as much as they gave, I never really settled."

"Is that why you live in Bay Ridge, not New Jersey?"

"Maybe. I love them and we keep in touch. *Shit.* They helped me pay for college. Even helped me get accepted into the New Jersey State Police. But then 9/11 happened and I joined the marines. Met Gray who became my family and then life happened. And now, here I am."

"Yeah, honey, here you are." I reached up to press my lips to his. I let my empty glass fall to the carpet and sank both hands into his hair, tugging him closer.

"Jesus, babe!" He groaned into my mouth.

I gasped as he hoisted me up, only to drop me back so that I sat astride him. He buried his tongue into my mouth and heat flooded me as I brushed up against his burgeoning erection. Our tongues swirled and I couldn't stop the whimper when he gripped my hips and gently glided his cock through my wetness.

Yes!

His mouth left mine and drifted down my neck. He pressed his hand into my back, arching me forward and curled his tongue around my nipple. I squirmed and pushed my breast against his stiffened tongue.

I loved his mouth on my breasts.

He sucked harder and I flexed wantonly against his gliding cock.

"Luke!"

He tilted his head and his husky voice murmured in my ear. "Now, babe, why don't you give Mira a call, let her know we're gonna be late."

I couldn't keep up. My brain was frazzled with images of 'Young Luke' raging at his father. And now, his rock-hard cock and sinful mouth were driving me into a frenzy. "What? Why?" I stammered, riding his hardness, desperate to feel him rub against my clit again.

"Wrap your legs around me," he ordered and stood up.

I did just that and reached up to trap his earlobe between my teeth. And bit.

"Fuck!" He hissed and released me to fall on the bed. He followed me down and covered me with his body. "We've been doing a lot of talking, baby, and I haven't got nearly enough of you yet." His mouth hovered over my breasts and he reached across me and grabbed his phone. "Call, babe," he murmured. And then he used his free hand to push my breast into his mouth.

"Oh God. I can't talk when you do that!" I wailed, wrapping my legs around his hips and arching up so I could slide my aching folds along his length.

He lifted his head and tilted his hips, simultaneously catching my hardened nub and smiling that lazy smile which should be banned. Tremors ricocheted and I greedily angled to catch his cock. "Luke," I groaned, "I need you inside me. Now!"

He rolled over to his back, taking me with him. "Dammit, Luke!" I reared up and straddled him. He had picked up the cell phone and was pushing keys. And he was grinning!

I bent over and bit his lip.

"Fuck!" He buried his hand in my hair and pulled me away. "Mira, everything good?" He nodded and I couldn't stop poking out my tongue when he winked at me. He tightened his fist and murmured, "Mmmhmm, sounds fun. Listen, we're gonna be late." There was a muscle jumping near his jawline and I bent, feeling him pull against my scalp. "I don't know how late. Jesus, I've got my hands full with her mother!" I nibbled on his jaw and laved it with my tongue, loving the sexy scrape of his stubble. "If you can't cope, call Gray to help, she can paint *his* fingernails!" Luke tossed the phone aside and his hands fisted into my hair.

He ab-curled up and tried to roll me but I dug in with my knees and gripped his shoulders. "If memory serves, honey, it's your turn to hold the headboard." And I raised my brow in challenge.

He froze, those gorgeous blues narrowed on my determined face.

My breath hitched as we sat motionless.

Will he let me have control again?

I exhaled noisily as his hold on my hair softened. Then he tilted his head and his mouth devoured me, deep and wet. "Have at it, baby," he said huskily and flicked his tongue along my kiss-swollen lip. "I'll give you all the control you want if I get to have this pouty mouth wrapped around my cock."

Yikes!

Then I settled down to give him exactly what he wanted.

And I loved every lick of it!

Chapter Thirteen
I'm Not the Enemy

King Security Head Quarters, DUMBO, Brooklyn
The Next Day
Katya

"Stop sulking," he whispered in my ear.

"I'm not sulking."

"You are, babe. It's cute as hell, but you're still not taking Lily out and about today."

"I don't see why not. Gray could come with us."

"I already told you, he's tied up. I'm meeting with him and King right now."

The elevator dinged and Luke stepped back, gesturing for Lily and me to exit.

Too damn bossy! I pressed my lips together to hold back my irritation.

"It's the Magic Princess and her Glitterbug!"

Blake approached and knelt down, his arms wide for Lily to give him a hug. She happily gave him what he wanted, and any residual resentment I harbored towards him melted when he looked up and winked at me. How could I stay annoyed at a man who so easily put his Armani covered knee on the floor, just to hug my daughter?

"Blake, when you're finished groveling at the feet of my daughter, how about you take Katya and Lily upstairs and amuse them while I meet with King."

I stiffened and turned to Luke. "I don't want Blake to *amuse* me. You said Grigori has more information about Lev. Why would you exclude me?"

Luke met my anger calmly but his eyes narrowed. "Blake," he said, not looking away from me.

"Come on, Glitterbug, let's go swing like a monkey." Blake took Lily by the hand and nudged her back into the elevator.

I wanted to scream, but I gritted my teeth. "I won't be long, baby-girl." My attempt to smile must have failed because Blake raised an elegant brow and minutely shook his head. The elevator door closed and I swung back to Luke. "I don't appreciate—"

"Take a breath, Katya." He stepped closer to me.

"Dammit, Luke. Stop handling me."

"You're not giving me any choice."

"You kids fighting?"

I stiffened as King came up behind me.

"Stay out of it, King," Luke muttered.

"He won't let me join your meeting about Lev," I complained, shooting imaginary poison darts at Luke.

"He's right. You can't." King was emphatic.

My hands shot to my hips and I turned to glare at King. "Why not?"

"You aren't part of my team."

I sucked in a breath. "You don't trust me?" I gasped at Luke.

"Katya." I turned at King's insistent call. His hand was on his hip and a lethal looking handgun showed under his jacket. "This has nothing to do with trust. In this situation, you're the victim and we have the job of protecting you. And, if you haven't noticed, Luke's distracted when you're around. Right now I need him on his game."

"That's not fair." I tried to throttle back my fury but my chin lifted at his arrogance. "Goddammit, I'm nobody's victim! I'm a survivor."

"And we're going to keep it that way. Now, please, do as Luke asks and let us do our job."

I hesitated under his unrelenting glare. He nodded abruptly and walked away. There was no doubt the man was used to being obeyed.

"Babe," Luke murmured.

I shook my head. I was angry. Hurt. Humiliated. *How can you shut me out?* But the words died in my throat. I turned away, and walked towards the stairs leading to the gym.

"Dammit, Katya!" Luke called.

I didn't turn back.

****

I sat stiffly on the leather couch in Blake's favorite waiting room. Lily was happily swinging on the rope and I was fuming. Or sulking?

This morning I woke up tired but in a good way. Last night had been late but it had also been so worth it. Lying in bed, my whole body tingled as I relished how thoroughly Luke had made love to me. And then I smiled like a Persian cat licking cream when I remembered how he had let me ravish him.

I'd taken my time in the shower and then found Lily and Luke downstairs in the kitchen. It had all seemed perfectly normal.

Too perfect.

Too normal.

A frisson of fear curled down my spine.

But I shrugged it off.

Yesterday, everything changed. *Dammit!* Luke and I had changed. We told each other secrets. Painful, soul-destroying stories that we whispered as we held each other, stroked each other. I wanted to believe we had a chance.

A chance at a future together.

I needed to believe!

But now he'd shut me out.

How had my day gone from basking in a heavenly morning afterglow to tamping back this creeping panic?

My skin was clammy and I tried to slow my breathing.

Luke's shut me out!

He'd left me stranded inside my head, the craziness of the last three days tugging on my sanity. Pulling me off balance.

I didn't feel safe.

He's shut me out. Just like my father!

"Blake!" I jumped up and went across to where he was spotting Lily on the rope.

"Come on, Glitterbug, time to come down." He helped her to the floor but his eyes were narrowed on me. "Go and get some water, munchkin." He gave her a gentle push towards the water dispenser and then waited until she skipped away before turning back to me.

"I need to go out, get some fresh air, coffee—"

"Princess, you're spinning out. Slow down." He stepped closer and took my arm but I pulled away.

"I need to get out. Now!" He was right, I was spinning out. There was a ringing in my ears and I could feel the walls pressing in on me.

"Katya, let me call Luke—"

"No!" I grabbed his arm and pleaded, "Please, Blake, I just need a moment on my own. Please!"

I don't know what he saw, probably his magic princess looking more like a deranged witch, but he tilted his elegant face and gave me what I needed. "There's a place across the street. Sells the best hot chocolate on the east coast. Will that do?" He raised a perfectly shaped brow.

My teeth were clenched so tight all I could do was nod.

"Okay, then." He took my hand.

Blake led Lily and me across the street and right into a sublime chocolate fantasy—*Pascal's Chocolat!* A chocolate shop and cafe decked out with floor-to-ceiling mahogany shelves, packed to the brim with hand-made chocolates in every shape you could imagine, all beautifully packaged and displayed. Lily and I stared in wonder at giant daisies of bright orange and yellow, spun from sugar and strung from the ceiling. Small, marble-topped cafe tables were lined along the windows, around which people were closely huddled, indulging in the ecstasy of Pascal's signature hot chocolate. The place was redolent with the aroma of rich chocolate and the contented buzz of its customers.

I turned to Blake and blurted, "How is this not your favorite waiting room?"

His eyes widened infinitesimally and then his mouth tipped into a small smile. "Princess, sugar's good, chocolate's better, but nothing beats hot alpha bodies rolling around on sparring mats, pushing up against each other, sweating—"

"I got it!" I gulped. And I did. A picture of Tane

and Matiu sparring, bare-chested, shot into my head. Did those sexy tattoos cover more than just their arms?

Blake shrugged an Armani clad shoulder and grinned outright. "Yes. I do believe you've got it."

And I burst out laughing. The cement in my stomach loosened and as my laughter faded, chocolate scented air filled my lungs and my smile remained. *This is exactly what I needed.*

"Mommy," Lily called plaintively and tugged on my hand. "I want chocolate milkshake."

"Okay, sweetheart." A banner at the counter rested over trays of freshly baked cookies. It boasted: Voted best chocolate chip cookie in NYC. I pulled on Lily's ponytail. "Stay with Blake, I'm going to pop into the restroom." Looking up, I made note of the restroom sign in the back corner of the shop. "Blake, I won't be a moment. I'll have a hot chocolate and a choc-chip cookie, thanks."

"Sure, princess." He winked and urged Lily into the queue at the counter.

I made my way to the back of Pascal's, through mounds of chocolate and bonbons. In the restroom I freshened my face and smiled into my reflection. It was a great idea to escape for a little while. My panic had completely dissipated.

I overreacted, I admitted to myself as I exited into the small passage. Luke wasn't shutting me out. He was just doing his job.

A hand circled my wrist and my heart thrashed. My arm was yanked behind me. "Don't scream or my men will hurt your daughter," a familiar voice snarled in my ear. Lev? I tried to look behind me, but he forced me against the wall.

"Look down," he ordered harshly.

My head dropped reflexively and my body spasmed. He had a vicious looking knife and it was pointed right up against my side.

"Be still and quiet, Katya, and listen to what I have to say. Draw attention and I'll hurt you but your daughter will suffer worse. *Da?*"

Oh God, it was definitely Lev!

We were crammed against the wall in the small passage, out of direct sight of Blake and Lily. "What do you want," I whimpered.

"I want what belongs to me." Hot breath wafted over my ear and a violent shudder shook my body. "I want Nicu's stash and the money he stole from that last transaction. I know you met with him, Katya. Where is it?"

"I don't n-no," I stuttered, shaking my head. *God! Where is everybody? Anybody!*

"Then find out. Now!" He snarled into my ear. "I want that money by the end of today or you, my pretty little Dalca princess, will lose everybody you love." Lev licked my cheek and my skin crawled with a million ghostly cockroaches. "Still so beautiful," he crooned. "Your father shook my father's hand and gave you to me." I cringed away from him, my eyes squeezed closed. I couldn't stop another whimper as his tongue raked my cheek again. "I want what's *mine*." He pulled my arm tighter until a hot poker pierced my shoulder and I gasped in pain. "I want *everything* your bastard father promised me! *Understand?*"

I nodded, terror clogging my throat.

"Good. *Da sveedaneeya*, pretty Katya. I'll be in touch later."

The pressure on my shoulder released but I remained frozen, pressed up against the wall. A door closed behind me and I flinched. *Is he gone?* I slowly turned my head. The passage was empty. My breath hitched and I started to shudder.

Deep breaths, girl. Lily's waiting, get control.

My legs steadied and I finally moved. It felt like I'd been gone a lifetime but when I cleared the passage and looked for Blake and Lily, they were still at the counter. Clutching my bag tight to my chest, I made my way to them. Blake took one look at my face and stiffened.

"What?" It was not a question, but an order.

"Lev," I whispered. "He w-was here."

"Corner table, over there," he pointed and hustled us over to the just vacated table. He thrust me in a chair and took up a protective stance alongside us. I grabbed a confused Lily and tugged her into my lap, hugging her to me.

"Mommy?"

My heart churned at her frightened call. "Shh, baby-girl. Mommy got a fright but everything's okay now." I rocked her and looked up at Blake who was already on his phone.

"Luke! We're in *Pascal's*. Lev was here." He nodded sharply at whatever Luke was telling him, not a single hair out of place, but his cultivated urbanity was gone, replaced by an alert sleekness that was both terrifying and comforting. "Nope, I didn't see him but he got to Katya. She's fine but shaken." He listened, muttered an assent and hung up. "Sit tight," he ordered, looking down at me. "They're coming to fetch us."

Shitsofuckit! Luke is going to be crazy mad.

"I want Daddy," Lily whined, burying her head in my neck.

Me too! "It's all right, baby-girl, he's coming now." I hugged her shaking body tighter.

As difficult as it was to admit, I needed Luke.

I needed him now!

****

Katya

Thor's evil twin!

That's what Luke looked like when he came storming into *Pascal's Chocolat*. His eyes raked over me but he didn't say a word. Just scooped Lily up into his arms and barked at Gray to take point. "Katya, stay close behind me." He grabbed my hand to place it on his belt at his back.

Blake took up the rear and we moved smoothly out of the chocolate emporium. We must have had gawkers, but I didn't notice. My heartbeat was echoing in my skull.

Gray didn't mess around. He crossed the road fast but I hesitated, instinctively checking for traffic. Luke's head whipped around when he felt me tug on his belt. "What?" he asked, eyes super alert.

"Um, traffic—" I said but I was confused because there wasn't any.

"Open your eyes, Katya, everybody's in the street. They're holding the traffic to get you clear."

I searched and my eyes widened. How could I not have seen them? Matiu and Tane were further up the street, standing in the middle, guns drawn at the ready. Cars were backed up behind them.

"Move, Katya, now!" Luke growled and wrapped his hand around my wrist, pulling me across the street. I looked the other way and there was King and Mira, a mirror image of the twins, armed and formidable, holding back oncoming traffic.

Shit! Shit! Shit!

Terror constricted my throat. The impact of my stupidity was dawning on me: I had put Luke and his team in danger. *And Lily!*

Gray herded us into the HQ elevator and the doors closed. Luke was still holding Lily, her little arms tight around his neck.

"Luke," I croaked and swallowed hard to clear the building thickness.

He turned to me and I flinched. The anger burning in his eyes was like a physical blow. "Not now," he warned.

The elevator doors opened and we all traipsed out. Fine tremors rippled over my body. I tucked my arms tight against my stomach, clutching my elbows. Luke murmured to Lily then handed her to Blake.

"Take her to Eva's office, I need some time with Katya," he said.

My little girl didn't even look at me, she just snuggled into Blake's arms and went quietly with him. Luke remained where he was, his back to me. His hands were on his hips, holding back his jacket and I noticed he was also armed, a large black handgun resting on his hip.

Luke and his world seemed suddenly, frighteningly unfamiliar. They had moved so quickly to protect me. But who were they? What were they?

"Luke, I'm really sorry," I whispered.

He spun around and stormed over. "Jesus fuck! What the hell were you thinking?"

"I'm s-sorry." His fury poleaxed me and I gripped my elbows till my knuckles were white.

"I know it wasn't Blake's idea to take a stroll outside. So what the fuck, Katya? Do I need to put a collar and chain on you?"

His intense blue eyes were dark and inky and for once, they didn't make me tingle. They made me mad as hell.

A collar and chain! Who does he think he is? He doesn't own me.

"I don't need you!" I hissed, lifting my chin at him. "Where were *you* when Lily was taken and Dani was shot? Where were *you* when Lily was three years old and her temperature was raging out of control?" My voice rose as memories slammed into me. "Where were *you*, Luke, when doctors put her in an ice bath and refused to answer me when I begged them to tell me if she was going to be okay? *Where were you?*"

"Babe—"

Heat roiled up inside me, choking me, and I backed away from him. "Where were *you* when she came home crying after her first day at kindergarten and asked why she didn't have a daddy?" My voice rasped, pain spewing from me.

"Tell me, Luke, Mr. Protector, where were *you* when I waited for you, crying, in New York?"

The elevator doors pinged and King and his warriors poured out. I backed further away, towards the door leading to the stairs. I said I wasn't a victim, but right then, adrenaline pouring through my system, I felt like one. Vulnerable prey, surrounded by hungry predators. I took one last desperate look at Luke and I bolted.

"Fuck!" I heard Luke growl as the door closed behind me.

I ran up the stairs, my pulse racing but my heart heavy. I didn't stop until I reached the gym and threw one of the huge windows open. Thrusting my head out, I took deep, gasping breaths.

Terror and fury were a lethal combination. I felt out of control.

Across the way, the Brooklyn Bridge stood unwavering and the briny smell of the East River filtered through the air. I closed my eyes and breathed, pushing back the panic that had reared its ugly head.

I heard him enter the gym, but I didn't turn or open my eyes. He came up right behind me and covered my arms with his. Lifting them from the window frame, he crossed them over my body and enfolded me, pulling me flush against his hard torso. Resting his chin lightly on my head, he breathed steadily.

After a while, his head shifted and I felt his breath at my ear. "I'm sorry, baby," he murmured. "I was an asshole. But you scared the shit out of me."

His quiet voice softened the knot in my stomach.

"I was also pissed," he continued, "and when I'm that angry, I can be a jerk. But babe." He squeezed me gently. "You can't run. You need to learn to stand fast and handle it."

I shook my head and pushed my arms against his, but his embrace didn't loosen. "Luke!"

"Babe!" His husky voice reverberated in my ear.

"How do I handle it when you're an aggressive jerk?"

"Give it right back at me, like you just did."

"It hurts me when you're like that," I admitted.

"And it scares me."

His arms tightened. "You don't ever have to be scared of me, Katya. I'll never hurt a hair on your head. Never!" His sincerity rang deep.

I tilted my head and he met my searching gaze. "When I'm scared, I run, Luke. It's how I'm built."

He turned me to him, cradling my face. "Fuck, babe, don't you know? When you hurt, I hurt. When you cringe from me, bolt like that?" His brow creased and he leaned closer, his lips brushing mine. "That hurt burns right through to my soul."

My eyes closed and he tucked my head to his chest. "Don't run from me, Katya. I'm not the enemy." I curled my arms around his shoulders as his fingers combed through my hair. "Let me protect you. Just for now. I'll keep you safe from Lev, and then you can be free to make decisions. For yourself and Lily. Good ones, the right ones, not driven by fear."

With each stroke of his fingers, his words penetrated my panicked brain. The havoc slowly receded. I softened against him and let his heat chase away the last of the tremors that had sent me running for solitude.

"Luke?"

"Yeah?"

"I'm sorry I overreacted."

"Me, too, baby. I'll work on reducing my tendency to be an asshole."

I smiled up at him. "You're not an asshole."

His brow creased but he didn't reply.

I took a steadying breath. "I know I overreacted, but why did you shut me out?"

He frowned. "You mean from the meeting?"

I nodded.

"Babe, we haven't had much time to talk about what we do here."

I nodded again.

"I'll explain more when you're not being stalked by scum, but I need you to understand: King's team is highly trained and considered the most effective response team in the world."

My eyes were popping. I couldn't pretend I wasn't impressed. "And the team includes you?"

"Fuck, you're gorgeous," he muttered and brushed his thumb across my lips. "Yeah, babe, the team includes me. And the team can't do what they do if you're in the mix. We need to be free to share ideas, make connections, run scenarios, without worrying it will upset you. It's a zone where anything can be said, and that's how it works best."

What he said made sense. "King was angry—"

"King's complicated. He's definitely not open to outsiders gate-crashing his inner circle."

"He doesn't trust me?" I whispered.

"He doesn't know you," Luke answered firmly. He cradled my face and pulled me to him. "I'll promise you what I promised your father." His expression tightened with sincerity. "It will never happen again. I will never leave you out in the cold. From now until I die, you and Lily will always come first."

His vow rang true but still I resisted his pull. "How do I trust what you promise?"

"Because I'll never give you a reason not to."

Every beautiful inch of him was focused on me. And as I drowned in the infinite blue of his gaze, my spirit unfurled and I finally let go of the last of the toxic panic that was strangling my heart. Going up on tiptoes, I threaded my fingers into his hair and pulled him down to meet my mouth. I didn't tease, I just swept my tongue past his sensual lips and entwined it wetly around his. "*Mmm.*" My throaty groan reverberated into his mouth as his heady taste flooded through me. Tingles prickled my scalp when he fisted my hair to angle my head so he could take control. Then he sucked my tongue deeper.

Wet. Hot. Delicious.

My knees wobbled and I swayed against him. His hand tightened in my hair and he cupped my ass, lifting me against his surging hardness. I sank into his heat, lost in the intoxicating taste of him.

"*Ahem!*" A determined cough from somewhere behind us. Luke lifted his head and I moued.

"This better be good," Luke threatened, glaring over my shoulder.

My brain was fogged and I could barely breathe through the clamoring desire.

"You okay, baby?" His voice was husky as he slowly released me and steadied me on my feet. "Babe?"

He was smiling wickedly.

I widened my eyes and purposefully licked my lips. His eyes darkened and I smiled smugly.

"She okay?" King asked from behind me. I turned to see him eying us. "You doing okay?" He stepped closer, his disconcerting gaze narrowed on me.

Heat bloomed in my chest and rushed upwards. *Dammit!* Blushing like a schoolgirl again. But his sincerity caught me off guard. Where was the arrogant beast I was used to? "Um, yes, I'm fine," I stammered.

He nodded, raising his hands to his hips in the familiar King stance.

"King." I took a tentative step towards him. *Suck it up girl.* He deserved an apology. "I'm sorry. I'm really sorry. I put you and your team out there, and it was stupid and selfish. I'm sorry."

His eyes flickered to Luke then back to me. He dipped his head, once. "It happened and it's over," he said, his English brogue deep and pronounced. "Blake briefed us on what happened, including Lev Boykov's threat." Luke lifted an arm and circled my shoulders, pulling me to him. King studied us, then zeroed in on Luke. "This needs to be resolved before something happens that we can't control," he said.

"Agreed. Any idea how?" Luke replied.

"Some," he said enigmatically. "I've been in touch with Petrov. He has new intel but he insists he'll only meet with you."

"Fuck. I don't want to leave Katya and Lily."

"It can't be helped. We'll watch out for them," King promised. "Lily can stay here. Blake and Mira can keep her occupied. I think it's best if you see Petrov alone." He looked at me. "If you want, I can spare Gray and he can take you to visit with Dani?"

I stared at him and the back of my neck tingled. Something was off.

"Babe?"

I looked up at Luke and decided to ignore the niggling doubt. I wasn't sure I liked King, but Luke trusted him. *Didn't he?* "Okay." I linked my hand with Luke's. "Go and see Grigori. Hopefully his information is good. Maybe it will lead to Lev's arrest." I swallowed back the queasiness triggered by the memory of his revolting tongue on my cheek and squeezed Luke's hand. "Go, honey. It'll give me a chance to spend some time with Dani."

Luke searched my face. He must have been reassured, because he made me promise not to give Gray a hard time and then he was gone.

I followed King downstairs to see Lily before I left for the hospital. He walked us down the corridor that led to the war room and stopped at the office the blond bombshell had emerged from when I was running— again!—from Luke.

"She's in here, with Blake and Eva," King said. "I'll go find Gray. Tell Blake to buzz when you're ready. Gray will collect you."

He seemed aloof, unwilling to engage in any further conversation. "King, is everything okay?" I was tentative, the prickling spreading from my scalp to the rest of my body.

He stared at me and nodded abruptly. "It will be," he said gruffly. "I'll make sure of it." Then he was gone, striding down the corridor and disappearing into the war room.

I didn't feel reassured. *What isn't he telling me?*

I rubbed at the goosebumps on my arms and eased the office door open. The room was unexpected. It looked more like an elegant sitting room than an office. Lily was kneeling at a small, glass coffee table, colored pens scattered over the surface. Warmth pinged my heart. Her tongue was caught between her teeth and she was scribbling madly. Blake sat behind her, lounging on a comfortable two-seater, busy with his phone. The blonde bombshell—Eva, I guessed—sat at her chrome and glass desk, working on her laptop.

I walked in and she immediately stood. *Yowza!* This woman was definitely no skank. She was curvy in all the right places, her hair and make-up immaculate. She wore a pale-blue, classic pencil-skirt and blazer, but there was nothing classic about how it molded to her hour-glass shape. My eyes widened as they skimmed over her pushed-up D-cups, clad in a cream, satin camisole.

"Katya," she greeted huskily. "I'm Eva." She came over to me and held her hand out.

"Um, hi." I shook her hand, relieved she totally ignored our last ignominious meeting.

She looked across at Lily. Then her pale-blue eyes cut back to me and I instinctively stiffened. "You should take better care," she murmured tightly. "If you lose her, you will never recover."

I stared into her icy gaze and shivered at the piercing truth of her words. She nodded abruptly and then slipped past me and out the door.

"Katya?"

Blake. I hadn't noticed he had moved from the couch and was standing beside me. "I'm sorry, Blake," I whispered, squeezing his hand. "I was so stupid—"

"Princess, enough." He gently tugged my hand. "You were panicked and it was my fault too. I know better."

I searched his hooded eyes. "Why don't we just agree that we were both careless?" I smiled tentatively and my heart skipped a beat when he pulled me against his lean body and hugged me tight.

"Would hate it if something happened to you, princess."

"I frightened Lily," I whispered into his ear,

fiercely blinking away tears.

He eased back and studied my face. "Yes, but she's a strong little girl. She'll be all right."

"I don't know. It's a lot to process for a child. All of it." I was worried.

"She likes the idea of having a daddy." Blake looked over my shoulder and his expression hardened.

Careful to keep my body angled so Lily couldn't hear me, I leveled my gaze at him, not liking his accusing tone. "I'm not running away, if that's what you mean." My temper flared. "Not that it's any of your business."

He smiled tightly and inclined his head. I met his enigmatic gaze and nodded, and then I turned to Lily. It was time to face my daughter. I approached and toed off my shoes, momentarily luxuriating in the thick, white rug. I knelt down and shuffled up next to her. She continued scribbling, refusing to even look at me.

My baby-girl, so stubborn.

"What are you drawing, baby-girl?"

"I'm not a baby." I swallowed hard when I saw her lower lip tremble.

"No, sweetheart, you're not a baby." I reached to stroke her long, sun-streaked hair. "But you'll always be *my* baby-girl."

Finally she looked up. Tears shimmered in her midnight eyes. I opened my arms and with a heartbreaking sob, she clambered into my lap. Wrapping her up tight, I crooned against her head. "Shh, Lily. It's going to be all right." I rocked her gently. "I promise you, baby-girl, everything's going to be all right."

Chapter Fourteen
A Gift For Lev

Katya

"You look fit to be tied, darlin'."

We were heading to the hospital and I was brooding. Lily was scared and confused. She didn't understand why Luke and I had argued. How did I explain to a five year old, the complexities of my relationship with Luke?

Gray interrupted my thoughts. "Want to share?"

I looked at him. He was an enigma. Always charming and amusing, sometimes cutting, but he invariably held himself apart. Except from Lily, of course. And his unusual gray-blue eyes missed nothing. "I'm fine," I shrugged.

"Must be something." He glanced at me. "You're scowling."

He was Luke's best friend, surely I could trust him? "I can't decide about Blake," I said hesitantly. "He's warm and friendly, until he's not." I shook my head in exasperation. "Can I trust him?"

Gray was wearing sunglasses so it was difficult to read his expression but he answered me readily. "Blake's like a Venus flytrap," he explained. "He's a dichotomous blend of beauty and death. But he's fiercely loyal to King and the team."

"Does that extend to the team's women and

children?" I asked pointedly and he smiled.

"Since you and Lily are the first, we'll have to wait and see." He checked the SUV's mirrors and then grinned across at me. "But it looks like he's already smitten with Lily and trust me, you're not far behind."

"How do you know?"

"Well darlin'," he drawled. "You might have noticed that he can be cutting with his nicknames—" I nodded when he raised his brow at me. "Well, that's a reflection of his opinion of your character," he clarified. "I think with the bestowment of Magic Princess, you're doing okay."

Would hate it if something happened to you, princess.

Blake's hug had been so tight, his words sincere. I bit my lip and rubbed at the knot in my neck. "I think *he* thinks I'm going to hurt Luke," I blurted.

"And are you?"

"No! Of course not."

"Well, that's good."

I stared daggers at him and the corner of his mouth quirked but he didn't look away from the road. "Blake has a soft spot for Luke," he said after a moment, "which is why he might be holding out with you."

"Luke, why?"

"You're not blind darlin'. You must have noticed how Blake drools over Luke."

My face heated and I winced. "A lot like I do?" I said, sheepishly.

His laughter filled the SUV and I grinned back. "No, darlin', not quite like you. Luke likes Blake plenty, and trusts him, but he definitely doesn't swing both ways."

I sat back and rested my head against the seat. My tension began to seep away.

"Katya?"

My stomach tightened again at his sober tone. What I could see of his face was blank but my eyes drifted down and both his hands were wrapped tightly around the steering wheel.

"Yes." I held my breath.

"I've never seen Luke look at anybody the way he looks at you."

Oh my God! I silently exhaled, terrified he'd stop talking.

"When we returned from New Orleans, I knew something had changed in him." He glanced at me but I sat frozen. "It was you." He looked forward again. "But I only really understood a year later, when I lost you in New York."

What? "I don't understand," I murmured.

"At Union Square." He ran his fingers roughly over the short growth along his jawline. "I was with Luke. *Fuck*! I've never seen him so torn."

My hands curled into fists but I remained silent.

"He sent me after you. He needed to find out where you were living." His voice was tight. "That fucking piece-of-shit Petrov waylaid me and you were gone." I cringed as his hand slammed the steering wheel. "When I called Luke to tell him I had lost you—" He turned and I swallowed hard at his contorted face. "Fuck. I thought I had lost him as a brother. It was a long time before he forgave me."

"I'm sorry," I said hoarsely. His anguish was palpable.

"You don't need to be sorry, Katya. Find a way to

forgive him because what the two of you have—" His voice deepened with intensity. "That's a gift you don't walk away from."

I impulsively reached out and clasped his forearm. "Gray, I *have* forgiven him."

His hand covered mine. It was warm and rough, like Luke's, but there were no tingles. "Darlin'," he said, his voice rough. "You might have forgiven him in your heart, but your head is still hesitating."

My hand jerked on his arm.

"Tell me I'm wrong, sweetheart."

You're wrong!

However hard I tried, the words remained lodged in my throat.

The miles passed and the strained silence between us relaxed. I kept my hand on his arm. His warmth was comforting and his silence held no judgment.

I decided that I liked Gray.

I liked it even more that he loved Luke.

"Luke mentioned you don't speak with your family." *Shit, Katya. Not your business!* "That's all he said," I added quickly when he turned to scowl at me. "It's just that, I know something about being cut off from family and I only wanted to tell you how sorry I am."

My chest eased when he relaxed and shrugged. "I was in love with my brother's fiancée," he said evenly. "Bad shit happened and I walked away."

"When are you going back?" I asked quietly.

"My family is here now." He shrugged again. "Luke is more a brother to me than my own brother ever was."

So bitter.

"Luke says it's never too late to reach out to family," I whispered.

He turned to me briefly before looking back to the road.

Seconds later, his hand returned to cover mine. But he still didn't answer, and we drove the rest of the way in silence.

****

Katya

"What are you frightened of, KitKat?"

I was in a chair pulled up close to Dani's bedside. Elbows propped on the bed. "It's not that I'm frightened," I said. "My heart trusts him, but my head keeps interfering. Or maybe it's the other way around?" I dropped my head, pulling at my hair. "Dammit, Dani, everything's going too fast, it's barely been four days and I've already slept with him!"

"Was it good?" Dani said breathlessly, her eyes huge.

A blush rushed up my chest and I buried my face in my hands.

"Come on, KitKat, spill," Dani teased.

I looked at her through my fingers and my blush traveled inward, warming my heart. She was still weak but it was so good to see her bouncing back. "Amaze-balls," I whispered, dropping my hands.

"I haven't heard you say that word in years." She smiled and her whole face lit up. I gently wrapped my hand around hers and grinned back. "You know—" Her warm coffee-brown eyes narrowed, "it's not really four days, it's more like six years."

"What do you mean?"

"I know you never got over him. You look more

alive now than you have in all the time you've lived with us." I ducked my head but I didn't let go of her hand. There was a reason Dani was my best friend. "Look at me, KitKat." She tugged weakly at my hand, waiting until I raised my head. "You never know when life is going to come screeching to a halt."

"I know that! Jeez. Don't you think seeing you shot isn't seared on my brain?"

"Then stop listening to your head," she said fiercely, straining towards me. "Dammit, give Luke a chance to prove himself."

"You're going to hurt yourself!" I cried and eased her back against the pillow. I was careful not to touch her where the drip needles had left dark bruises.

"And Katya," she said stubbornly. "Don't you teach Lily to be scared of love."

"I'm not doing that!" I denied hotly.

She scowled and her rich, brown gaze searched mine. "Then what are you doing?"

Last night flashed into my mind: The intimacy of sitting in Luke's lap, naked, listening to him open up his soul. "I'm learning how to love," I said softly. "I just need everybody to give me some space to do that. Jeez, even Lily is giving me a hard time."

Her hand squeezed mine. "Okay, sweetie, I get it."

I nodded and my shoulders sagged in relief. Talking with Dani always made me feel better, but I could see she was getting tired. "You need to sleep and I need to get back to Lily." I stood up.

Her eyes flickered to something behind me. "He's here again," she whispered.

"What? Who?"

"Him!" She hissed, rolling her eyes at the door.

"My shadow."

I glanced over my shoulder and frowned. Matiu? Tawny eyes met my questioning gaze but his expression remained stony. I turned back to Dani and whispered loudly, "I think he likes you."

"He thinks he's my guardian angel."

"That's good, isn't it?"

"No!"

"Why?" I teased and smiled smugly at her obvious agitation. "He's sleek, like a big, golden panther. And those tattoos!" I bent down to her and whispered. "Oh my God, Dani, do you think they cover his whole body?"

Her eyes widened and she began to giggle. "Cut it out, bestie. That's my fantasy, not yours."

"You do know I can hear you, don't you?" Matiu's voice rumbled from the wall.

We looked his way and I squeezed Dani's hand. He was lounging against the wall, his arresting face transformed by full lips pulled into a sensual half-smile.

"Go away or I'll sic my brother on you!" Dani threatened. But it didn't sound very intimidating. I giggled again.

Matiu just raised his brow, his face once again inscrutable.

Dani tugged at my hand and I leaned closer. "He frightens me," she whispered.

"No, I don't," Matiu growled. My heart skipped a beat and Dani and I stared wide-eyed at each other. "I awaken her."

"See," Dani said, her pupils huge.

And I did see. Love 'em and leave 'em Dani was being hunted by a panther.

"You asked me to give Luke a chance." I watched her forehead pucker. "What about you, girlfriend?"

She scowled and I grinned, the heaviness of the last few hours falling away. I peeked across at Matiu but he was gone. How did he do that?

Dani's eyes began to flutter closed. "Not sure you're going to be able to love and leave this one, honey," I whispered.

She smiled but didn't answer.

"He looks to be the persistent type." I murmured to myself and watched her drift off to sleep.

****

Once I was sure Dani was sleeping peacefully, I crept out of the ward and joined Gray. He was waiting for me, pacing restlessly alongside the nurses' station. His mouth tightened as I approached and my tension returned when his eyes skittered away to do a full sweep before returning to me. His eyes had darkened to slate-gray and a frisson of fear curdled my insides. "What's wrong?" I stopped in front of him.

He stepped beside me and his hand settled on my lower back, urging me forward. "Nothing," he said roughly. "Let's go."

"Gray?" I called, skipping to keep up with him.

"Everything's fine, Katya," he clipped, but he slowed his pace so I could keep up.

We moved quickly through the corridors and as we hit the main reception area he grabbed my arm to stop me. "Katya." His eyes were narrow, his brow furrowed. "No matter what happens, you must believe we will never let anything bad happen to you."

I searched his face and shivered, cold fingers of dread stroking down my spine. "Gray, what's happening?" I implored. "I don't understand."

"Katya!"

I whipped around to see who had called out my name.

"Anna?" I automatically met her reaching hands with mine, taking in her bruised and bleeding face. "Oh my goodness, look at you! What happened?"

"L-Lev," she sobbed, lifting her hand to wipe at the blood trickling from her split lip. "It-it w-was Lev."

Her face was a mess, smeared make-up blending with blood and tears.

Gray tapped my shoulder. "Take her to the restroom, help her get cleaned up." He was barely looking at Anna or me, his eyes constantly roving the reception area.

"Why would Lev hurt Anna?" I asked, forcing him to look at me.

"It doesn't matter right now," he insisted. "Clean her up and we'll talk after."

"Please, Katya," Anna sobbed. "He s-said he w-wants the money, I have to ask you for it."

Anger flushed through my body. *That bastard!*

"Maybe we should take her to the ER?" I suggested. "Let them check her out."

She shook her head vehemently, her long blond hair flying around her like a cape. "No, Katya," she pleaded. "Just some help in the bathroom and I'll be fine."

I tried to read her ice-blue eyes but they were darting all over the place. The back of my neck tingled. I should feel sorry for her but I didn't. I just felt on edge.

"Come on, the restroom's over there." Gray

pointed towards the back of the reception area, near the exit. I herded Anna along, Gray striding along beside us. He was hyper alert, his phone gripped in his hand. Anna ducked her head, like she didn't want to draw attention to herself.

I looked at Gray, a sinking feeling in my stomach. *What the hell is going on?* He pushed the restroom door open and held it for us. Anna entered and I stared quizzically up at him. "What?" I mouthed silently.

He scowled and shook his head, gesturing for me to follow Anna.

Fine!

I stomped in after her. I'd help the beaten-up skank and then maybe he'd take the trouble to tell me what the bejeezus was going on here!

"Rinse your face with cold water," I told Anna who was standing by the vanity, watching me through the mirror. "Go on, I'll get some paper-towel." I tried to smile encouragingly as I edged past her and reached for the dispenser. Her eyes followed me.

Cold.

Vicious?

I quickly looked away, shrugging off a shiver of revulsion.

I reached for a paper-towel, but a hand roughly fisted my hair and yanked my head back. Adrenaline spiked through me. "*Sooka!*" Anna spit in my ear. "Nicu's little princess!" She shoved the muzzle of a gun under my chin. It dug into my jaw and forced my head up. "You are Lev's now. Lev's and mine!" Her spittle sprayed my cheek.

"What are you doing?" I croaked, her grip on my hair strained my neck, forcing me off balance.

"Taking you to Lev."

She dragged me by my hair and I stumbled backwards. *Shit!* My scalp burned. "Anna! Why are you doing this?" My hands swung up and tried to loosen her grip on my hair. "Stop it!" She yanked my hair harder, pushing the gun into my temple.

"Quiet!" She hissed. "If your watchdog comes in, I will pull the trigger." She tapped the gun against the side of my head. "*Da?*"

I blinked rapidly, her hold on my hair too tight for me to nod.

"Good." She pulled me backwards several more steps. Her hold on me was vicious and I was helpless to stop her. "Now," she spat, spinning me round to face the window. "You're going to climb out, bitch. If you try and call to anybody, I'll shoot you where you stand."

"You're crazy," I gasped. There were no bars on the windows, and they were easily large enough for me to climb through. But how high up were they?

"Open the windows. Both of them," she ordered.

My fear escalated and I began to tremble. Her voice was ruthless. I knew she would shoot me without a care. *Shit. She would probably enjoy it.* Inhaling a shuddery breath, I reached out and unlatched both windows, pushing them wide.

"The drop is not high," she said, moving alongside me. "We will climb out at the same time."

Her face was contorted, the blood congealing, turning her into a nightmarish clown.

Gray, where the hell are you?

'No matter what happens you must believe we will never let anything bad happen to you.'

Gray's promise rang empty. Anna's eyes were cold, and I wanted to run. Run for my life. The gun jerked in my face and I turned to climb out the window.

The drop was short and I landed on bent knees without a problem. Before I could even think of escape, she was next to me, her gun prodding my side.

"Walk!"

I searched frantically for a way to escape. *Somebody must see and call for help!* But nobody was there. Just like in *Pascal's*, there wasn't a soul to witness my ordeal.

The skank had everything planned out, leaving no opportunity for me to maneuver. She hurried me through a fire-escape, down two flights of stairs and into the basement parking. An ominous black van loomed. I stopped short as the side door slid open.

No! I didn't want to get into that van.

Punch! I doubled up, gasping for breath.

"Get in the fucking van!" She demanded, and shoved me hard.

I stumbled, falling awkwardly through the open door. A hand reached out and pulled me the rest of the way inside, forcing me flat on my stomach. "No!" I screamed, but Anna's punch had winded me and it came out as a croak.

"Drive!" She ordered, and I heard the sliding door slam shut.

Darkness shrouded us and I looked up to see a bulky shadow clamber between the front seats and behind the steering wheel. *Whoosh!* I was slammed flat, a knee shoved into my back. Panic ripped through me as I fought to breathe. *Shit!* Her weight was forcing the air from my lungs. I went limp. My hands were yanked behind me, and some sort of cable was looped around my wrists. I tried to wriggle but I couldn't breathe. The cable was pulled tight.

I can't move. Oh God! I can't breathe.

"Listen up, *sooka!*" She clawed my hair, forcing my head up and hissed in my ear. "You make a sound and I'll gag you. Understood?"

I nodded as best I could and she shoved my head down, her weight lifting from my back. Air filled my lungs. I wheezed painfully, and rested my cheek against the rubber of the van floor.

How did Luke hook up with such a vicious cow?

The engine fired and the van moved. Fast. We screeched out of the parking and soon, daylight poured inside. I tried to get more comfortable. Every time the speeding van took a turn or a bump, I was tossed around like a sack of potatoes. I rolled to my back and looked for Anna. She was leaning against the side of the van, eyes locked on me, both hands gripping her gun. She licked the encrusted blood from her split lip and grinned at me.

With some effort and more than a little pain, I maneuvered myself into a seated position and leaned against the opposite side of the van. I forced myself to stare her down. She didn't move. I licked my own lips. My breathing had eased some, but my mouth was parched. "Did you do that to your face?" My voice was ragged.

She cocked her head and pouted. With her swollen lip and smeared make-up, she looked grotesque. "I had some help. Didn't I, Boris?" She bragged loudly to the driver. "It hurt, but it was worth it. I fooled you. *Da?*"

I clamped my teeth tight as she smiled smugly at

me. My gut had crawled with warning, but it had never entered my mind she would hurt herself.

"Why?"

"A gift for Lev." She smirked, her tongue lapping at her lip again. Her eyes flashed wildly, and I recoiled as she lunged forward. "With Lev's knife at your throat, your father will do anything to see you safe, including handing over the location of his hidden cash." A scary madness lurked in those eyes and I pressed back against the van. "For years, I sucked up to Nicu. I was forced to be Arkady's toy. It made me sick to my stomach. For what? Nothing!" Her mouth twisted into a sly grin. "Except, of course for Luke."

My nape prickled and my skin went clammy. She lounged back, a flush creeping over her face. "Now, he was a pleasant relief," she crooned. "That man of yours, he fucks like a machine. Goes at it for hours. Creative too."

Puke shot up my throat and I swallowed desperately.

Fuck you, skank!

I clenched my teeth, doing everything I could to keep my face blank. I knew I failed when she cackled, her eyes glinting with evil satisfaction.

"Lev?" She raised a perfectly tweezed brow. "He may not fuck as good as Luke, but he's mine. And with Nicu's money, we'll rebuild, take control of New York. Soon, we'll take over the whole East Coast. Nobody will be able to stop us!"

Chapter Fifteen
Skank Crumpled at My Feet

Astor Place, East Village, NYC
Luke

Luke parked in a loading bay opposite Astor Place Cube. He jabbed the button to open his window and squinted into the mid-morning sun to look for Grigori Petrov.

Where is Nicu's shit-for-brains shadow?

He glanced at his watch. He was a few minutes early, traffic to the East Village had been unexpectedly light. Relaxing in his seat, he rubbed his temple, the beginnings of a headache making him frown. Leaving Katya had not been what he wanted and he was pissed.

Why didn't King squeeze Petrov for his intel over the phone?

Pinching the bridge of his nose, he closed his eyes. *Fuck.* King was up to something. Whatever it was, it better not spill over onto Katya. His woman had enough of her own shit to deal with. Seeing her bolt from him hurt like hell. But he understood. Nicu fucked up as a father and his own asshole behavior cut her deep. His body tightened. *This morning he'd been an insensitive jackass.* He had to learn to take more care with her. Be patient until she learned to trust again.

Massaging his temple, he checked his rear-view mirror. *There.* Petrov had emerged from the corner of

Lafayette and was coming up behind his SUV. He opened his door and climbed out, circling around to meet Petrov head-on.

The beefy Romanian stopped and put his hands in his pockets.

"Petrov," Luke greeted curtly and raised his hands to his hips, drawing back his leather jacket so the man wouldn't miss he was armed.

"Hunter," he bit out, hooded eyes boring aggressively into Luke's.

They stood on the sidewalk, mentally circling each other, like two fighting dogs ready to scrap.

Shit. He didn't have time for this. "What's so important you need to talk to me in person?" Luke demanded.

A line appeared between Petrov's thick brows. "It was you." He jutted his chin at Luke. "King call me, he say it urgent I meet with you. So I come."

Luke stilled, the hair on the back of his neck springing to attention. "You didn't call?"

"*Nyet!*" Petrov shook his head.

"Fuck!" Luke swore through gritted teeth.

"What? What is the matter?" Petrov's frown deepened. "Is it Katya? Something is happen to her?"

"I've gotta go." Luke turned and started back to his SUV, pulling his phone from his pocket. "I'll be in touch later," he called over his shoulder.

What the fuck has King done?

He swiped his finger on the quick dial for his boss and climbed back into his vehicle.

Petrov hadn't moved.

"Come on, answer," he muttered under his breath, drumming his fingers on the steering wheel.

"Yes?" King's English brogue was blunt.

"What the fuck?"

"Sorry, Hunter." he said abruptly. "I had to get you out the frame."

A flame of fury ignited deep in Luke's gut. "What have you done?"

"What needed to be done."

Luke was used to King's brutal arrogance and mostly it just amused him. Today? He wanted to lay him out with his fist. "Where's Katya?"

Silence rang down the line and acid started to burn a hole in his stomach.

"King?"

"We tagged Anna hanging around the hospital," King said. "Gave her an opening to Katya."

"Jesus fuck! Tell me you didn't."

King ignored Luke's outburst. "Anna took Katya. Brought her to a small warehouse in Jersey. Near the Roosevelt Stadium."

Luke squeezed his eyes shut, his hand nearly crushing his phone.

"Hunter, nothing is going to happen to her. The whole team is here. We've neutralized Boykov's perimeter guard. As soon as we clock him, we'll take him down."

"You used my woman as bait?" Luke accused, his voice a painful rasp.

"Call Gray," King barked, then Luke heard nothing but blood rushing through his ears. The fucking asshole had hung up on him!

He inhaled deeply and quick-dialed Gray.

Let me protect you. Just for now. I'll keep you safe from Lev.

He forced a deep breath. His promise to Katya hung like a dead weight on his chest.

"Hunter."

Gray's betrayal burned much deeper than King's.

"Location?" He snapped.

"I'll text it," Gray said. "Luke, she's covered. Trust me, brother. I won't let anything happen to her."

"Lev's vicious. He's far too fucking unpredictable."

"We know that and we've got her covered," Gray insisted.

"You know nothing!" Luke roared and turned the ignition. "If anything happens to her, *brother*, I'll take out the fucking lot of you!"

His phone pinged and he ended the call. He programmed the warehouse address into the GPS and put the SUV in gear. Checking his rear-view mirror, he cursed under his breath, "Thank fuck!" Petrov had ducked. He didn't need questions from the Romanian pit bull.

I'm coming, baby.

Luke thought about Katya's temper and propensity for drama. *Shit!* It was going to take him at least forty-five minutes to get there.

Please, God, don't do anything stupid, baby. I'm coming.

****

Lev's Warehouse, New Jersey, NY.
Katya

Smack!

I recoiled in horror as Lev viciously hit Anna in the face.

"Stupid whore!" He grabbed her by the blouse and

shook her so hard, her head jerked back and forth. "What the fuck have you done?"

My stomach heaved as his spittle landed on her cheek.

"I-I b-brought a g-gift for you," she stammered, lifting a trembling hand to her face.

"A gift?" He sneered and shoved her. She stumbled backwards and before she could steady herself he advanced on her.

Punch!

Quicker than a snake, he sank his fist into her stomach and she dropped like a stone.

Ouch! I bit my lip so hard I tasted blood.

"A gift!?" He screeched again, standing over her body now sprawled flat on the filthy, concrete floor. "That gift," he snarled, pointing at me, "is going to have King Security crawling all over us. *Pizda!*" *Cunt!* He cursed and spat on her.

Anna's happy delirium had turned to crap in a blink. She was bleeding on the floor, and I didn't give a rat's ass. But watching Lev attack her like a mad dog, I couldn't stop trembling. I knew no woman deserved *that*.

She had been repulsively smug when she grabbed me by my hair and yanked me out the van. My scalp had burned so bad, I had to clench my teeth so I wouldn't beg the vile bitch to let me go when she frog-marched me into the warehouse.

If you could call it a warehouse.

It was more like a large double garage. Grimy walls, once painted beige, were peeling and patchy, some spots nearly black with filth. The ceiling was double volume and the small windows were boarded up. Old, fluorescent lights flickered a weak yellow beam that barely reached the corners of the room. The concrete floors were pitted and covered in oil or some other foul, dark substance. A door hung ajar, probably leading to Lev's 'office'. That's where he had emerged from when Anna called for him.

Against the wall, next to the door, there was a broken trestle table and a filthy plastic chair. The rest of the place was empty, except for a shiny red sports car with black finishes. It was garish and out of place in this squalid, musty rat hole. I presumed it belonged to the monstrous pig now standing in front of me.

If you walked past Lev Boykov in the street you wouldn't notice him. He was an average looking man. Average height. Average build. Average nondescript hair with an average, neatly-groomed goatee.

Until you looked into his eyes. Then average went swirling down the drain.

He had washed-out green eyes, like the muck that settled on an insect-ridden swamp, with small, beady pupils that dilated when they locked onto something he wanted.

And right now, they were locked on me.

"Ka-aa-tya," he crooned, drawing out my name.

Anna moaned and I couldn't stop my gaze darting towards her as she rolled over and tried to drag herself to her knees.

"No!" I gasped as Lev bunched his hand into my hair and forced my body to bend over backwards. Then he slammed his mouth down on mine and jammed his tongue inside. I gagged as his tongue rubbed up against mine. A hand ripped my shirt and cruelly grabbed my breast. My agonized scream was muffled by his mouth

293

pressed to mine.

I tried to arch away but my hands were still tied behind my back and his grip on my hair was forcing me off-balance.

"Lev!" Anna gasped.

He lifted his head and I inhaled desperately.

"Just getting a little taste, *Katyonak*," he said to Anna and licked his lips.

He punched Anna then called her Kitten?

I gritted my teeth, trying to ease the throbbing pain in my lower back. I could feel Lev's erection jabbing into me. His pupils blazed as he ground himself against me. *Jesus! No!* Agony stabbed and my knees buckled as he repeatedly dug his fingers into my breast.

Where are you Luke? Gray? Anybody!

My heart raced. *How the fuck can this be happening?*

"Lev!" Anna whined loudly and finally he lifted away. I couldn't tell if she was pissed at him or pissed at me. I didn't care. He yanked me upright and my legs sagged, tears flooding my eyes.

No! Dammit, Katya, don't you dare.

I locked my knees and looked down, determined not to cry.

"Soon, my little Katya. Soon, we will play," he crooned maniacally in my ear. "But first, you will tell me all about the money. Yes?"

He stepped back from me. "Anna!" he called. "Were you followed here?"

"Of course not." Her wooden tone was spooky.

"You are sure?"

"Yes, I'm sure."

The smug bitch from the van was gone. She was a

mess: her blouse torn and her face bleeding. But it was her eyes that sent cold shivers curling down my spine. Her pupils were so dilated they obliterated nearly all the ice-blue from her gaze. She looked demented.

"Go, sit there." Lev shoved me towards the dirty, plastic chair.

I backed away slowly. I didn't want to lose sight of either of them. Lev paced after me, his eyes never leaving me. They glowed with such an obsessive lechery that I started to hyperventilate, a terrifying claustrophobia leaching me of strength. *Shit!* I stumbled, the back of my legs getting tangled in the chair.

"Careful, pretty Katya." He jumped forward and grabbed my upper arm, preventing me from crashing to the ground. His fingers squeezed, biting cruelly into my skin, then he unceremoniously dumped me into the chair. His beady eyes studied me, like I was a specimen under a microscope. Then, like he'd made a decision, he nodded abruptly. "Watch her," he clipped at Anna. "And call Boris. They're to keep their fucking eyes open. We're moving out in ten minutes." He stepped away towards the door and disappeared.

My breath rasped and I couldn't think clearly, my body shaking with full body tremors. Anna managed to gain her feet. She didn't reach for her phone. She remained frozen. My heart thrashed when I noticed her gun, pointing down by her side, gripped tightly in her hand. I pulled against the cables that secured my wrists but they were too tight to give even an inch.

"You need incentive," Lev said walking back into the room. He held up a phone and his lizard eyes paralyzed me, their coldness more terrifying than his earlier depravity.

"What?" I croaked and cleared my throat. "What do you mean?"

"It's time for somebody to die," he said calmly and pressed a number on his phone.

I sucked in air, everything inside me suspended in disbelief as he lifted the phone to his ear.

"Do it now," he ordered. "Make sure you don't fuck up. I want him dead within the hour." He nodded brusquely, "*Da!*" And punched the phone with his thumb.

Luke!

A burning heat burst from my core and scorched through me.

This repulsive little man thinks he can murder my beautiful Luke. No!

I pushed off from the chair and with all my strength I barreled into the monster who was trying to destroy my life. My momentum drove him off his feet, but with my hands still secured behind my back, I had no balance and I went to the ground with him.

Oomph!

I landed on top of him and his arms wrapped around me, trying to shove me away but I tangled my legs with his.

"Fucking *sooka!*" He snarled, his head bobbing just above mine.

I'll give you bitch.

I dipped my chin then jerked my head up. *Ouch!* Pain ricocheted through the crown of my skull as I slammed him under his chin. His body slumped and I panted, licking tentatively at the split in my lip. I must have bitten it again when I head-butted him.

Clip-clop. Clip-clop.
Anna!

Lev groaned and I swallowed back a wave of nausea, revolted that I was sprawled over his body. Using my legs, I rolled off him and looked up at Anna.

She wasn't looking at me, she was standing next to Lev, her gun pointed at his torso. And her face was distorted by rage. "Fucking men. I'm sick and tired of you fucking men!"

Bang! Bang! Bang!

I tried to scramble away but it was difficult on my back. My weight was pressed down on my arms, which were already scraped raw from the concrete. Ice-blue eyes shifted from Lev and zeroed in on me.

"Anna, please," I whispered, the bite of cordite a horrifying reality check. But her face remained blank and she raised the gun and pointed it at me. "Don't, *please—*"

She stepped casually over Lev's bleeding body and stopped, staring down at me. Her gun was clasped steadily in both hands and I held still, cold sweat trickling between my breasts as I stared into that terrifying muzzle.

"You will take me to the money or I'll shoot pieces off you until you do," she rasped.

Before I could respond to her sick demand, a violent crash thundered over us. Anna spun around and I saw a dark Hummer ram through the roller-door entrance and slam into the red sports car. Brakes screeched and the aluminum garage door groaned, hanging off its hinges and swinging precariously. Two car doors flew open. Out of the corner of my eye, I saw Anna turn back to me and my whole world went still as

I stared into death.

Bang! Bang! Bang!

Anna's body contorted like a puppet and then, as if somebody had cut the strings, she crumpled to the floor. Her head landed right next to mine, her face covered by her long, blonde hair. *Thank God!* I didn't want to have to look into her dead eyes.

"Bloody hell! What the fuck did you think you were doing?" King's green eyes blazed with fury as he crouched down next to me.

Tears welled up and I collapsed back, the remaining strength in my body draining away. He gently rolled me to my side. With a snip my wrists were released and I whimpered as blood returned to my hands and shoulders.

"Come on, let's get you up," he said quietly and lifted me to my feet. Holding me against him, he called over my head, "Tane, fetch me a sweatshirt from the Hummer."

I sagged against him, tears flowing down my face. "Shit, I'm crying," I croaked into his chest.

"Brave girl," he said into my ear and cupped my head. "But also a stupid girl!"

"What? *Ouch!*" My lip stung and I gingerly licked at it, glaring up at King.

He shook his head and grimaced. "What did you think you were doing? Going after Boykov like that?"

Alarm bells rang but before I could unscramble my brain, Matiu called out, "King, Boykov's still breathing."

He eased me away and looked over his shoulder. "Call an ambulance, but make sure the bastard's secure."

"Here you go, sugar."

I looked up at Tane. He was holding out a large sweatshirt. *Damn!* My blouse was torn open and my cleavage was clearly on display.

"Um, thanks," I whispered taking the offered covering and wiping away at the stubborn tears wetting my face.

"Put it on," he ordered gently. "Luke's coming and he'll go ballistic if he sees you like this."

Luke!

Loud voices came from the entrance.

"Stay with her," King said curtly and hurried towards the scuffle.

"Here, sugar, let me help you with that."

"What?"

Tane carefully unclasped the sweatshirt from my tight grip and eased it over my head. My heart lurched as my vision was blocked, but the gentle giant pulled the collar down and then helped me with the sleeves. I was strangely uncoordinated, my attention split between the argument continuing in the entrance and the dead skank crumpled at my feet.

"What the fuck, man? You're supposed to be my brother!" *Luke. Didn't Lev order him dead?* He was yelling at Gray who was striding next to him. "I can understand *him*," Luke said, gesturing to King who was on his other side. "But you?"

His midnight-ink gaze narrowed as it swept over me. "Jesus fuck!"

And then I was swept up. Enfolded into warmth and security. My eyes flooded again and I collapsed against him.

"Jesus, baby, I'm so fucking sorry."

He cradled me against him and I sobbed, finally giving into the terror that had threatened to paralyze me more than once today.

After a while I composed myself and tuned into the conversation raging over my head.

"It was my call," King insisted. "We had Anna clocked. Caught her hanging outside the hospital and deduced she was waiting for your woman." I looked sideways and caught his eyes.

I thought I saw regret glimmering in their green depths.

His gaze briefly narrowed then moved back to Luke. "It was time to clean this mess up," he snapped.

Luke's arms tightened around me. "So you used my woman as bait?"

"Yes!" King nodded sharply. "She was never in danger, we never lost sight of them."

"That's not your fucking call to make!" Luke snarled.

"Yes it is!" King roared. *Yes, roared!* "This is still my fucking outfit. I make the calls, Hunter. You may not bloody like it, but that's how it is. And that's how it's going to bloody stay!"

He stormed away.

My jaw dropped. Thane Kingsley was really scary when he lost it.

"Let's get this shit cleaned up! And get this fucker to a hospital!" King shouted at no one in particular, pointing towards Lev's still-unconscious body on the floor.

"I'm going to kill that bastard," Luke muttered to Gray over my head.

Kill? Acid leaked into my stomach and I curled my

fingers into his sides. "I thought Lev ordered you killed?" I murmured.

Luke fingers were in my hair, gently easing out the knots. "What do you mean, baby?"

Still soaking up his warmth, I pressed against him and explained about Lev's phone call. "Whoever answered," I said. "He ordered him to kill you."

He stilled but kept me in his arms. "Gray, find his phone," he said.

I breathed in his musky scent, letting the familiar tang dilute the fear that was still rippling through me.

"It's a cell number," Gray called. "I've got Mira tracking it."

Luke nodded and dipped his head. "Okay, baby," he murmured, easing away from me. "Let's get you out of here." He wrapped his arm around my shoulders and pulled me tight to his body, guiding me away from Anna and around Lev, using his torso to block my view.

"I think your taste in women sucks," I mumbled.

He barked in surprised laughter and scooped me up into his arms. "Yeah, baby," he said, smiling down at me as I looped my arms around his neck. "I fucked up there. But things are definitely looking up for me." He spoke against my mouth, and then gently kissed me, careful to avoid my split lip.

Yes.

I tucked my head into his neck.

Things are definitely looking up.

****

Luke

Luke clenched his fists.

Too close. Too fucking close!

He waited impatiently at the entrance to the

warehouse, one eye on Katya who was sitting in the back of his SUV, Matiu cleaning up her grazed wrists. He clenched his fists again. There was nothing Matiu could do to help the bruises starting to appear on her breast. *Fucking hell!* He squeezed his eyes shut. She hadn't wanted to show him what was beneath the sweatshirt swamping her, but he knew she wouldn't be wearing it unless it was to hide something.

Something that bastard Lev did to her.

His heart pounded and he clenched his jaw. *How the hell did King let it get so out of control?*

Drumming his fingers against his belt, he let the fury simmer as he watched King finish his call to Mira and walk across to join him.

"It's a burner phone." He stopped a few feet away and eyed Luke warily. "Mira's working at tracking it."

Luke nodded abruptly. "My gut's twitching," he said through clenched teeth. "I want to know who the hell Lev gave that order to."

"Won't be long, Mira's on it." King turned to leave.

"King," Luke called, taking a step closer and squaring up to him. "Tell me something," he said steadily, his eyes boring into King's. "If you had Katya covered, why the hell was she rolling around the floor in Anna's blood?"

"Your woman's got a temper, Hunter," King replied heatedly. "We were about to breach when she leaped off her chair and took that motherfucker down!"

Luke blinked and clenched his jaw so tightly he thought he might dislocate it.

How could Katya be so fucking reckless?

King stared him down, his eyes ruthless. "We had

to be careful on entry," he explained. "I didn't want that asshole using her as cover."

"And Anna?" Luke asked, a clear picture of the dangerous scenario developing in his head.

"That cold bitch shot Lev point blank," King said. "Bloody hell! When she went after Katya I wasn't taking any chances. We used the Hummer as a distraction and I took her down myself."

Luke knew his eyes reflected his surprise. "You took out Anna?"

King's head cocked. "You care?"

"Fuck no!" Luke denied harshly, a wave of revulsion raising goosebumps all along his arms. "Jesus, my skin crawls knowing I had my prick in that piece of trash." He shuddered.

King's mouth twitched. "Well, we had no choice but to take her out. She had a gun on Katya and she was moving to pull the trigger." He shrugged and looked towards Katya where she was sitting in the SUV. "It wasn't a hard choice to make."

"DEA and NYPD is itching to speak with Katya," Gray said, joining them.

"I'll handle them," King replied.

"How the fuck did you let this happen?" Luke stepped closer to Gray. "I get his move." He lifted his chin at King. "But you? I thought you had my back, man?"

Gray stiffened and his normally blue eyes darkened to a stormy grey. "I've always got your back, Hunter, and you fucking know that!"

Luke hesitated. *Shit. He did know that.* "I get that Gray, but this did not play out how I wanted it to." He gestured to Katya. "I never wanted to put her at risk like

303

that. Never!"

Gray and King didn't reply but they looked away from him and towards Katya. Luke sensed their regret and decided there was no point in pushing it.

This whole thing was jacked up, but at least Katya was safe. And Lev was no longer a threat.

"You love her?"

What the fuck?

Gray's question came out of left field. His brain scrambled and he hesitated, running his fingers roughly through his hair. "Christ! It's only been, what, four days?" He muttered.

"Bullshi-iit!" Gray drawled. "It's been six years and you know it, Hunt."

"That long?" King threw in with a smirk.

Holy hell. They're like old women cackling around the pot.

Luke looked past them to Katya, who was gingerly sliding out of the SUV. She looked shell-shocked and bruised up but beautifully alive. His heart pulsed and warmth skittered through his veins. "Shit." He looked back at Gray and King. "I was a goner from the first time I glimpsed her through my scope."

Gray smiled but King gave him a penetrating stare. "Then it's good it's over so you can get on with it," he said. "Close the deal and start your life, before you fuck it up again."

Fuck!

King was an asshole but he wasn't wrong.

****

Katya

Whatever they were talking about, it looked intense.

Luke looked across at me and the corner of his mouth lifted. An answering awareness prickled in my chest and I tentatively licked my swollen lip. *Ouch!* It stung. But not as much as my bruised boob ached. Or my lacerated wrists burned. Or my arm, which had fingerprint marks where that vile pig had enjoyed cutting off my circulation, throbbed. Luke said something to King and Gray and then walked over to join me. He stopped right up close to my body. I inhaled deeply and reached out to lay my hand against his heart.

"What were you all talking about?" I asked.

"They were briefing me on what went down." He covered my hand with his. "Mira's tracking the cell phone, we'll have a bead on it soon."

"Why do we have to wait?" I wanted out of this place and I desperately wanted to hold Lily in my arms.

"I'd prefer to know who this killer is before we make a move." He gently pulled me against his body.

"You're worried?"

"My gut's burning."

That's not good.

I leaned back and he let me go, pacing a few feet away.

"What the fuck were you thinking?" he growled, spinning back to me. "Going after him like that?"

I jerked back. "What? Who?"

"Jesus Christ, Katya!" He closed in on me again. "Your arms cuffed behind your back. Anna armed and Lev a crazy fuck!" My jaw went slack as I watched him agitatedly run both hands through his hair. "And you fling yourself at him like you're fucking Buffy? Jesus, woman!"

I remembered the fear that had raced through me when I heard Lev give the order to have him killed.

How dare he read me the riot act?

"Buffy?" I questioned, stepping so close to him that there was no space between us. I lifted my chin and stared at him mutinously. "Show your age much?"

"This is not a fucking joke, Katya!" He was snarling and his eyes were flashing.

I didn't understand why he was so mad at me. *Had he been frightened for me?* His anger ignited mine and numbed what my brain was trying to tell me.

"So I should have sat on my butt and waited to be rescued?" Temper spewed from me. "I don't need your permission to act, Luke."

"What about what I need, Katya? Do you ever consider that?"

I flinched, his ferocity slamming into me. Trapped by flaring, midnight eyes, my chest heaved and heat rushed through me. Cupping my flushed cheeks, I tried to step back but the SUV prevented my escape.

"We've got a problem."

"For fuck's sake, could you give us a moment here?" Luke glared at King.

"It wasn't you, it was Nicu," King said, totally ignoring Luke's outburst.

"What?" I whispered, grateful for the support of the SUV.

"Lev's target," King explained urgently. "It wasn't Luke, it was Nicu."

"You've called the warden?" Luke said, his hand reaching to curl around mine. I gripped it tight because King didn't answer immediately. His head was bowed and deep in my bones, dread unfurled and started to slither through me.

"We're too late." He lifted his head, his moss-green eyes boring into me. "Nicu was found in the showers, he's got multiple stab wounds."

My legs shook and I sagged against the SUV. Luke let go of my hand and pulled me tight against him.

"He's dead?" I whispered.

"No." King lifted a hand to reassure me. "He's in bad shape but he's alive. He's being taken to Phelps Memorial. It's only four miles from the prison and they have a state-of-the-art surgical department there."

Papa!

"I'm sorry, Katya," King said. "I never expected Lev to make a move like this."

"Why not?" I snarled, leaning towards him. "That man is vile. You should have expected it—and worse!"

King jerked his head back. His shock was weirdly satisfying. "I know you may not care," I told him. "But you had no right to use me without my permission."

He nodded but remained silent.

I looked up at Luke. "I need to go to the hospital."

Luke's mouth was set in a hard line and a tic was twitching madly in his jaw. He didn't look at me, his eyes locked on King.

"Luke?" I trailed my hand to cup his jaw.

His eyes flickered and he finally dropped his gaze. I stretched up on tiptoes and gently brushed my lips across his tight mouth. His hand moved up to cradle my head and he pulled me tighter against his length.

"I'm sorry I scared you," I whispered against his lips.

His hand tightened in my hair, and he briefly closed his eyes. I felt him exhale and he let me go, kissing me lightly on the corner of my mouth. "Let's get you to your father," he said.

Yes, Papa first.

Chapter Sixteen
Gypsy Eyes

Katya

The drive to Sleepy Hollow seemed endless. I kept fidgeting and Luke suggested I try and nap as it would take us nearly an hour and a half to reach Phelps Memorial. I ached in so many places it was impossible to remain comfortable in one position for too long.

King called with regular updates about my father—each time these translated to the same thing, 'still in surgery, no change in his condition.' I stared at the passing landscape and smiled grimly. Luke was correct when he said King was a complicated man. I wanted to stay mad at him but he kept stepping in to help when it really mattered.

He'd spin his magic and people would jump to do his bidding. *Swoosh!* He waved his wand at the police and *abracadabra*, they'd backed off and agreed to delay my statement until tomorrow.

I cautiously wet my swollen lip. *Please, King, wave your wand and save my papa.*

I didn't want to be an orphan. I had run from my father as far and as fast as I could, but the distance was never enough to wipe his presence from my mind. Or my heart.

"Is it wrong I still love my father and want him to be okay?" I whispered.

"What's that, baby?"

I shifted so that I could look at Luke without getting a crick in my neck. "I was just wondering," I said to him again. "Is it wrong I still love my father and want him to be okay?"

"Why do you think it's wrong?"

"He's done really bad things, Luke." I swallowed hard. "How do I move past that? How do I forgive him?"

Luke reached across and gently uncurled my fist. He linked his fingers with mine, resting our joined hands on the console between us. I let his calm energy seep into me. Several miles swept by before he spoke.

"You might have heard this before, babe, but there is a difference between good people who do bad things, and bad people who are just born evil."

"I think I understand that," I said. "But I'm not sure where my father falls on the good-and-bad scale."

"I know what bad looks like, Katya." Luke squeezed my fingers. "Nicu is not an evil man."

God! I really wanted to believe him.

"Your father has always loved you. He fucked up in how he showed it, but he did his best to keep you safe." He loosened his grasp on my hand so he could indicate and change lanes. "*Hell.* Compared to my father, Nicu should get father-of-the-year!"

"Luke! *Ouch!*" I gingerly touched a finger to my stinging lip. "Don't make jokes," I mumbled, lifting my finger away to check if there was blood. "It hurts."

"Sorry." I met his eyes and they didn't look sorry. "Split lips tend to happen when you head-butt scumbags."

I scowled at him but held my tongue. Luke

indicated again as we passed the exit sign for Sleepy Hollow. "How long to the hospital?"

"Not long. About five minutes," he said, all humor gone from his voice. "Babe?"

I looked up and he reached for my hand again, lacing his fingers with mine. "Ye-es?"

"Maybe it's time to heal," he said quietly. "For both of you. Time to forgive and move forward."

"Maybe," I said.

I took slow, steadying breaths as we approached Phelps Memorial. I wondered if Luke needed me to forgive my father to give him hope that I would forgive him too. I looked down at our linked hands. Mine, so much smaller and softer than his. They looked perfect together.

Don't you know? I have forgiven you, Luke.

I squeezed his hand and vowed he would hear those words before I closed my eyes tonight.

****

Déjà vu.

Hospital. Surgery. ICU. Family waiting-room. And somebody I loved fighting for their life. My father had been stabbed seven times. Miraculously, he was still breathing. Barely! The surgical team lost him twice on the table, but managed to bring him back. According to the regular updates we were receiving, the surgeons were in the homestretch and we should remain hopeful.

"More coffee, baby?"

I tore my eyes away from the pale-blue doors that led to the surgical theater. Luke was standing by the small coffee machine. *Four days!* I hadn't seen him in six years and it had taken him only four days to break open my secret box of pain and shatter it into so many pieces that I would never be able to bury them again.

"Did you know my mom was pregnant when she died?"

Luke went so still even the air around him seemed to hang motionless.

"I was so angry with her." I carefully wet my lip. "No matter how many times she told me how exciting it was going to be, I just stayed mad." I looked up at Luke. "You see, I was jealous. I loved my papa so much, I didn't want to share him."

"That's normal, baby." Luke closed the gap between us and crouched down in front of me. "You were only ten years old."

"I know." He looked so concerned I ran my fingers along the side of his face. "My mom knew too and she never got upset with me. But my mom was wily," I said with a small smile. "She took me with her for her second trimester ultrasound. She wanted me to be with her when she learned if the baby was a boy or a girl."

"Shit, babe." Luke's voice was husky and he lifted my hand from his face and gently kissed my palm.

"Yeah. I guess she knew that once I heard the baby's heartbeat, saw it curled up in her belly on the monitor, the idea of a brother or sister would be more real to me." A tear trickled down my cheek and Luke cupped my face, using his thumb to wipe it away. I smiled but my chest ached. "And she was right. When the doctor told us it was a boy, I got so excited. All my jealousy just flew away."

"Where was your father?"

"He didn't come. Uncle Alexi drove us. My mom wanted it to be a surprise. She gave me the photograph from the scan so I could show him when we got home."

Luke's eyes closed and he dropped his head. "But you never made it home." His voice cracked and when he lifted his head, tears shimmered in the depths of his beautiful eyes.

I shook my head and inhaled deeply. I needed him to hear it all.

"In the car, on the way home, mom and Alexi were bickering over names. Alexi was adamant the baby's name would be Nicolae. 'All first born sons in the Dalca family are called Nicolae,' he insisted. My mom laughed him off. 'The Dalcas live in America now,' she said, 'it's time for new traditions.'"

I closed my eyes and let the memory of my mother and Alexi surface.

Mom smiling, excited. Alexi, shaking his head, always so earnest.

I felt Luke move from the floor to sit beside me. When he took my hands in his, I opened my eyes and turned to him. "Alexi stopped the car at a crossing and reached across to my mom. I remember he cupped her cheek and said something like, 'Silvia, my beautiful American princess. Nicolae is a good name, a strong name. In my country it means victory of the people. This is a good thing, no?' My mom turned and winked at me and then she reached up and covered Alexi's hand on her face. 'Yes,' she told him and leaned across the seat to kiss his cheek. 'This is a good thing,' she said."

Luke searched my eyes, his face grim. "You never told your father?"

I shook my head, pulling my hand from his to wipe my face.

"Why not?"

I squeezed my eyes tight, willing away the memory of what happened next. "Because until we crashed," I said, my voice breaking. "That was a beautiful day. The best day." I swallowed hard and opened my eyes. "My father didn't directly kill them. But the choices he made? He was responsible. And I don't think I ever forgave him."

"Christ, Katya!" Luke gathered me up, cradling me on his lap.

I snuggled into his tight embrace, my hand settling against his heart. "Does that make me an awful daughter?" I whispered.

"No, baby. It just makes you human." He stroked his fingers through my hair. "You loved your mother, but it's okay to remember you loved your father, too. Don't you think you've both grieved for long enough?"

Luke's words made sense. I felt his heartbeat drumming steadily beneath my hand.

"I think he loved you all so much he's never forgiven himself for your mom and Alexi's death." His chin rested lightly on my head. "His paranoia over your safety kept you cloistered but when you ran, he let you go. He still protected you from afar, but he finally let you be free."

I fiddled with the material of his shirt, creasing it between my fingers. "He knew where I was all the time, didn't he?"

"Yeah," Luke murmured and I felt him nod. "Hector told me he got a call from Nicu the day after you left. He said your father gave him a heads up you'd be coming and he was to help you out however you needed."

"My father mentioned something like that

yesterday, but I wasn't sure what to believe."

"Nicu called Hector again, soon after you arrived in Encinitas. Told him to keep you safe and send him regular updates or he would drag you back to New York."

I wasn't surprised by this. Ever since I was ten years old, my father had never left me unprotected. "You know" I looked up at Luke, sliding my hand from his heart to curl around his nape. "That circle of protection he put around me might have kept me physically safe, but it also isolated me from the love I so desperately needed from him." Staring at him intently, I stroked my thumb along his jaw. "Whatever happens between us, Luke, please don't make that same mistake."

He nodded and leaned in to press his lips to my forehead.

My eyes swam and I pressed myself tightly to him.

I'd been so lonely. Only one day together and then six years apart. But that one day marked me for a lifetime. *And I'd missed him!*

"He knew where I was all the time we were apart but he didn't tell you," I said into his chest. "He kept you away from me. From Lily."

"No, Katya." Luke leaned away to cradle my face and his eyes burned fiercely. "Your father carries the weight of a lot of bad on his shoulders, but not that. That one's all mine." He stroked my hair away from my face. "I made choices, Katya. They were the wrong ones and I have to bear the pain."

I didn't want him to carry that burden.

"Luke, I understand why—"

Swish! Thwack!

315

The blue doors swung open and hit against the wall. Before I could finish trying to ease Luke's guilt, he had me off his lap and on my feet, ready to hear the surgeon's prognosis about my father.

****

Katya

It was three hours later when Doctor Sharma finally let us in to see my father.

My lip was stinging because I kept biting it in frustration. *Dammit!* My father had come through recovery ages ago, but the nitpicking surgeon with his immaculate British accent wouldn't allow visitors until my father was fully conscious and had agreed to see me.

He was in a private room attached to ICU. I saw the armed guard stationed outside and gripped Luke's hand. In all the craziness, I had forgotten my father was still a prisoner. We signed a form, and the guard nodded it was okay for us to enter. Luke opened the door, nudging me inside with his hand at the small of my back. It took me a moment to orientate in the dimly-lit room.

Papa!

My breath hitched and a wave of dizziness had me lurching backwards. Luke's arms swept around me before I could hit the floor. I let him support my weight as black spots danced in front of my eyes.

"Deep breaths, baby."

His voice in my ear helped ease my nausea, but my skin was clammy and my legs no longer belonged to me. "He looks so small." My voice broke.

"Katya?" My father's voice called from the bed, surprisingly strong.

"Ready?" Luke whispered, his arm still wrapped firmly around my waist.

I inhaled deeply and nodded.

Luke stayed by my side as we approached the bed. My father was lying flat, his body connected to a multitude of tubes and intravenous lines. He was awake and alert, his intelligent gaze narrowing as it swept between the two of us. Then he saw the state of my lip.

"What happened?" He wasn't asking me. His demand was barked at Luke.

"Lev," Luke said. "And Anna."

My father's face contorted in pain. I knew it wasn't because of his wounds, and my vision misted.

"I'm fine, papa. Just a little bruised." I reached for his hand but stopped, my stomach churning when I saw it was cuffed to the rail at the side of the bed.

He nodded but his eyes remained closed.

I didn't know what to do except stand still, Luke's warmth at my back. Minutes passed and I thought he had drifted back to sleep but then he opened his eyes and focused on Luke.

"Tell me," he rasped.

It seemed they had a shorthand because Luke understood exactly what he meant by those two words. He briefly took my father through the events that led to me being taken by Anna and then what had happened afterward. My father listened without interrupting. When Luke finished he remained quiet, his eyes a mirror image of my own, studying me.

Gypsy eyes. That's what my mother used to call them. And I had loved that we shared something so special.

"Hunter." Luke's arm tightened around me. "Call

your old boss. He needs to come down here, with the DEA."

"You're giving up the money?" Luke asked.

"Call them," my father said, ignoring Luke's question. "Set it up for me to meet them in forty-eight hours."

"Why the delay, Nicu?"

"I need to speak with Katya. Alone." My throat thickened at the growing weakness in his voice. "After. It is her choice to share with you or not."

****

Luke

It was well after midnight when Luke finally parked his SUV at home.

After Katya finished talking with Nicu and he drifted off to sleep, he had suggested they stay overnight in a hotel in Sleepy Hollow. Her face had immediately dropped, her swollen lip looking so pouty that he had leaned in and taken a delicious swipe. She hated the idea of staying away, wanting only to be home with Lily.

Home. Shit! That sounded good.

He didn't think she even registered she had referred to his house as 'home' more than once. They didn't talk much in the car. He left her to her thoughts, not probing about what her father had discussed with her. It was about the cache. He had no doubt. But as Nicu had said, it was her choice whether to share with him or not.

Breathing deeply, a sense of rightness warmed him.

His beautiful Katya.

So frightened to give her trust. But it didn't matter. He would never allow the knowledge she held to blow back and hurt her. Or Nicu. Because when Nicu hurt, Katya hurt. And he wouldn't be a party to that anymore.

Katya went upstairs to check on Lily while he got an update from Gray and Mira. Lev was in a coma, his condition remained unstable. *Crap!* He wished the scumbag would just die. One less piece-of-shit psychopath to worry about.

Gray retreated upstairs and he smiled grimly as he locked up after Mira. They were both avoiding him. *Traitorous fuckers.* His temper flared when he thought how close Katya had come to a bullet. *Fuck!* If he even thought of the finger marks bruising her flesh, he knew he'd lay Gray flat. Or any other member of the team who got too close. It was going to take some doing for him to see his way clear to letting go of the fury that consumed him every time he thought of the danger they had put her in.

He made them omelets, their first meal of the day. When they were finished, Katya was fidgety and he knew she wanted to talk. He suggested a nightcap, and he sipped a bourbon while she fiddled with a glass of red wine. He closed his eyes and rested his head against the couch.

What a fucking day!

"Luke."

He opened his eyes at her tremulous call. He was sitting in the corner of the couch, legs stretched out and she was curled up next to him, but they were not touching.

"Yeah, baby?" He let his eyes drift over her and his chest burned. *He was so damn proud of her.* Over the last four days she had been put through the wringer. Most people would have curled up and died. But not

Katya. His woman just sucked it up and came out swinging. Every single time. He reached for her hand, clenching his jaw when he glimpsed the angry red abrasions circling her wrist. Her resilience humbled him.

"This morning, in the gym," she said hesitantly and he rubbed his thumb reassuringly across her knuckles. "When you said you needed to protect me. What did you mean by that?"

Her violet eyes were serious and he stared, fascinated by her incredibly long lashes. He sucked in a breath when she continued, realizing he hadn't answered her.

"When you didn't meet me in New York, you said it was because you needed to protect me. How is that different from how you want to protect me now?"

A flicker of awareness raised the hair on Luke's neck. Katya was perfectly still, her simple question ringing with such far-reaching depth that Luke immediately sat up and put his glass down on the table. He sensed his response to her question would have a significant impact on whether they moved forward together. Or parted ways.

"Katya." He hesitated. *Fuck. All he could do was tell the truth.* "When we first met in New Orleans, you took me by surprise. I was on mission and I refused to pay attention to what my gut was telling me. I buried my feelings and I went undercover, focused only on what needed to be done. A year later, I betrayed you again. At the time, I convinced myself that finishing the mission and bringing down Nicu and the drug rings was crucial to your safety and your chance to live a free life."

Katya's head tilted, but her face betrayed no emotion. He reached for his glass and took another sip. *Christ!* His stomach was like a lump of cement. He briefly closed his eyes, grateful for the fortifying burn of the liquor.

"It was jacked up," he said, turning to look at her. "My need to protect you was all mixed up with this fucking hold you had on my gut. *Shit!*" Katya jolted but her gaze never left him. "So I did the only thing I knew how to do. I shoved all that confusion away and I clung to the mission." Pain shattered the cement in his stomach as he watched tears shimmer in the depths of her eyes. "That's right, baby," he said huskily as he took her hand and lifted it to his mouth. "I didn't know how to deal, so I put the mission first." His lips settled over her lacerated wrist and he squeezed his eyes shut. He felt her hand settle on his head and stroke his hair. "That decision hurt you more than anything else I could have done," he finally admitted.

"I miss your ponytail."

"What?" He looked up. Tears trickled down her cheeks.

"Your ponytail." She sniffed, scrunching up her nose. "I liked it better when your hair was longer."

"So, I'll grow it for you." He cradled her cheeks, using his thumbs to wipe away her tears. She rewarded him with a tentative smile. "Are those tears for you or for me?" he asked.

"Both of us," she whispered and reached up to cover his hands with her own.

They stayed like that for several moments until she took a deep breath and let her hands drop. "The red wine's not working," she murmured. "Could you pour some bourbon for me, please?"

He leaned forward and briefly settled his lips against her forehead. "Sure, babe."

Yeah.

If she was ready to open up they were going to need it.

****

Katya

My need to protect you was all mixed up with this fucking hold you had on my gut.

I watched Luke pour me a generous measure of bourbon. His words were swirling around my head, wreaking havoc with my heart. *Crap!* Who was I kidding? His raw honesty had bypassed my heart and burrowed straight into my soul.

"Here you go," he smiled. "Drink up and tell me something wild."

"Like what?" I took the glass and my hand jerked, the touch of his fingers sending a tingle fluttering up my arm. *Jeez!* The potency of his touch still took me by surprise.

"Like the fact that you love me."

What!

His poker-face stared blankly at me and then he winked.

"Not funny!" I scowled at him.

He chuckled and settled down beside me. For the first time, I noticed shadows beneath his eyes. *Damn.* Luke was exhausted. No more procrastination. It was time to say what I needed to say so we could both get some sleep.

Taking a sip of bourbon, I steeled myself. "I know everything about my father's secret stash of money."

Luke nodded, his poker-face back in place.

"He sent me the information a long time ago." I gripped my glass tightly. "It came just before he was arrested." *Does he think I'm a coward for not speaking up earlier?* No matter. I wanted him to hear it all now. "Soon after I got back from New York, Hector gave me this sealed envelope. He said it was from my father. It took me days before I had the courage to open it." I swallowed back the last of my drink and looked searchingly at Luke. He eased the glass from my hand and linked his fingers with mine.

"Babe, there's nothing you can say or do that will keep me from you. Nothing."

I licked at my lip which was stinging from the booze. Luke spilled his guts to me and I hadn't run.

He won't run from me either.

Taking what felt like my millionth deep breath, I continued. "Inside were clear instructions to the money and how to access it." I spoke rapidly. "There was also a note from him. I read it so fast I don't remember what it said. Just something about the money being for my security. I stuffed everything back in the envelope and buried it in my cupboard."

"Why?" Luke asked quietly, his hand still holding mine.

"I was so angry with him. And I was frightened. He knew where I was and I didn't want to have to think about *that*." Looking down, I noticed again how well our hands fit together. "After he was arrested, I wouldn't read anything about the case or let Hector update me. I was scared if I let myself get involved, let myself feel even a little bit, then I wouldn't be able to stop myself from flying home to help."

"Help how?"

I squeezed Luke's hand tightly. "That's the point," I said huskily. "At the time I wasn't sure if I wanted to help him escape or help the police to convict him."

"What's changed now?"

"I'm still not sure why I didn't tell the police or King or even you. I guess, when it came down to it, I couldn't betray my father." I stared pleadingly at Luke. "I still can't."

"I guessed that, babe." Luke brought his other hand up to cup my cheek. "Your father's going to do that for you, isn't he? He's going to tell the DEA where to find the money."

Nodding, the words poured out of me. "He said the man who stabbed him was another prisoner who used to work for Arkady and Lev. He knew about the money. He promised his people would keep coming after me and Lily until they got the money."

"Fuck!" Luke jerked to his feet.

"I told him it was all over. Anna was dead and Lev was critical. He said if Lev survives, he's not convinced the police have enough to convict him of kidnapping. That the whole thing could be blamed on Anna. She took me, she shot Lev and she was going to shoot me." I shrugged at Luke helplessly. "I think he has a point."

"There's got to be something else, Katya." Luke impatiently ran his hand through his hair. "It's not adding up. What else did he say?"

"He said that even if all the money's gone, it still isn't enough to stop Lev's thugs. There's a safe hidden with the money. Inside is a lot of information. He said there's enough there to bury Lev and his organization forever. He wants to give it all to the DEA." My breath hitched. "He says that's the only way he knows to keep Lily and me safe."

"Fuck! That's the information we needed four years ago." Luke paced in front of the fireplace.

"Yes. But if he gives the DEA the money, it will give them the ammunition they need to re-indict him. He could end up with an extended sentence."

Luke stopped pacing. "He knows that, doesn't he?"

I stared at Luke, my vision blurring. "Yes. He said he has to take the chance to ensure my-my—" The words stuck in my throat and I started crying again.

"Shit, babe, c'mere." Luke sat down and pulled me into his arms. "It's the only way to keep you safe, isn't it?"

"Y-yes," I sobbed, clinging to his warmth as he rocked me in his arms. When I quieted, he murmured in my ear.

"Why the delay, Katya? Why does he want to wait forty-eight hours?"

"He wouldn't say, but I think it's to give me time to take the money." Luke's body stiffened.

"Take the money?" He pulled away, his mouth set in a hard line. "You're kidding?"

"No." I stared determinedly back at him. "Will you help me?"

I held my breath.

Would Luke go against everything he believed in to help my father?

Suddenly he relaxed. Recognition, or something like it, dawned on his face, and his mouth twitched. "Shit, babe, breathe." He reached for my hand. "You're right. The money needs to be gone. If Nicu's going to give his cache up to the DEA, then they need to find it empty except for the safe with the intel on Lev and his scumbag cronies."

"You'd do that for my father?" I exhaled sharply.

"No, Katya." He pulled my hand to his lips. "I would do it for you." His tongue settled in my palm and he gently bit my hand. Heat shot up my arm. "So. You going to add this stash to your million dollar inheritance?"

"W-what?" I was fixated on his mouth nibbling at my hand.

"The money, baby. You going to hang on to it? Save it for a rainy day?"

"No!" I pulled at my hand. "Stop that, I can't think!" His sinful grin only added to the heat flaring between my legs. "Luke!" He let go of my hand and I blinked rapidly, trying to remember his question.

Oh, the money and a rainy day.

Pushing back my desire, I moved to the edge of the couch. "I don't think it could ever rain hard enough for me to spend that money," I said fiercely and hugged my waist. "If we had another Noah's Flood, I wouldn't be convinced to spend that money. It's dirty!" I hugged myself tighter and stared Luke down. "I don't think I could ever be clean again if I spent one single dollar of it."

Luke's smile gentled. "Okay, babe. I get it. Now tell me—" he moved forward to join me on the edge of the couch. "That lawyer of yours, is he trustworthy?"

"Who? Why?"

"The way I see it, you've got two choices. Either we destroy Nicu's hoard, or we hand it over to your lawyer to distribute however you want."

What he said made perfect sense but my throat

thickened. Luke hated drugs and anybody connected to them. "You've dedicated a lot of your time putting people like my father away." I settled my hand on his thigh. "You'd really do this for me?"

"Don't you know by now, baby? I'd do anything for you. Whatever you need."

I searched his beautiful face and my pulse hitched.

"You want to know why?" He asked.

I nodded jerkily.

"Because, baby—" His husky voice sent shivers rippling down my spine and my pulse started to race. "I love you."

Oh God!

He cradled my face and pulled me so close, his breath kissed my mouth. "It's o-only been four days," I stammered. "How can you f-fall in l-love with me in four days?"

"No, babe." My stomach fluttered as his breath whispered over my lips. "It's been six years. I fell in love with you when we first kissed in *The Apple Barrel Bar*. They were playing 'I Want To Make Love To You' and all I could think about was being buried deep inside you." I whimpered and his hands slid back, threading through my hair. "*Christ!* You whimpered just like that, right into my mouth. And it was like you burrowed straight into my heart."

I clung to his thigh, panic and need dueling so hard in my head it was difficult to think. But this was important. *It was critical.* "That was a different Katya."

"Not different, just younger," he reasoned. "Sometimes, baby, life is about timing." He dropped his hand and tucked it under my knees, scooping me into his lap. I settled against him as he leaned back into the couch. "I don't think that younger Katya was ready for the likes of me. And knowing what I know now, I wasn't ready to take her on either."

I had an inkling I understood what he meant but I liked listening to how his head worked.

"What do you mean?" I slid my hand up to curl around his nape.

He relaxed and circled me loosely with his arms. "It's taken me time to learn that thinking you're doing good doesn't always mean you are. Sometimes, being inflexible means you cause more hurt and damage than you know." He gently pulled my hand away and settled it against his cheek. His eyes searched mine and my stomach tightened. "I learned that when I saw Lily. My shit decisions hurt you both."

"I forgive you, Luke!"

His head cocked at my breathless outburst.

Jeez! Who am I to offer Luke forgiveness?

"Oh! That came out all wrong," I was getting flustered and my hands shot to my face when I felt the heat rushing up my neck.

"It makes me happy you forgive me, babe."

I could hear the laughter in his voice and I split my fingers to look at him.

Oh, yeah! He was grinning.

I buried my head again. "I'm sorry, I didn't mean it like that," I groaned.

"So how did you mean it?" His husky voice in my ear only made me flush deeper, hotter. I gripped his shirt and didn't answer until his hand sank into my hair and tightened, tipping back my head. His mouth settled gently over mine. "Fuck. I want to kiss you but I don't want to hurt you."

I love you!

I swallowed hard. *Dammit, Katya! Just tell him!*

But I could only drown in his beautiful gaze, his familiar scent swirling around me. The words I desperately wanted to say to him remained locked up inside me.

"Breathe, Katya," he whispered, smiling against my mouth. "There's no hurry, baby. I'm not going anywhere."

How does he know?

"I'll be here when you're ready," he promised. "And trust me, baby. You will be ready."

So patient and so goddamn alpha at the same time.

Yes, that was Luke.

My Luke!

I pulled out of his arms and raced from the room, calling over my shoulder that I'd be back. Careful to be quiet so I wouldn't wake Lily, I searched my bedside drawer until I found what I was looking for. Skipping back downstairs, I climbed back into Luke's lap and triumphantly held out my treasure.

"What the fuck is that?"

I grabbed his hand and started to wind the cord around his wrist. "It's from your hair," I explained, unable to look at him quite yet. "In New Orleans. When you left the room with my memory stick, I found it."

Luke went rigid.

"I don't know why, but I kept it."

He stared at his wrist as I tied the cord. "Shit," he swore, his voice hoarse. "I was in there, wasn't I?" I looked up and his eyes locked with mine. "Right from the beginning, you let me in. How the hell did I get so fucking lucky?"

"Will you make love to me, Luke?" I trailed my hand down his jaw. "Please. I don't want to go to sleep with the memory of that pig's hands on me. I only want to feel yours."

"Christ, baby," he groaned and pulled me against him. "You're exhausted and all bruised up."

I started to undo the buttons of his shirt. "So, we can take it slow and easy," I whispered and leaned in to settle my mouth against his exposed chest. "Can you do that for me, honey? Slow and easy?"

He relaxed and lifted me to straddle him. "I can do whatever you need, gypsy."

I paused and looked at him. "Gypsy?"

"You said your mom used to say you had gypsy eyes?"

I nodded and my arms lifted as he slid my borrowed sweatshirt off and threw it to the floor.

"She's right," he murmured and scowled at my torn blouse.

"Right?" I put my hand under his chin, lifting his head so I could kiss away his frown.

"Yeah." He nipped at my fingers. "They're so goddamn beautiful. Full of magic and mystery. Gypsy eyes." I gasped when he grabbed my hand and sucked my finger deep into his mouth. Desire bloomed and I squeezed my thighs together as he slowly pulled it out, his tongue swirling. "But I could always call you sugar lips."

Oh Lordy! His voice was so deep and his eyes so dark. My nipples hardened and I reached up, quickly removing my blouse.

"Gypsy's fine," I breathed. "Or baby."

"You like baby?" He pulled me closer, his hot

mouth settling on my breast as his arms circled around to undo my bra.

"Mm-hmm." I pushed harder against his searching lips. My bra dropped and he sucked my nipple into his mouth.

Aah!

"Slow and easy," he drawled against my wet, hard nipple.

"Forget that!" I jumped to my feet, tugging at the button of my jeans. Luke cracked up laughing, but he also scrambled to undress and was deliciously naked by the time I climbed back onto him. I was slick and wet and he was sublimely hard.

"Christ, baby!"

I settled astride him. My pussy ached for the touch of his pulsing heat.

Yesss!

I slid against him, my soaking folds coating his velvety hardness. His hands gripped my hips and he pushed up against me but he didn't let his cock penetrate me.

"Oh, God," I groaned as the tip of his cock nudged against my clit.

"You like that, baby?"

"Ye-ess," I moaned and tried to move quicker.

"Slow and easy, babe."

"Luke!"

"Slow—"

I gasped as his thumb flicked fluid from the tip of his cock and rubbed it over my hardened nub.

"And easy—"

He circled my clit, his thick erection still buried between my wet folds. "Ride me, baby," he ordered and started to rock me against him, his thumb pressing and circling.

"Oh, Lordy!"

And so we made love. Slow and Easy.

Until it wasn't!

Because when he finally sank inside me, I was panting and my nails were digging into his back.

But by the sound of his groans he didn't seem to mind.

Neither did I.

Chapter Seventeen
Breathing Room!

Lincoln Correctional Facility, Manhattan, NYC.
Three Weeks Later
Katya

I was so horny!

Totally inappropriate, considering I was in a correctional facility. And I was watching my daughter on the swing, giggling at the two most important men in my life who stood on either side of her.

A lot had happened in the last three weeks. But the thing I most wanted to happen hadn't. So I was horny.

I studied Luke.

He was relaxed but his eyes constantly swept the visitor's yard, alert as ever. The sleeves of his white shirt were rolled up and as he pushed Lily's swing with one arm, my temperature rose at his casual strength. We had started running together every morning after sunrise, so he was now sporting a light tan.

Damn! I reached for my bottle of water and gulped down half of it. The man was even more impossibly sexy than ever before. I took another sip and squinted at him. *Nope.* He was watchful but he definitely wasn't tense.

Unlike me.

Breathing room. That's what he called the last three weeks. *Breathing room!*

And breathing room equaled no sex. *Nadda!*

After the hullabaloo had settled, Luke suggested Lily and I move out to a furnished apartment that was vacant in the King Security building. King, I'd learned, was loaded. Seriously loaded. He owned the HQ building and rented the apartments on the upper floors to selected friends and colleagues. Luke said he wanted me to have breathing room while I waited for Dani to be strong enough to travel home.

Huh! Breathing Room!

I had just about broken out in hives when I thought about moving out of Luke's house. I refused to admit he had become my anchor in all the craziness that had taken over my world. And I didn't have to because Lily rescued me from self-admission, when she threw a doozy. 'I don't want to leave Daddy!' She sobbed hysterically and heartbreaking tears rolled down her cheeks, succeeding in doing what I couldn't: melting Luke's resolve.

So we stayed in Bay Ridge.

Suddenly we were living like a family.

We would breakfast together before Luke went off to work. Lily and I shopped, explored New York and spent time with Dani. At night, Luke was home and we either cooked or he would take us out. We did it together.

Happy families? Well...

All I got from him were gentle kisses.

On my forehead.

Or the crown of my head.

Or the corner of my mouth.

That's it!

Sheesh! I got what he was doing, and I even

appreciated it. For a while.

Breathing room? I was so over it. *Lordy!* I missed his heat! But most of all, I missed his warm touch. *That* always had the power to set my world right.

Lily squealed and I smiled, relaxing on the bench. She was doing great. Two visits with Judith Crawford and Lily was deemed a 'very well-adjusted child, secure in her place in the world.' Lily was processing the recent events, Judith said, all she needed was time and space.

She missed Encinitas and her friends, but she was totally enamored with her daddy. And she had bonded with Gray and Mira like they were family. My chest tightened like it did every time I thought about what was going to happen next. I had to make a decision. Dani was healing and it was nearly time to return home. Fumbling with my water bottle, my mind raced. Lily needed to be settled and I had a life in Encinitas. *But what about Luke?* He didn't only have a life here in New York. He had family. I hadn't met them yet, but I knew he had plans to make this happen soon. And Gray? He was family too.

Luke.

He said he loved me. And even when I didn't say it back he didn't hesitate to help me save my father.

After we'd done it 'slow and easy' and his touch had burned away the memory of Lev, the very next morning he stuck by his word and helped me hide the evidence that had the potential to bury my father.

We had stolen away, like two secret agents on a deep cover mission. I thought he'd pop a vein when I told him the money was hidden in a leased warehouse in the Brooklyn Navy Yard. *Lordy!* That was right alongside DUMBO, King Security's backyard!

Like my mother, my father was wily, only in a different way.

Several years ago he'd taken a twenty year lease on a warehouse in the Brooklyn Navy Yard, close to the Steiner Studios Lot. He'd used a shell company whose business was described as film set construction. The DEA had never discovered it.

We parked outside the large building and used the first of a list of codes my father had given me to open the door. Luke was silent, his face still set in stone. Shrugging, I pushed inside. There were no windows, so the room was dark. A staleness permeated the air, like nobody had been inside for a very long time.

Click!

I swiveled towards Luke as light swept the room. He was standing by the wall, his hand still covering the light-switch. He raised a brow but his lips were tight.

He's sulking!

My chest eased and I smiled to myself as goosebumps raised along my arms. *Okay.* I was nervous but I was mostly excited. Being on a mission with Luke, uncovering secret stashes. *Exciting!*

"Come on, let's look around." Luke urged me forward.

A clever facade had been created so a casual observer would only see a number of large film sets stacked and stored. The most prominent set was laid out at the back of the floor space, as if it was on show. It looked like the inside of an upmarket condo and even had an assortment of set dressing that included furniture and paintings.

"Shit. Nicu's a clever bastard!" Luke's expletive

came when we opened what looked like an ordinary wooden door positioned in the back of the set. Instead of opening into nothing, we came up against a stainless-steel safe door over eight foot in height. There was no door handle, only a state-of-the-art keypad.

Luke moved back and butterflies churned my stomach. I stepped forward with the sheet of codes. My fingers shook as I carefully tapped in the long list of digits.

Bleep! Whirr!

Luke snatched me back against his body as the giant door whooshed out and then slid sideways. My eyes widened as a light flickered on automatically.

And then the butterflies went crazy!

"Jesus fuck!"

That's exactly what I was thinking.

On the other side of the door, packaged in plastic-wrap and stacked in piles almost to the ceiling, was millions of dollars in cash. We edged forward, cricking our necks as we slowly made our way between the towering walls of money. My tongue was thick and kept sticking to the roof of my mouth.

Jesus fuck!

Trying to calm my hammering heart, I didn't know what else to think.

The room was about five-square yards. When we reached the back, I grabbed Luke's hand and tugged him over to a small safe on the floor in the corner. Kneeling down, I punched in a final set of codes.

Twenty minutes later I was still hovering over Luke while he paged through the documents and scanned the laptop we had discovered in the safe.

"Is it enough? Please, honey, tell me if it's

enough." Impatience and fear made my voice frantic.

"You going to keep calling me honey?" Luke's lashes swept up, his beautiful eyes hot and glowing.

My tapping fingers froze. *Yowza!* "Do you want me to?" I asked breathlessly.

His mouth twitched and he straightened. "There's enough," he said. "Enough to bury Lev and most of his scumbag associates. *Hell*, Arkady's lucky he took a bullet. This information would have put him away for life."

Luke closed the laptop and returned it, with the documents, to the safe.

"So, baby," he said, hands on hips and staring at the neatly, stacked towers of money. "You got any idea what you wanna do with this?"

Neither of us had anticipated so much money. Luke roped Gray and King in and by the end of the day the money was locked and loaded and on its way to a secret 'King' location. Meanwhile, I called Mr. Connor from Connor & Stanton Attorneys. It took a little longer to get Mr. Connor on-board: he was reluctant to get involved in the cleaning of dirty money. Until King stepped in, and *Whoosh!*—his magic wand did its thing. Admittedly, it took longer than a day, but now, three weeks later, most of the money was where I wanted it to be. Helping people who needed it most.

I hadn't yet informed my father what I'd done with his money. *Yikes!* I was planning to do that today.

Oh, Papa! He was pushing Lily on the swing. Her head tossed back, engrossed in a story he was telling her. I blinked rapidly as my eyes filled. Maybe he would be a better grandfather than he had been a father?

Yes, I would give him every chance to show her.

Lounging back, I let the afternoon sun warm my face. In two days Lily would meet her great grandmother and grandfather. I'd eventually plucked up the nerve and called Mary Langworth. She was reserved but clearly excited to hear from me and we made immediate arrangements to join her and Frank for Sunday lunch at their home in Greenhaven, Rye.

But there was a complication. Or rather, a nuisance factor: Julian, my cousin. The very same cousin who abandoned me in his tree house when I was ten years old. He was staying with my grandparents, in their pool house, and when he heard I was coming for lunch, he reached out.

I wrinkled my nose, the discomfort from his earlier phone calls returning.

He called during breakfast to invite Lily and me sailing on Sunday morning, before lunch. He was totally buddy-buddy, which was weird since we hadn't been in touch for over twenty years. When I told him that we weren't free to join him, because Luke had an important meeting at HQ, he was distraught, and by the time he hung up I could hear him weeping. It left me with a guilty knot in my stomach. I wondered if lingering resentment over a childhood prank was keeping me from a reunion with him.

He called me again while we were en route to visit my father. "Please, Katya, reconsider. I really want to spend time with you and Lily. Please."

His sincerity echoed through the car speaker, prodding at my conscience. Uncertain, I looked at Luke. He reached over and muted the phone speaker.

"Go up earlier and spend some time with him," he suggested. "I'll join you for lunch."

Julian's intensity was unsettling, but he was family. And I wanted Lily to know her family. I took Luke's advice to heart and it was settled: Lily and I would go earlier and sail with Julian. Luke would join us at my grandparents for lunch.

"Katya."

My father's voice startled me.

He had lost weight but he was healing well. The DEA had been livid when they found no money at the warehouse, but the information from the safe proved invaluable in ending the evil threat of Lev and his posse of greedy scumbags. This was especially good because Lev, like the cockroach he was, had survived surgery and doctors projected he would make a full recovery. King stepped in and used his superpowers to facilitate a deal that reduced my father's sentence and he was transferred here, to the Lincoln Correctional Facility, a low security prison that encouraged family visits and re-integration. I think King was still trying to earn my forgiveness.

"The warden said I qualify for a weekend furlough in three months," my father informed me as he sat down on the bench opposite.

Okay! I'd let King off the hook today.

"Lily's beautiful. She reminds me of your mother."

I smiled and looked across at the swing where Luke was pushing her as high as she could go. "But she's also like her dad. Stubborn but with a heart of gold."

My father grunted, his expression difficult to read.

"Do you hate Luke for what he did to you?" I asked.

"Do you?"

I rested my elbows on the table and clasped my hands under my chin.

Did I?

I shook my head. "As much as I loved you, somebody needed to stop you. Even if it was just to stop you from hurting yourself."

His eyes flicked from me to Luke and he shrugged. "His job is to protect those who can't protect themselves. And to put bad men away." My clasped hands tightened at the intensity of his gaze as it shifted back to me. "How can I hate a man for that?"

"And are you a bad man, Papa?" My throat constricted, trapping the air in my lungs.

"Maybe I'm a good man who did bad things?" He grimaced. "That sounds better, don't you agree?"

Yes!

I dropped my hands and leaned closer to him. "Why did you?"

"Why did I what?"

"Do bad things."

He sighed deeply, staring into space as several moments passed. "Life in Bucharest was tough," he finally said. "I grew up with very little. We were often hungry. Cold. My father worked long hours and my grandmother did her best but we suffered." His brow drew together and he said fiercely. "I didn't want that for my family."

I sat motionless, ignoring the sun beating down on my exposed head. *This was huge!* Papa never spoke about his past. I didn't want him to stop.

"I thought being a good husband, a good father, meant making sure you wanted for nothing. I didn't think being a criminal mattered, so long as you and your mother were taken care of." His hands fisted, then opened to lay flat on the table. "The problem was, I was too good at it." He grimaced again. "The best."

"No, Papa." I shook my head emphatically. "The problem was you stopped giving us what we needed most of all, your love."

"I never stopped loving you!"

"Maybe not," I conceded. "But you stopped showing it. In fact, you stopped showing up at all."

We glared at each other, the air pulsing with our angry words.

Lily squealed and we both looked across as Luke caught her up and started to tickle her.

"Your mother would be so proud of you."

My heart skipped and tears prickled my eyes. "And what about you Papa? Don't you want her to be proud of you too?"

"I'm working on it, *prinţesa mea*, but I might need a little help."

I blinked madly and swallowed hard when he reached for my hand.

"You up to the task?" He asked gently.

I nodded jerkily and he smiled.

"That looks like a sad smile," I said hoarsely, my throat thick.

He patted my hand but didn't reply.

"I need to go potty!"

I inhaled sharply and quickly wiped my cheeks, Lily's piping voice a welcome interruption.

"You okay, baby?" Luke's concern was apparent.

"I'm good." But his eyes narrowed at the waver in my voice. "Really, honey. I'm good."

He studied me for a while then nodded. "Come on,

sunshine," he called to Lily, swinging her up into his arms. "Let's go potty."

With the intensity between us diminished, we sat quietly and sipped our water.

Father was fading and Papa was taking his place.

My stomach fluttered then calmed. An unfamiliar sensation warmed me. Hope.

"So how does over sixty million dollars disappear into thin air?"

I nibbled my lip. *How to tell him what I'd done?*

"I hear you're working in the library?" My coy tone was ruined by the blush racing up my neck.

His head cocked and then he was smiling and shaking his head. "I was informed by the warden the library just received a generous donation. A million dollars?"

I grinned, my lingering tears chased away because his smile was no longer sad. "You won't be short of reading material for the rest of your stay."

"What about the rest of the money?" He asked wryly.

"Selected charities across the country." I didn't elaborate. He didn't need to know I'd focused on the vulnerable who were most impacted by drugs. I didn't do that for him, I did it for Luke.

"Well, *you* most definitely don't need the money," he declared.

"No. Mom's inheritance is huge." I fiddled with my empty water bottle. "I think it worries Luke," I murmured.

"Should it?"

"No! Jeez! If I've learned anything, it's that money does not bring happiness. Even you know that!" All he did was raise an eyebrow. Irritated, I crossed my arms and glared at him. "I don't want to live in the lap of luxury," I insisted.

"And have you told him this?"

"Yes. I told him I want to start a foundation that means something to me."

"And?"

"He gets it. I think." I squinted at my father. "I think he's still adjusting to the idea that I'm super wealthy."

"Come." He stood up. "Let's go under the tree. You're burning."

We walked over to the swing and I sat down, gently rocking myself. While we waited for Luke and Lily to return, I told him about our planned visit with the Langworths.

"Your mother would be pleased."

When I told him about Julian and how he'd hounded us to go sailing, he smiled.

"That makes me happy."

"Why?"

"Do you remember that your Aunt Lizzie drowned?"

The back of my neck tingled. "No…"

"It was about sixteen years ago. Julian must have been about eighteen."

"What happened?" I gripped the swing-rope, my eyes riveted to my father.

He put his hands in his pockets—jeans!—not that awful green prison uniform. "They were sailing near Frank and Mary's home in Rye." His lips pursed in thought. "There was an accident and Lizzie drowned. Julian was devastated."

"That's awful!"

"Yes. I'm glad to hear he still sails. It was something he and Lizzie always did together."

He was staring over my shoulder and I turned to see what had distracted him.

Luke and Lily. She was sitting on his shoulders, little hands clutching at his hair as he walked towards us.

"The three of you a package deal now?"

God! Luke and Lily. They looked so alike.

"I'm working on it."

"He going to help you with that?"

"He said he loves me."

"And you?"

I pulled at the frayed swing-rope and stared at Luke.

"Besides Lily, I know he's everything to me," I finally said, dragging my eyes away from them to look up at my father. "I know that deep down, but I can't seem to say the words."

He circled round to stand in front of me. "What frightens you, *micuta mea*?"

"He might leave!" My worst fear burst from me. "Or change."

"Aah," my father sighed. "You mean like me?"

I couldn't speak past the lump in my throat.

"Katya, always so melodramatic." He bent and his hands reached to gently cup my face. "We men. We are slow learners, but we do learn." His thumbs brushed my cheeks before he dropped his arms and straightened. "Your man, look at him with your daughter. Do you not think he has learned a harsh lesson?"

Moving behind me he reached down and started to

push me on the swing. "Don't run from everything you have ever dreamed of having, Katya. Life can surprise you and not always for the better. If you don't reach out and grab what belongs to you, you will always be longing, dreaming but not having. Yes?"

I kicked my legs to build momentum. Tilting back my head, I closed my eyes and let my Papa's words reverberate through my bones.

When I sensed them settle, I smiled.

Hope felt good.

Chapter Eighteen
A Bad Feeling

En-route to Greenhaven, Rye.
Sunday mid-morning
Luke

Fuck! His balls were blue.

Luke shifted uncomfortably in the driver's seat and smiled wryly to himself. If Katya didn't get her shit together soon, his hand was going to become permanently glued to his cock. *Christ!* She'd been so goddamn provocative this morning, stuffing her face with pancakes smothered in syrup. When she licked her fingers and batted those long lashes at him, he just about come in his pants.

Yeah. His woman was pushing his buttons, but he'd be damned if he'd give in and let her have what she wanted.

He brushed his hair back irritably. It was getting longer now, soon it would be long enough to tie it up. The cord on his wrist caught his eye and tingles spread through his chest, his irritation fading. His old hair-cord: it remained around his wrist, a constant reminder of the awe he'd felt when she put it there. It was never just sex between them. He wasn't sure what it was, but it was definitely more than just sex. *Fucking earth-shattering!* That's what it was.

"Your girl's a stubborn witch."

Luke glanced at Gray then back to the road. "Lily?"

"Well, she's stubborn too," Gray grinned. "But she's not a witch. I meant Katya."

Luke smiled grimly. Katya refused to talk to Gray unless she had too. "She hasn't forgiven you for letting Anna get to her."

"Tell me about it," Gray grumbled. "She holds a mean grudge."

"You blame her?"

Gray looked away and stared out the windscreen.

Luke shrugged. Gray would have to get over it. To be honest, he also carried residual pain over what had gone down. He focused his attention on the road. They were coming up to the Bruckner Interchange and navigating through it could be a bitch. He didn't relax until he was clear away on the I-95N to Mamaroneck.

Gray was still silent. Luke briefly wondered if he'd screwed up, inviting him along. The meeting this morning finished quicker than expected and Gray seemed at a loose end. It was a Sunday, so Luke had impulsively invited him to join them for lunch.

"Katya seems more relaxed."

"Yeah," Luke said, relieved Gray had broken the silence. "She had a good visit with Nicu on Friday."

Gray nodded. "So what's up with you?"

"Nothing."

"Yeah, right. You're on edge, Hunt."

Luke shrugged, holding tighter to the steering wheel. "I'm still squirrelly about her and Lily going off on their own. Katya wasn't keen either. She's got mixed feelings about Julian."

"How so?"

"Not sure."

"You check him out?"

Luke glanced at Gray and raised his brow.

"Right." Gray laughed softly.

"Eva's doing some work on it for me, should hear from her soon."

"So, what else?" Gray pushed.

"There have to be something else?"

"Uh-huh. You've been crusty for a while now. What gives?"

Luke sighed, letting several miles pass before he spoke. "I'm giving her some breathing room."

"Breathing room. What the fuck is that?"

"I want her to have space to decide what she wants to do," he said defensively.

"Okay." Gray sounded baffled. "You're living together, so how exactly do you give her breathing room?"

"No sex."

Luke knew he was doing the right thing. *So why did he feel like such a fucking idiot?*

"She has trust issues," he added, trying to explain his decision. "I don't want to clutter her head."

"Sex clutters her head?"

"How the fuck should I know?" He grumbled. "It seemed like a good idea at the time."

"Fuck! Saint Luke!" Gray snorted.

"Saint Blue Balls, more like it," he said wryly.

Gray smiled and relaxed back in his seat. "She staying or going back west?"

"I'm not sure. We haven't really discussed it."

"If she goes, you'll go with her."

Luke looked at Gray. His friend wasn't asking a

question.

"Yeah. It won't be easy, but I'm not going to make any more crappy decisions."

He belonged with Katya and Lily. If that had to happen in Encinitas, San Diego, then so be it.

"And holding back sex is a good decision?" Gray asked sardonically.

Luke laughed, the tension melting from his tight muscles.

Shit. If they did move west, he was going to miss Gray.

His cell phone rang and he activated the hands-free from the steering wheel. "Yeah."

"Luke, it's Eva."

"Hey, Eva. I'm in the car with Gray. You're on speaker."

"Listen. You mentioned this morning that Katya and Lily were going sailing with Julian Langworth."

"Yeah." Luke's shoulders tightened, the tension returning full force.

"I looked into him, like you asked. I've got a bad feeling—"

"Talk to me!" Luke accelerated, moving quickly over the speed limit. *Fuck! When Eva had a bad feeling it was best to pay attention.*

"You know his mother died when he was eighteen?"

"Yeah. Boating accident." Luke's skin crawled.

"She left Julian a sizable inheritance, but it turned out to be less than expected."

"Explain."

"Elizabeth Langworth received a large inheritance when she turned thirty," Eva said. "But she lived wild and over the next ten years, she made a serious dent in it. When she died, Julian inherited what was left, but he could only receive the money twelve years later, when *he* turned thirty."

"Yeah. It's a clause in the will. Katya had a similar inheritance from her mother that she only now received. Draconian maybe, but not odd," Luke said impatiently.

"Hear me out, Luke," Eva said, her tone urgent. "He took control of his inheritance five years ago. Even though his mother had been reckless, the fund was still substantial because it had twelve years to recover."

"Okay." Luke gritted his teeth, trying to be patient.

"Not okay," Eva said. "In less than five years he's not only gone clean through his inheritance, he's got himself hocked up to his eyeballs."

"How?"

"He lives large and he's had a series of bad investments. I've got Mira on it because it looks like more than that."

"Drugs?"

"Yes. The pattern looks familiar. We'll be more certain once Mira's done her thing."

"Okay." Luke's mind raced. "So that stinks, Eva, but you said you had a bad feeling. There must be more."

"It's the Preston Inheritance. It can only be inherited by direct descendants of the original patriarch, Herbert Preston. That means—" Eva paused.

"I know what it means," Luke bit out.

"No, Luke, I don't think you do," Eva insisted. "Katya just took control of over one-hundred and fifty million dollars."

Luke felt Gray jolt up in his seat. "I know that."

"Did you know if something happens to Katya and Lily, then Julian inherits all that money?"

Luke went motionless, his eyes locked on the road ahead, his foot pushing the accelerator as far as he dared. "Tell me, Eva, when his mother drowned, where was it?"

"Off Mamaroneck Beach."

Fuck! That's where Julian moors his boat.

"And was it suspicious?"

"The police investigated, but they couldn't find any evidence of suspicious death," Eva said.

"But you got a bad feeling?"

"Yes."

"Thanks, Eva."

He hung up and passed his phone to Gray. "Call Katya."

Gray tried repeatedly but Katya didn't pick up. Each time, her phone rang four times before going to voicemail.

"Call Mira. Get a number for Mary Langworth. And tell King to track Katya's phone."

"On it." Gray punched out numbers and then turned to Luke. "We jumping the gun here?"

"Fuck, Gray! It's Eva. When she says she has a bad feeling—"

"Shit!" Gray pummeled the dashboard then sat back and inhaled deeply. "I'll get King to contact the coast guard. Mira can guide them to the boat using Katya's GPS on her phone."

Luke nodded tightly as the SUV sped down the I-95. It would take a while for Mira to locate Katya and it would be at least fifteen minutes before he and Gray got to the yacht club.

Jesus! He had to keep his head.

Crashing on the highway wasn't going to help Katya and Lily.

Please be safe. Please be safe. Please be safe.

Luke found himself silently repeating it like a mantra.

He'd give anything for his girls to be safe. Even his own life.

****

Mamaroneck Beach and Yacht Club, NY
Luke

Exactly fifteen minutes later, Luke slammed the SUV into park and was out and running towards the beachfront. "Grab the binoculars," he shouted to Gray over his shoulder. "They're in the trunk."

Following his nose, he raced through the rolling gardens until he spotted the dock. His stomach was still churning and he couldn't get rid of the bitter bile clogging his throat.

Her phone signal's disappeared. She's either switched it off or...

Mira hadn't had to finish her sentence. Katya's phone was dead. There was no way she would ignore his calls and just switch off her phone. He swallowed again as he jumped onto the floating jetty. His gut was burning.

Goddammit! Eva was right to have a bad feeling.

Running to the end of the jetty he searched the bay littered with several different types of leisure boats.

Jesus Christ! How the fuck was he supposed to find her?

The last location Mira had been able to track was just off the Mamaroneck Jetty.

"Hey, buddy, you need some assistance?"

Luke swiveled and stared blankly at the tanned, middle-aged man standing in a small powerboat alongside the jetty.

"You okay? Can I help you?"

"You spot her, yet?" Gray panted, running up and stopping next to him.

"Julian Langworth," Luke called to the man. "Do you know which is his boat?"

"Yes, but what's the problem?"

"Just tell me if you can identify his boat," Luke snarled.

"Luke, I think I've got it," Gray hissed, looking through the binoculars. "A Sea Ray powerboat. Name on the side is *The Lizzie*."

"That's it," the man confirmed.

Luke squinted into the midday sun in the direction Gray was pointing. "Is it the one not moving?"

"Yeah. Shit! Katya's in trouble." Gray passed the binoculars to Luke. "That fucker's got some type of rod pointed at her."

Luke snatched the binoculars and focused in on the boat. It was floundering in the swell, but he could clearly see Katya and Lily seated in the mid-section. *Fuck!* Even from this distance, he could tell something was wrong. Lily was clinging to the back of her seat, crying. He moved the lens to Katya. She was also curled against the back of her seat, shrinking from the asshole waving a long fishhook in her face.

"Hey, buddy. We need to borrow your boat."

Luke heard Gray clamber into the stranger's boat but he kept focused on the scene out in the bay, trying to get a read on what was happening. Julian was bent towards her and then he suddenly straightened, allowing Luke to zoom into Katya's face. *Fuck! Fuck!* She was terrified.

"Gray, we need to move now!" He spun from the water's edge and moved towards Gray who was talking to the man in the small powerboat.

"Shit, Luke, there's no fuel."

"What?" Luke froze, about to climb on-board the boat.

"There's no fucking fuel. He's just come in from fishing and was about to fill-up."

"I'm real s-sorry, guys," the man stammered, clearly freaked out by their intensity.

Luke's heart raced as he weighed up different options, discarding each one as quickly as it arose. "*Jesus Christ!*" His curse echoed uselessly and he raised the binoculars again, searching for Katya. The last time he'd felt this helpless he had been twelve years old.

"What are you doing, baby?" Katya had moved to the edge of her seat and swung her legs down. She was talking to Julian but kept looking at Lily.

"You want me to call King? He can call the police, maybe an ambulance—"

"Sit tight. Something's going down." Luke kept the binoculars glued to his face. "How long for this guy to fill-up on fuel?"

"Hey, buddy," Gray called. "How long to refuel?"

"About twenty minutes. I've got to take the boat around to the pump. Hey, should I call the police?"

"You got a pair of binoculars?" Gray asked, ignoring the man's question.

"Um, yes."

"Pass them over."

In his peripheral vision, Luke saw Gray reach out to the man. "Fuck, Gray, we don't have time to get to her." Sweat covered his brow and he blinked rapidly, but he daren't look away. Katya was about to make a move, he knew it. "Careful, babe," he muttered under his breath. "Watch that fucking hook."

"Holy shit!"

Gray's curse echoed his own silent one. *Jesus fuck!*

From her perched position on the lounger, Katya had launched herself at Julian. Her hands were clamped around the staff of the fishhook and she was in a tug of war with her motherfucking cousin. Julian was slim, but he was still stronger than her, and Luke could see she wouldn't be able to hold on for long.

"Come on, darlin'. Be creative," Gray implored.

Like she heard his muttered plea, Katya suddenly let go of the hook with one hand and drove the heel of her palm into Julian's face. He reared backwards and Katya let go of the hook to grab on to the sunroof to keep her balance.

Luke's jaw clenched so tightly, he thought it might crack. "That's it, baby, come on. *Take him down!*"

Please God. From his mouth to her ears!

Julian flailed, his hand raised to his face. It looked like his nose was bleeding. Katya lunged forward and Julian's body lurched.

"Fuck! Did she just stomp on his foot?" Gray shouted out.

"Yes, baby. Do it again." And then his beautiful woman angled her body side-on and kicked her leg out, making good contact with Julian's knee.

"Brother, your woman is something else!"

"Fucking sure she is." Luke croaked, his mouth parched as he watched Julian tumble to the deck. Katya was still standing, tentatively kicking at Julian who didn't seem to be moving.

"I think he knocked himself out," Gray said.

Luke remained motionless, focused only on what was happening out on the bay. Katya gestured to Lily, who scrambled to her feet and launched herself into her mother's arms. Hugging Lily, she gingerly climbed over her unconscious cousin and seated their little girl in the cockpit. Luke inhaled deeply, pride warming his chest, as she started to work at the controls of the boat. Half-listening to Gray on the phone to King, organizing for help from the local police, he watched the boat lurch forward and then settle. His eyes prickled with tears as it turned and slowly began to make its way back to shore, Katya at the helm.

"Well, would you look at that," Gray drawled, coming to stand close to Luke. "Every time we come to save your woman, she's busy saving herself."

Luke's legs felt weak. *Jesus, it wouldn't do for him to pass out!*

"You going to faint on me, Hunt?" Gray nudged him on the shoulder.

"No, you fucker, I'm not going to fucking faint!"

"Good. Being a marine force recon sniper and all—"

"I'm not gonna fucking faint!"

Gray snorted then stepped aside to ask the man to move his boat to make a space for Katya. They waited together at the end of the jetty as *The Lizzie* motored closer. Luke shuddered. Such a beautiful, tranquil setting, totally oblivious to the evil lurking on its

357

waters.

It seemed like hours later when he dropped his binoculars and smiled as Katya caught sight of him. He waved. Katya turned to Lily, who jumped to stand on her seat and wave back at him.

His eyes filmed over. *His girls. Fuck, he loved them!*

Katya slowed the boat and eased it alongside the floating jetty, bumping against the buoys rigged as a fender.

"Kill the engine, baby," he called to her and leaped onto the back of the boat. He glanced at Julian, who was lolling, face-down, on the wooden deck.

"Toss me the stern line," Gray said to Luke, pointing behind him at a looped rope.

Luke untied the rope and tossed it over to Gray to secure the boat.

"Luke!"

"Daddy!"

Luke turned. Katya and Lily had stepped over Julian and were scrambling over the L-shaped lounger to reach him. He stretched out over the aft seat which was folded closed and lifted Lily into his arms. "Hey, sunshine, how you doing?" He whispered into her ear as she clung to him. Keeping his arms wrapped tight around her, he lifted his head to look at Katya. "Hey, baby—"

Movement behind her. Julian was conscious! He was inching back and reaching under the seat in the cockpit. Luke's pulse raced. The fucker withdrew his hand holding a small caliber handgun.

"Shit!" Luke pulled Lily from him and forced her flat on the deck of the stern. "Gray! Gun!" He drew his weapon but Katya, already crawling over the aft seat, was in his line of fire. "Down, Katya!"

Fuck! Julian's gun pointed at Katya and Luke knew he couldn't risk taking the shot. His heartbeat exploding, he made a desperate grab for Katya and managed to wrap his arms around her, spinning them both to the aft deck.

Bang! Bang!
Bang! Bang! Bang!

Chapter Nineteen
Double Déjà-Vu

Mamaroneck Beach and Yacht Club, NY.
Sunday midday.
Katya

Luke's spine-chilling cry froze me in place and I barely registered the horror on his face before his arms were wrapped around me and the world spun.

Bang! Bang!

Bang! Bang! Bang!

He pulled me over the aft seat. I had no control as we slammed onto the wooden deck, but my heart jumped. I couldn't mistake how Luke's body jerked against me. Exactly in time with the gunshots!

"Luke!" My voice was a faint rasp, Luke's body a dead weight lying on top of me.

Oh God, no!

"No…no…no!" I struggled to free myself.

Please, no! Not my beautiful Luke.

Whoosh! My lungs expanded as suddenly his body was rolled off me.

"You hit?"

"Gray? What—"

"You hit, Katya?" Gray's fury penetrated the terror numbing my brain.

"I…no…" I croaked.

Am I hit?

I did a mental scan as I blinked up at Gray. "No, I'm fine," I said more steadily. But my calmness vaporized as I watched him yank off his T-shirt, wad it up and push it against Luke's chest.

Oh God, no! Blood was pooling all around Luke's still body.

"Luke!" I rolled over and scrambled to my knees. "Luke!"

"He's taken two hits," Gray snapped. "First one's a through-and-through, back to shoulder. The other one creased his skull."

"Luke!" *Please, God, no!* Blood was flowing from the side of his head, just above his ear. I used my hand to try and stem it.

"Katya!"

I stared up into Gray's eyes. They were a thunderous grey.

"I need you with me here, sweetheart. Yeah?"

Lily?

Hysterical sobs were coming from the corner of the boat. I jerked my head so quickly towards the sound a searing pain ripped down my neck. "Lily? Baby?"

"Katya!"

I whipped back round to Gray.

"Lily's fine. She's in shock but she's fine. Luke's not."

I closed my eyes and inhaled a deep, shaky breath. Luke's blood was seeping through my fingers. It was warm. There was too much of it!

Breathe, Katya. Breathe, baby. I could hear his voice in my head.

Opening my eyes, I met Gray's burning gaze. "What do you need me to do?"

"Climb back in the boat, find some towels," he said.

"Don't worry, I'm on it." A middle-aged man with a good tan jumped onto the boat and into the cabin. "Jesus Christ!"

At the man's shocked expletive, Gray and I stared at each other. "Julian," Gray said. "I shot him. He's dead." He looked up towards where the man was in the cabin. "Hey, buddy. Hurry!"

Julian was dead. *Bang! Bang! Bang!* I remembered hearing the other shots as Luke and I dropped to the deck.

Gray shot him, but not before Julian's bullets struck Luke.

"I was in the way, wasn't I?" I stared at Luke, willing him to move. "He couldn't shoot my bat-shit crazy cousin because I was in the way."

"Here you go." The man handed Gray a pile of white towels. "What else can I do?"

Gray handed me a towel. "Compress the bleeding on his head as much as you can." He moved his blood-soaked T-shirt away and replaced it with one of the towels. He looked up at the man. "Is there somewhere to land a chopper?"

"A chopper?" The man looked dazed.

"Helicopter," Gray said. "I'm calling in a helicopter, I need a safe place for it to land."

"Oh, shit, yeah." The man looked behind him towards the clubhouse, repeatedly running his hands through his short hair. "Um, yes! There's a flat grassy area between the dock and the beach." He waved an arm to indicate the direction.

Gray nodded. He gently rolled Luke's body over

and placed another towel under his back. He was holding both towels now, Luke's body sandwiched between. "Katya, there's a phone in my back pocket. Grab it."

Nausea thickened my throat. I swallowed hard and reached around him to pull the phone from his pocket.

"Eight-one-eight-zero, unlocks it," he said calmly.

My hand was covered in Luke's blood and I nearly dropped the phone. Shaking, I wiped both against my shorts and with a trembling finger, tapped in Gray's code.

"Look under favorites," he directed me. "King's number is second up. Call him and put it on speaker."

I hit King's name and swallowed again. The first name on Gray's list of favorites was Luke.

King's phone rang once and he answered. "Gray. Katya and Lily all good?"

"No! It's a cluster-fuck." Gray's voice was low and hard. "Luke's hit. Bad. A low-caliber through-and-through, back to shoulder and he's been clipped on the head. I think it only creased his skull but he's out cold. I need air-evac. There's a flat grass area between the dock and the beach. Get the bird in the air then call me back."

King was gone. In the silence, Lily's wheezing sobs pulled at me. I needed to go to her.

"He's not moving, Gray. Oh, God, there's too much blood." I stared at Luke, willing him to open his eyes. *Come on, honey. I need you. Lily needs you.* "Is he going to die?" I whispered to Gray.

"He's not going to fucking die!" Gray looked over his shoulder. "Hey, buddy—"

The man stepped forward, wringing his hands.

"Yes?"

"The police should be here any minute. Ask one of those people to go and meet them and bring them to the dock." Gray indicated towards the jetty. It had been quiet when we arrived. Now a growing group of onlookers had assembled.

"I'll go," the man said.

"No. I need you to take over from the lady, here." Gray indicated me with his chin. "She needs to see to her daughter."

The man didn't argue. I wasn't going to either. My heart wanted to hang on to Luke, but Lily needed me more.

The next thirty minutes were the most agonizing of my life.

A surreal haze slowly settled over me as I sat on the jetty, close to *The Lizzie,* where Luke was fighting for his life. Lily was in my lap. Her hysterical sobs had faded to the occasional hiccup and I rocked her gently, my hands pressing her head tightly to my breast. I didn't want her to see Luke who was still spread-eagled on the boat-deck, the white towels now obscenely red.

King called back. A helicopter was en-route with a paramedic team and doctor on board. Luke was going to be flown to Mount Sinai Hospital where a surgical team was already on standby. The police arrived soon after. They looked inside the boat where Julian's dead body lay, and a mad scramble followed with lots of talking on the radios. More police arrived.

Throughout, Luke remained motionless. Bleeding.

I didn't move either. My full attention was glued to Gray's back. He was bent over Luke, working madly to stem the blood flowing from his shredded body. The police steered clear of me. I think it was King's magic again. He earned my undying gratitude, because I didn't have it in me to give a clear account of what had happened. I was too busy dealing with the silent scream that was slithering up from the depths of my soul, steadily stripping me of my attempt to maintain some level of control.

Luke! Wake-up! Lily's in shock and she needs you to wake up. Please!

"Gray—"

His head lifted and he turned to me, his eyes flickering down to Lily. "Hang in there, Katya. He's still breathing and the chopper can't be far out."

Thump. Thump. Thump.

Gray and I both looked up, searching the blistering, blue sky.

Tears welled as the thumping got louder. *There!* A helicopter came swooping over the roof of the clubhouse and began to circle.

"Katya!"

I turned to Gray.

"I need you to take Lily and move back."

I instinctively gripped Lily even tighter and shook my head. The noise from the helicopter was reverberating through my brain and I didn't move, struggling to compute what he was saying. *Move away from Luke?*

"Now, sweetheart, please. They're going to move in fast and they need room to work."

His head shifted and he looked over my head. "Here they come."

I swiveled. Two paramedics were running, one with a huge bag and the other with a backboard. A third man—the doctor I guessed—was running just behind them.

"Come on, darlin'. Deep breath. Take the Glitterbug and move further back." I looked back at Gray, his calm instruction penetrating my frozen state. "I promise, Katya, it's going to be okay. Move back, now!"

I scrambled back. Lily clung so tight, if she didn't loosen her hold, her arms were going to strangle me.

The emergency medical team moved in. At the edge of my vision, police were keeping the crowd back, but it seemed far away. My whole world was Luke and Lily. And, *God help me*, neither were doing too good!

"Stay here, I'll come back and fetch you," Gray ordered as he moved past with the paramedics, helping them to carry Luke who was strapped to the backboard.

They moved like a well-oiled machine, across the jetty and up the grassy bank.

Thump. Thump. Thump.

The noise from the helicopter got louder, the thumping reverberating through my head.

Luke. Luke. Luke.

Suddenly it was in the air. Up. Up. And then it was swooping away, over the clubhouse and gone. The thumping faded and I started to ache, a feeling of immense loneliness washing over me. My legs turned to jelly and Lily felt like a deadweight in my arms. I sagged to my haunches and slid her onto my knees. Methodically, I rubbed her back, my aching loneliness at odds with the frenetic activity around me.

Buzzing from the crowds still milling around the jetty.

Squawks from police radios.

Roaring from powerboats coming and going.

I tilted my head, trying to catch a distant thump but there was nothing.

No sound from the helicopter. No Luke.

A clawing panic closed in and I squeezed my eyes shut, but still the tears escaped.

"Katya? Come on, darlin', let me take Lily. It's time to go."

I stared blankly at Gray, clinging to Lily. "It was my fault," I croaked. "He took those bullets for me."

"Of course he did." Gray stroked Lily's head. "Did you expect anything else?"

I rubbed my cheek against my shoulder, trying to brush away my tears. *Shit!* Of course Luke would put himself in the path of bullets to save Lily and me. "I love him!" I blurted to Gray. "Oh God, I love him and I haven't told him."

"Of course you love him." Gray reached for Lily. "Come here, sunshine. Uncle Gray's gonna carry you now. Come on, baby-girl." Gray crooned to Lily until she reluctantly let him pull her from me. Her little arms immediately looped around him and she buried her face in his neck.

"Come on, princess." He took my hand and pulled me to my feet.

"Thank you, Gray." I held tight to his hand. "You saved our lives."

"I didn't have a choice, darlin'." He raised my hand and gently brushed it with his mouth. "You're Luke's heart. You're his family. That makes you my family."

****

Mount Sinai Hospital, Madison Avenue, NYC.
Sunday, close to midnight.
Katya

Double déjà-vu.

Hospital. Surgery. ICU. And somebody I loved fighting for their life.

This time, instead of a family waiting room, I was curled on a small couch inside Luke's room, Lily sleeping beside me. King and Gray paid off any remaining debt to me when they stepped in and organized this.

Beep. Beep. Beep.

My head dipped and my eyelids fluttered. The steady beeping of the heart monitor was a weird comfort. As long as it kept up its staccato beat, I could keep breathing easy.

Beep. Luke is breathing.

Beep. Luke's heart is beating.

Beep. Luke is alive.

I eased back against the couch, my fingers combing gently through Lily's hair. Her knees were tucked up close to her chest, her head resting on my lap. King wanted to take her home to Luke's house but I refused. This wasn't like the other times.

Dani was bad.

My father was difficult.

But Luke?

My chest ached and I looked down at my beautiful daughter. *My baby-girl.* The only way we were going to survive this was together.

Beep. Beep. Beep.

The doctor said Luke was lucky. *Why do they always say that? Lucky?*

The bullet that hit him in the back and exited through his shoulder had broken his clavicle and damaged shoulder muscle, but it didn't hit anything vital. With intensive physiotherapy, he would suffer no permanent damage. It was the shot that creased his skull that caused him to lose consciousness. It had bled profusely and there was swelling but the doctor said, besides bad headaches for a period, there would be no long-term impairment.

He was lucky.

I rested my head against the couch and closed my eyes.

Beep. Beep. Beep.

Oh God! Julian killed his mother so he could have her money.

His bitter vitriol pounded painfully in my head: "Selfish bitch. Spending all *my* money on her gold-digging *man-whores!*" He told me how he drowned her, and then bought a new boat and called it *The Lizzie. How twisted is that?*

I'd stared into his cold, dead eyes and known absolutely, that no matter how many millions I had to give him, it would never be enough. He wanted my daughter and I wiped from the face of the planet.

Beep. Beep. Beep.

Dani's words whispered through my mind. *You never know when it's all going to end.*

So fucking prophetic! How could I have been so damn stupid? Holding out on Luke.

I. Love. You.

Three words.

I was such a goddamn coward.

I loved him and I wanted a family with him. Luke,

Lily and Katya. We were already a family.

Beep. Beep. Beep.

I'd been so damn scared. Stuck in the memory of a ten-year old child. The memories of my childhood had the substance of a fairytale. Like will-o'-the-wisp, they weren't real.

My eyes filmed over.

Dammit! It had been right in front of me, I just didn't see. Dani and Hector, Carmen and Antonio—they taught me about family. But I hadn't been ready to learn. Real families. They're about love and laughter. But they're also about pain and loss. And most importantly, they're about forgiveness.

I finally understood. A real family is about living and sticking, not existing and running.

"Babe?"

My head jerked at Luke's weak call.

"Luke!"

I eased myself from under Lily, bunching a blanket under her head, and rushed to Luke's side. "You're awake!"

Midnight eyes stared hazily at me as I bent close to his face, my hand hovering over his.

"Yeah," he murmured and licked his lip. "Christ, feel like shit."

"You were shot!" I blurted, my heart hammering. "But the doctors say you're going to be fine." His eyes were slightly dilated and I found myself looking away, butterflies suddenly fluttering in my stomach. "Are you thirsty?" I asked, desperate for something to do.

"Yeah."

There was a glass of water with a straw on the small cabinet by his bedside. I reached for it and held the straw for him while he sipped.

"Enough?"

He blinked and I moved the glass back.

He looked past me and his eyes settled on Lily. "She okay?"

"Yes" His voice was a little stronger and I tried to smile. "She was terrified, especially when she saw you bleeding so much." I turned and looked at Lily. She was still fast asleep and I didn't want to wake her. "She'll be a lot better when she wakes and sees *you* awake." I turned back to Luke.

He nodded and his hand closed over mine.

Warm. So warm!

He was on multiple drips, in a hospital, shot to hell. *And still, his hand was so warm.*

"You gonna run again?"

I started at his gruff question. "No!" But for some crazy reason I couldn't meet his eyes.

"You going back to San Diego with Dani and Hector?"

My chest tightened. "Do you want me to?"

"What do you think?"

"You were shot because of me!" I blurted again. "I told you I didn't need you, and then you saved me." My other hand fluttered, pointing behind me, "...and Lily. And you got shot!"

"Mmm." His fingers gently squeezed mine. "Gray get that fucker?"

"What?"

"Julian," he murmured, his voice starting to fade. "Gray shoot that motherfucker?"

I clung to his hand and nodded.

"You love me, baby?"

Tears welled up as I nodded again, trapped by his blue gaze. *God! He really had the most beautiful eyes I had ever seen.*

"You ever plan to tell me?" The corner of his mouth lifted and his eyes fluttered closed. "Never mind, gotta sleep now."

"Luke!" I whispered loudly.

"Later, babe."

I waited but his eyes remained closed.

Oh, for goodness sake!

****

Luke

Shit! He had a mother of a headache.

Luke shifted. His shoulder had that deep ache that told him something was broken.

Beep. Beep. Beep.

Oh yeah. Hospital. Katya.

He looked towards the couch and found himself caught by a set of wide, midnight eyes.

Lily.

She was lying with her head resting on Katya's lap, her eyes wide open and locked on him. He winked and his chest tingled when her eyes went round. *Christ, she was a beauty.*

His gaze drifted to Katya. She was asleep, half curled into the corner of the couch, her head resting back against the hard cushion. *Damn.* She looked disheveled, still dressed in her boating clothes, her hair in an untidy ponytail. And there were black shadows lurking beneath her eyes. *Dammit!* She had stayed by his side all night, hadn't even gone home to change.

Lily moved.

Shh. He raised his finger to his mouth. She stayed

still and then like she couldn't contain herself any longer, she slid off the couch and moved slowly across to him. Her face was so sad and serious Luke carefully reached for the button that would raise his bed. He didn't break eye contact with Lily, but he could see Katya shift behind her and he knew she was awake.

"Hey, sunshine," he whispered and gritted his teeth. *Fuck! Everything fucking hurt!* He moved gingerly.

"Are you going to die?"

Luke's heart skipped a beat as he looked into his daughter's frightened face.

"Come here, sweetheart." He patted the bed and without hesitation, she clambered up. Using his unhindered arm, he pulled her against his side. *Fuck! Fuck!* He winced as pain shot through his head and shoulder but he ignored it, snuggling Lily closer to him. Her head rested on his bicep and her hand lightly stroked the dressing wrapped tightly across his shoulder.

"Do I look like I'm going to die?"

She tilted her head up and her eyes squinted as she considered him. He wanted to smile when she took her time to answer but he didn't.

After several moments, she shook her head. "No."

"Then no, I'm not gonna die." Her lower lip trembled and her eyes kept flickering away.

Damn! No matter the pain from his injuries, the fear in his daughter's eyes hurt him more.

"I scare you?"

She slowly nodded and one lone tear rolled down her cheek.

Christ! She was killing him.

"I'm sorry I scared you, sunshine. I got hurt but it's all gonna be okay."

He hugged her tightly and closed his eyes as she snuggled against him.

"Daddy?"

"Yeah?"

She rubbed her eyes and looked up at him, uncertainty all over her face.

"What is it, Lily? Tell me."

Her legs curled up over his and she fidgeted. "Uncle Julian—"

Dammit! That psychotic bastard had scared the hell out of his carefree, giggling girl. "He frighten you?" He was careful to keep his voice gentle.

She nodded and her little hand crept around his nape.

"Listen, sweetheart," he said quietly, tilting his head down to her. "It wasn't anything you or your mommy did. Sometimes, people get sick. But instead of being sick in their body they get sick in their head. They don't see the world right."

"Was Uncle Julian like that?"

"Yeah. In his head he got all mixed up."

"Uncle Gray shot him dead."

He closed his eyes and cupped her head, her broken whisper made his chest burn. "Does that make you sad, sunshine?"

Again, Lily took her time to answer. This time, Luke had no urge to smile. He looked across at Katya. She was sitting upright, curled into the corner of the couch, a balled up blanket held tightly to her stomach. His chest started to burn again. *She was so fucking beautiful!*

Lily's hand tightened on his nape and he looked down at her. "His eyes were all mean, Daddy. And he yelled at me and at Mommy and…"

"Tell me, baby," he encouraged, gently stroking her hair.

"He wanted to hurt mommy with his hook. She made him stop but then, then—"

She hiccupped and stared up at him.

"Then what, Lily?"

She started to cry. "You were blee-bleeding and mommy was crying."

"Shh, baby." Luke patted Lily's back. His mind raced as he tried to think how best to comfort his frightened little girl. *Christ!* She was too young to process what had happened. Maybe, for now, all she needed to know was that everything was going to be okay. He held her tight and spoke into her ear. "It's all over now, sunshine. I'm going to be fine, and you and your mom are safe. And that's how it's gonna stay."

Lily slowly calmed and he breathed deeply as Katya stood up and walked around to the other side of the bed. She reached across and stroked the hair out of Lily's face. "Hey, baby-girl," she whispered and bent in to brush her lips across Lily's brow.

Warmth spread through Luke's body as her eyes lifted to his. "Your daddy's going to be just fine, Lily, and so are we," she said huskily.

And then she smiled.

Luke's pain faded. Her intoxicating beauty was like his very own morphine drip. "Do I get a kiss as well?" His voice was deep and her eyes darkened as she leaned closer. Closer. And then her gorgeous, pouty lips settled over his.

Heaven!

Lily giggled and whispered into his ear. "Are we a family now?"

Katya's tongue lightly stroked his lower lip and then her mouth drifted to his other ear. "I love you, Luke."

He reached his hand around Lily, and knotted it into Katya's hair. For a moment he closed his eyes.

Jesus fuck! He was surrounded by so much beauty.

Then he dipped his chin and muttered at Lily. "Yeah, sunshine, we're a family now. Forever."

About the Author

Last year, Anni Fife closed the door on a twenty-year successful career in television production, to fulfill her lifelong passion, writing. In the space of one month, she closed her business, packed up her city life, and moved to a small seaside village. "My writing has always been constrained by client briefs," Anni says. "Now, I finally have the opportunity to write to the beat of my own heart."

Luke's Redemption is Anni's debut novel, and she hopes you enjoy it as much as she loved writing it. Anni likes to spend hours walking on the beach searching for pansy shells, more hours drinking red wine with her gals, and the most hours writing romance novels filled with women you can relate to and men you love to dream about. She is currently working on her second novel *Gray's Promise*.

~*~

Join Anni's Posse
and get regular updates and Bonus Treats at
www.annifife.com
Follow Anni's Posse, like her Facebook Page
https://www.facebook.com/AnniFifeAuthor/
Email Anni
info@annifife.com

~*~

To chat with Anni Fife and other Wild Rose Press authors of erotic romance, join us at
www.groups.yahoo.com/group/thewilderroses.

Also Available

Maybe I Do

by

Allie Fisher

https://amzn.com/B01EVJ9IEY

A controlling mother and a high school sweetheart who broke her heart—only two of the reasons thriving lawyer Katherine Boon left her hometown of Isle of Hope, Georgia.

Twenty years later "Kit" must return for a wedding. Her goal? To get her niece married and get back to her comfortable, normal, single life in California. The last thing she expects is a one-night stand that rocks her world or that said rocker is the man she hired to plan the wedding.

Devout bachelor Aiden Spencer might plan weddings, but he has no interest in one of his own…until he does the unthinkable. He falls for one of his clients. With a little help, he sets out to seduce his way into her bed and into her heart.

Also Read

Beneath Him

by

C. Shell

https://amzn.com/B01DYEJ6HG

No matter how many times I try to stay away from him, he keeps drawing me back in.

Sexy, relationship phobic, make-up artist Jessica Grayson runs into an intense stranger who takes her breath away. The chemistry between them is consuming and impossible to deny. But he's everything she's learned to distrust—rich, handsome, and alpha.

Alex Harlow is a private man with much to regret. From the moment he laid eyes on Jessica, he had to have her. Despite her attempts to keep things between them casual, Alex is determined to win her over. But how can he convince her to trust the chemistry between them—and him—when his life is surrounded by secrets that could destroy them both?

Thank you for purchasing this
publication of The Wild Rose Press, Inc.
If you enjoyed the story, we would appreciate
your letting others know by leaving a review.
For other wonderful stories, please visit our
on-line bookstore at www.wilderroses.com.

For questions or more
information contact us at
info@thewildrosepress.com.

The Wild Rose Press, Inc.
www.thewilderroses.com

Stay current with The Wild Rose Press, Inc.
Like us on Facebook
https://www.facebook.com/TheWildRosePress
And Follow us on Twitter
https://twitter.com/WildRosePress